ZOMBI DO OR

Westlake was dead.

He knew it. Felt it. But sometimes he couldn't quite believe it. Sometimes, death was like a bad dream, one he might wake up from at any moment. In those moments, the world went cattywampus and it was easy to forget, well, everything.

Everything except the hunger. The hunger never went away, even when he forgot everything else. It was always with him. The itch at the base of his brain, the churning in his guts.

Hungry.

He stumbled, his head full of red hornets. He slumped against a display window and dug the palms of his hands into his eye sockets. He was coming unraveled, stitch by stitch, tendon by tendon. Rotting on the vine. Meat sliding off the bone.

Meat. Hungry. Eat.

"Stop," he croaked. His voice was raw and ragged. Not his anymore. "Stop it."

More Zombicide from Aconyte

Zombicide
Last Resort by Josh Reynolds
All or Nothing by Josh Reynolds

Zombicide Invader
Planet Havoc by Tim Waggoner
Terror World by Cath Lauria

Zombicide Black Plague
Age of the Undead by C L Werner
Isle of the Undead by C L Werner

ZOMBICIDE

DO OR DIE

JOSH REYNOLDS

ACONYTE

First published by Aconyte Books in 2023

ISBN 978 1 83908 261 0

Ebook ISBN 978 1 83908 262 7

Copyright © 2023 CMON Global Limited

All rights reserved. The Aconyte name and logo and the Asmodee Entertainment name and logo are registered or unregistered trademarks of Asmodee Entertainment Limited. No part of this product may be reproduced without specific permission. Guillotine Games and the Guillotine Games logo are trademarks of Guillotine Press Ltd. Zombicide, CMON, and the CMON logo are registered trademarks of CMON Global Limited.

This novel is entirely a work of fiction. Names, characters, places, and incidents are the products of the author's imagination or are used fictitiously. Any resemblance to actual events, locales, organizations or persons, living or dead, is entirely coincidental.

Sales of this book without a front cover may be unauthorized. If this book is coverless, it may have been reported to the publisher as "unsold and destroyed" and neither the author nor the publisher may have received payment for it.

Cover art by Riccardo Crosa & Paolo Francescutto

Distributed in North America by Simon & Schuster Inc, New York, USA

Printed in the United States of America

9 8 7 6 5 4 3 2 1

ACONYTE BOOKS

An imprint of Asmodee Entertainment Ltd

Mercury House, Shipstones Business Centre

North Gate, Nottingham NG7 7FN, UK

aconytebooks.com // twitter.com/aconytebooks

*For Christophe.
Thanks for the support.*

*For Christophe.
Thanks for the support.*

CHAPTER ONE
Kahwihta

Kahwihta Trapper paused, head cocked, ears open. Listening to the soft shuffle of rotting ceiling tiles, the rustle of wallpaper peeling away from cracked plaster as mold grew beneath it, the hum of flies. The ambient noise of the apocalypse. But beneath that was the other; the crash of something ungainly staggering into a display window, the scruff of feet on dusty tile, the querulous groan of a hungry corpse.

She didn't hear any of that at the moment, thankfully. Just the sounds of the slow collapse of the shopping center. But that didn't mean it wasn't there. Sound did strange things in places like this. It was a liminal space, halfway between life and death. She glanced down at her companion. "Anything?" she murmured.

Attila whuffed gently. The dog kept pace with her, rather than bounding ahead or wandering off. He knew better than that, or at least she liked to think so. Attila was a lean black and brown mongrel of indeterminate parentage but substantial size. Big enough to knock down most zombies and fast enough to get away when he couldn't, he could smell them coming a mile away. He was as much an early warning system as a friend.

Kahwihta took his grumbling for a reply in the negative. "Good enough," she said, giving him an affectionate thump between the ears. The dog's tail wagged gently.

She started forward again, keeping her head on a swivel as Ramirez called it. Not that it made much sense; continually swiveling one's head seemed to confer little benefit when it came to spotting zombies. Maybe it was an FBI thing. Or maybe it was just a Ramirez thing. The older woman had a lot of sayings like that.

The shopping center was empty of human life. Plenty of birds and small animals, however. There were sparrows nesting in the air vents. Their song rose and fell like a more pleasant version of the tinned music that had once kept shoppers company.

At her feet, moss crept across the tiles like a spill of emerald oil. The roof had caved in in places, creating impromptu waterfalls that carried life into the enclosed environment. Flowers and ferns had crept free from their stands and the ornamental trees had become home to squirrels and birds. Here and there the moss shrouded bones – whether human or animal, she couldn't tell.

Zombies went after animals when humans were in short supply. Animals returned the favor when they could, which brought its own set of problems. That there were so many animals here was a sure sign that there weren't many walking corpses in the area.

Attila paused, growling softly. Kahwihta stopped. The

birds had fallen silent. She reached down and unclipped the industrial cattle prod from her belt. Zombies didn't like electricity much. Their muscle tissue was still susceptible to sudden contractions, even if they didn't really feel it. Just one of the useful things she'd learned over the past year and change since the apocalypse had rolled over the world.

It was hard to remember what it had been like before. Intellectually, the memories were still there, but emotionally, she might as well have been reading a history book. She'd been in college when the curtain fell. She'd been up in the Adirondacks, studying the biodiversity of the Saranac Lake area when it had all ended. She figured that was why she'd survived the initial outbreak. She hadn't even realized that the world had ended until she'd hiked down to town and nearly gotten eaten by the locals.

She was still a student, but her focus had shifted somewhat these days. Zombies were the hot new environmental catastrophe, worse than global warming and carbon emissions. She'd taken her share of hungry corpses apart in the months since it had all gone wrong – dissecting them down to the marrow to try to get a handle on what had happened. She had no answers, unfortunately. Just a lot of questions.

Not that it mattered really. Who was there to tell, after all?

Attila gave a sharp bark. Kahwihta followed his gaze and saw a section of moss a few feet away suddenly quiver and bulge. She took a step back and activated the cattle prod. It snapped to life with a crackle of ozone. The moss ripped like carpet as something that was more bone and topsoil than meat hauled itself into view.

Zombies were remarkably durable. They could endure

conditions that would cripple a living human with little degradation of their physical abilities. Shoot them, stab them, set them on fire, run them over, they'd just keep going unless you removed the brain or severed the spine. If there was no prey to hunt, they just… stopped. Went into hibernation where they were and waited for someone to wake them up. Of course sometimes they rotted away to nothing while they waited, but that took a lot longer than most people thought.

This one was well on its way over the river, as her grandmother might have said. But that didn't make it any less dangerous. It had enough muscle memory left to get to its feet and move in her direction. Dirt slid from its wasted form as it took a staggering lurch toward her. Attila barked again and sidled away from her, drawing the dead thing's attention. It didn't have eyes anymore, or a nose. It was acting on sound alone. Maybe vibrations – had it felt her approach somehow?

She watched it move, noting the jerkiness, the lack of plasticity. A broken thing. It swayed in Attila's direction, jaws falling open in a hiss. The dog backed away, still barking. The zombie took a step forward in pursuit.

Kahwihta lunged. The cattle prod stabbed into the zombie's exposed ribcage and a fat spark danced in the air. The zombie twitched, champing its jaws mindlessly. She yanked the cattle prod out and jabbed the dead thing again. It was more resistant than she'd anticipated; maybe it didn't have enough tissue left to contract.

Attila darted forward and clamped down on a wobbling leg. Swiftly, the dog yanked the zombie off its feet and retreated, dragging it away from her. Kahwihta followed, reaching into her satchel for her hammer. It was just a standard ball peen hammer with a rounded head, but it did the job well enough.

Attila let go as she approached. The zombie made to push itself to its feet, but too late. She caught it in the center of the head with her first swing. It went down like a sack of potatoes. She hit it again, just to be certain. When it didn't move, she jabbed at it with the cattle prod, inspecting the remains.

The radio clipped to her belt crackled to life. "*Kahwihta?*" a woman's voice asked. Ramirez. She had the sort of voice that Kahwihta associated with people in charge – direct and authoritative.

Kahwihta thrust her hammer back into her satchel and unhooked the radio. "Here."

"We heard barking. Everything OK?"

"Just a zombie. Well past its expiration date. What about you?"

"Nothing. Found him yet?"

"No. But I think we're close. How's Terry?"

"Shaken up, but in one piece."

"Thanks to Westlake," Kahwihta said.

Ramirez was quiet for a moment. Kahwihta could almost see her face. Finally, she said, "*Are you sure?*"

"Which one of us is the expert?" Kahwihta asked with more confidence than she felt. "He hasn't gone feral, boss. Trust me."

"I do. And don't call me boss."

"You got it, boss." Kahwihta broke the connection before Ramirez could reply. Long conversations could be dangerous outside of a designated safe zone. Not that they'd seen many zombies since they'd arrived at the airfield. A few here and there, but no big groups.

Given the condition of the place, no one had expected any walkers to still be around. Zombies would travel hundreds of miles to stand on the wrong side of a chain-link fence, so long as there were human beings in sight. But take humans out of the equation, and zombies wandered off. It was something Kahwihta was still trying to puzzle out. How did they know when there were no more people in an area? The answer might well hold the key to building a true zombie-free zone. Unfortunately, there didn't seem to be a biological reason for it. At least none that she could determine.

The walker that had attacked Terry had been the first they'd seen in the mall. It had been waiting in one of the stores. Lurking in the employee washroom. Maybe it had been there since the beginning of the end. Locked in by someone and left as a nasty surprise for the next person to come along. In this case, that had been Terry.

He was a new face; one of the Atlantic City crew. A scrawny kid, a few years her junior. He'd probably still been in high school when the world had ended. He didn't talk much. None of the folks from Atlantic City talked much. Kahwihta didn't blame them. What was there to talk about? Few people liked to swap survivor stories; most just wanted to keep their heads down and make it to the next day.

Another member of their group, Ptolemy, talked about it a lot. He called it generational trauma. Like the sort that affected the survivors of wars. People could only take so much before they withdrew into themselves. Even the most boisterous or outgoing person could only keep it up for so long under these conditions. Eventually, everything became muted – gray all day, every day.

Kahwihta felt like that sometimes, though she tried her best to keep her mind occupied. Animals had it easier. Every day was new, and exciting. Not enjoyable, perhaps, but exciting. She glanced down at Attila and smiled. He scratched himself, ignoring her. "Good dog," she said, still thinking about Terry and the toilet-walker.

It had nearly taken the kid out and had banged him up pretty bad. Most walkers weren't very strong, but some could throw hands with the best of them. This one had tackled Terry to the ground while he scavenged toilet roll, and nearly had him until Westlake had intervened.

Things had become confusing pretty quickly after that. Everyone had been surprised, even Attila. Kahwihta wondered about that, too. Maybe something in the bathroom had masked the smell, or maybe he just hadn't been paying attention. Dogs could be as unobservant as people.

Terry had gone down, the walker on top of him. No one had reacted in time, except Westlake. He'd swooped down on them and wrenched the zombie back, away from Terry and… and then what had happened, had happened.

"Damn it, Westlake," Kahwihta said. He'd been doing so well, at least until they'd reached South Carolina. It had been weeks without an incident, without so much as a flicker of uncertainty. And now it was all over.

He'd ripped the walker's throat out with his teeth. Just like an animal.

Just like a zombie.

Ramirez had almost put a bullet in him then and there. But Westlake was quicker, thankfully. He'd scrambled away, vanishing into the labyrinth of the mall. Kahwihta had gone after him without waiting for the others. To their credit, they hadn't tried to stop her. They knew as well as she did that they needed him in one piece, preferably with a working brain.

Westlake had been turned months ago. They'd thought he was dead, but he'd somehow wound up in Atlantic City, trapped in a makeshift arena fighting an oversized zombie wrestler, and hadn't that been a surprise? Kahwihta still wasn't sure just what kind of zombie Westlake was, and she'd seen a lot of them. She'd never known of one that retained its sentience after turning.

The problem was, it didn't seem to be a permanent state of affairs. Westlake was still a corpse, albeit a talkative one. Like any corpse, like the zombies themselves, he was decaying. And his mind was getting worse. Soon, he might not be Westlake anymore. Maybe today was the day. But she hoped not. She liked him. Had liked him, since their first meeting in the Adirondacks.

She stooped and held a scrap of cloth, torn from Westlake's shirt during his struggle with the walker, to Attila's nose. "Find him, boy. Before he gets himself into any more trouble."

CHAPTER TWO
Westlake

Westlake was dead.

He knew it. Felt it. But sometimes he couldn't quite believe it. Sometimes, death was like a bad dream, one he might wake up from at any moment. In those moments, the world went cattywampus and it was easy to forget, well, everything.

Everything except the hunger. The hunger never went away, even when he forgot everything else. It was always with him. A fellow traveler. The monkey on his back. The itch at the base of his brain, the churning in his guts.

Hungry.

He'd known junkies who described their addiction as a voice, echoing up from the base of their skull. This was the same. He was hearing it, but it wasn't there. Not really. Just an impulse that his dying mind was trying to communicate in a way that he could process.

Did the others hear it that way? Were they like dogs responding to their master's voice? Or was it so much a part of them that they didn't even perceive it? Did it just go quiet one day and they never noticed?

Westlake thought about neurons popping like overheated bulbs and city blocks going dark in a blackout. He was hard-pressed to say which was worse… the voice, or the silence that must inevitably follow.

He stumbled, his head full of red hornets. He slumped against a display window offering holiday deals and dug the palms of his hands into his eye sockets, trying to press the hunger back into its box. It was getting harder by the day.

Speaking of which, what day is it?

The thought, so sudden and out of place, stung him. His hands fell away, and he found himself looking at his reflection in the cracked glass. There was enough left of his face for it to be recognizably his, but probably not for much longer. The thought didn't bother him as much as it once had. It hadn't been a very pretty face to begin with. Fit for mugshots, not television. He noticed, almost absently, that his mouth was stained with something dark.

Westlake touched his face in ugly wonder, and his fingers came away wet. Blood. Was it blood? He closed his eyes, trying to force a replay of the last ten minutes, the last hour. There was a cigarette burn on the film reel of his mind.

He knew he was in a shopping center – a mall by any other name. One of the hundreds of retail outlets that occupied this part of America.

What part is that?

Westlake didn't know. He had known, he was sure. But the memory wouldn't come now. One mall looked like any other. All corporate brands and chain eateries. Why was he here? Who had he come with?

What day is it?

The thought again. Persistent. Like the hum in his ears, or the feel of his ligaments loosening. He was coming unraveled, stitch by stitch, tendon by tendon. Rotting on the vine. Meat sliding off the bone.

Meat. Hungry.

He cracked the glass with his fists. Inconsequential thoughts slipped and slid through the runnels of his brain.

Who has an Arbor Day sale?

He stumbled back, glass in his hands, his reflection fractured and elongated. There was no pain, except for the hunger. It thrashed within him like a wild thing, and he ground his lacerated hands into his face, trying to wrestle it into submission before it overwhelmed him.

Hungry. Eat.

"Stop," he croaked. His voice was raw and ragged. Not his anymore. "Stop it."

"Westlake?"

His lips split as he bared his teeth and spun, eyes fixed on the speaker. A young First Nations woman, dressed in clothes that had seen better days. For a moment, he didn't recognize her. Names, places, dates... they all slipped through his fingers like sand these days. Then, iron bars of self-control slammed down like it was lights out at Joliet Correctional Center, and he straightened. "Is he alive?"

Kahwihta nodded. "You didn't touch him. The only one you took a bite out of was the walker." She paused. "You damn near tore its head off, by the way. Whatever else, your jaw muscles are still intact."

"Wonderful," Westlake muttered. It was coming back to him in bits and pieces. They were in South Carolina. Some shitbox retail site on the coast, near Charleston International Airport. A day's drive from a private airfield chopped out of the salt marshes; an airfield known only to a precious few – fewer now. "Did we – did you find it?"

Kahwihta shook her head. "Not yet."

Suddenly out of strength, Westlake sagged back against another display window, and sank down until he was seated on the floor. He looked at his hands and then, with a sigh, began to pull out the pieces of glass still embedded in them. Kahwihta crouched beside him – but not too close, he noticed. He wanted to smile but couldn't quite make it work.

She watched him for a moment, before asking, "Do you feel it?"

He didn't look at her. "The glass? No."

"That's not what I meant."

He paused. Then went back to cleaning his hands. "I know what you meant. Yes. I feel it. I always feel it."

"Even when you – when you're fed?" she asked, stumbling slightly over the phrasing.

Westlake glanced at her. "Yeah. Even then."

"Is it stronger then, or weaker?"

Westlake didn't reply. He knew what she was asking about. The hunger was a constant source of worry for all of them, not just him. Indeed, it was a greater worry for Kahwihta and the others. If he turned feral, they'd be the ones on the receiving end.

The lights in the shopping center hadn't been on in months, but there were plenty of windows on this side of the building. Lots of muddy gray light filtering in through smeared glass. Enough to see the extent of things. Water damage, scorch marks from an electrical fire... bullet holes. Always bullet holes these days. A ubiquitous sign that a place had already been cleaned out and picked over. But hope sprang eternal. Looters missed things, or were eaten before they could pilfer much.

Though this place had been largely deserted even before the apocalypse. Just a few stores left open to keep up appearances. It was – had been – a way station for Narcos and other sorts of traffickers coming north on the I-77 corridor. Like a bed and breakfast for assholes. There was food, water, ammunition, medicine... whatever might be needed, all socked away in a set of offices at the back of one of the stores. Only he couldn't remember which one. He looked across the hall at the cracked display window. "Arbor Day," he murmured. Kahwihta said nothing.

"Arbor Day," he said, more firmly this time.

"Weird holiday. What about it?" Kahwihta asked.

"Did the apocalypse happen on Arbor Day?"

Kahwihta paused. "No, I think I might have remembered that. Why?"

"No one has an Arbor Day sale." Westlake pushed himself to his feet and went to the display window. "This is it."

Kahwihta's eyes widened. "Are you sure?"

"Yeah. Positive. It's in there."

Kahwihta looked at the security shutters over the doors. They'd been padlocked shut. "Right, so, is there a code to unlock the shutters, or...?"

Westlake smashed his fist through the cracked glass. No alarms went off. No power and the backup generators had long since been drained. He kicked out the rest of the glass and climbed into the window. Kahwihta followed him. "If there's anyone – anything – in here, it knows we're coming."

"That's what the mutt's for," Westlake said, as he plucked glass from his arm.

"Admit it, you just didn't remember the code to unlock the shutters," Kahwihta said teasingly. Westlake grunted.

"We're in, that's all that matters." She was right, but he didn't want to admit it. The truth was his old life was just ashes in his head. He could sift through them and find answers, but it was getting harder by the day. Soon, there wouldn't be anything left of the old him. He'd be a shadow of himself and nothing more. Or worse than a shadow.

One more job. Maybe two, at most. That was all he was good for.

It would have to be enough.

He led Kahwihta through the empty store, toward the back. According to rumor, the store had once sold men's clothes. But there was nothing on the shelves now except dust and cobwebs. It had been that way for years. The stockroom was the only part that had seen any activity in that time. That was where the real business went on.

The stockroom was locked, of course. Another padlock. But that was easily solved. One good thing about being dead, he'd become a lot stronger. He twisted the padlock off, warping the door in the process. He tossed the broken padlock aside and noticed Kahwihta staring at him. "What?"

"Most zombies can't do that."

"Hey, you said it yourself… I'm special." He kicked the door open and went in. It was as he remembered. At least he thought it was. It looked like a stockroom, but for a survivalist's bunker. Tins of food, bags of dried pasta and rice, crates of bottled water. First aid kits, too, and some general antibiotics. He judged there was two or three weeks' worth of food, if properly rationed. The medicine was more important, but there wasn't much of it. He sighed. "Less than I thought."

"I thought you said there was ammunition?"

"There was, last time I was here." He paused. "Wait." A dim memory flickered and he looked down at the floor. Of course, they wouldn't leave that kind of thing out in the open. The food and the rest could be explained away, but not the guns. He dropped to his hands and knees and ran his fingers along the tiled floor until he found the hidden seam.

"What are you doing?" Kahwihta asked.

"Tiles are linoleum. See? If we – ah. There. Help me peel it back." With her help, he dragged the linoleum back, revealing the steel trapdoor set into the floor. "There we are." It resembled the door to a bank vault. Westlake stared at it in consternation. "Crap."

"You forgot the code, didn't you?"

Westlake sighed and sat back on his haunches. "No. It's a digital lock. No power, no way of getting it open."

"Luckily, we have explosives."

Westlake glanced at her. "That kind of noise will bring every zombie in the area running this way."

Kahwihta nodded. "Maybe. Maybe not. The question is, is it worth the risk?"

Westlake ran a hand over his scalp. "There'll be guns down there. Ammunition. Cash." He glanced at the radio on her belt. "We'll let Ramirez decide."

Attila turned toward the door and growled softly. Outside,

broken glass crunched. Westlake got to his feet and went to the door. Attila stepped aside to let him pass, deftly avoiding his offer of a scratch. The dog was wary of him these days. Westlake felt a peculiar sadness at that, but he pushed it aside and turned his attentions to the store. It was dark, but he could feel something.

Kahwihta called it his 'zombie-sense'. He knew when they were around. Not necessarily where, or how many. Just that they were there. Kahwihta figured it was how they managed to inevitably congregate into groups.

Normally, he tried to ignore the feeling. This time, he embraced it, and it told him that there was something out there in the store. Maybe they'd heard the breaking glass. Or maybe they'd simply come, following their own 'zombie-sense'. Either way, the result wasn't going to be pretty.

More glass crunched. An empty rack toppled over. It sounded like there was a bunch of them out there, though he couldn't see anything. Attila was growling loudly now. Westlake knew how he felt and clenched his fists. He'd left his shotgun behind in his hurry to get away from the others. He carefully closed the door as best he could and looked back at Kahwihta.

"Maybe tell Ramirez to hurry while you're at it?"

CHAPTER THREE
Ramirez

On the roof of the mall, Estela Ramirez lowered the radio and cursed in Spanish, then in English, and then, for a bit of variety, in French. When she'd finished, she looked at the others gathered on the rooftop. "They found the cache."

"What's the bad news?" Coop asked. Ramirez glanced at him. He was a big man, ex-military, muscular, tattooed, dressed in black fatigues and a combat rig. A GSG-16 assault rifle with a suppressor hung across his chest. The getup made him look like an extra from an action movie, back when there had been such things as movies.

"Zombies found them. We need to break camp and saddle up. Five minutes. Half of you with me, Calavera will take the other half to get the trucks and meet us by the south loading dock. If we manage to salvage anything, that's the closest exit."

The others snapped into action. They'd had enough practice over the past few months. There were six of them, besides Westlake and Kahwihta, all experienced survivors and scroungers, with that brittle edge and tension twitch that came from too much time in the open. Coop was probably the calmest of all of them. Terry was a bundle of nerves. Then, he'd almost been eaten, so that was understandable. Imogene and Riggs, the other two survivors from Atlantic City, were almost as shaken.

And then there was El Calavera Santo. The big man stood some distance away, his eyes on the horizon. It was hard to tell what he was thinking, given the luchador mask that covered his face. He wasn't nervous. Excited, maybe. But not nervous.

She sighed and ran her hand through her hair. She'd been a damn good FBI agent once. Now she was riding herd on a bunch of twitchy survivors, trying to get them through the summer. They'd managed winter, though it had been tougher than she liked to admit. Between the resources of the Villa up in the Adirondacks, and what was left of Atlantic City, things had been just about manageable.

But the city was almost tapped out; almost everyone who wanted to make the journey to the mountains already had, and Ariadne was having to take the yacht farther down the coast to find places that were still worth looting.

Thinking of Ariadne St Cloud made Ramirez frown. She, Calavera and the others had helped her take control of the city from her whackadoo brother, who'd set himself up as a warlord. She'd been reluctant to get involved in their feud at first, but Ariadne's brother had been the sort of asshole who was only going to get worse if left to his own devices.

Granted, they'd made some friends out of the deal besides Ariadne. There had been a few survivor groups scattered about the city, and outside it. Most of those had made common cause with them to oust Ariadne's brother. Afterwards, many had taken them up on the offer of sanctuary, believing the mountains to be safer than the city. Ramirez figured that was debatable – cities didn't have zombie bears, after all – but more hands made for swift work.

With the influx of willing workers to the Villa, they'd managed to erect new fences and start up gardens. They'd even managed to restock the lake with fish… ones that hadn't been feeding on submerged zombies for almost two years. It wasn't pretty, but it was working. The question was, for how long?

How long could they make it work? How long until something drew the dead back into the mountains? What then?

Ramirez shook her head, trying to banish her worries. It was hard. Worrying was what she did. It was why she was still alive. But too much of it was worse than not enough. She distracted herself by watching as the camp was broken down.

The roof had been perfect. Only a few doors to watch, and it was still mostly structurally sound. Anticipating it would take a few days to fully clear the mall before searching it, she'd had tarps set up to keep out the weather and provide refuge from the heat. She'd only visited South Carolina a few times prior to the end of the world, but what she mostly remembered was the weather. And the mosquitoes.

There weren't many of those around at the moment, thankfully. Kahwihta had a theory that mosquitoes and zombies didn't mix. Ramirez figured it was simpler than that. The bugs, like the dead, went where there was food. And that wasn't here.

She looked out over the parking lot, scanning it with a

pair of binoculars scavenged from one of the sporting goods stores below. It was a weed-wracked wasteland, full of mossy cars and stunted trees pushing up through the asphalt. From what Westlake had said, this place had had one foot in the grave prior to the apocalypse. The zombies had just tipped it all the way in. She paused, watching something that might have been a coyote or a large dog trot through the maze of rusted-out cars.

"Anything out there?" Calavera asked, as he wrapped athletic tape around his hands. The big man had crept up on her so quietly that she'd barely noticed.

"Nothing. Just the usual wildlife. Whatever is down there shouldn't be too hard to deal with." She winced as she said it. Inviting trouble, her abuela would have said. She looked at Calavera. The luchador smiled confidently. "You'll be careful," she said.

"I am the very soul of wariness," he said, and she almost believed him. The truth was, Calavera was never what you'd call careful. Dependable, yes. But not careful. He took too many chances. It was almost like he believed he was invincible. Then, looking at him, it was hard not to believe it. "You as well."

She gave a lazy salute. "I'll take it under advisement."

Calavera laughed and turned. "Riggs, Terry, with me," he said, smacking his fist into his palm. "Let us be as quick as possible." The three of them headed for the stairs closest to the parking lot exit. Ramirez and the others headed the opposite way.

Coop took point. Ramirez didn't even have to ask. The ex-soldier had been a member of Ariadne's private security detail before such things had become meaningless. She'd lent them his muscle, and Ramirez couldn't say he hadn't come in handy. But his loyalty was with Ariadne and nobody else, a fact she knew better than to forget. He headed down the stairs, weapon at the ready. Ramirez followed, her sidearm in hand. Imogene brought up the rear, flashlight aimed over their heads and ahead of them.

"Isn't he, like, already dead?" Imogene groused. "I thought zombies didn't bother their own." She didn't care for Westlake much. Ramirez understood. Westlake hadn't exactly been her favorite person before his death. And being a walking corpse only seemed to amplify his worst traits.

Ramirez glanced back at her. "Westlake might be dead, but Kahwihta isn't. Now keep the flashlight steady." Imogene was on flashlight duty due to the lack of a firearm. She claimed a dislike of them stemming from her pre-apocalypse life. Ramirez didn't press the issue, especially given how good the younger woman was with the array of cutting implements she carried. Chef's knives, mostly, which made Ramirez wonder if Imogene had been a chef or a line cook of some description. Regardless, she could flense a walker to the giblets in less time than it took most people to get a shot off.

It took no time at all to get downstairs. They'd propped the door open ever so slightly and oiled the hinges after arriving at the mall, so it made no sound when Coop pushed it open. Silence was the golden rule of the new world. Noise – any noise – had a chance of attracting unwanted attention.

Ramirez had been as surprised as anyone by the almost utter lack of zombies in the mall. It was surprising, after the hell of Atlantic City. But just because hordes of them weren't crammed into the building didn't mean they weren't close by. They could have been in the sub-basements, or in the woods on the other side of the parking lot. So far, only a bare handful had shown themselves.

They made their way through the quiet corridors. For Ramirez, it was odd to see a place like this so silent. In the movies, the malls were always places of shelter. In reality, few people had decided to make their stand in the local outlet mall.

She wondered how many of them would still be standing in a few years. How much of anything would still be standing in the next decade? The modern world had required constant maintenance; most people didn't see it, but as an FBI agent, she'd quickly become aware of the invisible infrastructure underpinning the country, as one of her teachers at Quantico had described it. Thieves like Westlake knew it and used it, so she'd learned what she could about it as well. In a few more years, maybe less, the interstates would begin to disintegrate; dams would burst; buildings would collapse.

The old world was slowly vanishing. And what was coming next was unknowable. Part of her was frightened by the thought of it. Another part was almost relieved. Once the last of all that had been was gone, it'd finally be time for something new.

A crash echoed through the mall. A rack falling over. Coop froze, and Ramirez stopped Imogene with a hand on her chest. They waited. Scurrying sounds followed, fading into silence. "Rats," Coop muttered.

"Keep going," Ramirez said.

They followed the noise to a broken display window. Glass

crunched underfoot. Ramirez paused, listening. There were sounds from inside the store – lots of crashing and banging. She nodded, and Coop climbed through the display window. She and Imogene followed. As she climbed inside, Ramirez saw that something was going on in the back of the store, where the door to the backroom was. She gestured, and Coop edged forward as Imogene raised the flashlight.

The light washed across the commotion, illuminating… rats. Far too many to count. At the touch of the light, the humanoid mass turned from the door, shedding vermin as it did so. A face – what was left of a face – surfaced for just a moment from within the rats. A stretched-out mask of tattered meat, beneath which squirmed more of the infected animals.

"Holy God," Coop muttered. He raised his weapon and the rat-thing lurched toward them. Coop and Ramirez fired, but the mass barely slowed. Rats burst like rotten fruit, but the thing beneath kept lumbering forward.

"Fall back," Ramirez said. "Fall back!"

As they retreated, she saw dark forms scurry across the floor. More rats. Where had they all come from? They'd seen no sign of the damn things when they'd arrived. Imogene called out a warning and Ramirez ducked aside as a rat leapt at her from a shelf. The younger woman threw a knife into the rodent. It continued to squeal and thrash, even with the knife pinning it to the floor.

"Definitely infected," Imogene said, reaching for another knife.

The rat-mass closed in, the squirming lumps that passed for its arms reaching out. Coop emptied his magazine into the thing with no effect and reloaded, cursing. Ramirez was about to order both he and Imogene out of the store when she heard Westlake shout, "Fire in the hole!"

Ramirez grabbed Imogene and threw her backward as something sputtering and orange crashed into the rat-mass. Glass shattered, and burning alcohol spattered across the teeming forms of the rats. Flames whooshed up. With a communal shriek, the tottering monstrosity staggered sideways and toppled over. Burning rats fled in all directions, squealing – but not in pain, something told her. Frustration, perhaps.

Coop raised his weapon as a new figure stepped over the burning mass. Ramirez lifted a hand, stopping him. "Don't. It's Westlake."

"Who else would I be? The Easter Bunny?" Westlake bounced a second bottle of alcohol on his palm. "Molotov cocktail. Gets them every time." He kicked aside a burning rat and handed Coop the bottle. "Hate to waste it, but I've never been big on vodka. Especially these days."

"Is Kahwihta…?" Ramirez began. She heard a dog bark, and Kahwihta followed Westlake out of the backroom. She looked at the burning heap with obvious interest.

"Fascinating… in a horrible sort of way, I mean. I've never seen infected animals do that before." Ramirez grimaced. The worst of it was, Kahwihta did sound impressed. Her interest in the dead had been almost cute at first, but of late it was starting to seem unhealthy.

"What about those pigeons in Atlanta?" Imogene asked.

"That wasn't quite so coordinated," Kahwihta said. "I have a feeling they'll be back, though. We should probably get while the going is good."

"What about the cache?" Coop asked.

"It's there," Westlake said, hiking a thumb over his shoulder. "But the good stuff is sealed in a vault. We'll need party favors – loud ones – to get it open."

Coop frowned and glanced at Ramirez. "Want me to check it out?"

Ramirez nodded. Coop sidled past Westlake, who had what might have been an offended look on his face. He looked at her. "Don't trust me?" he asked.

"I just want to be sure."

"My mind's rotting, but it's not quite all gone yet." He tried to smile as he said it, but the muscles in his face did a jitterbug instead. Ramirez looked away.

"I know," she said. "Terry's fine, by the way."

Westlake was silent for a moment. Then, "Good."

Coop returned. "Some good stuff back there, but not a lot. And he's right. The safe's built into the floor, so we can't even dig it out. Not that we have the tools – or time – for that. No way we're getting the rest of it without blowing that hatch." He made it sound like a question. Ramirez paused. They had some explosives, mostly for clearing obstacles on the road. But setting off something in here would make a lot of noise, and possibly bring a chunk of building down on top of them.

She looked at Westlake. "What's in there, exactly?"

Westlake shrugged. "Guns, ammunition, that sort of thing." He paused. "Then again, maybe nothing. It depends on who used it last."

"So, for all we know, it's empty." Ramirez gnawed her lip for a moment and then said, "Leave it. We've got enough guns to kit out an army. It's ammunition we're short on."

Coop looked like he wanted to argue, but thankfully kept his mouth shut.

"I'll start gathering up the rest of the stuff," Imogene said. She had a roll of garbage bags stuffed into her belt and she tore one off as she headed for the backroom. Ramirez motioned to Coop.

"Help her. And do it fast." She looked down at a smoldering rat and grimaced as she heard a distant scurrying sound. "I have a feeling we're not going to have much time."

CHAPTER FOUR
Calavera

To Calavera's eye, the parking lot was an overgrown wasteland. Rusted-out cars stretched as far as the eye could see, some covered in a thick shag of moss or swallowed by kudzu. The pavement was cracked and buckling, allowing tree roots, weeds and wildflowers to spread across the lot. At the far edges, the chain-link fence had collapsed, either due to the weight of kudzu vines or from storm damage.

It was no longer a place of civilization, but a haunt for wild beasts. Like so much of the world, it was being reclaimed by its original owners. Or so Santa Muerte whispered to him in his dreams. Sometimes, in the quiet hours of the night, she showed him the world to come... a kingdom of forests, built on roots of steel and concrete. The dead had risen, but life would continue after a fashion, even if mankind was no longer here to see it.

"It's fugazi, man," Terry said, stepping back from the open hood of the truck and snapping Calavera from his reverie. The vehicle was one of two they'd managed to salvage at the airfield. Terry wiped his hands with a rag. "These heaps start to come apart every time we crank the ignition. I'm surprised they've lasted this long."

"Luck has been on our side," Calavera said. Terry was the youngest of the group, a new recruit from Atlantic City. Dressed in an outsize hoodie and jeans that were a size too large for his underfed frame, he wore an archaic cross-draw holster he'd picked up somewhere, containing an equally old-fashioned Colt revolver.

He wasn't a particularly good shot, but he was getting better. In any event, his skillset lay elsewhere. Terry was something of a mechanic, which made him infinitely more valuable to their operation than another gunslinger.

"Yeah, well, you know what they say about luck," Terry said, as he turned back to the engine of the truck. "It always runs out, sooner or later."

Calavera patted him on the shoulder. "Perhaps. But not yet, I think. We have a way to go yet, and Santa Muerte is with us still."

Terry swallowed and nodded. "If you say so, big guy." He bent over the engine and went back to work. Calavera stepped around him and went to the second of their vehicles. It was still in working order, thankfully.

Riggs lay in the back, reading one of the guidebooks he'd scavenged from a tourist center near the airfield. Calavera didn't begrudge him his inattention. Reading material was always in short supply, though books were easy enough to come by these days. It was simply that few people ever thought to loot a bookstore. He paused, finger marking his place. "Well?" he asked.

"Terry believes that he can get it working."

"I'll believe that when I see it," Riggs said. He was a skinny man, dressed haphazardly in a concert t-shirt, Bermuda shorts, a trench coat and a cowboy hat that had seen better decades. His face was hidden behind a battered gas mask, the kind you normally didn't see outside of movies. He always wore it, even when there was no need. Calavera figured him for a germaphobe of some description. Or maybe he, like Calavera, found some comfort in the mask. Riggs' oddities were largely tolerated due to his skill at crafting smoke bombs out of spare parts and cleaning supplies. The ingenious devices confused walkers, if only temporarily.

"We must trust in his abilities, as we do in yours." Calavera leaned against the side of the truck, rubbing his hands. They ached from inactivity. Some days everything ached. Most days, in fact. He was getting older, slower. It was hard to stay at fighting weight on starvation rations. He pushed the thought aside firmly. Worrying was for after, as Santa Muerte told him. Always after. After what, he was not certain. Just... after.

Something thumped onto a nearby car. Calavera saw a tall, gangly bird perched on the vehicle's sagging roof. "Is... is that a stork?" Terry asked, staring at the large bird in confusion.

"It's a heron," Riggs said. "Great Blue Heron, to be exact. A Lowcountry treasure, according to these guidebooks we scored." He tapped the book in question and flipped a page. "I wouldn't get too close."

"It's staring at us."

"That's why I wouldn't get too close." Riggs closed the book and sat up. "Look but don't touch, as my mother always said."

"Why is it staring at us?"

"It's probably never seen a human before. At least not a

living one." Riggs scratched his neck, careful not to dislodge his gas mask. "Or maybe it's hungry. Who knows?"

Calavera peered at the bird, trying to ascertain its physical state. Some animals were more resistant to zombification than others. Birds were not among those, however. Pigeons, crows, even songbirds, were susceptible and far more dangerous than even the most persistent walker. For whatever reason, the process of decay was slowed in them, which meant they retained the ability to fly for a good deal longer than one might hope.

The heron, however, seemed to be uninfected. It lazily took wing a moment later, and soared skywards, draping its shadow over them momentarily before vanishing over the top of the mall. Calavera relaxed, but only slightly. "Terry?" he inquired, softly.

"Almost," Terry said, glancing at him. "The connections are corroded. I'm doing what I can, but I think this will be this hunk of junk's last ride."

"Let's get something stylish next time," Riggs said.

"Something lacking in cargo capacity, you mean," Calavera said. A distant twitch of motion caught his attention and he turned toward the woods that rose to the far side of the parking lot. Birds circled slowly in the air above the trees. "Riggs, the binoculars."

Riggs tossed him the binoculars. Focusing them, he could make out the birds better. Well enough, at least, to see that they were following something. "What is it?" Terry asked.

"Turkey buzzards," Calavera said, lowering the binoculars. Past the birds, the sky had taken on that particular deep blue tinge that he associated with rain. "And a storm," he added.

He handed the binoculars back to Riggs. "The buzzards are following something."

Riggs sat up. "Something singular, or plural?"

"Does it matter?"

"Nope. Can we get moving yet?"

Terry started up the truck with a triumphant shout. Calavera looked at Riggs. "I believe that is a yes. Keep a safe distance from us, just in case something else goes wrong." Riggs saluted smartly and clambered into the cab of his truck. Calavera climbed into the back of Terry's truck and thumped the roof. "Around the back. South loading dock."

Terry started the truck moving. Out over the trees, the buzzards became agitated, as if whatever they were circling had suddenly picked up speed. Calavera frowned. They hadn't seen many zombies in the area. Kahwihta had theorized that the creatures had moved elsewhere, in search of prey. He feared that they hadn't gone as far as all that.

The pair of trucks quickly navigated the parking lot, heading for the south loading dock. There were fewer vehicles here, other than a single delivery truck. Calavera considered trying to get it running, but decided against it. The trucks they had were enough for the task at hand. Anything else was a distraction.

The loading dock was a small concrete landing, extending from the side of the building behind the dumpsters. A pair of shutter doors allowed entrance to the mall. One of them was padlocked. The other wasn't. Unfortunately, it was occupied.

The walker stared at them blankly as the trucks came to a stop. It was trapped by what looked to be a set of palate straps that were tangled around its chest and one arm. Someone had lowered the loading bay door, pinning the straps to the ground. The walker was caught fast, unable to move more than a few inches in either direction. It stumbled back and forth, empty gaze fixed on the trucks. Its lower jaw was missing, as was most of its throat, leaving it unable to make any noise louder than a wet grunt. A swollen, black tongue flopped limply in the ruin of its mouth.

Terry winced at the sight of the zombie. "Christ."

"I doubt he looked that bad, even after three days in the tomb," Riggs said, as he climbed down out of his truck. He held out his fist. "Rock, Paper, Scissors?"

Calavera scooped up a chunk of shattered masonry laying on the ground, wound up his arm and sent it hurtling toward the zombie. It punched into what was left of the corpse's skull, pulping it and dropping the dead man to the loading dock. Terry and Riggs looked at him. Calavera shrugged. "We do not have time to play games. You two stay back and cover me while I get the door open. If there is something in there, I would rather it not chew my face off."

He sprang lightly onto the loading dock and gripped the bottom of the door. It wasn't locked, thankfully, but it was rusted out and in need of maintenance. He took a deep breath, centering himself and thrusting down the faint flicker of unease that accompanied opening unfamiliar doors these days, and began to drag the door upwards, kicking the fallen walker out of the way as he did so. Unseen gears squealed in protest, and it resisted him for a few moments. He kept his eyes on his feet, half-expecting dead hands to reach through the gap and claw at his ankles. Thankfully, nothing of the sort occurred.

He heard a muffled shout from inside, and the telltale boom

of a handgun. Something was happening, and it probably wasn't good. "This way," he bellowed, at the top of his lungs. "Hurry!" He grunted and the shutter door moved upwards by another few inches. He heard the sounds of running feet, panting and then a bark as Attila shot through the gap and bounded off the loading dock, tail wagging.

"Rats!" Imogene yelped, as she scrambled under the door. Calavera looked down in shock as Ramirez and the others followed her. Westlake was the last, and fat, black rats clung to his dead flesh, biting and gnawing.

"Get 'em off me," he rasped, clawing at his attackers. "Get them off me!"

Ramirez grabbed Westlake by the back of his shirt and dragged him across the loading dock. "Calavera, drop the door!"

Calavera attempted to do as she'd asked, but his efforts had somehow jammed it. As he worked to force it downwards, he heard the sound of rats scurrying toward the light. Not just a few, but hundreds. He cursed softly and strained against the metal, matching his strength against that of the building. Finally, with a crunch, the blockage gave way and the door started to drop – but not quickly enough. A dozen rats squirmed through the opening even as he slammed the door down. He retreated as they swarmed about him.

Gunshots sounded. One by one, the rats ceased moving. Calavera turned to see Coop lowering his rifle, and he gave the other man a nod of thanks. Behind him, the door shuddered slightly and then went still.

Ramirez and the others were helping Westlake. The dead man was cursing virulently as the rats were pried off him and dispatched. "Why the hell are they coming after me?" he growled. "Usually anything dead just ignores me."

"They're not dead," Kahwihta said, poking one of the rats with her cattle prod. "Just infected. Not that it's a virus, mind. Whatever you want to call it, they have it, only it hasn't killed them yet."

"I thought animals died fairly quickly after eating tainted flesh," Calavera said, as he joined her. He nudged the rat with his foot, repulsed and impressed in equal measure.

Kahwihta shrugged. "They do. They're supposed to. There's still so much we don't know about the causes behind all of this. Maybe rats are immune. After all, these look pretty healthy despite being, well, evil."

"Save the science lesson," Riggs shouted. "It's time to go." He was hanging half out of the cab of his truck and pointing behind him. Calavera looked and saw an indistinct number of shapes rushing along the fence-line. The flock of buzzards swooped low overhead, calling out to one another in their eagerness for the feast to come.

"Runners," Calavera said, flexing his hands in readiness. Behind him, the loading dock door rattled. He and the others turned. It rattled again, and something pink and twitching forced its way underneath. The rats, it seemed, had not given up their pursuit after all.

"Time to go," Ramirez said, helping Westlake to his feet.

CHAPTER FIVE
Ptolemy

Calvin Ptolemy looked up at the wide, carnivorous sky, and shuddered. It was simply too vast an area for his perceptions to handle. It was not beautiful, even at its bluest. The clouds hid jungles; who knew what sort of tigers lurked in them?

"What are you looking at?" a woman's voice inquired.

"A womb of infinitude," Ptolemy said, turning to the hangar. "Did you know that it was once postulated that the upper atmosphere contains an ecosystem all its own?" Through the open doors he could see the plane that had brought them to South Carolina. It was a private jet, large enough to carry twenty or so people, plus luggage. The hangar was large enough to accommodate it, just.

"Never heard that. Wouldn't surprise me, though. Lots of weirdness up there in the wild blue yonder." The woman – Gable – was tall and built like a runner. She spoke with a faint twang; Australian, Ptolemy thought. Or perhaps New Zealander. He'd never asked. It was a personal question, and their relationship was professional. "So, you want the good news or the bad news first?"

"The good, please." He pulled a small notebook out of his pocket and a scrap of pencil. He endeavored to keep a running tally of such matters when possible. Lists were the lifeline of survivor communities.

"She's running fine now. I cleared out the fuel line and refueled from the reservoir here. We're ready for takeoff whenever the others get back."

"And the bad news?"

Gable slapped the hull of the plane. "Right, she has maybe enough muscle for one more run – two at most. After that, I wouldn't want to take her into the air." Ptolemy assumed she knew what she was talking about. Gable was a pilot, and a good one. She'd been flying planes for almost a decade before the end of the world and had leapt at the chance to do so again, even if it meant the high possibility of a gruesome death.

She'd been one of the few survivors holed up at Atlantic City International Airport. A few passengers, some flight crew and a handful of pilots had forted up in the first-class lounge, surrounded by hundreds of zombies. Ptolemy and his friends had done what they could to clear it out, with a bit of help from the other Atlantic City survivors.

The airport was still largely full of undead, but they'd managed to isolate a single runway. It wasn't much, but it was enough for Gable's fellow pilots to ferry people to the Saranac Lake airfield in the trio of working planes they'd managed to salvage. There weren't many people left in the city these days; only the volunteers willing to contribute to the ongoing salvage operations. Gable was one of them. She'd agreed to fly the group south, for as long as the plane worked.

"That is good to know," Ptolemy said, making a note of it. "Anything else?"

Gable wiped her hands with a dirty rag. "If you want to keep flying, we need to get the engines converted over to ethanol. We're slack on fuel. There's barely enough here to get us to the next airfield. If… when we get back, we might want to think about stripping the other two planes and consolidating parts. Fewer planes means the fuel stretches further, and more parts available if something goes wrong. Which it will, because most modern planes are about one bout of bad turbulence from the scrapheap."

Ptolemy dutifully made the notes in his book. Gable watched him with her head tilted. "How many more runs, do you think?" she asked.

Ptolemy paused. "That depends." They'd fallen into a rhythm of late. Land at a convenient airfield, take what could be salvaged, then half the group would head out to whatever site Westlake had told them about. After two or three runs, the plane was full, and their haul could be ferried back to Saranac Lake. But it was getting harder to find the airfields, or anything worth salvaging.

"On your zombie mate, you mean."

Ptolemy snapped his notebook closed. "Yes. Westlake's knowledge of hidden byways, cross-referenced against that of Miss St Cloud, has allowed us to suss out a number of potential salvage sites."

"Only there wasn't much in that last one. The last few, in fact." Gable stuffed her rag in the pocket of her trousers.

Ptolemy eyed her warily. Gable was a good pilot, but like many professionals of her caliber, she thought her skill endowed her with authority. Coop was much the same. Neither of them liked being told what to do. Neither did he, come to that. But every survivalist worth his trail mix knew that someone had to be in charge.

"Your point?"

"Not worth the fuel we're burning, is it? Maybe we ought to shoot through."

"The fuel will go bad whether we burn it or not," Ptolemy said. "Better to use it than waste it, in my opinion."

"Yeah, well, not just your opinion, is it?" Gable smiled at him in a friendly fashion. "We should all get a vote, don't you think?"

"No."

The reply came not from Ptolemy, but from a lean, shaggy-haired woman, dressed in the remnants of a park ranger's uniform and scavenged fatigues. She held a camouflaged longbow in one hand and had a quiver of arrows slung over her back. She stepped past Ptolemy and jabbed a finger into Gable's chest. "No, you don't get a vote. I don't get a vote. Nobody gets a vote. We are not a democracy."

Gable stepped back, hands raised. "No drama, Sayers. I was just asking."

Elizabeth Sayers frowned. "But it's a question you keep asking. I find it annoying. Stop asking it. Stop annoying me. Just shut up and see to the plane." She turned to Ptolemy. "We've got a problem." She moved away from the plane.

"What sort of problem?" Ptolemy asked, following her out of the hangar and onto the airfield proper. It wasn't much to look at; overgrown, stacks of empty fuel drums and rusted machinery, and plenty of dead planes. It reminded him of every other airfield they'd seen in the past few months. It might as well have been a graveyard.

"The kind we can't do anything about. Look." She pointed in the direction of the coast. The sky was less blue there, more gray. And an unsightly gray at that. A heavy hue, Ptolemy thought. "See that?" Sayers went on. "That is a storm. And it's hurricane season."

Ptolemy blinked. "Ah. You think…?"

"I know." Sayers ran her hand through her mop of hair. "We've got maybe two or three days on it. If we head back today, we might just miss it entirely. If we stay on the coast, there's a good chance we'll get swamped." She glanced back at the hangar. "Gable's mouthy, but she's a good pilot. I doubt she wants to test her luck flying through a hurricane."

Ptolemy was about to reply when the radio clipped to his belt gave a belch of static. *"Ptolemy? This is Ramirez, over."*

He unclipped the radio. "This is Ptolemy. Are you heading back?"

"We are. But we've got company."

Ptolemy was about to ask the obvious question, when he saw the dust cloud and the buzzards. "Ah. Roger. We will prepare the appropriate welcoming committee." He lowered the radio and turned to Sayers, but she was already heading for the ladder that led to the roof of the hangar. Ptolemy retrieved his shotgun and checked it over.

The Benelli M4 tactical shotgun had become akin to an extra appendage for him. It was something reliable in an unreliable world. The gun was one of the few remaining pieces of the arsenal he'd assembled before the end of the world.

He shouted a warning to Gable and climbed onto the bed of a rusting fuel truck. The dust cloud was getting bigger, and the buzzards were closer. Rats, dogs, birds, and pigs in great numbers were all sure signs of a zombie population. The animals that fed off mankind's scraps were still doing so, even now. Wild animals knew better, mostly. Not always, but mostly. Whatever made zombies the way they were didn't affect animals in quite the same way, but it did affect them.

The trucks reached the fence and sped along the bumpy dirt road that led to the entrance of the airfield. As they neared the gate, Ptolemy could finally make out their pursuers. There were ten of them, maybe twelve. It was hard to get an exact count on something that moved that fast.

The runners were lean things, all sinew and leather, their features indistinct with decay. None of them were clothed, having discarded that along with their humanity in the years since the end of the world. As he watched them draw close, Ptolemy couldn't help but wonder what they might have been before. Most runners had been joggers, athletes and the like, at least according to Kahwihta, though she had no answer as to why they became leathery speed demons upon rising from the dead.

Behind him, Gable came out of the hangar with a hunting rifle in her hands. "How many?" she asked. Her voice was shaky. She was still frightened of them, even after all this time. Ptolemy glanced at her and gave what he hoped was a reassuring smile.

"Ten by my count. A small pack, nothing too troublesome.

Aim for the ones at the back. Sayers will handle the ones at the front."

"What about the bloody ones in the middle?"

Ptolemy dropped down out of the truck and hefted his shotgun. Gable frowned, but nodded. She settled herself behind an empty fuel drum and focused the weapon's sight on the approaching zombies. Ptolemy strode a short distance away, careful not to put himself in her line of fire. The day they'd arrived he and the others had set up a variety of obstacles around the obvious weak points in the fence. Things a human could easily avoid, but ones that zombies would find harder to get around.

The trucks crashed through the gate and slewed toward the hangar. He caught a glimpse of Calavera on the back of one, struggling with a runner that had made it onto the vehicle. Then the vehicles were speeding past, leading the runners into the line of fire. Unfortunately, the obstacles didn't slow them up much. Runners were far more agile than their slower kin.

Even so, one stumbled and fell, an arrow embedded in its eye. Gable fired then and another runner jerked, as if it had been stung, but kept moving. He heard her curse. It was hard to hit a moving target. That was why he rarely bothered trying.

Instead, he kicked over a pile of fuel drums and sent them rolling toward the approaching zombies. He didn't expect them to stop the runners, but they might slow them down a little. As he'd hoped, they scattered. Several of the zombies continued after the trucks but the others milled about, momentarily distracted.

Ptolemy raised the shotgun and fired. An unobservant

runner twisted in place, snapping blindly at the air as half its skull vanished, before collapsing to the ground. The others turned toward him as he'd hoped. He retreated toward the rusted-out truck and hauled himself back into the bed, all too aware of how close the runners were now.

He heard the *hiss-whap* of Sayers' arrows punching into flesh, and turned to see one of the zombies topple onto its face, an arrow jutting from its skull. Another hit the back of the truck and scrambled toward him, jaws wide, exposing a mouthful of jagged, broken teeth. He swung the shotgun up and fired. Once. Twice. The runner staggered back, portions of its torso and shoulder missing. Ptolemy fired again, shattering its head.

He heard the crack of Gable's rifle and clambered to the back of the truck. The runners had scattered, some going after the vehicles, others closing in on Gable. She was retreating toward the hangar, reloading as she went. Or trying to, at least. Ptolemy sighted and fired, knocking a runner sprawling. The thing kept going, dragging itself along the ground after the pilot. Two more headed for him and the truck.

He blew the first one's head off. The second made it onto the truck and lunged for him. It was too quick, and he found himself slammed back against the cab. He managed to wedge the shotgun between them and hold his attacker back, but it was stronger than he'd expected. Fear curdled in his gut, threatening to become panic. He fought it down.

The runner forced him back, snapping at him like a wild dog. He had a knife on his belt, but couldn't risk letting go of the shotgun. Then, with a growl, something struck the zombie in the back, knocking it off the back of the truck and to the ground. He looked down at Attila and nodded in thanks to the dog.

On the ground, Kahwihta deftly jammed her cattle prod into the zombie's head, causing it to twitch and convulse in an unpleasant fashion. She gave Ptolemy a thumbs up as she drew an icepick from her belt and thrust it through the runner's eye and into its brain. "Miss us?" she asked.

Ptolemy nodded. "Always," he said.

CHAPTER SIX
Florida

Westlake stood at the edge of the hangar, looking out at the night. Cicadas sang noisily in the trees and lesser insects kept time. Once, he'd found such natural sounds annoying. Now he felt nothing at all, save perhaps the calm of the grave.

Inside, the others were discussing their next move. Normally, he liked to be involved in the planning stages, but not this time. His mind still wasn't firing on all cylinders; hadn't been for some time. He could feel himself slipping in and out more often. For someone who'd once prided himself on his focus, it was unsettling to realize it wasn't there anymore. He looked down at his hands, bound in gauze and electrical tape. He was held together with spit and bailing wire, and it wasn't going to last.

Part of him didn't mind. He'd run out the clock already; it had all been overtime since the Villa. But another part of him was annoyed... no. Angry. Angry that he couldn't do more for them. Angry that his mind and body were failing, that he was becoming worse than useless. That wasn't how he wanted to go out. That wasn't how he wanted to be remembered. Not that he'd ever given it much thought, but death had a way of changing your priorities.

He frowned. The conversation behind him was getting loud. That was happening a lot more these days. The Villa survivors were used to working with one another, but the Atlantic City survivors weren't. They had their own ideas about how to do things.

He wondered how things were going back at the Villa with the influx of survivors. More hands made for swift work, but some of those hands might not appreciate being made to erect fences and plant potatoes. For now, everyone was concentrating on survival, on getting through the next day. But what about tomorrow? What about next winter?

There'd be trouble eventually. There always was. Maybe they'd get through it. Maybe they wouldn't. He probably wouldn't be around to see it either way.

He shook his head and stepped out into the night. Imogene was on watch, and she started at the sight of him. "What?" she said, half in challenge. She fingered one of her knives as she looked at him. She was scared; they were all scared, but he could smell it on her. The way he'd been able to smell it on Terry.

"Go inside. I'll keep watch."

"Yeah?"

Westlake nodded. Imogene hesitated, and then went. Westlake watched her vanish into the hangar and turned to face the night. For an instant, he wondered if it might be better for everyone if he just walked away now. They wouldn't notice until he was gone. But then what? It wasn't as if there was anything out there waiting for him.

"Going somewhere?" someone asked behind him. He heard the scrape of a lighter and turned. Coop stood behind him, lighting a cigarette.

"Just clearing my head," Westlake said. He studied the other man warily. He didn't much care for Coop. Coop didn't much care for him. He'd met guys like Coop before, almost always cops or cop-adjacent. Hard guys, with flat eyes and an inflated sense of their own authority. Bit of training, bit of blood, and they thought they were hot stuff. To his credit, Coop hid it better than most.

"Seems like it's plenty empty to me. Anything even left in there?"

Westlake frowned. "That a joke?"

Coop sniffed. "You see me laughing?"

Westlake grunted and looked out at the night. "I don't suppose you do much of that. Don't worry, I'm not planning to wander off."

"I'm not worried about that." Coop blew a plume of smoke into the air and sidled toward him. Westlake noticed that the other man had his hand resting on his holstered sidearm. "Tell me the truth… back at the mall, were you really going after that walker, or did it just get in the way?"

Westlake looked at him. "You accusing me of something?"

"Yeah, I think I am," Coop said. He pointed at Westlake. "I think you had a little lapse. I think something in what's left of your brain went pop and you decided to chow down."

"Is that what you think?" Westlake wanted to smile. He'd figured Coop wouldn't let the issue drop, no matter what Ramirez said. Coop thought he was the alpha dog. There was always one in every group who wanted to be in charge, but who definitely shouldn't be. That was Coop. Good at shooting, not so much at being a team player.

Coop nodded amiably, all smiles. Just two friends having a chat. "Yeah, it is. What about you, Westlake, what do you think?"

"I think I'm one foot in the grave. But you ain't the one who's going to bury me."

"Want to try me?" Coop said. He wasn't smiling now, and his hand was steady on his weapon, ready to draw it at a moment's notice.

Westlake chuckled. "I'm not the one with the problem, cowboy."

"Oh, I'd say you have a big goddamn problem," Coop growled. "And I'm just the guy to solve it for you." His arm tensed. Ready to draw. Westlake almost wished he would. Better to get it out in the open and handled than to let it fester.

"Are you now?" Ramirez said. She stepped out of the darkness, hands in the pockets of her jacket. Westlake wondered how long she'd been there. He didn't mind. Ramirez had been coming to his rescue in one way or another even before the apocalypse. "What problem is that, Coop? Care to fill me in?"

Coop frowned, but relaxed. Ramirez studied him. "No?" she said, when no answer was forthcoming. "Must not be a problem then. Take a walk. Check the perimeter and make sure nothing is creeping up on us in the dark. Runners don't usually travel alone. I'd hate to wake up tomorrow and find a horde of walkers clogging up the runway."

Coop made as if to protest, but then turned away with a grunt and ambled off. Ramirez watched him go, and then said, "You shouldn't antagonize him. He doesn't know you as well as I do."

"You don't know me very well at all," Westlake said. "And you should be more worried about him. A guy like that is more trouble than he's worth."

"Says the convicted felon."

"That just means that I know what I'm talking about." He crouched and picked up Coop's dropped cigarette. He watched it smolder and then stuck it between his lips. He inhaled creakily, drawing the last gutters of smoke into his lungs. It seeped out of the myriad tears in the flesh of his torso, squeezing between the layers of duct tape and clothing. Annoyed by the lack of sensation, he stubbed the cigarette out on his palm.

Ramirez watched the display with a raised eyebrow. "Are your lungs even still working?" she asked, half in jest.

"When I think about them," he said, flicking the remains of the cigarette away. "Which isn't often. I use them to talk, and that's about it. Even that's getting harder."

"I'm sorry."

"For what? It's not your fault."

"It sort of is."

Westlake grimaced. "Not really." He looked back at the hangar. "What's the consensus? Have we come to a decision?"

"Not really." Ramirez blew a strand of hair out of her face and peered toward the end of the runway. "Sayers says there's a hurricane coming. Two, maybe three days. That narrows our window significantly. Is there anything else around here? Charleston is – was – a major port. Is there something…?" She trailed off and gave him an expectant look.

Westlake stared out into the night. How many of the old hideouts had they already hit? He couldn't remember. They'd been going in a straight line, though. Taking it state by state, widening the parameters of the search. So, what was left on the east coast?

Not much, was the answer. Big cities were a no-go. Too many zombies, too much risk. That left the out of the way places, like the mall. The off-book safehouses and temporary accommodations available to a certain class of professional criminal.

"Westlake?" she pressed.

"Florida," Westlake said softly. Ramirez looked at him.

"What about it?"

"There's an airfield in Florida, in the Everglades. Refueling spot for drug traffickers."

"And?"

"And it's the big one. This place was a resort for international fugitives. Not as big as the Villa, but fairly large. It was built for big-time Narcos to hide away in when they made their occasional jaunts to the States." Westlake looked at her. She seemed doubtful. Then, she always looked that way. "No one knew about it except guys like me, and I can't imagine many Narcos left their fortified compounds for a hidey-hole in the swamp. But there's no telling whether it would still be there afterwards if Sayers is right and there's really a hurricane coming."

"You think we should hit it now, is what you're saying."

Westlake nodded. "Before it's too late."

"For whom? Us, or you?"

He looked away. "Does it matter?"

"Yes. The way you went after that walker… that wasn't like you. I nearly put a bullet in your head right then and there myself."

"So why didn't you?"

Ramirez hesitated. He wondered if she even knew the reason herself. Finally, she said, "I suppose I knew better. Besides, if you'd turned, I doubt you'd go for Terry… not when I'm standing right there." She gave him a crooked smile. He emitted a wheezy laugh and she wagged a finger at him. "Admit it, I'm right."

"I choose not to answer on the grounds that I might incriminate myself."

Ramirez nodded. "That's what I thought." She cleared her throat and changed the subject. "Why Florida?"

"Florida is close," Westlake said slowly. "Won't take us but a few hours to get there, and then we can go back to the mountains and hunker down for the summer."

"And then what?" Ramirez asked.

Westlake wasn't sure how to answer that, so he said nothing. The truth was, he wasn't thinking that far ahead. Couldn't, not anymore. Once, he'd been able to plan years ahead, lay the groundwork for jobs he might want to do at some point in the future. But these days, it was hard to think beyond the next week, even the next day. Maybe Coop was right, and his brain was decaying like the rest of him.

"Do you ever wonder what will happen to them, when it's all used up?" Ramirez asked. Westlake looked at her. She smiled in a brittle way. "The old world, I mean. When the last of the gas is gone, when all the insulin and the bullets are – poof! What then?"

"People got along fine without most of that for a long time." Privately, he figured things wouldn't change much. People would still be people. They'd still need someone to tell them what to do. Ramirez was good at that.

"People died."

"They do that regardless," Westlake said. "Nowadays, they even come back." He flexed his hands. He couldn't feel anything in them, not even the pull of tendons. They were so much dead meat. But he could still use them, though he didn't know how that was possible. Kahwihta had some theories, but he no longer had the patience to listen to them.

"No," he added, after a moment. "I don't wonder. I can't waste the braincells worrying about things I have no control over."

Ramirez snorted. "You were never very philosophical, even when you were alive."

"I had my moments," he protested.

"Few and far between," she said. Then, "Florida, huh? Saving the best for last?"

Westlake gave a phlegmy chuckle. "Something like that."

CHAPTER SEVEN
Sayers

"I'm not flying this bloody plane into the path of a hurricane, you absolute whacka," Gable said loudly. "I mean, not to knock your plan and all, but that's the most idiotic nonsense I have ever heard."

Sayers looked up from her book and fixed the pilot with a steady stare. Given that she was across the hangar, Gable didn't notice. That was probably for the best. She and the others were on the far side of the hangar discussing their next move. Except it wasn't a discussion, really. Ramirez had decided, and now everyone had to go along with it whether they liked it or not. That was how it went these days. The new hands hadn't quite figured out how the ranch was run yet, but they'd learn in time.

Ramirez raised her own voice in reply, and Sayers turned her attention back to the book. It was hard to concentrate, but it was one of Calvin's favorites so she was determined to finish it, even if the subject matter wasn't particularly to her taste. She heard someone approaching and sighed. Coop joined her, the wooden pallet she was using as a seat creaking beneath his weight.

"I thought you were on watch," she said, not looking at him.

"Kahwihta took over. Nothing out there anyway. Except bugs."

She knew he was wrong about that, but didn't press the matter. He might confuse it for a desire to have a conversation. Unfortunately, he didn't take the hint.

"Mind if I ask you a question?" he asked.

"Have you seen the yellow sign?" she replied, carefully dog-earing her page and closing the book. Coop blinked in puzzlement.

"What? No. What are you talking about?"

She held up the book. "Chambers. *King in Yellow.*"

"I thought Raymond Chandler wrote that."

"Not this one," Sayers said, setting the book down. "Something I can help you with?"

Coop studied her for a moment, and then reached into his combat vest and produced a crumpled pack of cigarettes. "Care for a smoke?"

Sayers frowned. "We're in an airplane hangar."

Coop selected one for himself. "So?"

"There's fuel fumes in the air. One errant spark and we could go boom."

Coop lowered his lighter. "Is that your way of saying no thanks?"

"What do you want, Coop?"

Coop sighed and took the cigarette out of his mouth. "You

seem like the practical sort. You handled yourself pretty well in Atlantic City. I think you're smart enough to see how things are going."

"Badly?"

Coop's smile surfaced like a shark's fin before vanishing into a scowl. "Westlake tried to eat Terry today. Ramirez won't admit it. Neither will Trapper. Your pals seem to think he's still human, but we both know that's not the case."

Sayers was silent for a moment. Then, "Which one's Terry?"

Coop paused. "The kid."

Sayers nodded, though that didn't really clear it up for her. "Fine. And?"

"That doesn't bother you?"

Sayers looked down at the book, running her finger over the title. She wasn't sure why Calvin liked it enough to bring. He'd built a small library at the Villa, mostly books with a practical bent, but there were some surprises in there. Collected volumes of Dickens, Hurston, and Wright. Books of poetry and big fat art books. "Everything bothers me," she said finally. It was one of the reasons she'd become a park ranger. Long periods of isolation, and only intermittent contact with the public. "Being out here bothers me. Working with people I don't know bothers me. People interrupting me when I'm trying to read." She looked at him. "Come to the point or leave me alone."

Coop snorted. "Fair enough. Westlake's dangerous, and so's Ramirez. We keep following their lead, we're all going to wind up dead or worse."

Sayers almost laughed. "Hate to break it to you, but we're going to wind up that way anyway." She looked at him. "The world's winding down. The only question is how long you last and what you do with the time left."

"That's two questions," Coop said with a frown. "And I'd like to last as long as possible. What about you?"

Sayers didn't reply. He was still dancing around it, but she knew what he wanted. Coop reminded her a little of her father; he'd thought the only good operation was one he was in charge of. Then, he might not be wrong. Thus far, things weren't going too well. Low on fuel, low on ammunition, and too far away from the Villa to hoof it back if something went wrong with the plane.

"I don't worry about things I can't control. Neither should you."

"But what if we could? Control it, I mean." He looked at Ramirez and the others. "Maybe we tell her it's time to go home... minus some dead weight."

"What's this we stuff?" she asked, picking up her book.

"Come on. I know you don't like her – or this."

"So you thought you'd come ask me to back whatever dumbass play you have in mind?" She snorted. "The problem with guys like you, Coop, is that you think everyone is as pragmatic as you. You think that if you puff out your chest and act all bad, that the others will fall into line like good soldiers. Only we're not soldiers, we're survivors. And that's a whole different type of hierarchy."

Coop had a puzzled look on his face, and she sighed and stood. "I'm going outside." She ambled out of the hangar, hoping the night air would clear her head. It was almost as loud outside as it was inside. City people never realized how loud the country could get, even now. Every animal for a hundred miles was up and out, foraging, fighting and the other thing. Not to mention the zombies.

Kahwihta was on watch. She sat outside near the fuel drums, playing with an old mason jar. Attila lay by her feet, head propped up on a battery powered lantern they'd salvaged from a sporting goods store. The dog looked up as Sayers approached, and she gave him a gentle scratch as she sat down beside Kahwihta without waiting for an invitation.

"Coop is planning a coup," she said.

Kahwihta nodded. "Ramirez knows." She rolled her eyes. "Everyone knows. He's not exactly subtle. I thought spec-ops guys were supposed to be smart."

"Guys like him don't do well without a proper chain of command. They see it as a problem to be solved – usually by putting themselves in charge. That's not how things work at the moment, though."

"He'll figure it out," Kahwihta said, still watching her jar.

"Maybe." Sayers looked at her. "What are you looking at?"

"Insects," Kahwihta said softly. She had a mosquito caught in the jar and was watching it bump against the sides. "We know animals turn. Warm-blooded, cold-blooded, doesn't matter. What if insects turn as well? Can you imagine swarms of undead mosquitoes? Or locusts?" She gave the jar a shake and looked at Sayers. "Sometimes I think you're right. I think it's all over bar the shouting. That nothing we do matters because we've already lost the fight. But if that's true, we wouldn't have lasted this long."

"Not exactly a scientific argument," Sayers said.

Kahwihta smiled. "Science isn't the only way to explain the

world. It's just one possible route." She looked at Sayers. "I think Westlake is the way he is because of random chance, fate, and the hand of God. I think we've lasted as long as we have because we were meant to, we're good at it, and we've had more than our share of luck."

Sayers shook her head. "I don't follow."

"What I mean is, I've got all the theories, but nothing to back any of it up." She fixed Sayers with a measured look, one that Sayers found somewhat unsettling. Then, she'd always found Kahwihta a bit weird. "That's all any of us have… just theories. No facts, just feelings."

"Gut instinct has always served me well," Sayers said. She paused, listening. Attila stiffened, a ridge of hair prickling on his back. Kahwihta frowned.

"What is it?"

Sayers didn't answer. She went to one of the upright fuel drums and watched the water that had collected there. It rippled gently, as if from some deep tremor. There was an ugly pressure in her head, as if her skull were a balloon about to burst. That usually meant it was going to start raining soon. She looked back at Kahwihta and gestured silently for her to arm herself. Then she started toward the gate.

They'd wedged it shut as best they could after the sudden arrival of Ramirez and the others, finally sticking one of the trucks in front of it. Kahwihta followed her. "Coop said he walked the fence," she murmured.

"Coop was looking for two-legged threats," Sayers replied. "Stay back a moment and keep quiet. I need to listen." She took the fence a pace at a time, senses straining against the muffling folds of night. There was something out there. There was always something out there. The question was, did it want to get in here?

She kept moving, checking the fence. Once upon a time she'd have rigged some cans on a string or even a few boobytraps, but she'd learned the hard way that making noise was the worst thing you could do, especially in unfamiliar territory. Better to risk something sneaking up on you than having a stray breeze or falling branch alerting every zombie in the area to your presence.

Sayers paused, feeling eyes on her. She peered out through the fence, trying to spot whatever it was, half-expecting something dead and rotten to lunge at her. Instead, she heard a grunt to her right. She turned and stopped.

A coyote stared at her through the fence. She'd known there were coyotes all up and down the east coast, but it was bigger than the ones in Saranac Lake. More like a pit bull than anything else. Maybe it was, or had been, a crossbreed. Now it was something altogether less pleasant. From the look of it, it was having a bad time; mange, maybe. Or maybe it was rotting on the bone like every other zombie.

A twig snapped and she glanced left. Another one crouched near a small gap in the chain link. Behind her, Attila's growling had risen a few decibels. Eyes shone in the dark beyond the fence. She made a quick count; there were a dozen at least. Probably more, waiting where she couldn't see them.

The problem with zombie animals was that they retained a modicum of natural cunning. Human zombies, barring a few, had as much smarts as a shark that had just smelled blood. They went after their prey with single-minded fury, and not much else. But zombie animals were smarter than that. Nastier. Sneakier.

More dangerous.

She heard Kahwihta approach and quickly motioned for the younger woman to stop. There was no telling if there were coyotes already past the fence. There were plenty of gaps, and some coyotes knew how to climb. "What is it?" Kahwihta asked, softly.

"We have visitors," Sayers said. "Keep back, and keep hold of that mutt. I don't want him getting in my line of fire." She reached back for an arrow. As she moved, the coyote retreated. The others followed suit until there was nothing in sight. But she could hear them, running the fence line, yipping and snarling. Attila was barking now, flinging himself toward the fence despite Kahwihta's best efforts to hold him.

To her right, something growled. Sayers spun, nocking an arrow even as she twisted around. She loosed it just as the coyote sprang from where it had been hiding. The arrow caught it in its open mouth and followed the path of least resistance to its brain. The animal collapsed in a twitching heap. Howls filled the night. She looked at Kahwihta.

"Back to the hangar – now."

CHAPTER EIGHT
Take Off

The rest of the night was spent listening to the coyotes prowl around the airfield, yipping and howling. Kahwihta didn't mind much. The Adirondacks were full of animal noises. This was a bit different, granted. Most of the animals in the mountains weren't infected, which these coyotes definitely were.

They'd had to kill a few more before Calavera and Coop had gotten the doors shut. Sayers had done most of the work, putting arrows in them. But Terry and the others had contributed when one had managed to squeeze in before the doors were fully shut. They'd beaten it to a pulp with whatever was to hand before Calavera had tossed it outside. She'd heard the others fighting over it for a while and wondered if there'd be anything left of the carcasses come morning.

She dozed a bit, her head resting back against a tool cabinet, one hand laying protectively on Attila's neck, just in case she had to make a grab for his collar. But he seemed content to stay by her side, so long as the hangar doors were shut. She knew Ramirez and the others thought he was dumb, but he was smart enough not to go looking for trouble. That put him well above most people, in her estimation.

Attila suddenly lifted his head. She stiffened, listening. Something snuffled at the base of the hangar wall. Then it was gone. Light streamed under the corrugated metal. It was morning. Birds were singing.

Imogene sat down next to her suddenly and offered her a baggie of dried apple slices. "Bit chewy, but still edible." She rubbed Attila's ear, and he gave a contented grunt. "Think they're gone?"

"Possibly. Coyotes are generally crepuscular."

Imogene stared at her. Kahwihta selected an apple slice and smiled. "Means they're more active in the early evening than later at night. Though urban coyotes are more often nocturnal – or were. Who knows what zombie ones prefer?"

"Zombies don't seem to care one way or another," Imogene said, nibbling on a piece of apple. "Can't imagine these are any different."

"You'd be surprised. Zombification is a mystery box. You never quite know what you're going to get when you reach inside."

"There's a mental image," Imogene said. She took another apple slice and bit it in half. "So, you're some kind of expert on zombies or something?"

"Or something. Why?"

Imogene jerked her chin in Westlake's direction. "Is he getting worse or better?"

Kahwihta paused. "I have no idea. I've never seen one like him. Maybe he'll stay aware and lucid until he just... falls apart. Or maybe his mind will go, and he'll be just another walker. There's no way to tell, no way to predict it. All we can do is watch and hope."

"That doesn't sound very scientific."

Kahwihta shook her head. "You're not the first to point that out." She leaned back against the cabinet and looked at Imogene. "What about you?"

"What about me?"

"You're not a zombie expert, or a marksman or a luchador. So, what are you?"

"I was a line cook," Imogene said, tapping one of her knives. "In a restaurant downtown back in Atlantic City." She smiled thinly. "I was chopping vegetables when it all kicked off. Never been so glad I bought the good knives."

Kahwihta chuckled. "I was in the mountains. Didn't even know there'd been an apocalypse until I made it to town." She looked over to where the others sat. They'd set up a map on an old corkboard they'd found in the airfield office. It was one of Ptolemy's, covered in circles and x's, like some high school coach's strategy board.

Every cache and safehouse Westlake could recall had been marked on it. Those that were out of reach or located in areas that were considered too dangerous to travel to were marked in red. Everything else was black.

Right now, they were all staring at Florida as they ate a meager breakfast of dried fruit, expired candy, and flat soda. It was almost the last of their provisions. They were down to jerky, hardtack and whatever they could find in candy machines.

Westlake tapped the map. "It's here. Right smack in the

Everglades. The only way to find it would be to get a satellite looking straight down. Or to know where it was in the first place."

"Did you visit this one, at least?" Coop asked. Westlake glanced at him.

"Once, coming back from a thing in Cuba. Why?"

Coop smiled and spread his hands. "Just wanted to make sure you weren't bullshitting us, man. No offense."

"None taken," Westlake said after a moment. But Kahwihta could hear the lie in his tone. It was difficult, but she'd learned to translate his creaky monotone over the last few months. Westlake was angry, whether at himself or Coop, she couldn't tell. If it was Coop, she didn't blame him.

Coop had seemed nice enough when they'd first met. But after spending time with him, she'd come to realize it was all surface pleasantries. Coop was a dyed-in-the-wool jackass, and while his heart was probably in the right place, his head definitely wasn't. Especially if what Sayers had told her the night before was true.

She glanced at Ramirez, and saw that she already had her eyes on Coop. She looked annoyed, frustrated, and tired all at once. Coop didn't seem to notice, or maybe he didn't care. He wasn't the first idiot to try to put himself in charge. They'd had their share of 'Gone Galt' nutjobs in Saranac Lake, as Ptolemy called them. It never ended well for them.

Gable spoke up. "And there's fuel there? Trucks?"

"Fuel definitely. Vehicles, maybe." Westlake paused. "This place was the biggest Narco hideout in Florida. They considered it a forward operating base." He glanced at Coop. "You know what that means, right?"

Coop nodded slowly, a thoughtful look on his face. Kahwihta wondered if he were suddenly reconsidering whatever foolishness he'd been planning. She hoped so. Ramirez looked at Gable and said, "How long?"

"An hour, not much more depending on the storm winds. But if that is a hurricane brewing out there, we'd be crazy to fly into its path. We certainly won't be able to fly out again…" She looked around, as if seeking support, but found none.

"That's the beauty of it," Westlake said, his hand pressed flat to the map. "We can ride out the storm there. Get the plane into a hangar and take our time plundering."

"Unless it's full of zombies," Terry said. He didn't look at Westlake as he said it. Kahwihta wondered what he thought about what had happened at the mall. From what Calavera had said, Terry hadn't much mentioned it.

"Another reason to take our time," Westlake said. He looked at them. "This is the big one. Larger than anything this side of the Villa. It'll see you set for months, if not a year or more. You take everything that's not nailed down, load it up and go."

Kahwihta caught the phrasing of that, even if no one else did. She looked hard at him, and knew he was planning something. He had been for some time, she thought. Maybe that was why he'd been avoiding her since the mall.

"We've got maybe three days before whatever is brewing off the coast sweeps inland," Sayers said. "Probably less. We'll get heavy rainfall about eighteen hours prior, and the wind will start to pick up. The pressure we're feeling now? That's a sign the rain is on the way. So, if we're going to do this, we need to do it now."

Riggs cleared his throat. "What if we don't want to?"

"There's one working truck," Ramirez said. "You can siphon gas from the other one and head back toward the Villa. If you keep your head down, and don't do anything stupid, you should make it in one piece."

"Stupid like flying into the Everglades during a hurricane, you mean?" Imogene called out. She pushed herself to her feet. "Look, I enjoy a good airplane ride as much as anybody, but is this really the right thing to do?" She glanced at Kahwihta. "Let's just go back to the mountains. Leave it. This place will still be here in a month or two, right?"

"Maybe," Ramirez said. "Or maybe someone else will get to it first." She looked around. "That's the risk with a place like this. It's not going to be long before someone stumbles across it, or it gets destroyed or... something. And then it's not there anymore."

"It might not even be there now," Coop said.

Ramirez didn't look at him but kept her eyes on the others. "That's the risk we run. That what we need won't be there."

"And if it's not? If it's already been picked over?" Gable asked.

"Then we return to the Villa, and regroup," Ptolemy said, speaking up for the first time. "We go out again when we are rested and ready." He went to the map and studied it, his hands clasped behind his back. "There are no survivor groups in Florida."

"What do you mean?" Coop asked.

"I mean, there are no survivor groups in Florida. At least not any that I have been able to contact. I have spoken to survivors from Florida, but none *in* Florida."

"Which means it's all up for grabs," Westlake said, looking

at the others. He paused. "But every month that goes by, there's going to be less chance that place is still there. No one to look after it, no one to keep the swamp cut back, pretty soon it'll be a memory."

Ramirez spoke up. "That's why now is the best time. We're here, we've got the fuel, the guns. We may not get a second chance." She paused. "But I'm not planning to force anyone to go. Not even you, Gable. You can get on the truck with Riggs."

"I didn't say I wasn't coming," Riggs protested, but no one was paying any attention to him. Ramirez looked around, her expression one that Kahwihta thought of as "tired abuela". It was the sort of expression that made hard cases look at the floor and scuff their feet, suddenly ashamed of all the bad behavior.

"I'm going," Ramirez said, looking around. "So's Westlake. Who else?"

Calavera's hand went up immediately. Ptolemy followed suit, and Kahwihta raised her own hand a moment later. It wasn't that she particularly wanted to go, but she wanted to keep an eye on Westlake. Terry's hand went up as well, which was something of a surprise. Riggs and Imogene hesitated a bit longer, but raised theirs eventually. That left Gable, Coop and Sayers. Gable shook her head. "Galahs, the whole bunch of you." She pointed at the plane. "That's my plane there. She and I have developed a close relationship the likes of which you cannot conceive. So, I will not be leaving her in your heathen hands, thank you."

"Is that your way of saying you're in?" Ramirez asked.

"I reckon."

Ramirez looked at Coop and Sayers. Sayers, Kahwihta

noticed, wasn't paying attention at all. When she realized that Ramirez was looking at her, she shrugged. "I go where Calvin goes. Even if this is a dumb idea."

Coop laughed and stood. "I've always wanted to see the Everglades." He looked at Ramirez. Kahwihta wondered what he was thinking. Nothing good, she guessed. "Guess we're all in. What now?"

Ramirez smiled. "Now we get loaded up and get this bird in the air."

A few minutes later, Calavera and Coop got the hangar open, letting in a wash of morning light. Nothing rushed in with it. No coyotes, no zombies. Just birdsong and mosquitoes. Ramirez gestured. "Kahwihta, Coop, Sayers... keep an eye on the perimeter. Once that engine gets going, our friends from last night will probably come back."

Kahwihta took Attila out to where the coyotes had attacked. As she'd expected, the body was gone save for a few tufts of bloody hair. She retrieved Sayers' arrow from the ground and examined the tip. The blood had a tarry consistency that was in keeping with most zombies she'd studied.

Attila growled softly, and Kahwihta looked up. Something was dragging itself toward her through the long grass that clustered around the fence. She rose slowly to her feet and tightened her grip on the arrow.

It was a coyote, or what was left of one. It hauled itself along on broken forepaws, its head wobbling unpleasantly around the arrow Sayers had put through its neck the previous evening. Attila started toward it, teeth bared, but Kahwihta waved him back. She watched the dead thing crawl toward her.

It reminded her of Westlake in a way, refusing to surrender to the inevitable. She thought of the look she'd seen on his face in the mall. She didn't intend to let Westlake end up like this. She leaned over and drove the arrow through one of its eyes. It stiffened and flopped to the ground, unmoving at last.

One way or another, she'd spare him that.

CHAPTER NINE
Flying High

"The wild blue yonder," Gable said, tapping the instrument panel. "Only place on God's good green Earth more dangerous than the bloody ocean." She glanced at Ptolemy. "Keep those darling peepers peeled, if you please. Don't want to run into a flock of zombie budgies if we can help it."

"Once was enough," Ptolemy murmured, writing in his notebook. She laughed.

"Too right." They'd hit a flock of mixed species coming into Myrtle Beach a week previous. Pigeons, sparrows, birds of prey... all together, all infected. The birds had swarmed the plane, divebombing it as she'd landed. They were lucky the engines were still intact.

It hadn't taken them long to get airborne. They had it down to a science these days. Load up, clear the runway, and grab some altitude. By the time the local wildlife started to follow the sound of engines, they were gone.

It had been quiet since then. Most of the group used the flight time to catch a few extra winks of sleep. Gable didn't begrudge them that, though she could use an extra nap herself. Caffeine was a distant, fading memory. They had some tea, but it was the kind Americans bought in cans. Disgusting stuff, even before it had expired.

These days, the old world was in the rearview mirror and vanishingly small. She'd concluded that she was never going to see Australia, or Sydney, again. Even if she could find a plane fit for the journey, there wasn't going to be enough fuel to get her home. At best, she'd be forced to land at some halfway point. At worst, she'd go down in the ocean and join the rest of the dead walking there.

Nothing for it really. She had to stay and make the best of things, whether she liked how it was going or not. It was that or give up.

She leaned forward, peering out the rain-spattered windshield. Florida unspooled below as an ill-defined gray-green mass of sawgrass marsh and freshwater swamp. They'd been in the air for just over an hour and seen little except dark clouds rolling in off the ocean. No birds, living or dead. Then again, birds probably knew better than to fly in hurricane weather.

Florida was basically no-man's-land at this point and had been since the apocalypse. Stories traveled fast, even with social media a thing of the past. Survivors bartered information like it was bullets or tins of mystery meat. Since leaving the airport, she'd learned that Florida was the proverbial black hole. Survivors went in and didn't come out. Every city was full of the walking dead, every road and interstate jammed with aimless hordes. Even the wildlife was slowly going bad.

She'd stayed out of the Outback, like any sensible person,

but she could imagine what had happened there. Zombie boars or worse... zombie koalas. There was no telling what sort of hell on Earth the Everglades had turned into.

She sat back in her chair, trying to get comfortable. It was harder these days, though she didn't know why. Too many months without taking a bird up, maybe. And hadn't that been a corker of a vacay? Lots of time to think about her life choices, in between moments of searing panic. She hadn't come to any conclusions worth recalling.

Gable smiled thinly. She'd never imagined being stuck in another country when the world ended. It somehow made things simultaneously easier and more difficult. Not that she'd been the only one in the airport. There'd been passengers and crew alike from all over; most of them hadn't survived. She glanced at Ptolemy. "Bit of a coincidence that, though, don't you think? Minute we get into the air, the birdies show up. Minute we land, it's the two-legged variety. God must have it out for us."

He looked up from his notebook. "What if coincidences are not coincidences at all, but the schemata of some infinite machine? The clockwork of history."

She snorted. "Fate, then?"

"What is fate but the retroactive assignment of meaning to diverse occurrences in order to bolster a self-narrative? You think, therefore you are. If you are, then what you think is meant to be." Ptolemy looked up from his notebook. "The truth is, if there is a pattern we cannot discern it, therefore whether there is or is not is of little consequence, save as a campfire debate. As Fort said, I think, therefore I am going to have breakfast."

Gable shook her head. "You're a weird one, mate."

"So I have been told." He reached for the radio and began to scan the frequencies. Mostly it was just static. It was always static these days. Sometimes there'd be a snatch of a voice, like a distant echo at the edge of your hearing. But it was always gone when they went back. The human race was over; nowhere left to run. Gable was careful not to share that opinion, however. Depression was a killer, as fatal as a zombie's jaws on your throat. It spread quickly, too.

She tried to think of something, anything else. She settled on Ptolemy. He was fairly good looking, despite being a bit of a dag. Away with the fairies, even on his good days. That made her feel a bit clucky around him, though she was careful not to show it. Too precious for the world, as her sister might have put it, were she not currently wandering about Sydney, looking for some unfortunate soul to nibble on.

Gable grimaced at the thought. She'd been on the phone with her sister when the shit hit the fan and the world went topsy-turvy. She could still remember that call like it was yesterday. The sound of her niece and nephew screaming, the dog barking… glass shattering.

She blinked the memory away before it could fully unfold, stuffing it back in the black box at the bottom of her mind. That was where she put all her bad thoughts and ugly memories. After the last year or so, it was stuffed to bursting. Sooner or later, it'd break open and she'd be a wreck. She'd seen it happen to others and could feel it in the offing – like an itch she couldn't scratch.

She thought again about the airport, and the fight to survive.

Taking on walkers with a fire extinguisher for the chance to raid a candy machine. Going through the unclaimed luggage, hoping for something – anything – useful. They'd found a fair few handguns that way. God bless America, land of the free and home of the heavily armed.

It hadn't been enough. For a while, she'd wondered if there was anyone left alive outside their fortified first-class lounge. Consciously, she'd known that if they'd survived it was likely others had as well, but subconsciously was a different story. Then they'd contacted Atlantic City, with Ptolemy's group. They'd learned about the Villa. About the sanctuary in the mountains.

She hadn't seen it yet. That was the most frustrating thing about the current situation. She hadn't seen it. None of them had seen it, in fact. Not even Coop. They'd heard plenty, but so far, the promised land was out of reach until they'd ended this supply run. Sometimes she doubted she'd ever get to see it at all.

"What is that?" Ptolemy's voice jolted her from her reverie.

"What is what?"

Ptolemy was leaning forward, craning his neck to see through the windshield, to the ground below. "I thought I saw something. A vessel of some kind."

"A what?" Gable looked at him.

"A ship."

Gable stared. "In the Everglades?"

He didn't reply. Instead, he reached for the radio and began to tweak the knob. "It looked well maintained. Perhaps there is someone alive down there. Someone who needs help or could be of assistance."

She shook her head. "Yeah, I don't think that's likely, mate. And I don't think you saw what you think you saw."

Ptolemy frowned and made as if to get out of his seat, but a sudden bout of turbulence forced him to forgo the idea. He mumbled a string of numbers under his breath; latitude and longitude, she realized. He really did think he'd seen something. She cursed under her breath.

It was always something with these people. They saw something, heard something, thought something, and it always led to them haring off into the back of beyond. In Philadelphia, Ramirez had ordered a detour to rescue a settlement. In Norfolk, it had been a radio signal from what Ptolemy insisted was an off the books military installation. Delay after delay, leading to wasted ammunition, wasted fuel… maybe eventually wasted lives. Maybe hers, maybe someone else's.

"Is that the fuel light?"

Gable blinked and sat up. Cursed. "It is, yeah. I told you we're flying light. We are running on fumes." Not even fumes, come to that, but she saw no reason to cause a panic. She'd landed birds on empty before, but it was never a pleasant experience.

"Thankfully we are close to the coordinates Westlake provided. It should be coming into sight soon."

"Soon ain't soon enough," Gable said, tightening her grip on the controls. She didn't feel like mentioning that Westlake's coordinates were taking them smack into the middle of the swamp. If he was wrong, they weren't getting a second chance. She tapped the instrument panel, trying to get it to realign with her wishes rather than reality. "We might be in for a bit of a bump."

"We have survived worse."

"Mate, I don't fault the confidence, but I'm not worried about us. I'm worried about the bloody plane." She activated the intercom and picked up the mike. "Ladies and gentlemen, this is your captain speaking, we are approaching the last chance saloon, all or nothing, do or die. The seatbelt sign is now on and you'd better do as it says, or there's a pretty good chance you're going to be splattered across all of the cabin. Fair warning, I'm not cleaning that up." She glanced at Ptolemy. "That goes for you, too. Buckle up and hold on to your butt."

She hauled back on the controls, fighting to keep the plane on an even keel despite its desire to wobble and flop. A splashdown, even one out here, wouldn't be a game-ender, but it wouldn't be pleasant either. Especially since they had no way of towing the aircraft to solid ground. She had to keep them aloft, at least until they reached the airstrip.

"Come on, come on," she murmured.

True to Ptolemy's word, she spotted it a moment later. A long stretch of nothing cut through the green of the Everglades, with a backstop made of water barrels and sandbags. Not the most professional strip she'd ever put down on, but it would do. "There you are, you beauty."

"Told you," Ptolemy murmured.

Gable ignored him and concentrated on taking the plane down without smearing them across the inviting stretch of runway. But even as she focused on the task, something – many somethings – brown and mangy flung themselves toward the descending plane. "Oh holy... hold on!"

"What is it?"

"Bloody pelicans!"

The first pelican hit the plane a moment later. It sounded like a water balloon bursting. The controls twitched in her hands as the rest of the flock arrived. Brown pelicans, at least thirty of them, all clearly infected given their behavior. The windshield cracked as a second bird struck the plane and pinwheeled away.

The runway rose up to meet them as the pelicans continued their assault. Gable lowered the landing gear and prayed one of the birds wouldn't get jammed in the mechanisms. The cracks in the windshield spiderwebbed and a thin whistle of air filled the cockpit. Ptolemy shrank back in his seat. "This happens far more often than I care to think about," he said.

Gable reached for the pistol hanging in its holster from the back of her seat. The glass started to buckle even as she drew it. The plane touched down as a stabbing beak pierced the membrane of glass and darted for her. She twisted aside, and the beak stabbed into the seat. Ptolemy cried out, but she ignored him, extended the pistol, and fired. The pelican vanished as the plane careened down the runway. She hit the rudder pedals, reducing speed as they approached the backstop.

Pelicans hit the cockpit like bullets, trying to get through the broken window. Gable emptied her weapon into the mass of beaks, trying to get the birds out of the way so she could see what was ahead of her. The plane began to slow, its rear end veering slightly as the landing gear bit into the dirt runway. It rolled to a stop. The pelicans pressed against the glass, eyes rolling as they gazed at her hungrily.

"Turn away," Ptolemy said sharply. Gable twisted aside as

Ptolemy shoved his shotgun into the broken window and fired. What was left of the pelicans tumbled away from the plane in bloody heaps. Gable brushed glass off her chest.

"Couldn't have done that earlier?" she asked, glancing at him.

Ptolemy climbed out of his seat. "I thought it best not to distract you while you were landing the plane." He paused. "A fine job, by the way. I thought for certain we were going to crash again."

Gable rose from her seat and kicked aside the head of a pelican. "I hate this bloody country."

CHAPTER TEN
Dixie Jewel

Daniel Jessop, first mate of the *Dixie Jewel*, watched the plane pass overhead and sighed. He lowered the binoculars and looked at the others. "No markings. Private aircraft. Probably out of Tampa."

"It's going the wrong way for Tampa," Phipps said. He'd been stout at the beginning. A lawyer, or maybe a politician. Now he was skin and bones. Jessop figured he'd been sneaking his rations to the kids, but chose not to say anything.

"Does it matter?" Grillo asked. She was a short woman, not petite but muscular. A swimmer, once upon a time. She'd been the ship's purser, before things went south. She and Jessop were the only officers left, other than Captain Ogilvy. And Ogilvy wasn't good for much these days. He mainly stayed in his cabin talking to ghosts. "We've got our own problems," she added.

That was something of an understatement. The *Dixie Jewel* was a passenger liner – a cruise ship, in the popular parlance. She'd been anchored at Port Everglades, in Fort Lauderdale, when the world had ended. Ogilvy and the other captains had decided to take as many vessels as they could offshore, look for safe harbor somewhere else.

They'd loaded up everything they could salvage, and as many survivors as they could find, and raised anchor just as Fort Lauderdale was overwhelmed by a veritable tsunami of tourists-turned-zombies. It turned out most of the coast was the same – ports and resorts turned into the hunting grounds of the dead. Even the airwaves were dead, save the occasional burst from some survivor settlement. Most were too far inland to reach. Others were too far away, given the relative lack of fuel for the ships.

They'd had nowhere to go. They'd spent a month anchored at sea, only a few miles from Fort Lauderdale, the ships tied together by mooring ropes so that they couldn't drift apart. But what had seemed like a good idea at the time had, in reality, been a nearly fatal mistake. Turned out water wasn't much of an impediment to the dead. They'd swarmed the vessels, drawn by the pulse of the engines. They'd had to cut the other ships loose and head away at all speed.

By the time they'd reached a safe distance, the weather had turned against them. A storm surge had battered them into the Everglades, and crippled the ship to boot. They'd thought that was the worst of it, until the dead had poured out of the sawgrass and trees like someone had rung a dinner bell.

When they'd left port, there'd been nearly one hundred people on board the *Dixie Jewel*. They were down to less than twenty now. In his private moments, Jessop wondered how long they had before the ship was nothing more than a rusting hulk full of dead bodies – walking or otherwise. But he was careful not to let the despair of those moments infect his interactions with others. He was still first mate, and that meant he was in charge while the captain was… indisposed.

Jessop looked at Phipps. "What do our stores look like?"

Phipps ran his hands through his thinning hair. "We've got maybe two days of food left. Longer, if we cut the rationing even tighter." He looked tired, Jessop thought. Then, they were all tired. They had to sleep in shifts thanks to the accident, and the thought of what was belowdecks didn't make for a restful slumber.

"Cut it," Jessop said. "Water?"

"Plenty of that if the rain keeps up," Grillo said, smiling slightly. "Which we know it will, given the season." She looked out over the swamp. "You know what gets me? If we could get to the engine room, get things shipshape, we could probably use the hurricane to get us moving back out to sea."

"Feel free to try," Phipps muttered.

Grillo looked at him, and then at Jessop. "Might be worth a go. Better than sitting here and starving to death, right?"

"There's nearly a hundred zombies down there," Jessop said. He turned away and rested his elbows on the rail. He looked out at the Everglades. Once, he'd have enjoyed the view. But after staring at it every day for several months, it was starting to pall slightly.

The Everglades had once been beautiful. Now they were just a green hell, full of the unshriven dead and the things that ate them.

Feet thudded on the deck. Jessop turned and saw one of the other survivors, a woman named Deborah something-or-other, hurrying toward them. She had a rifle in her hands, and a worried look on her face. "James and Willy saw something over on the right side–"

"Starboard," Jessop corrected absently. He hitched up his gun-belt and went to meet her. "Did they say what it was?"

"No. Just something. In the water."

"A boat?" They'd seen a few boats here and there, but none had ever come close to the cruise ship. Maybe they were worried about how many zombies might be aboard. Or maybe they were worried about the breathing passengers.

"Just something," she said, turning back the way she'd come. Jessop and the others followed her. It took them several minutes to reach the other side. The *Dixie Jewel* wasn't the largest ship on the water, but she was substantial enough to comfortably carry a few hundred passengers plus crew.

There was music playing when he got there. One of the other passengers, Shamekia, had proven to be something of an engineer and had hooked up the PA system to a spare solar generator, allowing them the luxury of music pumped from an old laptop. It was an eclectic mix; some country, some gospel, at least one house mix that sounded like a cross between Mongolian throat singing and a psychedelic haze.

Jessop spotted Willy and James standing at the rail, looking down at something. He joined them – and froze. It was big; no, not just big. Massive. The size of a truck. Bigger. An island of spikes, piercing the water and vanishing. Something that might have been a tail sending waves of murky water crashing over nearby walkers. He gripped the rail tightly, knuckles white. He felt a faint tremor run through the hull as whatever it was prowled around the bottom of the ship.

"It's looking for a way in," Grillo murmured.

"If it doesn't find one, it can probably make one," Jessop replied hoarsely. The ship shuddered slightly, as if buffeted by an unseen wave. He'd seen his share of monstrosities since they'd come to the swamp – the alligators were the worst – but nothing that big. It didn't bode well, that was for sure.

"What is it?" Phipps hissed in a low voice. Maybe he was worried about their visitor hearing him. "Another one of those goddamn alligators?"

"Too big to be a gator," Willy drawled. He was older than most, with lips and beard stained yellow from a lifetime chewing tobacco habit. He spat over the side, unconcerned about what might be swimming beneath them. "Might be one of them there dinosaurs."

"Dinosaurs are extinct," Grillo said.

"If humans can come back to life, why not dinosaurs?" James asked. He was younger than the rest of them, barely more than a kid. Willy patted him on the shoulder.

Grillo shook her head. "It's not a dinosaur."

"Then what is it, ma'am?" Willy asked, in a tone of challenge. Grillo bristled, but Jessop cleared his throat before she could say something she might regret. Things were tense enough as it was. He didn't want to have to worry about what was left of his crew tearing each other apart over flared tempers.

The ship shuddered again, more violently this time. Jessop instinctively grabbed the rail to steady himself. He could hear shouts of alarm from below. "Go check the hatches," he said, gesturing to Willy and James. "Make sure they're still sealed. I don't want any of those things getting out." The two hurried off. Another convulsion ran through the vessel as the half-glimpsed shape circled around to the port side. There was a loud splash as something that might have been a tail rose from under the water and fell back, propelling the unseen monstrosity along. "Somebody turn off that damn music," Jessop snapped. The music was a luxury; a way of giving people something to alleviate the tedium. But it also attracted the dead. Maybe it was doing the same with whatever this thing was.

As the music clicked off, the ship ceased shuddering. The monster had vanished as quickly as it had come. Phipps leaned back against the wall, away from the rail, his face in his hands. "Jesus Christ… how much worse can things get? Zombies aren't bad enough?"

"Never rains but it pours," Grillo said. She held out her hand. "And on that note…"

Jessop frowned and looked up at the sky. It had an ugly hue to it, like a newly minted bruise. "How many days, do you think? I give it maybe two, if we're lucky."

Deborah spoke up. "We should ask Willy. Apparently, he can tell a lot about the weather by how much his knee swells."

"I'll keep that in mind," Jessop said. Down below, the massive shadow on the water had seemingly departed. He heard the crunch of a tree falling somewhere in the swamp and saw a flock of birds rise over the canopy and flee from something he couldn't see. Whatever it was, it was heading away for the moment. But it was going to come back, sooner or later. He could feel it in his gut. "I'll go update the captain."

"Why bother?" Grillo asked bluntly.

Jessop gave her a stern look. "Because he's still captain, that's why." They'd had this conversation too often of late. Grillo wasn't the only one who felt that way, he knew. Ogilvy had retreated into himself after they'd lost contact with the other ships. Jessop knew he blamed himself. But they needed him.

Jessop left them there and went to the captain's cabin. The door was shut, of course. Ogilvy rarely came out these days. Jessop knocked politely, waited though he knew there'd be no reply, and opened the door. The cabins had needed keycards back when things had worked, but since the power had gone out, nothing locked unless they did so manually.

The cabin was dark, the window covered by a jacket. The interior smelled of unwashed body and spoiled food. No gnats, though. No flies. There weren't many insects around these days, not even mosquitoes. Jessop had noticed that early on, though he didn't know what it meant. Maybe it was just the weather, or something else. The thought worried him, nonetheless. One more thing to keep him up at night.

Ogilvy sat slumped in a leather chair, a bottle by his feet. The captain had enjoyed the occasional tipple prior to the apocalypse. Since then, he'd crawled fully into the bottle and hadn't surfaced in some time.

"Captain?" Jessop said softly.

Ogilvy grunted wordlessly. Jessop sighed and crouched near the chair. "Captain, it's time for the daily report."

"We're all dead," Ogilvy croaked.

Jessop frowned. "Not yet."

"I heard... something," Ogilvy muttered. He gestured aimlessly. "Out there."

"Just an alligator," Jessop said smoothly. "We chased it off." He started rattling off the day's reportage, and wondered if he ought to mention the plane. But he could tell Ogilvy wasn't really listening. The captain didn't have the capacity for the day-to-day anymore. But he was still the captain, until he was removed from command. And no one was doing that while Jessop was upright and breathing. The chain of command was all they had left, and he'd be damned if he was going to be the one to break it.

"The boats," Ogilvy said suddenly.

Jessop paused. "What about them?"

"Did they come back?"

Jessop stood. "No," he said softly. The *Dixie Jewel* was equipped with a small flotilla of lifeboats, as well as inflatable rafts, jet-skis and other methods of transport. For a while, they'd sent out a boat every few weeks, hoping to find extra supplies or some way of moving the ship. So far, none of them had ever come back, and Jessop had decided it wasn't worth risking any more lives.

"How many?"

It was a familiar question. Ogilvy asked it every time. "Eighteen, counting us," Jessop said gently. Ogilvy looked at him for the first time.

"No. I meant the others."

Jessop swallowed. "I... don't know." He didn't like to think about the dead down in the hold. When they'd first sealed the hatches, the banging had been incessant. These days, they were fairly quiet. Maybe they were hibernating.

"I can hear them, you know. Moaning into the vents. They blame me for what happened, Jessop... and they're right. It's all my fault." Ogilvy bent forward and buried his face in his hands. "It's my fault." He jerked around so suddenly that Jessop took a step back. "You should let them have me. They'll be at peace then, I know it."

"No, sir," Jessop said flatly. "No, I won't be doing that." He'd known Ogilvy was spiraling, but hadn't realized how bad it had become. Or maybe he'd just ignored it.

Ogilvy wobbled unsteadily to his feet. "They're my crew, my passengers… my responsibility… I have to go down there. You have to let me."

Jessop backed toward the door. "No, sir, I do not. My only responsibility is to keep everyone on this vessel alive for as long as possible. That includes you. But I'm afraid that for the remainder of our voyage you will remain confined to your cabin."

Ogilvy shook his head, as if he couldn't understand. Jessop took the opportunity to slip out and shut the door behind him. He heard Ogilvy mutter to himself behind the door, but thankfully he didn't attempt to barge out.

Jessop stared at the door for several long moments. He was going to need to put a guard on it, just to make sure Ogilvy didn't hurt himself or anyone else. He ran his hands through his hair and thought about the plane again. Then he pushed the thought aside and headed to find the others.

He wanted to double check those hatches.

CHAPTER ELEVEN
Airfield

Westlake looked at the hideout. It didn't have a fancy name like the Villa. No one was even supposed to know it existed. Maybe the people who'd built it had called it something, but Westlake didn't know what that was. He wondered if he had at one time. Was it one of those memories that had slipped from his head over the past few months? He pushed the thought aside. What was one more memory, after all?

The airfield was a thin strip of raised dirt, with a bulwark composed of a set of water barrels at one end. The trees had been cut back only to the narrowest possible margin, so as not to attract attention. The sawgrass was creeping back now, reclaiming what had been taken from it. In a year, maybe two, the airfield wouldn't be here anymore. That wasn't necessarily a bad thing. In his more philosophical moments, he was of the mind that what was happening now might actually be a good thing in the long run.

A few years before the apocalypse, he'd run a crew that

included a self-proclaimed anti-natalist, whatever that was. The guy had spouted off a lot about population density and failing resources. At the time, he'd sounded like an asshole. But maybe he'd been right. Maybe this was all nature's way of wiping the board clean. Once the humans were gone, the zombies would follow. Life would flourish again. Or not.

Westlake brushed the thought aside. He studied the hideout the way he'd once studied banks and delivery schedules. It sat at the far end of the runway, a low-topped square, single-story building. The roof was covered in camouflage netting to hide it from prying eyes in the sky. The netting stretched over the immediate area around the building, theoretically allowing for guests to move freely between the main structure and the outbuildings. There was a dock hanging off the back, marking where the sawgrass gave way to the swamp.

"Doesn't look very big," Coop said from nearby.

"Doesn't need to be," Westlake said. "There were never more than a dozen people here at a time." He looked at the others. "I'll take point."

Ramirez stopped him. "You sure?"

Westlake glanced at her. She had an expression look on her face that he didn't care for. She was worried about him. No, not about him. About what he might do. It annoyed him. He was used to Ramirez not trusting him, but this was something different. "I'm the most durable," he said. "If there's a boobytrap, or someone waiting with a gun, I'm the one most likely to survive. So yes, I'm sure."

Westlake went ahead while the others waited at the edge of the airstrip. From the look of the place, he didn't think anyone had been here in some time. But as he got closer, he changed his mind. Something was different about the place. Something new had been added. Decorations of some sort hung all over the place, rotating slowly in the humid air.

Drawing closer, he saw that the decorations appeared to be made from broken sticks, twisted lengths of sawgrass and animal bones. At least he thought they were animal bones. They hung from every beam and post in sight. Dozens of them, more than he could count. Someone had been busy, and not the Narcos. Some of them had the capacity for creepiness; some of them even had a flair for it. But this wasn't the usual "nail the snitch to a barn door by his scalp" nastiness. This was something out of a movie.

He didn't touch them. A good thief knew better than to touch anything that wasn't on a carefully curated list. Especially something unexpected. He felt no unease, no fear. Just a vague annoyance that there was something there where there shouldn't be.

The air hummed with an almost painful vibration, and he turned, looking out over the sawgrass and trees. He felt as if he were being watched, and he wondered if there were zombies nearby. It was a ridiculous thought. Zombies were like rats; you were always within ten feet of one, whether you could see it or not. Maybe it was just the birds. He could hear them in the trees, and wondered if they were happy the pelicans had been taken care of.

Up close, the hideout was a flat square of cement, reminiscent of a bunker. A generator shed sat a short distance away, and there were two other outbuildings. One, he knew, was a boatshed; flat boats were the only way to reach anything like civilization from out here. The other was probably a toolshed. The airstrip needed constant maintenance; that included cutting back the grass and repacking the earth that made up the runway.

There were boat chains on the doors and spent brass on the ground. Some shooting had taken place here, but it had happened months ago at least. Had there been an outbreak here? Had the dead woken up and surprised whoever was using the place? Or was the explanation more mundane?

He turned and signaled the others forward. Calavera, Terry and Ptolemy stayed with Gable to oversee the refueling from the pump set at the end of the runway. Ramirez and the others joined him in front of the hideout. "Anything?" Ramirez asked.

Westlake shook his head. "Nothing jumped out at me."

"What about this stuff?" Riggs said, indicating the decorations. "What is it? Some of that kitschy folk art, like they used to sell on the boardwalk?"

"I don't think so," Westlake said. There was something off about the birdsong, but he didn't know what. It just didn't sound right. He was starting to get that old familiar feeling, like when a job had been about to go south. He looked at Riggs. "Don't touch it."

Riggs stepped back, hands raised. "Wasn't planning to."

Sayers pushed past him. "Don't touch anything until it's checked for tripwires or IEDs. If someone was here before us, they might have left some surprises behind. I'll take the back and the dock."

Ramirez stopped her, gesturing to Kahwihta. "Kahwihta, go with her. Riggs, with me. We'll check the outbuildings.

Coop, you and Imogene go with Westlake and take the interior. See if you can find the storeroom."

"I don't need help," Sayers began.

Ramirez fixed her with a steady look. "No one goes anywhere alone."

Sayers stared at her for a moment, and then nodded and turned to Kahwihta. "Come on. Make sure the mutt doesn't touch anything until I have a chance to look at it first."

Ramirez crooked her finger at Riggs, who trotted over to her. She looked at Coop. "Take it slow, and by the numbers. No surprises."

Coop gave her a lazy salute in reply. Imogene had a crowbar and thrust it through the chain keeping the door shut. She hauled on it ineffectually for a moment, then looked at Coop and Westlake. "Care to lend a hand?"

"I'm on watch," Coop said, patting his weapon. Westlake wondered why Ramirez had put the two of them together. Maybe she was hoping he'd eat Coop. The thought almost made him smile. He nudged Imogene aside, handing her his shotgun as he did so. He took a tight, two-handed grip on the crowbar and started pulling it back and down inexorably. He wasn't any stronger than he had been while alive, it was just that his muscles couldn't get tired anymore. He could keep pulling until his arms unraveled or his shoulders dislocated, whichever came first.

Thankfully, the chain gave before either. He flung the pieces away and offered the crowbar to Imogene. She took it gingerly, as if afraid to touch it, and passed him back his shotgun. "Why do you even carry that thing?" she asked. "I've never seen you use it."

"It has sentimental value. Let's go. Stay behind me."

The generators had been out of fuel for a long time, and the interior was dark. Westlake figured it had been for a while, with no one to refuel them. The air inside was humid, and the paint was sloughing from the concrete walls in messy sheets. The carpet underfoot, cheap stuff, was damp and things were growing in the corners. He could hear the breeze and figured there was a broken window somewhere.

But what got most of his attention was the blood on the walls. Lots of it, gone brown and crumbly with age. He touched it, and some of it came away on his fingers. Instinctively, he sniffed them.

Hungry.

"Not that hungry," Westlake grunted. He forced himself to wipe his fingers on his shirt. There were impact craters as well, marking spots where someone had gone to town with an automatic weapon indoors. But no bodies, no bones. Just blood and brass and bullet holes. "Lots of blood," Imogene murmured, as he led them into the front room.

"Old blood," Coop noted. "Whatever happened here, happened some time ago. Lucky us." The room was somewhere between a living room and a waiting room, big enough for a dozen people to sit comfortably. A sliding door looked out over a patio. Two windows to let in the light. No curtains, though. Just a curtain rail and rings. Bookshelves, comfortable couches, a recliner. A flat screen television occupied the wall between the bookshelves. The screen was cracked; the couches were overturned.

"Yeah, but where are the bodies?" Imogene asked.

"You have to ask?" Coop said, indicating Westlake.

Westlake ignored him. He peered at the bookshelves, noting the mix of potboilers, local color, and guidebooks. Everything a visiting drug runner might need to familiarize himself with the area. There were gaps here and there, as if volumes had been removed at random. He turned away, following the flow of the building.

It was a simple setup. The living room at the front, the kitchen at the back, bedrooms and bathrooms sandwiched between. They took the other rooms one at a time. There were six bedrooms, two of which were meant to be shared by multiple people. The bedrooms had largely been stripped of bedding and mattresses. Two bathrooms, both the worse for wear; moss in the toilets and insects in the showers. "Toilet paper is all gone," Imogene said, looking in the cupboards under the sinks. "Towels, too. Not even a half empty tube of toothpaste."

"Someone has cleaned this place out," Coop said.

"Maybe," Westlake muttered. He'd been certain no one knew about the place. Maybe he'd been wrong. Maybe one of the locals had hit it first thing. Maybe that was what all the blood was about. Coop looked at him.

"Didn't you mention something about there being staff?"

Westlake nodded absently. "A few. A cook, groundskeepers, that sort of thing."

"Did they live here?"

"Not to my knowledge." Westlake paused and looked at the others. "But they might have decided to hole up here when things went bad." Why hadn't he thought of that? He shook his head, annoyed with himself. "They wouldn't have known about the cache, though."

"But they might have found it," Coop pressed.

Westlake turned away. "Maybe. But maybe not. Come on. Kitchen is this way."

The kitchen, like the rest of the place, was in a shambles. Someone had clearly cleaned it out, taking all the cutlery and tableware. Just like the curtains and the bedding and toilet paper. It had one door, leading out onto another patio area that overlooked the water. More of those strange decorations hung from the patio rafters, twisting gently in the breeze. The sight of them made Westlake feel vaguely queasy. Something about them struck him as wrong. Who wasted time making that sort of thing just to hang it up way out here?

"I'm not seeing any storerooms," Coop said accusingly. Westlake gave him a rictus grin and stamped on the floor. There was a muffled thump.

"Remember the mall?"

"There's nothing but swamp under us," Imogene said.

Westlake thumped a spot on the floor with the butt of his shotgun. It rang metallically. "That sound like swamp to you?" he asked.

He and Coop quickly pulled back the linoleum to reveal the steel hatch set into the floor. There was no lock on this one, just a pull-ring. He shoved his shotgun into Coop's arms and hauled it up, releasing a wafting plume of putrescence. The others gagged and reeled back as a cloud of flies boiled up out of the hatchway. "Jesus," Coop snarled, pulling his bandana up over his mouth and nose.

To Westlake, it just smelled familiar. Like a friend's cologne. "Back," he snarled, and attempted to slam the hatch shut. But too late. The zombie erupted from out of the hatch a moment later and knocked him sprawling. Two more followed, scrambling up and out of the dark aperture, their rotting features twisted into expressions of mindless hunger.

CHAPTER TWELVE
Hatchway

Coop shot the closest zombie in the head, the noise suppressor condensing the sound to a minimal 'phut-phut' exclamation. He spun to tag the second, but saw that Imogene had already put a butcher knife through its sinuses. She was fast; he liked that about her. There weren't many people who could react that quickly to an attacker.

That left the one who was tangling with Westlake. Coop hesitated, not because he was worried about shooting Westlake by accident, but because he was worried he might not. The plan had been gestating for some time; since Atlanta, at least. At first, Westlake hadn't bothered him much. The thought of a tame zombie had been cool, in a way. Only Westlake wasn't tame, and definitely wasn't cool.

Coop had known guys like him in the service, and then later in the private sector. People for whom the chain of command was a suggestion rather than a rule. People like that made bad situations worse. Westlake being dead only made that quality worse. You couldn't trust something that didn't know when to stay dead.

When the world had ended, he'd been acting as security for Ariadne St Cloud. He'd screwed the pooch on that one. She'd nearly been killed by her brother. Then again by the newly risen dead. That time he'd been on the ball, and had put the dead down, saving both her and his job. He'd stuck with Ariadne out of a sense of obligation. She hadn't been bad as far as bosses went. When she'd implied it might be wise to have somebody riding herd on Ramirez's little expedition, he'd volunteered like a good soldier.

He was starting to regret it now. Not just because of Westlake, but because as far as he could tell, the whole operation was FUBAR'd. Sure, they'd found some supplies, some guns, a few survivors, but none of it was worth what they'd spent to get it. Not in his professional opinion, at least. Ramirez was just too stubborn to admit it.

The problem was these days stubbornness got you killed. It got everyone around you killed, too. And Coop didn't intend to be collateral damage in anyone else's screwup.

He circled the two dead men, GSG-16 leveled, trying to calculate the variables on a believable friendly fire incident. Ramirez would be pissed, of course. The others too, probably. Maybe not Sayers. Or Terry. Gable seemed largely ambivalent. Really, he doubted any of them but Kahwihta liked Westlake. Even the dog seemed to hate him.

Westlake caught the zombie by the head and drove it against the floor again and again, until the dead man's skull burst and came apart in his hands. "Walkers," he said, as he wiped his hands. Coop held the gun on him for a moment longer, weighing the odds. Imogene was distracted, trying to work her knife free. Then Westlake looked up and met his gaze.

He knew.

Coop didn't know how, but Westlake knew. It rattled Coop just enough that he lowered his weapon and stepped back. Something that might have been an attempt at a smile crossed Westlake's ravaged features. Then he stood. "Just walkers," he said, again. "They must have popped them and tossed them down there as a surprise for anyone who came looking."

"I thought you said no one knew where this thing was," Coop said.

"I said maybe. Besides, things change. The real question is, what's still down there?" Westlake stood and cleaned his bloody hands on his shirt. He looked at Coop. "Want to take point this time?"

"Age before beauty," Coop said. Westlake gave a gurgling laugh and started down the cement steps that led into the cache below. The only light was from Imogene's flashlight, and what it showed was a square, cinderblock room roughly the size of the building above, full of steel shelves, packed with dry goods and boxes that might have been full of ammunition or nothing at all. A tarp-covered mass occupied most of the floorspace directly below them. Something about it made Coop uneasy.

Westlake stopped halfway down the steps. Coop waved Imogene back, just in case another rush of walkers was in the offing. "What is it?" he called down.

"Something's down here." Westlake sounded hesitant. Uncertain. From what Coop knew, the dead man's "zombie-sense" wasn't a hundred percent effective. Or if it was, Westlake didn't immediately recognize it as such. Yet another way in which he was undependable.

"More walkers?" Imogene asked.

Westlake shook his head. "I don't see any."

"Do your eyes even still work?" Coop asked. Westlake looked up at him.

"I don't know, you tell me."

Coop paused, his finger tapping the trigger guard. He glanced sidelong at Imogene. Then he lowered his weapon. "No offense meant," he said. Westlake peered up at him for a moment longer. Then he stretched a hand back up toward them.

"Let me have that crowbar again."

Imogene swiftly passed it down, and Westlake used the curved head to snag the edge of the tarp on the floor. Carefully, he pulled it aside. As he did so, Coop heard the jingle of a bell. Westlake took a step back up the stairs, and the jingling increased. Not just one bell, but many. Coop snatched the flashlight from Imogene and aimed it down at the tarp, which was now bunched and rolling back to reveal several walkers, all bound together by zip-ties, ropes, and rags. They were flat on the floor and began to flop about as the tarp was pulled aside.

"Holy God," Imogene breathed. "Their faces..."

"I see them," Coop murmured. The zombies' faces had been stripped to the bone by something or someone, with even the eyes removed, and a variety of bells and noisemakers tied to their rotten limbs so that every move they made unleashed a cacophony of sound.

"Jesus," Coop snarled. He wondered why someone would cut their faces off. Sadism – or more practical reasons? He leveled his weapon at the newly revealed zombies, but Westlake swatted the barrel aside with the crowbar.

"No." Westlake gestured for them to back away from the hatch. "They can't see us or smell us, but they can hear us. So just back away, and don't rile them up." He spoke softly, as if worried the zombies might be offended.

"Why don't we just shoot them?" Coop asked, keeping his voice low.

"Because of the grenades," Westlake said. Coop frowned and made to reply, but a moment later he caught a glimpse of what Westlake was talking about. He played the beam of the flashlight along the fishing line that was snagged around the zombies' ankles and connected to a grenade duct taped to the back wall. The more they moved, the more the pin jiggled in an unsettling way. More lines were attached to their arms and threaded through the exposed bones of their torsos, stretching to different points around the room. A grenade waited at the end of each strand, its pin twitching in time to the movements of the dead.

Coop whistled. "That is… elaborate." If anyone riled up the walkers enough, say by attempting to get past them to the shelves, they risked setting off an explosion. Ditto for just shooting the zombies. Someone had a nasty sense of humor. He was almost impressed.

"Yeah." Westlake flexed his fingers and looked at his hands in what might have been regret. It was hard to tell when the guy had a face like a peeled orange. "And my fingers aren't as light as they used to be. Otherwise, I'd solve the problem myself."

"Why haven't they set it off before now?"

"Bunker's soundproofed," Westlake said. "It was meant for people to hide in if the Feds ever got wind of this place."

Coop grunted. That made sense. Imogene drew one of her

knives. "We could use a knife," she said. "Just slot each one in turn, and then disarm the trap."

"Too risky," Westlake said. He was looking at something else now, a puzzled expression on his face. Coop followed his gaze to yet another wire, only this one was stretched to the wall and then up across the ceiling to a crudely made hole that led up somewhere else in the building. Coop handed Imogene the flashlight and stepped back from the hatch to listen, trying to hear past the noise from below.

There it was. More bells – cowbells, by the sound of them – ringing somewhere else on the property. "Crap," he said. Imogene looked at him.

"What is it?"

"They're ringing the dinner bell," Westlake said, as he climbed out of the hatch. "Noise like that will draw the wrong sort of attention." He carefully shut the hatch. "They'll quiet down in a minute. We need to find the others."

"No need, we're here," Ramirez said, as she stepped into the kitchen, Riggs at her heels. "What the hell is all that noise?" She spotted the downed walkers and frowned. "Shit. Where were they?"

"In our friend's secret cache," Coop said flatly. He glanced at Ramirez. "We need to cut those goddamn bells, and quick." From what he'd seen, they'd been wired separately to the grenades and the bells. Cutting one wouldn't set off the other.

"I'm on it," Imogene said, hurrying toward the door. Ramirez gestured, and Riggs followed Imogene.

"It's too late," Westlake said. He was staring out the door. Coop couldn't see anything out there, but it didn't mean it wasn't there. He shook his head and looked at Ramirez.

"It was boobytrapped. Besides these, there was a bunch of jury-rigged walkers down there set up to sound an alarm if someone came poking around." He paused. "Or blow the place up." That thought had only just occurred to him. Had someone meant for the grenades to go off? Why risk destroying a cache like this?

Ramirez's eyes widened. "What?"

"Grenades," Westlake said, still looking out the door. "Lots of them. Probably found them here, decided to make use of them."

"Who?"

"No clue."

"Surprise, surprise," Coop said. "Something else you don't know." He looked at Westlake. What was the dead man looking for? "We'll add it to the list, shall we?"

"Coop," Ramirez began.

"Let him talk," Westlake said. There was a smile on what was left of his face. Coop wanted to blow it off. "He obviously has something he wants to say."

Coop studied him. What was the game here? What was Westlake up to? He knew what Coop wanted, but it didn't seem to bother him overmuch. Then, maybe he was too far gone to be worried. Or maybe he wanted to die. Coop could understand that; being locked in a rotting shell probably wasn't a lot of fun.

Somehow, that made him even angrier about the whole thing. If Westlake wanted to blow his brains out, why not just do it and save everyone the hassle?

Finally, Coop said, "Yeah. A lot, actually. But we both know telling you anything is a waste of time. You're not the one in charge, after all." He shook his head and looked at Ramirez. "I told you. But you didn't listen. I thought you were smart, but clearly, I was overestimating you. This has all been for nothing – again." He pointed down at the hatch. "Another goddamn waste of time."

"Stow it, Coop," Ramirez said. "You have no idea what you're talking about." She spoke slowly, her tone mild. Like a mother disciplining a child. She always talked that way when she was trying to remind them who was in charge. It was irritating.

Coop pointed at Westlake. "I know that he's rotten; that his brain has the consistency of the stuff you find at the bottom of a garbage bin; and that this is the guy you're entrusting our lives to. A goddamn zombie."

The cowbells were abruptly silenced. "Finally," Coop said. The door to the kitchen banged open, and Riggs and Imogene hurried inside. He heard the dog start to bark and knew what they were going to say even before they said it.

"We have company," Riggs called out. He had his pistol in his hand, and his eyes were wide behind the lenses of his mask. "All that noise drew some unpleasant types out of the swamp. Lots of them!"

CHAPTER THIRTEEN
Council

Ramirez twitched aside a curtain and peered out through the window at the mass of dead meat outside. A walker covered in Spanish moss and mud staggered out of the sawgrass and past the window. It had a camera slung around its neck and wore a jacket with a cartoon character emblazoned on the back.

She watched it stumble one way and then the next, as if uncertain about the direction it should be going. Walkers were like that sometimes. Runners and brutes were more focused when it came to finding prey, but walkers tended to just wander around until they spotted food. The walker bumped into one of the poles holding up the camouflage netting, dislodging the novelty cap it wore, but it kept going, staggering in a circle around the building.

More of them came out of the sawgrass; tourists in Florida best, now thoroughly ruined by all the time spent wandering around outdoors. Even a theme park mascot, still disturbingly in costume. The others looked like withered scarecrows dressed in rags and tatters. They'd been pecked by birds and burnt to leather by the sun, but they were still moving. Still hungry.

She frowned as one walker in particular drew her attention. The dead woman's head was little more than a mass of nails, and more of the wood and bone decorations had been hung from her body. Other walkers were similarly decorated. Someone had taken the time to mark them, though she couldn't see any reason why a person might go to the trouble.

More importantly, perhaps, she could hear moans rising out of the grass, and knew this was just the first wave. She sighed. Another day, another horde.

"I count thirty-two walkers and something that might be a runner," Ptolemy said. He stood on the other side of the window, his eyes on the zombies. "Not good odds."

"We've faced worse," Ramirez said, trying for bravado. It came out sounding like a protest. Ptolemy didn't seem to notice either way.

"That is a fact, but even so the odds are not in our favor." He looked at her expectantly. She grimaced.

"I'm thinking."

He nodded. He wasn't visibly worried, which was something. He was silent for a moment, then, "The outrageous is the reasonable, if introduced politely. Charles Fort."

Ramirez blinked. "What?"

Ptolemy removed his glasses and wiped the condensation from the lenses. "When we were flying over, I saw something. It looked like a cruise ship, strange as that sounds."

"A cruise ship?"

"Yes."

"In the Everglades?"

"Gable said much the same. I was going to bring it up later, once we had reconnoitered properly, but…"

"Yeah," Ramirez said, and looked back out the window. The runway was crowded with bodies now, all heaving to and fro. It reminded her of Times Square back in the good old days. One of the walkers noticed her and started toward the window. An arrow sprouted from its head and it toppled sideways. Ramirez looked up, and detecting the thump of someone moving around above her. "I thought I told her to stay off the roof," she said.

Ptolemy shrugged. "She did not listen."

"When does she ever?" Ramirez growled. Sayers had never quite managed to become a team player. She'd more than earned Ramirez's trust since they'd taken the Villa, but sometimes it was hard to forget that she'd tried to kill them all more than once. Ramirez sighed again and shook her head. "A cruise ship. Fine. So what about it?"

"It might have supplies."

"It might be full of zombies."

Ptolemy nodded. "It might." He gestured to the window. "Zombies are ubiquitous these days. Wherever we go, there they are. As if they are waiting for us."

"They are," Ramirez said, as she let the curtain drop. "That's all they can do. Besides, we barely saw any in Charleston."

"Maybe they all came to Florida," Coop said, as he came into the sitting room. "We're locked up tight. Or at least as tight as this place can get. The defenses won't last long, though." As if to emphasize his point, a rotting fist thumped against a window, making Imogene flinch. "They'll be through the windows before we know it. The doors, too, if there's a brute out there. We need to get to the plane."

Ramirez shook her head. "Too dangerous." Gable and the others had abandoned the plane on the runway, still lacking in fuel. They'd only just gotten the pumps working when the first walker showed up. They'd managed to get inside before the horde arrived en masse, thankfully.

"So is forting up. Rule One in Atlantic City was never let yourself get caught in a so-called defensible position. Zombies don't give a shit about casualties and the more noise you make, the more of them show up. Pretty soon you're out of ammo, and they're inside."

"Sounds just as bad as getting caught on a plane without fuel, stuck out on an open runway," she said. "Neither seems like a good idea, but one's more roomy than the other."

"Fine," Coop said. "But we need a plan."

"I might have one," Ramirez said, with a glance at Ptolemy. She'd been thinking on it since they'd holed up in the building. "But I'm going to need volunteers." She gestured to Ptolemy. "Round up the others. Meet me in the kitchen. We need to have a council of war." She'd spread the others out to do what they could to fortify the building. Mostly that meant moving heavy pieces of furniture in front of windows and doors.

Coop snorted. "Is that what you call it?"

"I tried confab, but council of war tested better," Ramirez said airily, as she headed for the kitchen. It was the safest room in the building, with access to the dock and the runway. Coop trotted after her. "Besides, you're the military man. I thought you'd appreciate it."

"What I'd appreciate is not being trapped in here in the first place," Coop said.

Ramirez didn't reply. Coop had gone from being the most reliable member of the team to the most annoying very quickly since Atlantic City, and part of her wondered whether he'd been sent by Ariadne to sabotage their search efforts. That was unfair though; in all likelihood, he was just an asshole.

Calavera was already in the kitchen when they got there. He was looking through the pantries and setting aside anything worth taking. It wasn't much. Ramirez picked up a can. "Pumpkin?" she asked, giving the can a shake.

"I thought perhaps… pie," Calavera said. "We have those readymade pie shells back at the Villa, but precious little to put in them." He turned, bouncing a can of beans on his palm. "Someone has already picked it over, though."

Ramirez frowned. "You're sure?"

He nodded. "We are not the first ones to come here."

"That's obvious, given the meat-bags down there," Coop said, indicating the steel hatch on the floor. The walkers were still beneath them, but they'd quieted down some, at least so far as Ramirez could determine.

"Yes, but why leave anything?" Calavera asked, as he idly arranged the cans into a pyramid. "Why not clean the place out entirely?"

Coop frowned. "You think they left it here as – what? Bait?"

Calavera looked at Ramirez. "The bells, the booby trap… it is conceivable that we were meant to seek shelter here."

Ramirez nodded slowly, following his line of thinking. "Whoever it is wants us pinned down." She ran her hand through her hair. "Sayers tried the same trick once. I wonder what she makes of it."

"It's damn sneaky, that's what I think," Sayers said, as she came into the kitchen with the others. "Found an airboat tied up outside on the dock before the deadheads arrived," she continued. "Clearly boobytrapped. And more of those weird decorations everywhere. Like Calavera says, someone got here before us, and whoever they are, they marked their territory."

"What do you mean 'their territory'?" Ramirez asked.

Sayers nodded to Kahwihta. "Ask her. She's the one who said it."

Kahwihta frowned. "I said that's what they reminded me of. They look like curse markers, warnings for outsiders." She held up one of the decorations. "Or maybe someone just likes making weird shapes out of sticks."

"As interesting as this is, you mentioned something about a plan?" Coop asked.

"First, we make some noise," Ramirez said. "We get them all in close, keep their eyes on us. Then some of us make a break for the boat."

"The boobytrapped boat," Coop said doubtfully.

"I fixed that," Sayers said. She looked at Ramirez. "So, what? We take the boat and lead our friends out there away. Then what?"

"Then you circle back, we load up and get gone."

"Except that the plane ain't refueled yet, is it?" Gable interjected. "Take another hour at least. Those pumps out there are rusted shut."

"Which is why some of us will stay here, while the rest play distraction," Ramirez continued. "We'll take out the stragglers and get the plane ready."

"Sounds good to me," Riggs said, adjusting his mask. "We sit tight and quiet, then when the horde goes stumbling after the boat, we pop out and get the job done."

"Or not," Coop said. He looked at Westlake. "Because there's another boobytrap below us in the room with all the supplies, and no way to disarm it without risking setting the whole thing off."

"So we don't load up," Riggs countered. "We just fuel the plane and get her ready to go. Easy-peasy." He looked at the others. "Look, I'll even volunteer to stay. What about you, Terry?" He nudged the younger man.

"No way," Terry said. He flinched as a rotted hand thumped against the back door. "I'm not staying here. I'll take my chances in the swamp."

Westlake cleared his throat. The death rattle sound caught everyone's attention. "I'll stay. Me, Riggs, and Gable can get the plane fueled and ready."

"You'll need more than three," Ramirez said. "We might be able to pull off most of those walkers out there, but some won't be so easily distracted. And who knows what else is out there, already heading this way?" She looked at Coop. "We'll stay. Sayers takes everyone else into the swamp."

"Are you volunteering for me now?" Coop asked in a low tone.

"I just figured you might want to keep an eye on Westlake." She looked at Westlake as she said it. He raised an eyebrow, but it might just have been a spasm. "Any objections? Anyone got a better plan? No?" She clapped her hands. "Then let's do this."

Westlake went first without being asked. Ramirez didn't try to stop him. He slid the fridge they'd been using to block the door to the dock aside and stepped out. The closest walkers barely registered his presence, instead heading immediately for the open door. Westlake fired his shotgun, diverting their attentions.

From what Ramirez had seen, the zombies were content to ignore Westlake until he attacked them. Then they couldn't dogpile him fast enough. Every walker in earshot of the shotgun blast converged on Westlake.

"Coop, Calavera," she said. The two men went next. Coop lined up his sights on the closest of the zombies and fired. Head shots weren't easy when the target was bobbing around in waist high water or staggering through thick grass, but he was a professional.

Calavera snatched up a cinderblock and chucked it, knocking several walkers sprawling. He caught another by the head and swung it around, driving it face-first into the side of the building. He shouted happily and spread his arms, inviting the zombies to attack.

Ramirez and the others, taking advantage of the breach the three men had created, exited the building, guns blazing. Riggs popped one of his homemade smoke grenades and sent it rolling away from the building. The smoke would keep the walkers occupied, but not for long. "Remember, once the boat goes, we head back inside," Ramirez called out. She picked off a walker as it fumbled at Westlake, and he gave her a nod of thanks.

As Sayers had said, the dock was festooned with more of the bent stick and sawgrass decorations. The airboat bobbed on the murky water next to the dock. Sayers headed for it, only pausing long enough to jam her hunting knife into a walker's skull. She got the boat's engine running after a few false starts.

Ramirez gestured sharply. "Calavera, you and the others go, we'll cover you!"

Calavera, Kahwihta, Imogene and Terry headed for the boat. As they did so, the wind shifted and the smoke cleared. The walkers surged toward them. Terry broke away from the group, firing his handgun. Ramirez went to his aid, grabbing him under the arm as he stumbled and was nearly swarmed. She hauled him up and sent him staggering toward the door. She turned back toward the others – and froze.

Kahwihta had stopped. She was looking down at something… an arrow. It jutted from her side, and blood swiftly stained her shirt. "Kahwihta…" Ramirez breathed, unable to process what she was seeing. The young woman slumped, eyes wide. Calavera scooped her up and leapt onto the boat, Attila just behind him.

Another arrow flicked across Ramirez's shoulder, pinning her to a crate by the edge of her jacket. She saw the others reacting now, aware of this new danger. They were all moving too slowly. Her fault.

She saw Coop howling curses as he stumbled to one knee, an arrow in his other leg. Westlake tried to catch him, but Coop jerked away and fell. Seconds later, an arrow sprouted from Westlake's back. "Everyone – *get inside*," Ramirez shouted. Out of the corner of her eye, she saw the airboat pull away from the dock.

Westlake swayed on the edge of the dock, bristling with

arrows. One last arrow hit him high in the throat, snapping his head back. He toppled backward into the water.

Ramirez' first thought was to help him. It was only when an arrow punched into one of the crates near her head that she realized the foolishness of it. If Westlake was still functional, he'd be safer in the water than on the dock. And if he wasn't, it didn't matter. Right now, the others had to be her priority.

"I told you we should have gone back to the plane," Coop snarled, as he dragged himself into cover behind a tarp covered pile of boat parts. "I goddamn told you!"

Ramirez ignored him. She was crouched behind a stack of wooden pallets. She had her sidearm out, but there was no one to shoot at. Their attackers might as well be ghosts. She spotted Ptolemy nearby, sheltering in the doorway. His eyes were wide, but he wasn't panicking. An arrow punched into the dock near her feet, forcing her to draw her legs up even tighter against her chest. "Ptolemy, help me get Coop inside!"

She forced herself to her feet, ready to go to Coop's aid, but as she made to rise, a guttural voice drawled, "Don't move. Don't even twitch."

Ramirez froze. At the edge of the dock, a walker staggered toward her, arms outstretched. A woman dressed in hunter's camouflage came around the side of the building and smoothly removed the walker's head with a single swipe from a machete. "That's the last of them on this side," she said, wiping her machete clean on her pants leg. "Brady and them are seeing to the rest."

Ramirez heard gunshots from the runway and figured that was "Brady and them". A moment later, Ptolemy, Riggs and Gable stepped out onto the docks, their hands in the air. She hoped the boat had gotten away, at least. Two more newcomers, both dressed like the woman, followed them, handguns aimed at their captives' heads. One wore a battered hockey mask with a pair of stubby deer antlers rising from the top. The other had long hair threaded through with feathers and chicken feet. Both were armed to the teeth, with bandoliers of shells and shotguns slung over their shoulders.

"We don't want any trouble," Ramirez began.

"Well, I'm sorry to hear that," the man behind her said. He stepped into her line of sight, a shotgun cradled in his arms. He was big, heavy with the sort of muscle you got from working outdoors, and was dressed in a set of camouflage overalls and a stained t-shirt. A baseball cap with a tattered brim completed the ensemble. What really caught her attention, however, were his eyes. They were an ugly shade of yellow. She felt a queasy flicker of fear in her stomach at the sight.

He smiled down at her, showing his teeth. "You may not have come looking for any, ma'am, but you sure have found it."

CHAPTER FOURTEEN
Escape

"Are you sure you know how to drive this thing?" Imogene asked. She sat in the front of the airboat, cradling Kahwihta's head on her lap.

Sayers ignored her, trying to concentrate on keeping the boat moving over the shallow waters. She'd only driven an airboat once or twice, and it wasn't like riding a bike. There was a lot you could forget, and the swamp had a lot more obstacles than the frozen lake her father had taught her on. She glanced at Calavera. "Is she alive?"

Calavera was bent over Kahwihta, gently cutting the arrow free of her flesh with Sayers' knife. He finally worked it loose and looked at Sayers. "For now. But she requires medical attention. There is no telling how much damage it did to her."

"Who were those guys?" Imogene asked, stroking Kahwihta's face.

"The same ones who set up the boobytraps," Sayers said. "The whole place was a trap and we walked right into it." She was annoyed with herself as much as Ramirez and Westlake.

She'd set enough traps in her life to recognize one when she saw it, but this one had escaped her notice until it was almost too late. She glanced down at her sleeve, and saw the ragged tear where an arrow had nearly caught her. Whoever they were, they were good shots. Bows were smart. Not much noise at all, less chance of drawing the dead down on you. Arrows were easy to make, if you knew how. Easier than bullets.

Someday, when they'd finished with the running around, she was going to push the people in charge to let her start training the other survivors to use the bow. Bows and arrows, swords, and shields, that was the way forward. To survive, humanity would have to downgrade. Relearn all those lessons it had forgotten over the centuries. She guided the airboat around a fallen tree, reducing the throttle as she did so. "Are we being followed? Did that part of the plan work at least?"

"Looks like some of the zombies are following us," Imogene said. "Should we be slowing down?"

"Yes," Sayers said. She could hear the groaning now. Air wheezing in and out of deflated lungs, whistling through gaps in torsos and heads. Zombies were walking bagpipes, and made a noise to match.

"Only they're catching up."

"That's the idea, remember?" Sayers said, as she tilted the rudder and let the airboat drift around a hummock.

"Yeah, I'd say the original plan went out the window when we were attacked by bow and arrow wielding nutjobs – no offense."

"None taken," Sayers said. "And what would you suggest we do, then? Speed up? And go where? In case you haven't noticed, we're not exactly in friendly territory."

"You're a park ranger, aren't you? Can't you find us a way out of the swamp?"

"I was a ranger in the Adirondacks. This is the Everglades." Sayers tapped the throttle, giving the boat a bit of speed. Walkers waded through the dark waters to either side of them. The sound of the fan was bringing them out of the swamp. "We'll go a bit farther and turn around, go back for the others." *Whoever's left*, she thought, but didn't say.

Calvin was back there. She'd seen him as she gunned the motor and sent them skidding away from the dock. He was still alive. He had to be. She wasn't going to leave him. Not again. Turning an airboat was no simple proposition, however. You had to be careful, otherwise you'd tip the whole craft over.

They skidded over a root network, and Sayers felt the reverberation through her tailbone. She heard Imogene curse, and then Attila began to bark as something fell from the trees above and slapped down into the front of the boat. The craft suddenly slewed sideways and she looked back to see dead hands clinging to the roll cage that contained the fan.

"Floaters," she snarled, reaching for the Mauser C96 in its holster on her hip. The weapon was the last thing her father had given her and once the ammunition ran out, it'd be no better than a paperweight. But right now it still had its uses.

"Not just floaters," Imogene called out. Sayers saw a rotted body, sans legs, thrashing toward her. The zombie wore the tattered remnants of a flight suit and had broken branches jutting from its torso. The remains of a parachute hung from its back and it had a helmet on, obscuring the top half of its face but leaving the jaws exposed.

"Wonderful. Wait your turn," Sayers hissed as she leveled her pistol and shot the dead man through the goggles of his helmet. Calavera stooped, caught the sack of dead meat by the back of its jumpsuit and slung it out of the boat. Water-bloated fingers scrabbled at the sides of the boat as she gave it some speed. If they could break free, the floaters would just sink back to the bottom. But if the boat stalled, the walkers would catch up and that would be that. "Break their hands," she said. "Cut them off, something!"

Imogene and Calavera went to work, chopping and hammering at the hands that clutched the sides of the boat as she fought to keep the craft from stalling out. Loose fingers rolled around the bottom of the boat, twitching like drowning fish. The boat lurched and then abruptly shot forward with a wet, snapping sound. They skidded over roots and careened through trees, the fan whining as Sayers momentarily lost control of the craft.

She managed to right it just before it tipped over and spilled them all into the drink. The walkers faded into the distance, hidden by the trees, but they were still coming. They wouldn't stop until they hit something or found new prey.

She angled the rudder, letting them drift around a knot of trees too thick to pass through. Beyond it was what appeared to be a clearing. As the boat passed the trees, she spotted it. At first, she thought she was seeing things. A vast mountain of pale steel, rising up over everything and casting its shadow on the shallow waters around it. Sayers stared at the sight in open-mouthed shock. "I'll be damned. A cruise ship. He was right."

"What?" Imogene asked. "What is that?"

"Calvin. He told me he saw a cruise ship when we were flying in. This must be it." Sayers reduced the throttle and saw figures on the upper deck. They weren't milling around, like zombies. Rather, they were at the rails, waving. No. Waving them off. But why would they–?

The airboat rocked suddenly and the fan whined. Calavera steadied himself on the side and said, "Something large just passed under us."

There were shouts now from the rail above. The waving had become more energetic, more frightened. Sayers let the throttle loose and sped them toward the ship. If they could reach it–

The boat rocked again, the fan rising out of the water. She was nearly spilled from her seat. She heard metal whine and part as something tore at the bottom of the boat. "Calavera," she cried. He leapt into the water without protest. The big luchador was crazy, but sometimes crazy came in handy. Whatever it was left the boat and went after him. She caught a glimpse of a scaly back and bony spikes, feeling her stomach clench in a sudden primeval fear.

Calavera surfaced a moment later. The water was a little higher than his waist. He slapped his palms against the surface, making as much noise as possible. "*¡Hola!*" he bellowed. "Come and get me, demon! Come and face El Calavera Santo!"

The demon – whatever it was – did as it was bade. It sprang from the water, jaws wide. An alligator, or something that had once been an alligator, she thought. Calavera dodged aside, no easy feat in the water, and the behemoth slammed down where he'd been standing. Calavera turned as it surged toward him like a torpedo, and one big arm snapped down like a vise around the creature's jaws.

He was propelled forward for a short distance before he somehow managed to stop himself and the beast. Sayers could see the muscles in his shoulders and arm bulge with effort as he fought to control the thrashing animal. He risked a glance in her direction. "Get to the boat," he roared. "I will hold it for as long as I can!"

Sayers didn't argue. She was already heading that way. Attila was still barking to beat the band, and she saw walkers stumbling out of the tree line, into the gap carved by the ship. That was all they needed.

They were almost there when a brute erupted from the water with a gurgling roar. It was an awful sight, covered in wet weeds and mud, its swollen flesh sloughing from its malformed bones. Its head bore a crown of fungus, and its jaws had been shattered – or expanded – into something more like the mandibles of an insect. It lurched toward the airboat, and they just managed to skid around it.

But not past it. Not entirely. The brute snagged the fan cage with one heavy hand, nearly ripping the mechanism off the boat. Sayers was thrown from her seat by the sudden stop, and Imogene was hard-pressed to keep Kahwihta from rolling into the water. The brute turned and tore the fan cage off, flinging it away in a display of inhuman strength. Its jaws spread wide like a flower of meat and bone, as it dragged the back of the boat down and attempted to clamber aboard.

Sayers fired her pistol, hoping for a lucky shot as the water rose and the brute closed in. Then, with a roar, Attila flung himself past her. The dog danced back and forth, barking and snapping at the zombie, distracting it. Sayers heard engines and saw a motorized rubber raft racing toward them. Someone aboard had a rifle and knew how to use it. Shots plucked at the brute's arm and face, causing it to turn.

Then, there was a sound of nightmare; a bone-deep bellow that set the birds to rising from the trees. She saw a scaly form strike the brute in the back. The alligator chomped down on the brute's side and attempted to roll, but the big zombie was too heavy for the reptile to drag down. Water surged over the sides of the half-sunk airboat as the two monsters struggled against one another. Thankfully, their struggle carried them away from the boat.

She watched them in awe. It was like something out of those old black and white horror films that Ptolemy loved. Just two ungainly shapes tearing away at one another. Unfortunately, their rescuers weren't coming any closer. Sayers couldn't blame them. She wouldn't want to get close to that pair of monsters either.

"We need to get to that raft," Imogene said.

"Only one way to do that. We have to abandon ship." Sayers holstered her weapon and slid her arms under Kahwihta so that she could awkwardly lift the younger woman. Kahwihta moaned in pain and leaned against her. Taking a breath, Sayers stepped off the sinking boat and into the water, bracing Kahwihta against her shoulder.

It was colder than she'd thought it would be, and it took everything she had to keep Kahwihta above water. Attila leapt off and paddled beside her, barking in concern. Imogene followed them, knife in hand. "Any sign of Calavera?" she asked.

"Calavera can take care of himself," Sayers said. "We have to get Kahwihta to safety or she's not going to make it. Now come on." Something brushed her leg as they left the boat behind. A fluttery touch that came from fingers. She lashed out with her foot as best she could, kicking the touch away. More touches, more caresses that turned to clawing. Luckily, they couldn't get much purchase.

"Sayers…" Imogene began.

"I know. Keep moving."

Attila growled and began to swim faster. Sayers tried to follow his example, but it was difficult. The brute and the alligator were churning the water, and small waves slapped against her back and sides. Fear warred with annoyance. She hadn't wanted to come here in the first place.

Something caught at her ankle; a hand rose from the water to her left, and Imogene cut it off with a chop of a knife. "One good thing about floaters is they come apart real easy," she said, stabbing at something under the water.

"Just keep them off me," Sayers said, forging toward the raft. As she came near it, she saw that there were only two people aboard, one at the tiller, and one with a rifle. The latter half stood and aimed the weapon at her.

"That's close enough," he said. He wore a uniform that had once been white but was now stained a dull khaki color. A bandolier of shells crossed his chest, and he looked like he knew how to use the weapon in his hands.

"We've got an injured person here," Sayers said. Something was moving around by her knees, fumbling at her legs. Floaters couldn't see – the soft tissue was the first thing to go, including the eyes.

"Bitten?" the man with the rifle asked intently.

Sayers tried to kick away the unseen shape groping at her legs. "No. Someone shot her. Now can you point that rifle somewhere else?"

The man hesitated, then set his rifle down and extended a hand. "My name's Jessop."

"Introductions later," Sayers said brusquely. "There's a floater pawing at my shins." She all but heaved Kahwihta into the raft, bent, snatched her knife from its sheath and drove it down into something spongy and unpleasant. Black blood billowed across the surface of the water. She jerked her knife free and saw Imogene helping Attila into the raft. Jessop looked nonplussed by the dog's presence, but didn't argue.

Sayers turned, looking for Calavera – but no sign of him. Then, a roar drew her attention to the struggle between the brute and the alligator. The brute was losing. The alligator had the zombie's arm in its jaws and was rolling over and over, attempting to tear it loose. Every walker in sight was converging on the fracas, drawn by the blood and noise. "Are you coming up or not?" Jessop demanded.

She was about to reply when she spied the familiar mask rising from beneath the water. Calavera, with a shard of metal torn from the airboat's hull in his hands. He scrambled up onto the alligator's broad back and raced up its length toward the brute even as it rolled. The metal punched easily through the brute's skull, causing it to drop. The alligator tore the arm loose and whipped away beneath the water, out of sight, leaving Calavera to swim toward them with long, smooth strokes. Sayers gave a small laugh. It was always a pleasure to watch the ex-wrestler work.

"Who the hell are you people?" Jessop asked in awe.

Sayers hauled herself into the raft. "Like I said, introductions later. For now, let's get somewhere out of reach of these walkers, huh?"

CHAPTER FIFTEEN
The Family

Zombies hung upside down from the branches of a towering oak, their struggles dislodging the curtains of Spanish moss that shrouded everything above the waterline. The zombies' legs were tied together at the ankles, and they flailed ineffectually at the airboats that slid just out of reach through the water beneath them.

Ptolemy took in this macabre scene with equanimity. He'd seen worse. Or so he tried to convince himself. Riggs shuddered beside him. "Jesus. Jesus, Jesus, Jesus," he muttered. "This is bad. Real bad." They were both bound by the wrists and ankles.

"What tipped you off?" Ptolemy murmured. He craned his neck, trying to spot the others. Their captors had wisely split them up into several boats, rather than risking them all in one. He spotted Terry in the nearest craft. The younger man looked shaken and somewhat worse for wear. Their captors had not been gentle. Ramirez and Coop had gotten the worst of it. He spotted Gable, slouched beside Terry. She looked frightened, but relatively composed. She met his gaze and gave a surreptitious nod.

He settled back, wondering whether Kahwihta still lived. He hoped so; the young woman had survived worse. They all had. But every survivor came to the point where their number was up. The sun was setting, and he could hear an alligator bellowing in the swamp. And the zombies, of course. They were always there, their moaning the score to the apocalypse. The sound moved oddly here, drifting sluggishly through the trees, eddying and spreading with no rhyme or reason.

"Pretty, ain't it?" the woman sitting at the prow of the airboat said. She had a rifle across her knees and her greasy hair was threaded through with feathers and bones and, incongruously, a hair clip in the shape of a cartoon unicorn. Her face had a familiar cast to it; she was related to the rest of their captors by blood, Ptolemy thought. She smiled down at him, her blistered lips leaking a colorless serum as she did so. Her eyes, like those of her companions, were an ugly shade of yellow.

"What?" he asked.

"Them sounds. The way them dead folks sing out in the swamp." She paused, a frown of consideration on her face. "You think it's a happy song or a sad one?" She sniffed. "I don't suppose it matters much either way, but I'd like to know." She poked Riggs with the butt of her rifle. "Why you wearing that mask? You think we smell bad or something?"

"Yeah," Riggs said tactlessly.

She smiled. "That's a bit rude." Then, with barely hint of effort, she clipped him in the face with the rifle's stock, knocking him flat in the bottom of the boat. He groaned, but didn't try to rise. She looked at Ptolemy. "We do smell ripe, though, I admit. Helps hide us from them dead folks, or so Elmer says."

"Elmer..." Ptolemy murmured, filing the name away. In situations such as this, one never knew what sort of information could prove valuable. "My name is Calvin," he said. "What is yours?"

"Jeannie-Ray Watkins," she said, looking him up and down. "That's a pretty name, Calvin. Pretty face, too." She leaned toward him, her yellow gaze flicking across his features. She reached out, as if to touch him, but the boat's pilot leaned over and caught her wrist.

"You know better than that, Jeannie," he said sharply. "Don't touch them before Wilbur gets a look at 'em."

"I was just looking, Brady," Jeannie said, yanking her hand free of his grip. "Maybe you should keep your eyes on the water. Last time out we hit a patch of them floaters and nearly capsized."

"That weren't my fault," Brady whined. "Damn bat or something dove at me, scared me shitless." He settled back. "Besides, we're almost home." He gestured, and Ptolemy saw something in the distance, rising out of the swamp like a tombstone in a forgotten graveyard.

It was a house, and not just any house; a plantation house, or something that had once been a plantation house before time and circumstance had warped it out of proportion. Jeannie turned and whistled sharply, communicating with the other airboats. More whistles answered her. Ptolemy watched and said nothing. Jeannie seemed to have forgotten him, and that was all to the good. Something in her gaze had unsettled him. Not lust; something more primal.

Before the apocalypse, he'd spent time with other survivalists. Some were simply off-the-grid types, like himself. Others were more into conspiracy theories – black helicopters, alien intelligences, and global cabals. While Ptolemy shared some of their beliefs, he found the idea of an organized global conspiracy to be laughable and had made himself largely unwelcome in their ranks.

There was yet a third type of survivalist. Those who were off-grid and exiled from society not through choice, but by circumstance or necessity. Those were the dangerous ones. The others had been largely play-actors, preparing for an Armageddon that none of them truly believed would happen. Even Ptolemy had doubted it in his heart of hearts.

But that third type didn't care about the end of the world, because they'd already abandoned society and its strictures. These were the ones who he'd feared would persevere despite the undead. The kind who would see the end of all things as an opportunity rather than a tragedy. Thankfully, they hadn't run across many of that sort since finding the Villa. But from what he could see, their captors were definitely of that class of survivalist.

"Darwinism: the survivors survive," he murmured. A favorite quote of his by Charles Fort. Fort, like Ptolemy, had been of a skeptical nature. He'd looked past the gossamer web of the world to see the spiders crawling around underneath. Fort had been a modern-day seer; an observer of patterns. Ptolemy liked to think of himself the same way.

The pattern he was seeing here was an unpleasant one;

humans reverted to barbarism very quickly when placed under existential threat. They became violent, erratic, and unpredictable. But what if they were already like that before the threat became known? What would happen then? What would they become?

Music rose from the distant house – not from a device, but from instruments held by real hands. Fingers plucked strings. Voices were raised in song; not a hymn, but some old folk song he recalled hearing long ago, though he could not identify it.

The boats puttered to a stop, bumping against a wooden dock that seemed to float atop the sawgrass. Wind chimes hung from the support beams and clattered in the stale breeze. An alligator skull had been mounted atop the mooring post, its snout pointing downwards.

A man stood at the edge of the dock – a big man. Bigger even than Calavera, which Ptolemy had not been sure was possible. The man was dressed normally, in denim and a t-shirt. No feathers, no bones, no war paint, or camouflage. He had a belt buckle in the shape of an alligator, with a large hunting knife on one hip and a revolver holstered on the other. His arms were crossed over his thick chest, and he glared at the approaching boats as if they'd somehow offended him.

"Cousin Wilbur," Jeannie said, in a tone that bordered on fearful. Ptolemy figured him for the boss. Or at least one rung up on the ladder. He checked on Riggs, who was stirring.

"Sit up," Ptolemy murmured.

"I think she broke my nose," Riggs mumbled. He touched the end of his mask and flinched. Ptolemy shook his head.

"I have a feeling there is worse in store for us than a busted nose. Now be quiet and keep your eyes open." The boat thumped against the dock, and Ptolemy looked up to see Wilbur studying them.

"Sort of scrawny, ain't they?" he rumbled. Like the others, he had a drawl. Unlike theirs, his voice was so deep as to be almost unintelligible. It was more like the grunt of an alligator than the voice of a man. "Maybe you should have thrown them back."

"There's more in the other boats," Brady said. "One of them is a big fella – but he got an arrow in him."

"How many of the rest of them got arrows in them?"

"Just the one," Jeannie said proudly. "The rest of them gave up when they saw us."

"Except the ones who got away," Brady added helpfully. Jeannie gave him a death-glare, and Ptolemy figured she hadn't been planning to mention that. That was useful. Wilbur was the sort of leader that one did not wish to share bad news with.

"How many?" Wilbur growled.

Brady pulled off his ratty baseball cap and pressed it to his chest. "How many got away?" Wilbur looked at him for several moments and then gave a guttural sigh.

"How many you bring us?" he clarified.

"Six," Jeannie said quickly. "One injured. Not bad, but he ain't going to be dancing anytime soon."

Wilbur grunted at this and hiked a thumb over his shoulder. "Get them offloaded. Cages are waiting."

Brady dragged Ptolemy and Riggs to their feet, cutting the thongs that bound their ankles. At Wilbur's gesture, a pair of young men came forward to take custody of them.

Both were dressed casually with no sign of the outlandish accoutrements of the others. But like the others, they had that jaundice gleam to their eyes – a nasty, yellow tint that made them look like human coyotes.

Ptolemy did not know what to make of that gleam. He'd heard stories about yellow-eyed people from a trucker of his acquaintance; of cars left abandoned on the side of the interstate and missing persons, but he'd only half-believed it. He wanted to ask them who they were, what they wanted, but he suspected he already knew the answer.

It was the wind chimes that clued him in. They were made of bones.

Not animal bones; too big. Too straight.

Jeannie patted him on the cheek, startling him. "See you later, Calvin. Take 'er easy." Then she turned away as he and Riggs were frog-marched down the dock. Chicken wire had been strung up between the dock posts, pulled taut across a makeshift frame of plywood and sheet metal. More wind chimes hung from the frame, and more of the strange decorations they'd seen at the airfield.

"You like those?" one of their escorts asked. "The kids make 'em special. Call them angel catchers, though I ain't sure they ever caught anything but mosquitoes." He smiled genially at Ptolemy, and then nudged him in the ribs with the stock of his shotgun, urging him to keep moving. "Granny likes them, so we hang them up all over."

"And who is this Granny?" Ptolemy asked, trying to push down his growing sense of foreboding. Fear would serve no purpose here.

The two young men looked at one another. "Granny

is Granny," the one who'd spoken before said, in visible bewilderment. "She's our granny. Our momma's momma."

"Daddy's momma," the other one corrected.

"Somebody's momma," the first countered.

"And she is in charge?"

"You ask a lot of questions," the first said, frowning slightly. Ptolemy, sensing the warning in the young man's words, fell silent. He glanced back and saw the others being shepherded out of the boats. Coop was struggling, but cursing loudly. Ramirez was silent, her face a flat mask, but her eyes watchful. Terry and Gable weren't struggling as much as Coop, but they weren't going along easy. Wilbur watched them, and when Terry shoved one of his captors, the big man felled him with a single blow.

He reached down and hefted Terry onto one shoulder like a sack of cornmeal, with no sign of strain. Then he pushed past the others and started toward the house. "Hurry it up," he growled. "I ain't got all afternoon."

Ptolemy kept his head down and asked no more questions. He was starting to understand why the others were scared of Wilbur.

CHAPTER SIXTEEN
Gator Bait

Westlake hauled himself out of the water and onto the mossy hummock, his body bristling with hunting arrows. It wasn't the worst he'd ever felt, but neither was it the best. There was no pain, of course, but he still had enough rudimentary sensation to feel the arrows poking into his crumbling organs. It was unsettling to feel his liver flapping around inside him like a wet plastic bag. But he'd lived with worse. So to speak.

He lay for a moment, trying to reorient himself. His last few moments on the dock had been confused ones. He'd never been shot with an arrow before. It had been a new experience, if not one he was eager to repeat. He squinted up at the sky, visible only in snatches between the heavy boughs of the trees. The day had given way to early evening. How long had he been in the water?

These days, he lost time easier than fingers. His attention drifted too often and for too long. That was why he hadn't spotted the ambush. Once, he'd have seen it coming the moment he stepped off the plane. His mind wasn't as quick as it had been – a thought he'd had before, but one that kept bobbing to the surface of his thoughts like a warning buoy in choppy seas.

The ambush had been quick, practiced. They'd done it before, whoever they were. More than once. They'd used the walkers to get close, to keep their targets distracted. They had to have had some way of hiding themselves from the dead, though. Maybe it had been as simple as standing downwind, but he didn't think so.

The others were fine. They'd been through worse. They could weather an ambush. Only… Kahwihta had been hurt. And Coop. The latter didn't matter so much, but the kid… the thought caused him a flicker of unease. A crumb of worry floating in the stew of his brain. She'd never been hurt before. Banged up some, yeah. In danger, more than once. But actually hurt – not since he'd known her.

Some criminals he'd known would have called that an omen. Westlake had never been superstitious, not like that. But even so, the thought clung to the underside of his mind like a lamprey. It was his fault she was hurt. His fault they'd been ambushed. Coop had been right, not that Westlake intended to tell him that. If Coop was still alive.

If any of them were still alive.

He needed to check. To go back and see if he could help. To see if there was anyone left to be helped. If not, he'd settle for payback.

He slumped against a tree and looked down at the arrows perforating him. Then, with a sigh, he reached to pull the first one out. He'd just managed to work it loose when he heard a reptilian grunt from somewhere close by. He paused and turned.

A dark, heavy shape moved through the water toward him. An armored back rose above the murk, revealing mossy scales and primeval scar tissue. A wide tail slapped the water with a sound like a gunshot. Two eyes like boiled eggs peeked up and fixed on him. Westlake straightened up and pushed himself away from the tree. "Wonderful. Can this day get any better?"

He'd never seen an alligator up close before. In the zoo, once, and that time he'd watched Vinnie Spinoza feed a bookie to one in Miami. That was it. The animals hadn't exactly made a favorable impression on him.

This one was weird, though. It drifted toward him unhurriedly, but there was something off about its movements, or lack thereof. For one thing, it didn't blink. For another, he couldn't hear its heartbeat. He hadn't noticed it at first, right after he'd woken up dead and realized what that meant. Later, he'd realized when he heard the living, he wasn't just hearing voices or the sound of breathing, but also the thrum of a pulse, the thud of a heart. Signals that meant life. That meant prey.

Hungry, it whispered. The killer urge. That's what the voice was. Not him, but the part of him that nestled in his reptile brain. He wondered what he would do if the others were dead. Or worse, if they were undead. Would any of them wind up like him? He hoped not. It wasn't any kind of life for a decent person, and they were all decent – barring maybe Coop. And Sayers.

Hungry, his hindbrain murmured. It was worse when he'd taken damage. Like his body was trying to fix itself, only there was no way to do that. Not on this earth. He tried to push it away, to focus on the threat before him. It wasn't breathing. Was it like him? A hungry thing, caught between death and life. Bad luck.

Bipedal zombies usually ignored him, unless he did something to provoke them. The four-legged kind weren't so accommodating. To them, he was just another meal. He looked around for a weapon and found a half-rotted log sticking out of the water. It would have to do. He grabbed it as the alligator surged toward him, malformed maw spread as if to swallow him whole.

Westlake turned – and jammed the log between the animal's jaws, preventing them from closing. The alligator immediately twisted away, making a concerned grunting sound. Its tail nearly took his head off in the process, forcing him to scramble deeper into the water and off his relatively stable perch.

It was an ugly thing, like a child's drawing of an alligator, all lumpy bands of scale over swollen musculature. Its jaws were filled with an excess of teeth, and not all the right kind. Its eyes were blank marbles, at least those in its head. The ones on its flanks were fat and yellow, like leeches. They blinked at random, glaring at him with mindless malice.

Its jaws bent; the wood creaked; splintered; snapped. Then it was coming for him again, a freight train of reptilian fury. He dove away from it, toward deeper water that swallowed him up greedily. He didn't need to breathe, so it was just a matter of finding his footing – and readying himself.

The alligator surged toward him, cutting the water like a knife, jaws swinging wide. He caught them, left hand on the upper jaw, right hand on the bottom. Gators had a strong bite, but a weak jaw, or so he recalled from television. Maybe that had been an oversimplification. He was about to find out.

The gator's momentum drove him backward, his heels digging in the soft mud. The beast was stronger than he was, and heavier. But he was deader than disco, and such things didn't mean much to him anymore. He held it at bay, letting the force of its charge reverberate down through his arms and legs, stalling it in place. The alligator slammed its tail against the water as it tried to break loose, but Westlake had planted his feet and he'd decided he wasn't going anywhere. Slowly but surely, he started to force the animal's jaws wider. Its struggles grew fiercer, but it couldn't get any leverage on him.

"Fight all you want, you sonnuvabitch," Westlake growled. "This only ends one way – and you ain't going to like it." He heard skin and scales tear, and then the top of the alligator's head came away in a geyser of tarry blood. Westlake let the body float away and stared at the bit he'd wrenched off. The dead eyes blinked. He felt his lips peel back from his teeth. He knew that if he'd still had salivary glands, he'd have been drooling.

Westlake raised the chunk of alligator meat, unable to stop himself from taking a bite. It tasted... foul, but sweet. He tore strips from it, cracking open the top of the skull to get at the shriveled brain meat within. It felt good to eat. To chew and swallow, to feel the rush of congealed blood rolling down his ravaged throat.

Hungry.

"Yeah, I hear ya," Westlake mumbled, chewing a tough chunk. Something was missing, though. A memory of a taste of something he'd never eaten. Or at least couldn't remember eating.

He'd been in a fugue state after he'd died and come back. He'd wandered for months, unaware and amnesiac. He often found himself trying to remember that time, but never successfully. Had he eaten anyone during it? Had he been just another walker, or worse? Or had he stopped himself even then from doing something he knew he could never take back? The thought would have kept him up nights, if he'd slept. As it was, it was always at the back of his mind, waiting to pounce.

It did so now, and he froze, staring at the ruined mass in his hands. The alligator's body was still twitching and splashing, but the eyes on its flanks were closed. He dropped what was left of its head into the water and staggered back, suddenly all too aware of the taste in his mouth and the need in his belly. He'd woken it now, given it a taste – it wouldn't be satisfied with dead meat, not for long.

HungryhungryHUNGRY–

"Shut up," he hissed, pounding on the sides of his head with his fists. "Shut up, shut up!" He looked down at the arrows still in him and felt a paroxysm of rage grip him. He began to tear them free without concern for what they did to his body. He just needed to do something, anything other than listen to the voice.

He heard a familiar grumbling roar and turned. Another alligator. It splashed toward him hungrily and without thinking he rammed the arrows in his hands first into its eyes and then into its brain, even as its jaws closed on his legs and knocked him onto his back in the water. He felt its teeth tear through his leg, but it let go almost immediately. It rolled, groaning in its death throes. But it wasn't alone. More of the beasts closed in. Three at least, maybe more from the sound of it.

Too many for him to deal with, with just his hands. He reached for another arrow. It was better than nothing.

A roar split the gathering gloom. Not the basso grumble of an alligator, but something much louder, made by something much bigger. Westlake heard trees splinter beneath a great weight, and water splashing. An alligator was lifted into the air by a powerful blow and sent hurtling away head over tail. He had the impression of something large and stocky, built like a tank. It moved with a curious lunging motion – not like an alligator, but not like any animal he'd ever seen either. Whatever it was, it sounded hungry.

Westlake took the opportunity and ran. Not well, and not especially quickly, but he damn well ran. Let whatever it was play with the gators if it wanted to. He stumbled through thigh deep water, disturbing snakes and insects in his awkward haste. He heard an alligator squeal somewhere behind him. Whatever had it wasn't being nice about it. A bear, maybe? They'd seen a mutated bear in the Adirondacks.

Only it hadn't smelled like a bear. And no bear was that big, even a mutated one. He wondered if it had been something like the creature he'd faced in Atlantic City – a zombified mass of meat and muscle, grown to inhuman proportions. He hoped not. One of those had been enough.

He paused only once, and that was because he'd caught sight of a runner loping through the swamp to his left, heading in the same direction he was. It wasn't the only zombie moving that way either. Walkers stumbled through the waters, groaning eerily. It was as if they were all running away from the same thing he was. He had a suspicion that whatever it was, it wouldn't turn up its nose at eating a few zombies as dessert once it finished with the alligators.

Westlake picked up the pace. He wasn't certain he was going in the right direction, but at the moment, anywhere was better than here.

CHAPTER SEVENTEEN
Cruise

The *Dixie Jewel* was lit up like a beacon. Solar powered Christmas lights hung from the rails, and a generator hummed as it powered several spotlights mounted on the upper deck. The spotlights swept the water below, startling the alligators that congregated around the husk of the brute Calavera had slain.

Sayers stood on the deck of the ship and looked out over the swamp. Calvin had been right, not that that was a surprise. Still, a cruise ship in the middle of the Everglades wasn't the sort of thing one expected to see. She just wished he was here to see it, rather than wherever he was. Somewhere out in the swamp, maybe. Or worse.

Kahwihta was in the ship's infirmary, still out of it. Attila refused to leave her side. Calavera and Imogene sat nearby, talking to their hosts. She had no idea where the others were. The last she'd seen of Ramirez and Coop, they were taking cover from another volley of arrows. And Westlake was probably dead for good this time. As for the others, well, if they were smart, they'd have headed for the sawgrass.

They'd been brought onto the ship via a provisioning hatch in the hull. The raft had been left to bob against the hull, secured with several stout lines, while Jessop had led them up through a narrow maintenance gantry to the uppermost deck.

She turned back to the others. People milled about, within earshot but not obviously eavesdropping. Some were manning the rails, others were just sitting quietly. According to their hosts, there were around eighteen people aboard the ship counting kids. There'd been more once, but things had gone from bad to worse. That was a story she'd heard before. They'd all heard it before and experienced it for themselves. They seemed amiable enough, but she wasn't sure what to make of them yet. Trust was earned, not given.

"We've been out here for months," Jessop said from where he sat nearby, giving his coffee a swirl. Sayers sniffed her own as she went to join the conversation. The coffee was real. Not instant, but definitely stale. She glanced at Jessop who added, "We've been drying out the grounds and reusing them. More like a placebo than anything. Lets people feel a bit…"

"Normal," Imogene supplied. "I understand." Sayers was content to let the younger woman guide the conversation. Imogene was a people person; more so than herself at least. Calavera volunteered little. He just sat, rubbing his hands as if they pained him.

Jessop nodded gratefully. "Frankly, we were starting to figure we were the only people left alive out here. At least until we saw the plane."

Sayers snorted. "Not likely."

"We're from Atlantic City," Imogene supplied. "Well, I am." She indicated Calavera and Sayers. "They're from the

Adirondacks. Our group came looking for supplies." She paused. "We were attacked."

"Alligators?" Jessop asked, and from his tone Sayers guessed he'd had a run in with the creatures before. Imogene shook her head.

"They had bows."

"Bows?" Jessop frowned in confusion. "Who the hell uses bows?" He glanced at Sayers. "No offense, ma'am."

Sayers grunted. "Doesn't ring any bells, then?" She set her cup down on the rail. Ripples formed on the surface of the liquid. She followed the distant sound of startled birds and saw avian forms rise against the murky stars a few miles away. But she said nothing about it and turned to Jessop. "That wasn't you out there, at the airstrip?"

"Airstrip?" Jessop looked at the others. The man named Phipps looked puzzled and shook his head. The woman, Grillo, did the same. Sayers didn't think they were lying. They didn't know anything about it. Maybe that was why they were still hiding on the boat. Off in the distance, she heard the sound of trees being broken in two. Something bellowed. It was bigger than an alligator, whatever it was. Calavera turned toward the sound, and she thought she saw something like interest flash in his eyes. He rose and went to the rail. She wondered what was going on inside his head. Usually, he was more talkative.

Jessop and the others looked nervous, particularly Phipps. Sayers figured they'd heard the sound before, even if they didn't know what it was. She smiled. "There's a hurricane coming. Any plans for that?"

Grillo looked at her. "Batten down the hatches and hope we don't capsize – or worse."

"What could be worse?" Imogene asked.

"The dead," Phipps said softly.

Sayers tensed. "There are zombies on this boat?"

"Ship," Jessop corrected. "And quite a few, yeah. All below-decks, thankfully. We've got the bulkheads sealed. There's no way they're getting out unless the hull suffers catastrophic damage, or someone lets them out." He stumbled over the last bit, and Sayers wondered about what that might mean. Nothing good, probably. He leaned forward. "You said there's an airstrip near here. What about a plane?"

"Unless whoever attacked us has stripped it for parts, it should still be there."

"And a pilot?"

Sayers looked back out over the swamp. "Out there somewhere. Or dead. Or both."

Jessop slumped. Grillo and the others looked equally despondent.

"Maybe not," Imogene said hurriedly. "If they managed to get away…"

"We could go look for them," Grillo said, sitting up. "Take one of the remaining boats and see if what they say is true."

"Why wouldn't it be?" Sayers asked.

Grillo looked at her, and Sayers smiled. She'd been told her smile wasn't a particularly friendly one, but that was fine with her. Grillo swallowed. "I just meant we could go looking for them. There's worse things than zombies in this swamp."

"Like whoever attacked us, you mean," Sayers said. "Or whatever it was that just bellowed out there."

"Just a gator," Grillo said.

"It's not a gator and you know it," Phipps said sharply. He

looked around. "It's a monster is what it is." He looked at Sayers. "We've seen it before, but never up close. It's always underwater or behind the trees."

Jessop made a placatory gesture. "It's just an animal, whatever it is. As to the other, we've been stuck on this boat for longer than it's been stuck in the swamp. If there is someone out there, we've never – huh." He sat back, a considering look on his face. "The boats."

"What boats?" Imogene asked.

Grillo looked at Phipps. "The boats," she said, nodding.

"What boats?" Sayers demanded. Jessop looked at her.

"We've seen boats. In the distance. Flat boats mostly. An airboat once. They don't get close. I figured them for locals. There were some people who lived in the Everglades, not many but some. A few are probably still alive."

"You think... what? Swamp folk attacked us?" Sayers wanted to laugh, but she knew better. She'd dealt with hermits before; hell, she was one, at heart. They could be vicious if provoked, and sometimes even if not. Stable people didn't generally choose to make their homes in deep wilderness, and she was including herself in that generalization.

Jessop looked uncomfortable with the suggestion. "Maybe. Either way, we should probably try to find your friends, don't you think?"

"And why would you help us?"

"How many people can fit on that plane of yours?" Jessop asked.

Sayers leaned back against the rail. "That depends." She looked at Imogene, who shrugged. And Calavera said nothing, still looking out over the rail into the darkness. Sayers sighed.

She didn't like being in charge. She didn't like dealing with people. "First, let's make sure the plane is in one piece and that we have a pilot. Then we can talk about getting your people somewhere safe."

Jessop glanced at his companions, and then nodded. "Fair enough." He paused. "We should check on your other friend first."

Imogene rose. "I'll do it." She looked at Sayers. "Why don't you see about helping them get a boat ready?"

Sayers gave her a two-finger salute. Grillo went to show her the way, leaving Sayers alone with Jessop and Phipps. Jessop swatted the other man on the arm. "Go round up a few volunteers, and make sure that they're armed. I'll take Miss Sayers to the boats and we'll see if any of them other than the raft are still seaworthy."

"So, the Adirondacks," Jessop began, as he led her along the deck.

Sayers grunted. She didn't want to encourage any further small talk. But Jessop wasn't the sort to give up easy. Maybe he was just desperate to talk to someone new. If so, he'd picked the wrong person.

"Must be nice. Can't imagine there are many zombies up there."

"More than you might think."

"Still less than here. It wasn't a day after we wound up here that they came out of the swamp. It was like the hurricane stirred them up and drew them all out of hiding. More than a hundred of them." Jessop paused, struck by the memory. "We didn't have a chance."

"Obviously you did. You're still here, after all."

He looked at her as if she'd slapped him. "There's only eighteen people left on this tub, lady." His hands clenched into fists. "Eighteen out of almost a hundred. That's not exactly a win/loss rate to brag about, is it?"

"Better than the alternative," Sayers said. She hesitated. Calvin wasn't here, but she could almost hear him sighing at her lack of sympathy. She looked away. "I'm... sorry. But it's impressive that you've managed to stay alive this long. It really is."

He shook his head. "Doesn't feel impressive."

"No, it never does." She looked around the deck, taking in the tarps set up to collect rainwater, the fishing rods mounted on the rails, the pool that had been drained and turned into a garden. According to Jessop, most of it had been done while they'd been at sea. It wasn't a bad start. But it had only ever been intended to be temporary. "Nice garden."

"It gets us by."

Sayers grunted. "We've got gardens and a greenhouse back in the mountains, but it's not enough." Sayers looked over the rail. "I don't think it'll ever be enough, honestly."

"A growing community requires resources," Jessop said.

Sayers laughed bitterly. "We're not growing... we're just surviving."

"Survival can be a form of growth."

Sayers shook her head. "You sound like my... like Calvin."

"Who's Calvin?"

She didn't reply. Who was Calvin to her? They'd danced around the issue for months, never quite managing the level of intimacy that they'd once had. Her fault. She'd betrayed him. Them. They'd forgiven her, she thought, though she hadn't asked for it. In truth, she didn't know that she wanted it.

"A friend," she said finally. "One of the ones we... left back there." She glanced at him. "If we can get your people to safety, we will. That's... what we do, apparently." She looked up at the darkening sky. The wind was starting to kick up a bit now, and the air tasted wet. "I just hope we have time to do it."

CHAPTER EIGHTEEN
Infirmary

Kahwihta dreamed of black waters. She was somewhere she didn't recognize, a wide frozen sea, its icy surface like a mirror of polished obsidian. Beneath it, an infinity of grotesque faces and hands pressed to the underside of the surface.

She stared at them for long moments, trying to understand what she was seeing. Their mouths moved soundlessly as their hands beat against the unyielding water-glass. Were they dead? Alive? There was no way to tell. Their features were indistinct smudges, like blurred faces in a bad photo.

She stood on the surface of the water and something – someone – was nearby, their back to her. As she approached them, the writhing of the things beneath the water grew more frenzied. Were they trying to free themselves, or warn her?

She wanted to stop. To turn and run. But she couldn't prevent herself from reaching out to whoever it was. As her hand touched their sleeve they turned.

It was Westlake.

He was worse. His skin was sloughing off in sheets, and his bones showed through in places, wet and yellow. His eyes were pustulant sores and his jaw sagged as if in greeting. His hands rose, and she saw that all the repairs they'd made to him over the past few months had unraveled, leaving his limbs a tattered mess.

She tried to speak but could find no words. There was only one sound in this place; an intermittent groan, like the settling of an old house, and it was coming from Westlake's open mouth. The sound grew louder as his yellow gaze fixed on her. He took a step. She found her voice. "Westlake…"

"Hungry," he moaned. His hands stretched toward her.

"No," she said, backing away. Beneath her feet, the ice began to crack. Black water surged up and slopped across her feet and legs. Westlake lurched after her.

"Hungry," he moaned again. It wasn't his voice. Not really. It was no one's voice and everyone's, all smashed together like shards of broken glass. It was the voice of every dead thing in the world joined together in one cry. He grabbed at her, and she tried to shove him back, but he was too strong.

He grabbed a handful of her hair and one of her wrists and yanked her toward him even as the ice ruptured beneath their feet. They plummeted into the water together, and the cold swallowed her up like a shroud and dragged her under. Westlake clung to her, clawing at her, splintering his own teeth in his frenzy to bite her. She did her best to push him away, but he wasn't the only threat. The things under the water were reaching for her as well, from every angle. She saw their faces clearly now, though she wished she couldn't.

There wasn't a single one she didn't know. Ramirez,

Ptolemy, Coop, Gable, Imogene... Hutch, Labrand... more; her family... her mother and father, grandparents, cousins, classmates... faces she'd only seen for a few moments, all now glaring at her from the dark, reaching for her with frantic hands. They grabbed her and pulled her in all directions with such force that she thought she might come apart at the seams.

Westlake came for her again, jaws spread wide – too wide – impossibly wide. His broken teeth were larger, and his body was swelling. Transforming. She kicked away, trying to scream even as cold water filled her lungs and hands dragged her deeper down into the dark. Deeper and deeper, until the light was just a fading memory and then–

Kahwihta awoke with a start, to find herself in an unfamiliar place and that everything hurt. She tried to sit up and stopped with a grunt of pain. Attila, laying on the end of the bed, whined and crawled toward her, tail thumping wildly. She stroked his head as best she was able and looked around.

The room was large, sectioned off by white curtains, and lit by an electric lantern hung from the ceiling. Mirrors were mounted in the corners of the room, and properly angled, allowed the light to stretch farther. Circular windows – portholes – were open, letting in the gray light of day and a humid breeze. "Where am I?" she croaked, tossing a questioning glance at the room's other occupant.

Imogene smiled and leaned forward. "Ptolemy was right. There was a cruise ship, and we are aboard it." She gestured about herself. "This is the ship's infirmary."

"What's left of it," a man said, as he entered the room.

He was short and dark, with a mane of curly black and gray hair, a grizzled beard and eyebrows that jutted like mountain ridges. "I'm Doctor Hawser. You are a very lucky woman."

"I don't feel lucky," Kahwihta said, as Imogene helped her sit up. Pain rippled through her, radiating outwards from a point just below her ribs.

"You are. A hairsbreadth lower, and you'd need a colostomy bag. A bit to the right, and you'd need a wheelchair. A bit to the left, and you'd have bled out. It hit you at just the right spot to make it hurt, but not to cripple you for life." He gestured for Imogene to move, and bent over Kahwihta, checking the bandage taped to her side. "Looks clean. Swelling is to be expected, but I think we avoided infection… though I hate to think what might have been on that arrow."

"Arrow?" Kahwihta asked. She could barely recall what had happened. "Like – bow and arrow? Someone shot me with an arrow?" She frowned. "It wasn't Sayers, was it?" Kahwihta was fairly certain Sayers was over her backshooting tendencies, but while she might have forgiven the former park ranger for her error in judgement, she hadn't forgotten.

Imogene shook her head. "We were ambushed. Someone was using the dead as cover to get close. At least we think that's what they were doing."

"The others?"

"We don't know. We barely made it out ourselves, and by the time we convinced Sayers to turn around, well… we were nearly eaten."

"Eaten?" Kahwihta blinked. "Zombies?"

"Alligators," Hawser said. "But yes, also zombies. Zombie alligators. As if the regular kind weren't bad enough."

Kahwihta rubbed her head. "You should try the mountains. We've got bears."

Hawser snorted. "Sounds like paradise." He stepped back. "We've got some painkillers left if you need them. Not many, but enough to take the edge off. Keep it dry, don't let any zombies stick their fingers in it, and you should be fine. Now, I've got to make my rounds, so I'll leave you two to it. Glad you're awake. Welcome to the Love Boat." With that, he was gone. Kahwihta frowned.

"Love Boat?"

Imogene shrugged. "He thinks he's funny. Me, I just think he's old." She looked at Kahwihta. "We're safe, for now. But apparently this place is on its last legs."

"What do you mean?"

Imogene ticked off the list on her fingers. "They're down to less than twenty people from a hundred. Most of that hundred are roaming around belowdecks. The ship's stuck. There are zombie alligators in the waters, zombie birds in the trees and a hurricane on the way. Plus, whoever attacked us is still out there." She paused. "Those weird decorations we found… do they think they're the ones responsible for those? Like, maybe they were territorial markers or something."

Kahwihta frowned. "Maybe. Though they looked more like something out of a bad horror movie." She touched her side, winced, and eased back down. "Anything other than walkers below?"

"Some. But the brutes can't get through the corridors easily, and the runners are all mixed up with the walkers. Jessop, the first mate, says they've cleared a few of the hatchways, but they didn't have much ammo to begin with and he's not inclined to use the rest until they have to." Imogene sat back. "Apparently there's a wealth of dry goods and canned food down there, but no way to get to it without unleashing a horde of zombies. That's probably the most screwed up thing about this – there's *years* of supplies down there, and we can't get to it."

Kahwihta considered this. "Do we know for certain that we can't?" she asked, after a moment. "Cruise ships load up through hatches in the hull. We could open those and the zombies might just wander out."

"They've thought of that. They've managed to keep one of the outer hatches clear. That's how they brought us in. But they're worried about other things getting in. And there's no power to open the largest hatches. It'd have to be manual. And that means going down near the water. Where the gators are." Imogene spread her hands. "They're in a pickle."

"Big pickle," Kahwihta said, still running the problem over in her mind. It gave her something to think about other than the pain. "Maybe we could help them with it."

"They'd be grateful, I think." Imogene looked at her. "Jessop's trying to be confident, but he's tired. They all are. If we could get them and the supplies to the Villa…"

"There is no if," Calavera said, from the doorway. "There is only when." He came over to the bed and looked down at them. "Sayers will be leading a team back to the plane to see if we can find the others. I am going with them."

"I'll go too," Imogene began, getting to her feet.

He stopped her with a shake of his head. "No. Someone needs to stay here with Kahwihta. I merely came to alert you to our departure." He paused. "We will find the others. I promise you."

Kahwihta heard something in his voice – an eagerness she'd heard only a few times before – and said, "That's not all you're looking for, is it?"

Calavera hesitated. "There is something out there. Something large."

Kahwihta sat back with a sigh. "And you intend to kill it."

"I intend to try, if the opportunity arises." He rubbed his hands, as if trying to massage away an ache. "Something tells me that it is not meant to live."

"It's not alive," a new voice intruded. The words were slightly slurred and came from a disheveled older man in a filthy uniform, leaning against the entrance to the infirmary. He stumbled into the room, still talking. "There's nothing alive out there now. Even the trees are dying. The water is sour." He went to the medicine cabinet and started to rummage through it. "The third angel has blown his trumpet, and the great star has fallen from heaven. Its name was Wormwood." He gave a little cry as he found what he was looking for, then turned around with a bottle of rubbing alcohol in his hands, and paused, peering at them blearily. "I don't know your names though. Did you come aboard in Tampa?"

"No," Calavera said. Then, gently, "Who are you?"

"Why, I am the captain of this fine vessel, as you might be able to tell from my uniform." The man gestured airily to himself. He looked down at himself as he did so and paused. "Oh my. I appear to have spilled something on it."

"The contents of a liquor cabinet by the smell of you," Imogene said bluntly.

He looked at her. "I assure you, young lady, that not a drop was spilled." He belched and thumped his chest with a fist. "But I do find I need a top-up. Anyone care for a drink?" He gave the bottle of rubbing alcohol a swish.

"No, thank you," Kahwihta said. He blinked and looked at her.

"Are you hurt?"

"Not badly."

He grabbed a stool and pulled it noisily over to the side of the bed and sat. "That's good. I'm glad. Getting hurt means you die. And when you die, you go into the hold with the others." He patted her hand awkwardly and seemed on the verge of tears. "I can hear them, even if they've gone quiet." He leaned close, and whispered loudly, "It's me they want, you know. Because it's my fault, you see. They trusted me and I failed them and now they are dead and it is my fault that they are dead."

Kahwihta wasn't sure how to respond to that. She could hear nothing. No echoes, no thumping at the hatches. The sort of thing you'd expect if there were a bunch of walking corpses trapped below. She felt a flush of pity for him; a lot of folks couldn't handle survivor's guilt.

The man swayed on his stool, looking around the room. "I want to go in the hold with them. That is what a captain is supposed to do. But Jessop won't let me. I should discipline him, but he's a good officer and I know he means well." He unscrewed the cap on the bottle. "So instead I drink. When I turn, I expect I will be very flammable." He stumbled over the word, and under other circumstances it might have been funny. But here and now, it was just sad. He gave Kahwihta an encouraging smile. "Don't worry. You will be safe here. Everyone will be safe on the ships. We'll sail away from all the horror…"

He trailed off, and his gaze became vague and absent. Hawser came back a moment later, followed by another survivor. "There he is," Hawser said. "Get Captain Ogilvy back to his cabin, please. And for the love of God keep him in there this time. Lord knows what he'll do if he gets out again."

"C'mon, sir," the other survivor said, taking Ogilvy by the arm. "Let's get you back now. You look like you could use a sleep."

"Thank you, you have the helm," Ogilvy mumbled as he allowed himself to be led out of the infirmary.

Hawser waited until he'd gone and said, "I'm sorry about that." He frowned, as if something had just occurred to him. "He stole my last bottle of rubbing alcohol."

"Looked like he needed it," Kahwihta said. She looked at Calavera. "Now what's this about looking for Ramirez and the others?"

CHAPTER NINETEEN
Captives

Night slid into morning. Ramirez, body aching, tried to find a more comfortable position in her cage. In the rising light, she could make out the house better. It had the bones of something from the turn of the century, but additions had clearly been made over the years since its construction. It had been made taller, wider, longer. Stretched between the trees and over the sawgrass by successive generations of inhabitants.

From where she sat, it almost had the look of something organic; grown, rather than built. The thought chilled her, and she turned her attention to the cage. It was one of a dozen stainless steel shark cages, each hung by a series of pulleys and levers from a cable stretching across the water.

The cable stretched away from the back of the house and to the edge of the swamp, where a concrete water break had been built at some time in the past. A walkway made from scrap wood and metal, enclosed in a chicken wire and chain link shell, led from the back porch of the house to the bulwark.

Below the walkway, a mass of zombies moved against one another, trapped by a makeshift fence composed of nets and buoys. Occasionally, a zombie would reach up, vainly trying to grab hold of a cage, but they were thankfully out of reach.

Ramirez leaned back and rubbed her shoulder. Everything ached. But she was alive, if a bit bruised. Their captors hadn't been gentle. Riggs was in her cage, and she could see Gable and Ptolemy in another some distance away. Terry was at the far end, in the last cage closest to the dock. But where was Coop? No sign of him. That didn't bode well. She wasn't his biggest fan at the moment, but she didn't want him dead. "Riggs," she said, glancing at him. "Riggs, you awake?"

No answer. There was a crust of blood on the side of his head, beneath his mask. Flies spun lazy circles around it. Their captors had bashed him hard. Maybe too hard. She tried to signal the others, but to no avail. She'd have to shout, and she wasn't sure she wanted to attract that much attention at the moment.

The other cages had their own occupants. Three men and two women, all of whom looked malnourished and the worse for wear. They lay limply in their confinement, clearly past the point of exhaustion and resigned to whatever fate awaited them. Ramirez grimaced. No help there. Maybe no help anywhere. She hoped the others had gotten away. She hoped they were alive. She thought of Kahwihta slumping, the arrow in her side... was she still alive? Maybe she was another name to add to the list of lost friends and family that Ramirez kept inside her head.

She hoped not; prayed not. Only prayers didn't seem to do much good these days. She flinched as something poked her.

She saw a child, dressed in filthy dungarees and a ratty t-shirt, holding a stick. "Y'all awake?" the child drawled. Ramirez couldn't tell whether they were a girl or a boy.

"I'm awake," she said, her voice cracking with thirst. She couldn't tell when she'd last had something to drink, other than it had been too long. "Who're you?"

"Dickie," the child said.

"That short for something?"

"Richelle. Named on account of my momma." The child – the girl – gave a sly smile. She was maybe eight or nine, or even a malnourished ten. She had a feral energy that the children at the Villa lacked. They were still frightened of the dead. Dickie, on the other hand, didn't seem all that bothered by the corpses in the water. "What's your name, ma'am?"

"Estela."

"Estela," Dickie repeated, sounding it out. "That's pretty." She rubbed her nose. She looked at Riggs, who sat hunched at the far end of the cage. "Why's he got that mask on?"

"He's afraid of bugs," Ramirez said. "Where are your parents, Dickie?"

"In the water," Dickie said, without a flicker of emotion. "Granny had Cousin Wilbur put them there when they turned. The way we do all them as turns." She smiled again, and Ramirez noticed that her eyes were an ugly shade of yellow, just like the rest of their captors. "Unless we feed them to God first." She paused. "I think we're going to feed y'all to God. That's good though, because if God eats you, you go right to Heaven. That's what Granny says."

"Is that what she says?" Ramirez asked, repeating the child's words.

"She do." Dickie rubbed her nose again, and then rubbed her hand on her dungarees. "Anyway, I'm going to go get her, on account of she wants to talk to y'all." She smiled again. "Was that big fellow your friend?"

Ramirez grabbed the bars of the cage and leaned forward. "Coop? You mean Coop? The one in black? Where is he?"

Dickie licked her lips and ran off, calling out to the house. Ramirez pounded a fist against the bars and cursed. She didn't have long to wait, as Dickie's shouts brought out the tall man she'd seen the night before. Wilbur, the others had called him. He was big, nearly the same size as a brute. Strong, too, as he'd carried Terry around with no real difficulty. He came out, squinted at her, and then went back in.

He reemerged a moment later, pushing a wheelchair down from the house toward the cages. Seated in the wheelchair was an old woman. Was this Dickie's "Granny"? Ramirez watched them draw close. They stopped a safe distance from the edge of the walkway, and the old woman said, "Get her down from there, boy. Bring her over here."

Wilbur grunted and did as she asked. He used the pulleys to draw her cage close enough for him to grab one-handed and he unlocked the door. She considered making a run for it. The odds, however, weren't in her favor. Better to let things play out for the moment. Wilbur opened the cage door and stepped back, gesturing for her to exit. Riggs hadn't moved at all. He might as well have been catatonic.

She climbed out of the cage slowly, watching Wilbur out of the corner of her eye. He was doing the same to her; she had a feeling he was hoping she'd do something stupid. He let the cage slam shut and caught her by the back of the neck, forcing her to stumble across the walkway until she was standing in front of the old woman.

The old woman was a withered stick figure, in a dress two sizes too big, and long untidy white hair. Like the others, her eyes were wrong – jaundice yellow, like something poisonous. Her wheelchair was an old-fashioned sort, like something scrounged out of a goodwill shop. A pistol belt hung from the back holding a 9MM.

She eyed Ramirez up and down, taking stock of her the same way Wilbur had. Then, she spread her arms, as if in welcome. "Allow me to introduce myself... my name is Keziah Watkins. This here is my property, my swamp... my world." She grinned at Ramirez. "And what's your name, baby girl?"

"Ramirez," Ramirez said. "Estela Ramirez."

"And what were you, Ramirez? Before it all went to hell? A cook, maybe? A maid?"

Ramirez's eyes narrowed. "I was with the FBI."

"Oh lord, you hear that, Wilbur? She's a Federal," the old woman croaked. "Thought there weren't any more such things. Thought they was all gone, eaten up by the dead." She leaned forward in her wheelchair and studied Ramirez through a veil of white, stringy hair. "Bring her closer. My eyes ain't what they were."

Wilbur shoved Ramirez painfully to her knees. Keziah wheeled herself closer and peered into Ramirez's face. "Was a Federal who put me in this chair, oh yes. Put a bullet right in the small of my back, quicker than shit." She traced Ramirez's cheek with a thumbnail. "Only fair, I suppose, as I'd given his partner the same. But by the grace of the good Lord, I survived. Spent damn near ten years in the state penitentiary. Missed my boys growing up." She glanced up at Wilbur. "When I got out, they was grown men."

"You have my condolences," Ramirez said, trying to keep her voice even. The old woman's thumbnail cut into her cheek – painfully – drawing a bead of blood on her skin. Ramirez didn't flinch. She didn't want to give them the satisfaction.

Keziah licked her bloody thumb. "How you still alive, Federal?"

"Just a born survivor, I guess."

The old woman laughed and looked at her son. "Hear that, Wilbur? She a survivor. We survivors, too, ain't we?"

"Yes, momma," he murmured. His odd, yellow eyes fixed on Ramirez like the scope of a rifle. The old woman patted his arm affectionately.

She looked at Ramirez again. "Yeah, we survivors. For a time, I thought we was the only ones. Then I learned different. God was looking out for us, I expect."

Ramirez frowned. "What do you want?"

"Who says I want anything?"

Ramirez shook her head. "We wouldn't be having this chat if you didn't want something. So what is it?"

Wilbur caught a handful of her hair and lifted her painfully off her feet. Cords of muscle bunched in his arm as he held her in the air. Ramirez bit back a scream of pain. "You being rude, Federal," Wilbur murmured. His yellow eyes flickered oddly as he studied her. "Maybe we should take a leg, momma. Teach her to be polite."

Keziah's voice was a whipcrack of command. "Put her down, boy."

Wilbur dropped Ramirez painfully to the deck. Ramirez rolled over onto her back and lashed out with her feet, trying to sweep Wilbur from his. But it was like kicking a tree trunk, with about as much reaction. Wilbur's eyes narrowed slightly, and his hand fell to the knife on his hip. "I said leave her be," Keziah repeated. She wheeled herself closer to Ramirez and looked down at her.

"Now, where were you doing your surviving at, exactly? Not the place we found you at, because we killed everyone who was living there already. No, y'all came from somewhere where you got access to planes. Planes means machines, and machines means gasoline and supplies."

Ramirez hesitated. Something told her that refusing to answer wouldn't end well. She swallowed. "New York."

Keziah nodded, as if this was the answer she'd suspected. "That do figure. Well, well. New York City. Ain't that a fine how do you do? And how many of you is there?"

"Enough to keep a plane in the air," Ramirez said carefully.

Keziah slapped her bent knees in amusement. "Good answer. Smart to play it cagey, Federal. Less you tell us, longer we have to keep you breathing. But breathing don't mean in one piece, you hear me?" She grinned, showing off teeth that had seen better decades. "Play me false, and we'll serve you up the way we served your big friend." The old woman snapped her fingers, and Wilbur pulled a sack off the back of her wheelchair. There was a thick, red stain on the bottom, and Ramirez felt suddenly sick. "He resisted a mite much for Wilbur's taste. Boy doesn't have much patience. He's just like his daddy, God rest his soul." She swung the sack before Ramirez's eyes.

"Coop," Ramirez whispered. Now she knew what Dickie had meant. A sick feeling clawed at the underside of her mind.

"Was that his name? Wilbur didn't inquire before... well." Keziah reached into the sack and dragged out Coop's head by its scalp. Ramirez flinched and looked away. Coop's face – what was left of it – was twisted up into an expression of pain and horror. "Don't mourn him overmuch now," Keziah went on, as she cradled Coop's head like a beloved toy. "He's going to feed my family for weeks... and if you ain't careful, you and them others will do the same."

Ramirez stared at her in horrified realization. Black nausea thrummed through her, and she bit back a sudden rush of bile. "Cannibals..." She'd heard the stories. Everyone had. But it just seemed like another post-apocalyptic urban legend, like zombified chupacabras or wolves that walked on two legs. But to have it confirmed so bluntly...

"Naw," Keziah corrected. "Just survivors. Like y'all. We make do best we can, like always. Lot of hungry mouths here, and not much to eat since the dead ones came to the swamp." Her smile widened. "And you ain't even met the hungriest one yet."

CHAPTER TWENTY
Expedition

The motorized raft cut across the water like an orange dart. Swamp birds rose on tattered wings, hurtling skywards. Whether dead or alive, Calavera couldn't say, but he feared it was the former. From what he'd seen of the swamp thus far, it seemed as if a new ecosystem were forming here – one based on the dead and the eaters of the dead. Even the trees seemed to be dying, if more slowly than humans and animals.

He knew this to be true, because he could hear Santa Muerte singing somewhere in the swamp. The melody of her song was sad and slow, a hymn for the dying. She was singing it for the world, Calavera knew. Mourning what had been and what would never be again. The world of the living was passing into history, leaving only ashes to mark its memory.

Normally, Calavera was not given to such melancholy thoughts. Not because he denied the obvious, but because he knew his purpose and was content in it. Santa Muerte had spared him so that he might do the same for others. But this time, he could not help but wonder if Santa Muerte's song was for him as well.

He thought again of the roar he'd heard, and the thing he'd seen moving in the swamp. He'd eagerly looked for any sign of it since their departure from the *Dixie Jewel*, but had seen nothing save a few fallen trees. "Looking for the dinosaur?" Willy asked, leaning toward him. The old man spat a stream of tobacco juice over the side of the raft.

Jessop had gotten two volunteers to accompany them; Willy, and a young woman named Shamekia. Willy was an older man, dressed like a hunter, in a camouflaged vest over a ratty t-shirt, with a rifle slung across his shoulder. Shamekia held a hunting crossbow on her lap and a quiver of bolts. From the notches on the weapon's stock, Calavera thought she knew how to use it.

"Is it a dinosaur, then?" Calavera asked.

"That's what I figure," Willy said, spitting another stream of tobacco as if for emphasis. "Dead people coming back, why not something else? Maybe it's one of them tyrannosaurus rexes, like in the movies. Or one of them ones like in that lake in Scotland." He seemed amused by the thought. "Wouldn't that be something?"

"Yes," Calavera agreed. It would be something. His hands flexed unconsciously.

Willy grinned. "You want to kill it, don't you?" He sniffed and scratched his cheek. "With that mask and all, you must think you're something special."

"I am El Calavera Santo," Calavera said simply.

Willy paused. "I knew it! I thought that was you!" He gave a whoop of delight and slapped his knee. "I saw you at the

Triple A hall a few years ago. You was fighting that fellow in the gold, what was his name?"

"El Rey Dorado," Calavera murmured, recalling the match. A good one. A bit too much time flying off the ropes, but the crowd had enjoyed themselves. He'd been a groomsman at El Rey's wedding later that month. He wondered where the other luchador was now. Where any of his old sparring partners were. Were they dead or worse?

"That's the one," Willy said. "Way you came off them ropes was pure magic."

Calavera nodded in thanks and turned back to the swamp as Willy continued to talk about the match. Their surroundings were starting to look familiar. He glanced at Sayers, who sat on the opposite side of the raft. She nodded, her face expressionless.

"We're getting close," Jessop said. It was as much a statement as a question.

"We are," Sayers said. Between them, she and Calavera had been able to describe the route they'd taken through the swamp well enough to guide them back. He'd thought they'd traveled farther than they had, but in the end, it was less than an hour's travel.

They'd waited for morning like sensible people. Calavera had dozed for an hour or two, but sleep had proven elusive. His head was too full for rest. Sayers, he knew, had felt the same way. Then, he'd never actually seen the woman sleep.

They broke through the tree line a moment later and the airstrip came into view. The boxy structure was as they'd left it... including the walkers that surrounded it. Sayers hissed in annoyance. "I thought they'd have wandered off by now."

"Maybe someone is still inside," Calavera said. But the back door was hanging open, and as he watched a jittery, bone-thin shape stumbled out of the kitchen and onto the dock. "Runner," he said, alerting the others.

"I see him," Willy said. He glanced at Jessop. "Want me to put him down?"

"Conserve ammunition," Jessop said, from where he sat at the boat's tiller. "If it doesn't bother us, we don't bother it."

Sayers made a sound deep in her throat, and Calavera glanced at her. From her expression, he could tell what she thought of that. She kept it to herself, thankfully. Sayers could be incredibly rude when she put her mind to it.

"Sometimes they ignore the raft," Shamekia said. "They don't seem to know what to make of it." She loaded her crossbow as she spoke, her eyes on the runner. "Sometimes they come right for it, no hesitation."

"Even the dead have their peculiarities," Calavera said, rubbing his hand. The humidity helped with his aches and pains, so it was more in the way of a habit. Overhead, the sky was going gray. It started to rain a moment later. Not heavily, but persistently.

Willy grunted. "Storm's coming."

"We've got time," Jessop said, but he didn't sound certain. "I'll take us over to the dock, but it doesn't look like anyone's home." He paused. "Anyone feel that?"

Calavera did. It was as if the raft were passing across roots. Only roots didn't bulge and twitch. Suddenly something punched against the bottom of the raft. Shamekia yelped as a flabby hand erupted from the water and grabbed at her sleeve. "Floaters!"

"Keep still, otherwise we'll capsize," Jessop bellowed. Willy drew a knife from his belt and hacked at the hands that fumbled at the side of the raft. Sayers did the same, cursing under her breath. Shamekia pointed.

"Runner coming in," she shouted.

The runner loped across the dock toward the approaching raft, its arms outstretched before it in almost comical fashion. For a moment, Calavera thought it was going to simply fall into the water, but instead its foot touched the head of a floater.

The runner darted so quickly across the heads of the floaters rising between the raft and the dock that it seemed almost to be dancing. Calavera tensed, waiting. Runners were tricky; fast and strong, unlike walkers and with better reflexes than brutes. They were, in his estimation, the most dangerous of the commoner varieties of the dead.

It was only a handsbreadth from the raft when Calavera's hands snapped out. His palms slapped against either side of its decaying head. It was like slapping a sandbag, but it did the trick. The runner's neck broke and it lost all control, tumbling into the water. Calavera waited, but the runner had been alone. They got bored quickly, if such creatures could be said to get bored. Whatever the reason, they were often the first to wander off once all available prey was gone.

He turned to Jessop. "Speed up now, before these floaters fixate on our position."

Jessop stared at him. "You just… just swatted it out of the air."

Calavera nodded. "You would have preferred that I let it aboard first?" he asked, somewhat amused by the man's reaction. Sayers and the others had grown used to his antics.

It was nice when someone was properly impressed. The luchador he had been still thrilled at applause, and he often found himself performing for an invisible crowd when he matched himself against the dead. If a thing had to be done, best it was done well.

The raft puttered to a stop and bumped gently against the dock. Calavera leapt out, and swiftly tied off the raft, keeping one eye on his surroundings. There were a few walkers still lingering here and there, and one bifurcated zombie hauling itself across the patio with its arms. That one he dispatched by the simple expedient of stomping on its head until it ceased moving. The nearby walkers spotted him then and started toward him. He heard the whistle-snap of Sayers loosing an arrow. A walker in a cheerleader's outfit slid down the wall, an arrow through its eye.

A second walker lunged for Calavera, the tattered windbreaker it wore bunching and billowing in odd places. Calavera slapped aside its groping hands and drove his other hand into its chest through a gaping tear in the windbreaker. He caught a handful of something and tore it loose in a burst of gore. The walker spasmed, but didn't fall.

Annoyed, Calavera punched it in the head, knocking it to the ground. He stamped on its back, breaking its spine. Then, with a growl, he gripped its head and tore it free of its neck. He tossed it over his shoulder into the water. Sayers and the old man, Willy, moved past him across the dock and toward the building. Willy lifted his hunting rifle and put a round through a walker's chest, then a second through its head.

"Save your ammo," Jessop called, as he climbed onto the dock. "Don't use any more than you have to."

"That's what I'm doing," Willy barked. "Not my fault it moved." He kicked open the back door and peered inside. Calavera joined him. "See anything?" Willy murmured.

"No. But that does not mean it isn't there."

He left the door and circled the building, heading for the airstrip. The plane was where they'd left it, apparently untouched by their attackers. Walkers wandered in its shadow, and Calavera backed away slowly, trying not to draw their attention. There would be time enough for that later.

Shamekia was waiting for him near the front door, her dark eyes sweeping the horizon. "All this time, we never knew this place was here," she said in a low tone, her eyes on the walkers.

Calavera nodded, even as he turned the question over in his mind. "I was told that was the point. Those who built it wished for it to remain undiscovered." He tapped one of the hanging decorations. "Only I do not think that they succeeded."

Shamekia looked at the decoration as it spun slowly. "Yeah, what is up with those?"

"Warnings," Sayers said, as she rounded the building. She glared at the younger woman until Shamekia absented herself. "I don't like this," she said, looking around. "It feels off. Why would they just leave everything?"

"Perhaps they got what they wanted."

"Or maybe they're still out there, waiting to see if we come back." Sayers stared at nothing in particular. "The bodies are gone. Did you notice that?"

"I did."

"Why would they do that, unless they were hoping to pull the same shit twice?"

"Who is to say that we are the first?" Calavera murmured.

He spied Santa Muerte standing near the plane, a woman – a skeleton – all in black. He watched her until a walker stumbled between them and she was gone.

Sayers grimaced. "Yeah." Calavera followed her around the building, back to the kitchen. Jessop was inside, stuffing tin cans into a gunny sack.

"Find anything?" he asked, as they stepped inside.

Sayers shook her head. "I think we need to get back on the raft and get out of here. At least until we know where the others are."

"We'll load up these supplies and then go," Jessop said, holding up a can of pumpkin mix. Calavera recognized it from before.

Sayers rose to her feet. "We need to go *now*."

Jessop frowned and made to reply when a rifle spoke. Outside, Willy yelped. Calavera raced to the door and saw Shamekia dragging Willy down behind a stack of pallets. "Can anyone get a bead on them?" she called out.

Sayers joined Calavera at the door, her bow in hand and an annoyed expression on her face. "Just like before. Only this time there's no airboat to get us out of here."

CHAPTER TWENTY-ONE
Bargaining

Ramirez sat on an extremely uncomfortable chair made out of bones – alligator bones, she hoped. But she didn't think so. At least not all of them. She was inside the big house, the dining room to be exact. She'd expected décor straight out of Ed Gein, but it was normal. Almost disturbingly so. Except for the chairs.

She sat back, trying not to think of Coop's head, or the expression on his face. Over the past few years, she'd become good at pushing that sort of thing down where it couldn't get at her. Maybe one day it would all come back up and hit her when she least expected it, but as long as it wasn't today, she'd be fine.

Coop had deserved better. And she intended to settle up on his behalf at the first available opportunity. She glanced to her left, where Wilbur sat at a window, peeling a moldy looking apple with a penknife. He met Ramirez's gaze, but said nothing.

She turned away from him and took in the rest of the room.

There were portraits on the walls; old-fashioned oils, rendered into imperceptibility by humidity and neglect. Framed pictures crowded the rest of the space, depicting several generations' worth of Watkins family outings, including the occasional mugshot.

Keziah, sitting across the table from her, smiled and said, "We've always been photogenic types. Never a bad picture."

"So I see," Ramirez said. The house smelled of damp and cat litter, but not a single cat in sight. No dogs either. No animals at all, although there were signs there had been some at one point. Given what she knew about the family's dietary preferences, she figured any pets had been first in the stewpot.

Keziah set a silver cigarette case on the table and opened it. Inside were rolling papers and a flat pouch made out of what looked like leather. She began to roll a cigarette, her eyes on Ramirez. "You're wondering about our eyes, aren't you?"

"I'm curious about a lot of things."

"The yellow tinge, the eczema, that's all on account of the dead, I figure."

"You... ate them," Ramirez said hesitantly.

"Not at first. But... well. Things change, don't they?" She paused. "I am sorry about your friend, believe it or not. But we did him a favor. That leg of his would have been the death of him. Infection was already setting in. And, well, waste not, want not." She rolled a cigarette. "My daddy taught me the key to survival in hard times is a well-stocked larder. We never had much, but we had enough to get through them first few months without even a flicker of worry." She looked at her hands, and despite herself, Ramirez couldn't help but follow her gaze. They were strong looking hands, despite being knotted with arthritis. They reminded her of her own grandmother's hands.

"We'd gotten by in better times being poachers or weed farmers," Keziah went on. "Then we made meth and sold poison when times were worse. Acted as guards for them fellows from down south whenever they'd come flying in to that little runway." She smiled fondly at the memory, then frowned. "But then the dead came into the swamp and that was that. Couldn't go nowhere, couldn't find nothing. The nearest towns were picked clean or overrun. We needed the gasoline for the generators and couldn't afford to waste it on no shopping trips."

Ramirez looked down at her. "So you started eating people?"

Keziah laughed. "Not live ones! Not at first. The dead were easier to get hold of, and most of them wasn't that gamey at the time. No worse than good roadkill." As she spoke, her yellow eyes flashed, and Ramirez had a sickening realization. She knew what eating the dead did to animals… but what about humans? Had it driven them insane, or had they always been this way? Keziah patted her hand, making her flinch.

"Later on, though, I thought it best we confine our consumption to organic stock, as it were. Did wonders for our digestion at least, I'll say that much."

"You're insane," Ramirez said without meaning to.

Keziah nodded. "Most like. But if the world itself is mad, then only the insane will prosper. That's from the Bible."

"No, it isn't," Ramirez said.

Keziah paused, as if considering this. "Well, it should be. You want a smoke?" She offered Ramirez the cigarette case.

"No, thank you."

"Probably smart. Need to keep them lungs pink. But I'm too old to worry about it." Keziah fished a lighter out of her clothes and lit her cigarette. She sat smoking for a moment, her eyes on nothing in particular. Then, "What do you know about the big boat?"

Ramirez paused. "What big boat?"

Keziah fixed her with a stern look. "The cruise ship stuck out there in the swamp. Got blown into the Glades by the last hurricane. What do you know about it? You come here looking for it? I figure somebody must be."

"No. No, we didn't come looking for it. We didn't even know it was here until we spotted it flying over."

"Why did you come, then?"

"To look for supplies," Ramirez said.

"There's food on that boat," Keziah said. "Ammunition, medicine… it was a bounty from God the day his storm blew it onto our patch. A way to save my family. And God has provided us with the means to take it." She pointed her cigarette at Ramirez. "By which I mean you, if you were wondering."

"Me?"

Keziah nodded. "You didn't think I pulled you out of that cage because I was in the mood for some girl talk, did you?"

Ramirez shook her head. "No, you made it clear you wanted something. I figured it was the plane." She looked up as a young woman came in bearing two plates of food. Ramirez added to the silent tally in her head. So far, she'd seen around twenty-five people in or around the house. A couple of children, like Dickie. Most were young adults, with a few older folks – Wilbur's siblings, she assumed, though Keziah hadn't said either way.

Maybe that was why they hadn't gone after the ship already. Not enough people for a frontal assault. Especially if someone was already occupying it. Attacking a cruise ship would be like laying siege to a medieval castle.

The young woman had the same eyes and general demeanor as the rest of the family; her skin was in a bad state, and though she'd made some attempt to hide it, her hair was coming out in clumps. She set the plates down in front of Keziah and Ramirez and sidled out without a word. "Thank you, honey," Keziah called after her. She indicated the plate in front of Ramirez. "Hope you don't mind. I expected as you might be hungry."

Ramirez was, but she damn sure wasn't going to eat whatever mystery meat it was on the plate. She pushed it aside and said, "So why did you kill Coop? To show us you meant business?"

"I told you, we needed the food," Keziah said, as she carefully stubbed out her cigarette and thrust what was left of it behind her ear. "You don't seem that broken up, if you don't mind me saying. Maybe we did you a favor, too, huh?"

Ramirez didn't reply. Instead, she asked, "And what about the rest of my friends? Are they food, too?"

Keziah nibbled on something that might have been a slice of ham. "That depends on you, Miss Federal. I do not deny we could use the meat. But I'd rather have something a bit easier on the stomach."

"Meaning the ship," Ramirez said. *And the people on the ship*, she thought, but didn't say. She tried not to think about it.

Keziah nodded. "The very thing."

"And I'm going to help you get it."

"If you're smart."

Ramirez was silent for a moment. "And what do I get in return?"

"Why, the lives of yourself and your friends, of course." Keziah spread her hands. "I ain't a monster, whatever you might think. Just a survivor, like I said. We all do what we must to survive in this fallen world."

"Sure," Ramirez said noncommittally. But what she was thinking was that maybe some people shouldn't survive. She pushed the thought aside. She had a feeling Keziah would happily cut her throat as make a deal. She'd dealt with felons like that before; psychopaths that remained friendly just long enough to get within striking distance. Of course, there were also ones like Wilbur, who didn't even make the pretense.

Keziah glanced at Ramirez's plate, but made no comment. Then, "I ain't promising they'll all be in one piece come the day, of course. But we'll do our best to keep them safe."

"I haven't agreed yet," Ramirez said.

Keziah was about to reply when a younger man – barely out of his adolescence – ran in and headed straight for Wilbur. The newcomer tossed an apologetic glance at Keziah as he murmured into Wilbur's ear. The big man growled something under his breath and stood. "Them folks on the ship have dealt themselves in," he said.

Keziah pushed her plate aside. "How so?"

Wilbur glanced at Ramirez, and then said, "The ones that got away – they went right to the goddamn ship. Like they knew where it was." He rounded on Ramirez. "She's lying, momma. Let me have a chat with her. I'll get the truth." He caught Ramirez by the throat and pulled her out of her chair with no more difficulty than as if she'd been a child. She dropped her fists onto his wrist, forcing him to release her. He stepped back, surprised, and she went for the knife on his belt.

She never reached it. Wilbur was quicker than she'd anticipated. He hit her between the shoulder blades and dropped her to the floor. She picked herself up slowly and caught him glaring down at her. He raised his foot, as if to give her a kick, but put it back down again at the sound of Keziah's voice. "I told you I want her in one piece, boy."

"She's lying!"

Keziah snorted. "So? Who wouldn't in her shoes? I damn sure would. Get her up."

"I don't need help," Ramirez said, hauling herself to her feet. Keziah looked up at her.

"No, I don't expect you do." She held up a finger. "You get one. Try it again, and I'll let Wilbur pick your bones."

Ramirez held up her hands in surrender. Keziah chuckled. "What was the plan, Federal? Grab a knife… cut my throat, maybe?"

"No. His." Ramirez looked at Wilbur. "He's the muscle."

Keziah patted Wilbur's arm. "That he is. Just like his daddy, God rest him. Bit smaller than his daddy, mind. But he makes up for it in other ways. Smarter for one thing." She looked up at him. "Speaking of which, you leave a guard on that plane?"

"I did," Wilbur said, his eyes on Ramirez.

"Who all you leave out there?"

"Brady, Cole and Jeannie," Wilbur rumbled. "I told them

to keep a sharp one on the place, just in case someone came back. Told them to stay out of trouble as well, but you know Cole... he's got some vinegar in him."

"That boy's nothing but," Keziah muttered. She looked at Ramirez again. "If your friends come back, we'll be waiting."

Ramirez said nothing. Keziah eyed her for a few moments. Then, "Walk with me, Miss Federal. Wilbur, take me outside. It's almost time for church."

Wilbur grimaced, but did as his mother asked. Ramirez walked with them, all too aware that they were both watching her now. She wouldn't get another chance to make a break for it. She was glad Sayers and the others had gotten away, at least.

"So, you have someone watching the ship, then?" she asked, after a moment.

At Quantico, she'd learned to get them talking and keep them talking. Most cases were solved that way. People gave away information without realizing how valuable it was. Maybe Keziah would give her something useful.

Keziah nodded. "We do. Can't blame us for that, can you?"

"No. I suppose not." Ramirez hesitated, weighing the next question. "Those other people in the cages... are they from the ship?"

Keziah gave her an appraising glance. "A few. Some we caught coming into the Glades, looking to get away from the dead. But the dead followed them." They were outside a moment later, looking out over the back, where the cages still hung over the zombie-packed waters. Ptolemy and the others were still in one piece, thankfully – but for how long?

Keziah pushed herself up in her chair and gestured with one long arm. From somewhere on the roof of the house, gospel music began to play loudly. "How long it been since you gone to church?" Keziah asked, eyes closed.

"I was never much for religion," Ramirez said absently. The rest of the family were gathering, young and old. The music had scared the birds out of the trees and stirred up the dead in the water. Why were they playing it so loudly? They were only going to attract unwanted attention. A moment later, she realized that was exactly what they wanted.

Out in the swamp, a tree snapped. The sound was loud, audible even over the music. Around her, the Watkins family began to sing. Softly at first, and then with more vigor. Only Wilbur was silent. She took note of it, filing it away.

Keziah began to clap, keeping time with the music. "Music is how you get God's attention. A preacher man taught me that while I was up in Broward. Said we must sing joyfully so that the Lord can hear our appreciation."

Another tree broke, and under its echo Ramirez detected the sound of something heavy moving through the swamp. She glanced down at the water and saw that the dead were being unusually quiet. Were they afraid of whatever was coming? It didn't seem possible, but she knew walkers sometimes scattered if a particularly aggressive brute was in the area.

Just out of sight, in the trees beyond the concrete water break, something bellowed. A thunderous, groaning cry that pounded at her eardrums and made her heart seize in her chest. "What is that?" she asked, staring at the trees.

"The king of tall trees and deep waters. The lord of wet shadows and shelter." Keziah looked up and gave her a thin smile. "Our ancestors knew he was here in this swamp. That's why they came out here, originally, or so my momma claimed. Said we had need of God, and so must prostrate ourselves in his garden. But it's only since the dead rose that he has revealed himself to us in all his savage glory." She spread her arms like an old timey preacher. "He protects us from them."

Her smile widened. "And we in turn see that he has his sacrifices. He knows we have one waiting when he hears the music." She glanced at Wilbur. "Take the one in the mask. I expect he'll give us a good show." Wilbur nodded and started toward the cage she'd shared with Riggs.

"What?" Ramirez asked, horrified. She stepped forward, finding herself looking down the barrel of Keziah's pistol. "You told me you wouldn't hurt them!"

"But as you said, you have not yet agreed to my terms. So, I think a bit of encouragement is in order, don't you?" Keziah showed her teeth. "Smile, Miss Federal… it ain't every day a woman gets to meet God."

CHAPTER TWENTY-TWO
In the Grass

Westlake lurched out of the swamp in a crowd of walkers, steadying himself on a theme park mascot that resembled an animated cougar as he stumbled on a root. The mascot grunted querulously as it swiped a felt and plastic paw at him, missing him by a country mile. It got turned around and started back into the swamp, still groaning. Westlake watched it go and then turned back to the others.

He'd been running with the pack – the herd? – all night and most of the morning. Safety in numbers, he figured. Plus, they were likely to be drawn to wherever people were, which was where he wanted to be. The walkers had largely ignored him, and those that hadn't, he'd dealt with.

It was odd. He'd never been alone among them this long, not that he could recall, at least. There was a certain, eerie peace to it. He'd first noticed it in Atlantic City. But it was stronger here, maybe because it was quieter. The dead here were less a malevolent horde than a group of animals. He wasn't sure whether that was better or worse.

Watching them, walking with them, he could see the advantages they had over the living. Not just the obvious ones. The dead by and large didn't fight amongst themselves unless there was a brute or a runner nearby. Then things got complicated. But they also communicated somehow: not by vocalizing, but by movement. Like a flock of birds wheeling and turning at some instinctive signal.

If he'd been a scientist, and not a thief, he might have been able to draw some conclusions from it. Kahwihta certainly could have. He filed his observations away for when he next spoke to her. If she was still alive. The thought made him uncomfortable. He supposed he should be glad that he could feel anything at all, but he could have done without the gnawing feeling of worry at the base of his skull.

One of the walkers moaned, scenting something on the wind. Westlake smelled it, too. He blinked – focused. The airfield was dead ahead. A raft bumped against the dock. That hadn't been there last time. The walkers had been drawn by the sound of the motor, the same as he had. He figured Sayers and the others had finally come back. But the zombies weren't the only ones who'd been alerted.

He slithered through the grass, following his nose to where three figures, draped in what looked like ghillie suits made from spoiled meat, were watching the hideout. The three smelled like zombies, but they weren't. They were using flayed skins to hide their scent from the walkers milling about in the grass. It was a good trick... unless the zombie was smart enough to understand what it was looking at.

He bit back a chuckle. Of course they were waiting. They'd likely figured someone would come back for the plane, at least. So they'd set a guard. And sure enough, someone had come looking. He squinted at the distant building and saw the familiar shape of Calavera prowling around the building, with others he didn't recognize. Had they found help out there in the swamp? If so, that was a lucky thing. Wherever Ramirez and the others had been taken, he suspected they were going to need help to get them back. But that could wait. For now, they had other problems.

He leaned against a tree, keeping it between himself and the trio. They were alert, careful. One had a rifle, the other two were carrying bows. The one with the rifle moved slowly toward another tree and scrambled up into the branches. The other two stayed crouched where they were, their attentions fixed on the airstrip. He needed to wait for them to split up, or their buddy with the rifle would just pick him off when he heard the commotion.

So instead, he sat and listened. His hearing hadn't been going the way of his other senses. In fact, it was better than it had been. Years of blowing open armored cars and vaults had left him with a persistent ringing in his ears. But that was gone now. Sometimes, he just sat and listened to the world move around him. But right now, he listened to hear what they were saying. Might be something useful.

"How many of them is it, Cole?" one said.

"I count about five, Brady, now keep your damn mouth shut until Jeannie gives us the go." Cole was the bigger one, heavy with prison muscle. Brady was smaller; younger, maybe. That made Jeannie the one with the rifle.

"It's just, Wilbur said we wasn't supposed to do nothing but watch," Brady continued, in an apologetic tone.

"Well Wilbur ain't here and we are. Now I'm in charge and I say we take them."

"If he gets here and finds us in a shootout..." Brady began.

Cole shoved him. "It'll be over by then. Now clam up."

Westlake figured their plan was to let Jeannie pick a target and start the ball rolling, the way they had before. He wondered if Cole and Brady had been the ones to shoot him. He wished he had a gun, or even a rock, but he'd make do with his hands. He needed to distract them somehow, and alert Calavera and the others at the same time.

He decided to go for the direct approach. He rose up behind them, head bent and at an angle to the tree. Cole turned first. Westlake caught him by the head, jabbing his thumbs into the other man's eyes. He had big thumbs, and they went in deep. Cole screamed shrilly and clawed at Westlake's forearms. Brady spun and went for the machete on his belt.

Still gripping Cole's head, Westlake shoved him into Brady, knocking the other man down. He tore his thumbs free and snatched the machete from Brady's belt. Brady was screaming curses. He tried to punch Westlake, and Westlake bit him.

It was all instinct. He saw flesh and went for it. One moment he was staring, the next he was sinking his teeth into Brady's arm.

Hungry.

And he was. So hungry. So damn hungry. He shoved Brady to the ground and reared back, blood on his lips and singing in his head.

The sound of the shot startled him. Jeannie fired again, not at him but at the building. She hadn't noticed what was going on with her pals yet. Or maybe she didn't care.

He looked down at Brady and slugged him. He heard Cole squeal and saw that a handful of walkers had been drawn by the commotion. They were crouched over the thrashing man, devouring him alive. Blind and in pain, Cole's struggles were in vain.

Westlake hesitated, smelling the coppery sweetness of the dying man's blood, and tasting what he'd taken out of Brady on his lips. He wanted nothing more than to drop to his knees and join them in their awful feast. Instead, he raised the machete – but again, hesitated. One of the walkers looked up at him, empty eyes rolling in ruined sockets. It had been hit with something sharp before, if the cleft in its skull was anything to go by.

The others were the same. Like him, they were ragged scarecrows, battered and hanging by a thread. And like him, they'd just keep going until they finally collapsed into pieces. The one that was looking at him glanced down at the length of Cole's intestine in its hands and then up at Westlake again.

Then, with an almost apologetic gesture, it offered him a bite.

Westlake stared, unable to comprehend what he was seeing. It wasn't the first time a zombie had reacted oddly to him, but it was the first time that the reaction wasn't a violent one. The walker lifted its offering higher, as if to encourage him. The others had noticed, and were watching him like wary animals, even as they chewed bits of their victim.

The one doing the offering suddenly flinched and slumped. The boom of the rifle caught up with the shot an instant later. He heard a woman screaming. Jeannie. Another shot and another walker toppled over, brains spilling into the water.

Westlake started toward the tree, moving as quickly as he could while keeping his head down. A shot plucked at his back and nearly knocked him to his knees. The rest of the nearby walkers were converging on the sound of the rifle, giving him some cover. But it wouldn't last long. She was a good shot, whatever else.

He reached the tree a moment later. She was up high, but not so high he couldn't reach her. He tried to count the shots in his head, hoping to predict when she'd need to reload. But the numbers got jumbled up in his head, so he decided to risk it.

He waited until her attention was on one of the walkers, then flung the machete toward her. She turned at the last minute and the blade only caught her in the shoulder. She fell out of the tree with a yell, and the walkers closed in. Westlake retrieved the rifle she'd dropped and left them to it. It ended quickly enough, though she put up more of a fight than Cole had, cursing and yelling as she flailed at her attackers with a hunting knife.

When she'd fallen silent, Westlake headed for the airstrip. He held the rifle up over his head as he walked. "I'm friendly," he called out. His voice sounded like a wheezy engine, but it was good enough.

"It is Westlake," he heard Calavera say.

"Who?" someone asked.

"One of ours," Sayers said, as Westlake reached the dock. A man he didn't recognize stared at him in open-mouthed shock.

"But he's..." the man began.

Westlake nodded. "Dead? Very much so." He studied the

guy, taking in the uniform, now stained and patched in places. A sailor of some kind.

"Long story," Sayers said brusquely.

Westlake looked at Sayers. "I took one alive. Unless my fellow undead have gotten to him. Out near the tree there." He pointed to where he'd left Brady, and hoped the injured man hadn't crawled off somewhere.

Sayers nodded and Calavera hurried toward the tree. She looked at Westlake. "How many arrows did they hit you with?"

"Enough to make me feel like a pincushion. The one I caught, he might be able to tell us where they took the others."

"If they're alive," Sayers said.

"They are. I heard them talking." Westlake felt something rub against his breastbone and pulled out an arrowhead. He held it up. "Must have missed one." Sayers didn't flinch. She wasn't like the others. She had a cold, pragmatic streak in her that he admired. In another time, she'd have made a good thief.

"Who are they?" she asked.

"Search me. All I know is that they seem familiar with the area." He paused, trying to sift through his memories. "Poachers, maybe. There were some local redneck types that had to be paid off to get this place built and left alone. Fentanyl dealers and meth heads. Harder to kill than cockroaches. If anyone could survive a zombie apocalypse, it'd be them."

The man spoke up. "We've seen people, at a distance. Why would they attack us?"

Westlake looked at him. "Why wouldn't they?"

The man frowned. Then, "Are you really… one of them?"

Westlake spread his arms. "You tell me." He glanced at Sayers. "Is Kahwihta...?"

"Alive. Our new friends here have a well-stocked infirmary." Sayers nodded to the man. "His name's Jessop. He's the first mate of the *Dixie Jewel*."

"And what's that when it's at home?"

"A cruise ship, stuffed full of supplies – and zombies."

"Sounds like another day in paradise," Westlake said. Calavera returned, carrying the whimpering Brady like a sack of potatoes.

"He says you bit him," the luchador rumbled.

"He's lucky I didn't strangle him," Westlake said. He flexed his hands and Brady made a sobbing sound. Calavera dropped him onto the dock.

"Keep him away from me," Brady howled as Westlake took a step toward him. Westlake paused and looked at the others.

"He knows where the others are. We need to question him."

Jessop frowned and gestured for his people to bind Brady. "We can do that back aboard the ship." He studied Westlake. "You bit him?"

Westlake tried to smile. "Only a little bit."

CHAPTER TWENTY-THREE
Altar

When the first tree had snapped, Riggs had known what was coming. Not the exact shape or the nature of it, but he got the idea. Something big and hungry; one more monster in a world full of them. He'd tried to ignore it, to pretend it was happening somewhere else, but the sheer noise of it all made that difficult. He'd never heard anything roar like that.

He wished he was anywhere else. That he'd never come here. They'd had a saying in Atlantic City: never volunteer for anything. Riggs had made that his mantra, and only broken it once in the months he'd huddled in the basement of a pawn shop with five other survivors. But breaking it had led him out of the basement, out of Atlantic City – he'd hoped it would lead him somewhere safe. As if that was a thing anymore. He couldn't even remember what safety felt like.

Come to that, he couldn't even remember his own first name. He could barely remember the last week. His mind went in and out, retreating into itself for its own good. It had been that way since the beginning of the apocalypse. He focused on the now, and not the past or the future. It was how he'd survived in the hell of Atlantic City.

He wished he could retreat into his mind now, and not be here. The roar came again and he clenched his fists against his ears. It was worse than the gospel music echoing down from the roof of the house. It was an ugly sound, reminiscent of every zombie moan and guttural grunt, but somehow worse. Whatever was out there, it sounded hungry.

He wanted his smoke bombs, a gun – even a sharp stick would do. They'd taken his coat and his hat, but left him his mask. They were polite, for a bunch of hillbillies. "Must be that southern hospitality I've heard about, ha-ha-ha," he muttered, sounding out each "ha". He could see Ptolemy and the others in the other cages. He wondered where they'd taken Ramirez. He recalled them taking her out of the cage but not much else. Coop was missing as well.

Another roar came from out in the swamp somewhere. It was getting closer, whatever it was. He reached for his cowboy boot and felt around for the gap between the leather and the lining. He'd learned that it was always good to have a little extra something on hand, just in case you ever wound up in a situation like this. He found the flat handle of the shiv, but didn't retrieve it from its hiding place. Not yet.

He had to be smart. What good was a knife while he was still in a cage? He looked around again. "Should never have left Atlantic City," he mumbled. At least there he'd only had to worry about zombies. He'd known it was too good to be true.

Even before the end of the world, he'd never trusted a sure thing. Nothing was safe, nothing was certain. There was trouble everywhere, in every atom of dust. People had started getting sick before the first zombie had shown up. Or so he'd heard; he'd never seen it himself. Just secondhand stories shared by other survivors. But it was enough to get him to start wearing a mask, just in case.

The gospel music got louder and their captors were starting to sing. Even the kids. That was the worst bit, though he couldn't quite articulate why. It was just… they had kids. The cage shuddered and started to move along its rope pulley. He looked toward the walkway and saw the big man who'd been waiting on them at the docks the night before. He was hauling Riggs' cage in, and Riggs felt a sinking sensation as he realized why. He knew what they intended for him, even though he didn't know the particulars. He'd seen this movie before and read the books.

"Oh, shit," he muttered, as the cage clanked and juddered toward its destination. "Shit, shit, shit. No, no, no."

The cage thumped against the walkway and the big man opened it up. "Get up," he rumbled. "We ain't got much time before he gets here."

"No!" Riggs pressed himself back against the bars, determined not to go. The big man growled low in his throat and reached in, grabbing Riggs' leg and hauling him out – or trying to. Riggs had hold of the bars. The contest that followed wasn't dignified in the least. Just a tug of war. Finally, the big man stooped and stepped into the cage. He slugged Riggs a few times, real quick and hard enough to rattle his teeth. The next thing he knew he was being dragged across the wooden walkway by one leg.

Riggs clawed at the boards. He heard laughter from the

house and risked a hand to give them the finger. It cost him, as the big man turned and bounced his head off the boards. Then he was up and over the other man's shoulder.

As he bounced along, he saw Ramirez standing with an old lady in a wheelchair. The old lady was holding her at gunpoint, and she didn't look happy. "Give them what they want," Riggs called out. "I don't want to die!"

Ramirez called out something, but he didn't hear it because whatever was out there decided to roar again. Maybe it was getting impatient. He started squirming, trying to break loose. Trying to reach his boot. If he could get his knife – what then? Maybe get away. Maybe find help. Someone had to be out there, right?

The roar again. Loud like thunder. Almost overpowering. Whatever it was, it was big; definitely not the sort of thing he wanted to meet face to face. He paused. The singing had changed to something else... chanting? "Are they chanting?" he demanded, momentarily forgetting himself.

"Yes," the big man sighed. He didn't sound best pleased.

"Why are they chanting?"

The big man didn't answer. Instead, he carried Riggs up onto the concrete bulwark that separated the property from the swamp. Two other members of the family were there waiting. Both men, lean and narrow with feral faces and filthy clothes. As Riggs' captor approached, they dragged a flat 'X' of plywood upright. It was a crude thing, clearly homemade. Its base slotted into a pair of steel plates embedded in the concrete, allowing it to stand upright without support.

Riggs started to struggle even more. "No, no, no, I've seen this movie!"

The big man dropped him onto the concrete. Stunned, Riggs managed to palm his blade. Before he could do much else, the other two hauled him to his feet and slammed him back against the X without a word. The big man waited, his hand on his pistol and his eyes on the swamp. The trees were shaking and the disturbed waters slapped against the concrete. "Hurry it up," he grunted. "We don't want to be out here when he arrives."

"When who arrives?" Riggs asked, as they stretched his arms, binding his wrists to the top of the X with rope. "What is that thing?"

The big man looked at him. "King Crunch."

Riggs almost laughed. "Sounds like a cereal mascot from back when you could get cereal." He looked down as they tied his legs to the lower struts of the X. "You don't have to do this," he pleaded. "I'll do whatever you want, just don't leave me out here…" Begging and pleading had never hurt his pride. You couldn't have pride dealing with the dead. They didn't care how you felt. But sometimes it gave you an edge against the living.

But they ignored him, finished up and hurried toward safety. Only the big man stayed behind, and then only long enough to lean toward Riggs and murmur, "That knife in your hand? I'd use it on yourself, if you can." Then he was gone, and Riggs was left alone to face whatever was coming.

The world shuddered as it drew closer. Birds screamed in the distance, and alligators bellowed. Riggs adjusted his grip on his knife and awkwardly began to saw at his bonds. Thankfully, the blade was sharp and the ropes were old and fraying. He had one hand free a moment later and started to work on the other.

Just as he freed that hand, something massive exploded out

of the tree line, rising from the water like a mountain surfacing from the ocean. Up – and up – and up. Then its shadow fell across the bulwark, swallowing Riggs up.

Riggs stared at the abomination – there was no other word for it – in horror. He'd seen big zombies before. Whatever it was that made the dead rise, it also changed some of them. Twisted them into horrible parodies of the human form. It did the same to animals on occasion, but never like this. Never to such a size.

The snapping turtle was roughly the size of a bus, and awful in its immensity. Barnacle-like growths sprouted from its tree trunk limbs and its shell was like armor plating, covered in moss and stunted trees. Its head reminded him of a bulldozer, with a cruel beak that looked as if it could rip through a battleship hull, and two ugly, pallid eyes that glistened with a foul seepage.

It lumbered toward the bulwark on two pylon-like legs, long forelimbs swatting aside any trees still in its path. He'd never seen a turtle walk on two legs outside of a cartoon, and something about the way it moved was even more unnerving than its size. Its limbs were out of proportion, more like those of a bear or an alligator than a normal turtle.

Riggs bent double, sawing at the bindings on his legs, his heart hammering painfully in his chest. The turtle raised its beak, as if to sniff the air. Could it not see him? He bit back a laugh, afraid that if he started, he'd never stop. One leg was free. One left. He began to pray under his breath, naming all the gods he could think of, starting with Jesus and working his way to Odin. He'd never been religious, but now seemed like a good time.

The turtle made a deep, guttural sound and scraped the top of the bulwark with one forepaw. The smell of it rolled over him like a wave; it stank of stagnant water and sour earth, of dead places and deader people. As he watched in horrified fascination, a patch of rough skin on its neck puckered and popped, releasing a splatter of noxious ichor. The last of the rope binding his foot parted and he half-toppled onto the concrete. He cried out inadvertently as he caught himself on his knees and palms, and the turtle's massive head snapped toward him. Its beak caught the X and splintered it.

Riggs scrambled to his feet, no direction in mind, just knowing he had to get away. His panting was loud in his ears, too loud. The turtle groaned in frustration and followed the sound of his feet on the concrete. It might be blind, but it could damn sure hear him. His knife wasn't going to be any good against such a monster. He had to get away. Had to.

He felt the heat of its breath wash over his back, but didn't turn around. He just kept going – straight for the edge. Not into the zombie pit, but into the swamp. Maybe he could get away, find help… find something. He tensed at the edge, then leapt.

For a moment, Riggs thought he'd made it. Then he was caught, smashed from the air by the blow of a massive claw. He flew back, struck the bulwark, and tumbled into the water at the base. It would have been funny if it hadn't been him.

The world went topsy-turvy, and was edged in red as he surfaced, spluttering, trying to breathe and failing. His mask was askew, and he could taste blood in the swamp water. He'd lost his knife in the fall, but he didn't waste time looking for it. He tried to rise but nothing was working and everything hurt. All he could do was flop and flail. He didn't want to drown here. Didn't want to die.

A shadow fell over him.

Riggs didn't want to look up, but at the last minute he gave in to the urge. He saw the thing's beak spread out and something wriggling within – its tongue, only it wasn't a tongue but a… a person. At least, that was how it looked to him. Like someone reaching out to embrace him. To hold him close and tell him everything was going to be fine.

But it wasn't fine.

Not at all.

CHAPTER TWENTY-FOUR
Plans

Jessop sat in Ogilvy's cabin, studying his captain. "I don't know what to do," he said. They'd brought the prisoner back, and the zombie – Westlake. He still couldn't quite get over that bit of it. A zombie that talked. He wondered if the others had the capacity to do the same. He thought of those in the hold, roaming the lower decks of the ship. Were they still capable of human feeling? If so, they hadn't shown it. But maybe they hadn't had the chance.

"About what?" Ogilvy asked. He was slumped in his chair, staring at the floor.

"These new people. They say they can get us out of here if we help them. But how do we know we can trust them?"

"You've always been a good judge of character," Ogilvy said.

Jessop sat back. "You're saying trust my gut?"

Ogilvy gave him a bleary look. "I'm not exactly shipshape, Daniel," he said simply. "My advice is worth less than this empty bottle of rubbing alcohol." He held up one of the bottles he'd stolen from the infirmary.

Jessop took the bottle. "You really shouldn't be drinking this." They could use it for something. To catch water, or as a Molotov cocktail. Everything got re-used these days, one way or another.

"Safer than water."

"That's debatable, captain."

Ogilvy shook his head. "I'm not captain anymore."

"You are until we formally remove you from command."

"Why haven't you yet?" It came out as an accusation. Jessop paused, wondering how to answer. He wasn't really sure himself, sometimes.

"Because you're the man who got us out of Fort Lauderdale. You saved a lot of folks, captain. You're owed a bit of consideration."

"A captain goes down with his ship," Ogilvy said. "You should have let me die with the others when we got blown off course." He stood abruptly and went to his sideboard, likely searching for another bottle. There weren't any. Jessop had ordered Hawser to clean out Ogilvy's stash. He'd waited too long to sober the man up, but things were coming to a head, he could feel it. He wanted Ogilvy dried out and competent if possible.

Ogilvy gave a triumphant chuckle, and Jessop wondered if they'd missed one. But when Ogilvy turned around, he saw it wasn't a bottle that the other man held but a pistol. An old-fashioned Colt Navy revolver, purloined from some museum during the evacuation. Or maybe Ogilvy had always had it. He aimed the weapon at Jessop and cocked it.

"I wondered where I'd put this," he said.

"Captain…" Jessop began, hands raised, a spark of fear

dancing across his thoughts. He cursed himself for dismissing the guard. He'd sent her away to get a meal, trusting that Ogilvy was harmless. Yet another mistake.

"I told you, I'm not your damn captain." Ogilvy blinked rapidly. He was unsteady on his feet; Jessop figured he was basically pickled at this point. "You're going to escort me into the hold now, with the other dead folks. I have to see them. I have to tell them I'm sorry…"

"They know, captain," Jessop said.

"Stop saying that. What kind of captain gets his crew killed?"

"Death is a part of life," a deep voice rumbled from the open door of the cabin. "Can a captain be blamed for rough seas or the dead rising?"

Jessop glanced back and saw Calavera standing in the doorway. He stooped slightly and squeezed into the cabin. Ogilvy stared at him in befuddlement. "Who…?"

"I am El Calavera Santo. I know from death." The big man reached out and gently pried the revolver from Ogilvy's hand. He flipped out the cylinder and showed it to Jessop. "Empty. He had no intention of shooting you."

Jessop sagged slightly, suddenly aware he'd been holding his breath. He balled a fist, wanting to strike Ogilvy, but let it drop after a moment. Calavera saw and nodded. "I was eavesdropping. I hope you will forgive me."

Jessop nodded. "Did you need something?"

"The prisoner has decided to talk. Sayers thought you might like to hear what he has to say."

"Great." Jessop looked at Ogilvy. The other man looked lost, almost shrunken. "Captain…" he began, but Ogilvy turned away and went to his cabin's porthole. Calavera set the pistol down and gestured to the door.

"Let me speak with him."

Jessop stared at him. "Are you a licensed therapist under that mask?"

"No. But I know what he is feeling." Calavera paused. "I might be able to help."

Jessop hesitated, then nodded. "Fine. I'll take you up on that." Maybe the masked man could help. At this point, he'd try anything, if it might bring the old Ogilvy back. He left them there and made his way back to the upper deck. The prisoner had been isolated in a section near the prow, under a lean-to. Sayers and Willy had conducted the initial interrogation, over Grillo's protests. She was waiting for Jessop when he arrived.

"Calavera said we've got some answers," he said. Grillo grimaced.

"We do, I suppose."

"That bad?"

"It's not great," she said. She nodded to Westlake, who stood looking out over the rail. "Have you decided what to do about... him?"

"Nope. I don't think there's much we can do. Sayers and the others seem to trust him. Guess we have to as well."

"And why are we trusting them at all?" Grillo asked in a low voice.

Jessop didn't look at her. "They might be our way out of here. Unless you want to go down with the ship like our captain."

Grillo blinked. "Not any better, then?"

Jessop decided not to tell her about the pistol. "No. None

of us are getting any better." He paused and turned to face her. "Our supplies are running out, and we're all worn down to the nub. We won't last much longer out here." Ogilvy had told him to trust his gut, and his gut was telling him that this was their best chance. "If they're throwing us a life preserver, who're we to ignore it?"

"If you say so," Grillo said grudgingly. She looked again at Westlake. "I still don't trust that thing." She raised a hand, forestalling his reply. "I know, I know."

Together, they made their way to the prow, where Sayers and Willy were waiting for them. "Calavera said you had something?" Jessop asked.

"Our friends out there were just scouts," Sayers said, without preamble. "It's more than just four or five raiders. It's a whole damn family."

"How many is a family, exactly?" Jessop asked, with a sinking feeling.

"More than us," Willy said. "And that ain't even the worst of it."

"So what's the worst?"

Sayers held up a knife in a leather sheath. "We went through his things. He wasn't carrying much, but what he was carrying was pretty nasty."

"It's a knife. So?"

"Sheath's made out of human skin," Sayers said. "Patches on his clothes are the same. Even his boots. Not badly, either. Someone took their time, did it right."

"You're sure?" Jessop asked quietly. He couldn't quite believe it.

Sayers nodded. She handed him the knife. "The hilt's bone."

"Alligator?" he asked, already knowing it wasn't. The spark of fear was back, and he tried to snuff it.

She shook her head. "No. And we found jerky on him."

"Jerky?" Jessop asked. "Like... beef jerky?" He didn't want to hear what came next, but he couldn't help himself. Revulsion swelled in him.

"Not beef," Willy said. He spit a stream of tobacco juice over the rail. "After it all went bad, I ran into a guy in Tampa who was of a... similar proclivity. Had his own smokehouse and everything. His stuff had the same smell and texture. Unpleasant bastard. But he was just one crazy. This seems like a whole goddamn bunch of them. And they been watching us since we got here." He glanced back at Brady. "Like wolves circling a herd of deer."

Jessop felt a chill go through him. "Jesus."

"Nothing to do with it, if you ask me," Willy said.

Jessop shook his head. "What else has he said?"

Sayers frowned. "They've got the others. Our friends and some of your people, by the sound of it. They're in the larder, as he put it."

Jessop shook his head again. He went over to the prisoner and looked down at him. The young man – Brady – met his gaze with yellow-eyed suspicion. "You going to kill me now?" he asked. As he spoke, Jessop got a glimpse of his teeth. All sharp, like they'd been filed. He repressed a queasy shudder.

"No. We don't do that."

Brady chuckled. "Guess you as dumb as Wilbur says you is, then."

"Wilbur?" Jessop glanced at Sayers.

"The leader – or one of them."

Brady cackled. "Hell, Wilbur ain't the boss. Even if he wishes he was."

"But this Wilbur, he's the one who left you to keep watch on that place. Why?"

Brady looked at him as if he were stupid. "To see if any of y'all came back, of course. Can't have folks running around the Glades willy-nilly. Anybody that we catch belongs to us." He looked around. "Goes for y'all as well."

Jessop spotted Calavera stepping out onto the deck. The big man nodded to him, though just what that was supposed to convey, Jessop wasn't certain. He turned his attention back to the prisoner. "So you're the ones who've been taking our people? Why?"

"This is our patch," Brady said sullenly. "You're the trespassers. Ain't this America? Ain't we allowed to protect ourselves? Life, liberty and all that crap?"

"We never did anything to you," Jessop said. "We never meant you any harm."

"It ain't about you," Brady snarled. "We just hungry, is all!" In that moment, his eyes glinting like those of an animal, the tendons in his neck standing up, Jessop suddenly understood what they were facing. Not just reavers or hostile scavengers, but something far more malign. He stood and went to the rail and was noisily sick over the side. There wasn't much to come up, thankfully.

Calavera joined him. The big man patted him on the back. "It is all right, my friend. There is no shame in revulsion when it comes to such matters."

"Cannibals," Jessop said. The word left an unpleasant taste in his mouth. "I thought I'd seen everything this world had to throw at us." He paused. "I've even seen a zombie shark. But this…"

"This is the world," Calavera said. "We must make do as best we can for those in our care." He leaned close. "You have done very well, Mr Jessop. We are here now, and we will help if we can."

"And if you can't?"

Calavera gave him another friendly pat on the back. "Then we will die together."

Jessop shook his head. "Jesus." He turned back to the others. "Well, I'm not turning my damn boat over to a bunch of cannibals, I can tell you that. At least not until we get everyone off. Then, as far as I'm concerned, they can have it."

Sayers leaned forward. "I talked it over with Kahwihta and the others. The way we see it, we've got three problems. The first is them…" She indicated the prisoner, who glared at her dully. "The second is where to go, if not here. And the third is how to get those supplies out of the hold."

Grillo frowned. "There's no way into the hold."

"There is," Imogene said. "You brought us aboard through it, remember?"

Grillo shook her head. "But it's still the same issue… we open a hatch, zombies come out. And we don't have enough ammo, let alone people, to handle that. Face it, those supplies might as well be in Charlotte for all the good they can do us."

"Unless we send a team in," Sayers said.

Jessop took his seat. "A team – volunteers, you mean?"

"Us," Calavera said, crossing his arms.

"What's the catch?" Phipps asked.

"The same as it always is these days. Zombies." Sayers looked at Calavera. "Ordinarily, this isn't something I'd suggest. But we're here and so are those supplies. Me and Calavera and maybe two or three other people can head down, find the supplies, and get them topside."

"There's a lot of supplies," Jessop said.

"So we improvise. We make sledges, we cache it up and bring it out a bit at a time. We clean out the zombies in the process, if we can. The more we put down, the easier it gets. Theoretically."

Jessop nodded slowly, running it over in his head. It could work, with additional people. He hesitated. "What about the second thing? A place to go?"

"The airstrip," Westlake croaked. Jessop jumped. He hadn't even noticed the dead man join them. "It's got everything you need. More easily defended than this place. Plus, we can bring people out when the plane's refueled."

Calavera nodded, picking up the thread. "It is a good bargain. The mountains are not safe, but they are safer than here. We have some supplies, walls, guns, and more hands make for quick work."

Grillo spoke up. "How do we know you'll keep up your end?" She glanced at Westlake as she said it, and Jessop could almost read her mind. How could they trust people who kept company with something – someone – like that? But what choice did they have? In any event, Westlake answered the question.

"They've stuck by me through worse," he said. He was staring at Brady as he said it. "Points two and three taken care of. As to point one, I think me and Brady here can handle it." He reached over and lifted the cannibal from his seat by the collar of his shirt. "You're going to show me where the rest of you live. We're going to pay them a visit and see what we can see. If you're a good boy, you might even live through it."

"What are you going to do?" Jessop asked. He didn't mind the idea of getting the prisoner off his boat as quickly as possible, but something about the look on what was left of the dead man's face didn't sit well with him. He'd seen that look before, on a walker looking to take a bite out of him.

"Case the joint," Westlake said roughly. "See if I can bust the others out."

"I'll come with you," Sayers began.

"No," Westlake snapped. And Jessop heard it – that grave-deep growl. Zombies didn't get hungry, not really. But they damn sure acted like it on occasion. Westlake visibly composed himself and tried to smile. At least Jessop thought it was a smile.

Sayers didn't blink. "Yes. You'll need help, and that's me."

"She's right," Jessop said. He looked at Sayers. "Go get our people, Miss Sayers. Then we can all see about getting the hell out of the Everglades."

CHAPTER TWENTY-FIVE
Wilbur

The camouflaged airboat skidded across the surface of the water, disturbing swarms of insects and sending unseen shapes crashing away into the water. Ramirez tested the rawhide strips that had been used to lash her wrists together and cursed under her breath. Wilbur sat across from her. One of his cousins crouched at the prow of the boat and another was in the pilot's seat. Both wore camouflaged hunting outfits, unlike Wilbur, who still wore his stained denim jacket and jeans.

Two other boats followed in their wake, with armed Watkins family members aboard both. Ramirez only had a vague sense of what their plan was, besides her part in it. She figured they meant to draw whoever was on that ship out and ambush them the way they had her team. Any warning she attempted to give would very likely precipitate a massacre. Not to mention the deaths of Ptolemy and the others – if they were even still alive to begin with.

She thought of Riggs and closed her eyes. Coop had been bad enough, but Riggs... God. The way that... thing had torn him apart. It had snapped what was left of him up and swallowed it whole. She'd seen plenty of monsters since the world had ended, but never anything like that.

There'd been a zombie in its mouth. That had been the worst bit. Not even a whole zombie, just... part of one. Wriggling on the end of its tongue like a lure. And more of them stuck to its shell like barnacles.

After devouring Riggs, it had turned and slunk off back into the swamp. Like it had gotten what it wanted. Keziah had implied that a similar fate was awaiting Ptolemy and the others if Ramirez didn't play along. She'd had no choice but to agree. Now she was relying on lunatics to keep their word and not just kill her and her people out of hand when the deed was done. She tested the bonds again, knowing it was useless, but needing to try. It wasn't in her to give up.

"You ain't getting out of those," Wilbur said suddenly. It was the first thing he'd said to her since they'd started this little expedition. She glanced at him and saw a considering look in his eyes. There was a brain in there, and it was working. Keziah might treat him like a slow child, but everything Ramirez had seen of him spoke to a startling degree of intelligence. A nasty sort of smarts, maybe, but it was still smarts.

"You're going to have to let me out of them. Otherwise, you'll tip off these folks you want to bushwhack. And then where will you be?"

Wilbur straightened and drew his revolver. He checked the cylinder and said, "Slow it down, Roy. Don't want them hearing us before we're ready."

"What about the walkers, Wilbur?" the one up front asked nervously. The sound of the airboat was drawing zombies out of the swamp. Ramirez could only wonder where they'd all come from. Maybe it was like the Adirondacks... they just wandered in and became part of the local ecosystem. The idea made her think of Kahwihta, and she pushed the sudden surge of fear for the younger woman down. Worries did her no good now. She had to focus on getting out of this in one piece.

"You got a rifle, Sandy... use it." Wilbur paused. "But not until you need to, you hear me? Don't need you panicking and drawing a bunch more of them down on us." He spoke calmly, but there was the hint of a snarl there. An ugly reminder that Wilbur wasn't quite human anymore.

She wasn't sure what he was – or what the rest of his family were. She could see the sickness in them, smell it. The yellow eyes were just the beginning. Most of them had a bad case of eczema, with added hair loss and something that looked like flesh-eating bacteria. At a distance, they looked tough, hardy. Up close, though, you could see the hollowness in them. They were surviving, but for how much longer?

Wilbur was the exception. He looked tough even up close. Rangy and big, with too much muscle. If the others were waning, Wilbur was waxing. She had a feeling that the apocalypse was the best thing that had ever happened to him.

"So, tell me something," she began.

"Quiet," Wilbur growled. He scratched at his neck, and Ramirez saw skin peel away. She closed her eyes and tried not to think about the bear she'd seen in the Adirondacks, its flesh peeling and its gut bulging with still-twitching zombies.

Was that what was happening to him? Was he changing into something other than human?

"I don't understand why you never tried it before, is all," Ramirez continued, watching the big man. The Quantico handbook said to get them talking and get into their head. Flip the script if you could. She didn't think that was going to be easy with Wilbur. It wasn't just his loyalty to Keziah. It was that he was enjoying himself.

Wilbur looked at her, his yellow gaze flat and wary. "Who says we didn't?"

"If you had, we wouldn't be doing this, would we?"

Wilbur grunted and said, "Think you're smart, don't you?"

"Top of my class."

Wilbur sat back against the side of the boat and braced his revolver against his knee. He studied her for several moments. Then, "We couldn't get none of the prisoners to agree to do it." He smiled, displaying teeth that were altogether too sharp and too white to belong in his mouth. "Lucky thing for you."

"Why the scam? Why not just creep over the side?"

"They're too cagey for that. Always got guards posted on them rails, and lights on the water. And the minute they knew we was out here, they'd be on alert. No, momma decided to play it sneaky, get them to lower their guard a bit."

She heard the frustration in his voice as he said it. There was the crack. Now to see if she could widen it any. "Not a fan of that?" she asked.

Something that might have been a smile flickered across his lips. "I do lack for patience, it must be said."

"But if she wants to take it slow, why not just… wait them

out? Keziah said there was only a handful of people on that thing. They can't sit there forever."

Wilbur pointed lazily at the slate-gray sky. "Feel that breeze, Federal? Taste that rain? It's hurricane season. Last big blow we had brought that ship and hundreds of them damn zombies into the Everglades. Who knows what this one will bring? Who knows if that ship will even still be there afterward?" He gestured with the revolver. "So, we take it now and see what we can scavenge before we lose the opportunity." He fixed her with a steady look and aimed the revolver at her. "And you are going to help us do that, miss top of her class. Or I will shoot you and leave you for the gators."

"Or worse – eat me, right?"

"Right," Wilbur said, smiling widely now. His eyes flashed as he said it, and she abruptly came to the sickening realization that for Wilbur, cannibalism wasn't a sad necessity. Whatever Keziah might claim, her baby boy was so far gone he might as well have been a zombie himself. He leaned toward her, still smiling. Showing off his teeth. "Bet you think we're a bunch of dumbass inbred backwoods hillbillies, don't you?"

"I was getting that vibe, yeah," Ramirez said.

Wilbur chuckled, though his cousins looked distinctly disgruntled. "You'd be mostly right, except about the hillbilly part, on account of us living in a swamp. Not much inbreeding, neither. Momma had her six brothers and sisters, and they all had kids of their own. When times got hard, they all came home. Just like momma knew they would."

"That go for you, too?"

Wilbur paused. "You trying to build a rapport, huh? They

teach you that at Quantico?" He licked his teeth, like a dog that's sighted a meaty bone. "Yeah, that went for me, too. I was all over, for a time. And then God called me home."

"Which God? Old guy with a white beard – or the giant turtle?"

Wilbur snorted and sat back. "Neither. It was a figure of speech." Something in his tone caught her attention. A sort of blanket dismissal. Another chink in the armor? Only one way to find out.

"You don't agree with your mother then?"

Wilbur looked at her. "Don't see what business that is of yours." Despite his words, there was no warning in his tone. He wanted to talk, just like his mother. How long since any of them had talked to anyone outside the family?

"Call it curiosity," she said.

"You do recall what that did to the cat," he said, but laughed as he did so. "Fine, since you ask so politely – no. No, I do not agree with momma on this particular bit of theological nonsense. It is just another brute creation of the Almighty, like ourselves."

"Yet you happily feed people to it."

"Only until I find something that can crack its shell." Wilbur hesitated. "King Crunch would have eaten us all long before now, if we hadn't started tossing him a sacrifice every now and then. Momma might have got the idea from some old film or other, but it was a good one."

"King Crunch?"

Wilbur snorted. "Some of the children named him that, on account he looks like a character on one of them cartoons that used to be on the television. Or maybe it was a cereal box. I can't quite recall. Whatever we call him, he is king in these swamps. Even the alligators know not to mess with him." He scratched his cheek with the barrel of his pistol. "Never know though… might be something on that ship I can use to kill that big sumbitch, huh? Then maybe I'll be king."

Ramirez almost smiled. That was what she'd wanted to hear. Wilbur wasn't happy with the status quo, not at all. She could use that. Maybe. "And what then?" she asked. He looked at her. Instead of replying, he pointed.

"There it is."

Ramirez turned and blinked. "Ptolemy was right," she said. The cruise ship was bigger than she'd imagined. She'd only ever seen them on television. Seagoing vessels were more the Coast Guard's thing.

"Right. This is my stop." Wilbur thumped the side of the boat and the pilot slowed it down. He holstered his pistol and picked up the bow and arrows, slinging the quiver over his shoulder. He glanced at Ramirez. "You be good now, because I'll be watching." He turned a stern eye onto his cousins. "That goes for you two as well. We're only going to get one shot at this, and I'd hate to tell momma that you two are the reason it didn't work." With that, he slipped over the side and into the water, as smooth as an alligator.

Ramirez looked at Sandy. "Swell guy," she said.

Sandy turned away. "Shut up, Federal."

"Make me," Ramirez said, smiling slightly. She had their measure now, she thought. She extended her wrists. "Better cut me loose now, before we blow this."

Sandy hesitated, then drew a hunting knife and cut her

bindings. The young woman bared her teeth at Ramirez. "Don't you try nothing funny now, or I'll gut you and feed you to the damn walkers one piece at a time."

Ramirez saluted. "Scout's honor."

Sandy grunted and hunkered, pulling a tarp over herself until she was hidden from view. But Ramirez could feel her readiness to act on her threat. She had to think of something. Some way of warning the ship.

The other two airboats had peeled off at some point without her noticing. Probably circling around the clearing that held the ship. As Roy edged their craft forward, she looked up and saw the ship was lit up in the gloom as Wilbur had said it would be.

Spotlights swept the water, illuminating the walkers that splashed in and out of the tree line. There were a lot of them, but the water made it hard for them to move. "Christ," Roy muttered. "Place is under siege."

"Rethinking this plan of yours?" Ramirez asked, rubbing her wrists. Roy muttered under his breath, but didn't reply. He slowed the airboat as they neared the ship, until a beam of light struck them. He raised his hand over his eyes and cursed.

"That's far enough," a voice said, amplified through a bullhorn. This was punctuated by a rifle shot that plucked at the water near the hull of the airboat. Ramirez didn't flinch. She'd known it was coming. These days, it'd have been odd if there hadn't been a warning shot. Roy made a sound in the back of his throat that might have been a whimper and cut the throttle. Sandy stayed where she was under the tarp.

Roy looked at her. "You're up, Federal. Make it good, draw

them all out into the open long enough for us to do what needs doing – or else..." He grinned and patted the pistol on his hip.

Ramirez looked away.

CHAPTER TWENTY-SIX
Succumbing

Sayers paused, one fist raised to signal Westlake and Brady to stop. Westlake jerked their captive to a halt and listened. The swamp wasn't quiet, especially as the sun was going down, and with a hurricane on the horizon. He could hear birds and gators; things screaming somewhere out among trees that bent and creaked in a constant wind. More, he could hear the dead all around them. The weather had them agitated.

It had him agitated as well, come to that. It was like an itch he couldn't scratch, and it was only getting worse. His head felt like there was a wasp loose in it. He'd wanted to ask Kahwihta about it before they'd left, but there'd been no time. He'd been pleased to see her alive, but to hear Brady tell it, every moment counted. Maybe when they got back. If they got back.

Sayers lowered her fist and started moving again. Westlake followed, dragging Brady with him. The latter hadn't given them much trouble, but Westlake could feel him gathering his courage the closer they drew to his home turf. He was going to try something. The only question was when. The thought didn't bother him as much as it might once have.

Sayers glanced back at him. "No mosquitoes," she said. "You notice that?"

"No food," he said. "Except for Brady's kin. And I'm betting they don't taste very good these days. Do you, Brady?" He looked at their prisoner. The peeling skin, the yellow eyes, the smell. It was just about detectable to his sense: a stink like a walker, only not quite. Maybe that was why the ghillie suits worked so well for them. They were rotting from within, turning cancerous because of their diet.

Westlake gave them a few months at most; a year, maybe, if they got supplies. They'd start to turn then. According to Brady, some already had. But the rest would follow in due course, until none of them were left. Until the Glades were quiet, save for the groaning of the innumerable dead.

That wasn't his problem, though. He was content to let Brady and his kin turn into undead freaks, so long as they got Ramirez and the others back safely. That was his job now. Nothing else mattered.

He stumbled on a root and cursed softly. The water wasn't as deep here, but that meant there was more to trip over. And the trees were as close-set as anywhere, all but blocking out the last dregs of light from the setting sun. "Should have used a boat," Brady said, watching him. "Only an idiot goes for a stroll in the swamp."

"Yeah, I bet you'd like that," Westlake said. "Your people would hear us coming a mile away." Traversing the Glades on foot wasn't fun, nor was it fast. But it drew a lot less attention than the motorized raft Grillo had used to drop them off at the airfield. They'd made the rest of the journey on foot, avoiding the few walkers that had followed them from the ship. They'd given Brady his ghillie suit back, and Sayers had appropriated her own from one of the would-be ambushers Westlake had killed. She didn't seem to mind the blood on it. Westlake didn't need any protection. The walkers had gone back to ignoring him.

Somewhere ahead of them, something heavy splashed through the water. Westlake spotted a snake swimming away from the sound. A moment later, a brute lurched through the trees, a burnt and tattered apron and ragged work uniform straining to contain its bulk. A novelty hat was pinned to its head by an errant splinter of wood, and its face was mostly a blackened ruin. It had no eyes, and its mouth was just a cavern. It listed blindly, fumbling its way through the swamp. Sayers drew an arrow from her quiver, but didn't loose it.

Westlake understood her caution. Brutes were harder than walkers to put down. Even getting an arrow into their eye or ear canal was no guarantee of hitting anything vital. You needed a sledgehammer just to crack their skull. Better to let it wander on by than draw its attention. Brady watched it lurch out of sight with something like regret. "Lot of meat on that one," he muttered.

"And already cooked by the looks of it," Sayers said, in a low voice. When the brute had passed out of sight, she looked at Brady. "How far now?"

Brady grunted and looked away. Westlake caught him by the neck and dragged him close. "She asked you a question," he croaked. Brady gave him a narrow-eyed glare and looked at Sayers.

"Not far. Should see the bulwark up past them trees. We put it up to keep the gators out of our fishing waters. Best keep your head down, though. Wouldn't want it to get shot off by anyone on guard duty." He smirked as he said it. "Or maybe don't. That'd suit me."

Sayers tapped her nose with the head of her arrow. "Noted," she said. She glanced at Westlake. "I'll scout ahead and see what we're up against. You keep an eye on him. I don't want to have to chase him down." A moment later, she was gone. Quick and quiet as a ghost.

"She freaks me out," Brady said.

Westlake nodded. "She freaks everybody out."

"You going to kill me?"

Westlake didn't reply. He wasn't sure yet whether he was going to or not. He was sure Sayers wouldn't blink if he decided to do it. Not like Calavera or Ramirez. Instead, he said, "Tell me something... those walkers in the bunker, whose idea was that?" He shoved Brady against a tree. Not hard. Just enough to get his attention. "Yours?"

Brady rubbed his arm. "No. It was Wilbur's."

"Which one is Wilbur?"

"My cousin." Brady grinned. "You'd know him if you saw him. He's a big fellow. Bigger than that guy with the mask, even."

"That seems unlikely," Westlake muttered.

"Believe it or don't, he'll settle your hash when he gets hold of you." Brady gave a high, jackal-yip of a laugh and Westlake hit him. Not hard, just enough to shut him up. Brady went down into the water, but came up again almost immediately, holding a stick. Westlake caught it just before it smacked into his head. They stared at one another for a moment. Then Westlake tugged the stick from Brady's unresisting grip.

"Stop it," Westlake said. He tossed the stick away. Brady stared at him.

"What are you?" he asked.

"You know what I am."

"You bit me. Am I going to turn?" Brady made a face. "I don't want to be no walker."

Westlake reached down and dragged him to his feet. "Who knows? Be a good boy and maybe you never find out." He looked at Brady. "So the traps were Wilbur's idea, huh? How many times have you guys pulled that stunt?"

Brady hesitated. "A few."

"And what happens to the people you take prisoner? You eat them?"

"Sometimes."

Westlake leaned close. "Then what are you worried about? Seems to me you're already halfway there." He patted Brady on the cheek. Brady flinched back.

"We only do what we have to, to get by," he protested. "If it wasn't for them we took prisoner, we'd have been eaten ourselves. King Crunch would have gobbled us up long ago."

Westlake paused. "King who?"

"Crunch. Grandmomma allows as he's God, but he looks like something else to me." Brady leaned against a tree and rubbed his arms. He looked around nervously. He stank of fear. His pulse was all over the place. "This is his territory out here. He's what's kept the dead from overwhelming us when they all got blown down into the swamp."

Westlake thought of the thing that had saved him from the

alligators and felt a vague stirring. Not fear, not exactly. But maybe as close as he could get these days. "So you feed people to him, as well as eat them yourselves. Nice little ecosystem you got here."

Brady glared at him. "You don't know shit, dead man." Brady's hand was down, reaching for something jutting from the water. Another stick – a bigger one this time. He had to give Brady credit for persistence, if not smarts.

"I know enough to know you're scared," Westlake said. "And scared people do stupid things." He paused, head tilted. "You think I don't see your hand reaching for that chunk of wood there? You think I can't hear your heart speeding up? What are you going to do, Brady? Hit me again? Maybe go for my skull?" Westlake smiled. "What's the plan from there? Shout a bit, raise the alarm?"

Brady stared at him, then he yanked the chunk of wood up and stabbed the splintered end into Westlake's chest. Westlake fell back and Brady went with him into the water. The chunk of wood tore loose and came down again, perforating his abdomen. Something that wasn't exactly blood anymore spurted into the water. Westlake felt no pain, only annoyance. Brady had been quicker than he'd anticipated. Then, maybe he was just slower.

Brady was up a moment later, splashing in the direction Sayers had gone, drawing in breath to shout. Westlake burst from the water behind him and caught him by the back of the head and neck. He shoved his opponent's head under the water without hesitation – and then held him there. Brady's hands clawed at the water and nearby roots, but Westlake had the leverage. When he'd finished, Brady was still.

Westlake stepped back, letting the body float. He stared down at it, almost puzzled. It had been easier than he remembered, killing someone. Once, he'd have hesitated, if only for a moment. Killing had never been a tool in his bag. It was messy, a sign you'd screwed up somewhere, somehow. Only amateurs left bodies behind.

Slowly, almost without realizing it, he rolled the body over. Brady stared up at him with wide, disbelieving eyes. Something twitched in the dead man's cheek. Then he convulsed and rose, as if on strings. Westlake retreated a short distance as the newly made walker twitched into motion. Then, driven by some hideous compulsion, he lunged forward and buried his fingers in the walker's throat.

Hungry.

The walker gave a gurgle and fumbled at him, trying to shove him away. But Westlake bore down, tearing apart the soft flesh of its neck and throat, exposing the bone. One twist was enough to render the zombie unable to move, leaving him free to indulge himself. Strong fingers tore aside the ghillie suit, exposing the midsection.

Hungry. Hungry. Hungry.

Digging in, he began to eat. It was as if he were outside himself, watching from a remove as his body – his hands – tore flesh and cracked bone. He watched intestines unspool and saw his teeth bite soft tissue, tear it, saw his throat swallow. Felt it slide down into the pit that was his stomach. Part of him couldn't understand why he'd resisted for so long.

The other part of him wanted to scream, to smash his skull against the nearest tree. To stop what was happening by any means necessary. But he couldn't. His body was on autopilot, no longer under his control.

More walkers arrived, emerging from the surrounding swamp, drawn by the smell of blood on the air. They shoved him aside, and he went without protest, still chewing on a piece of Brady. It tasted like nothing he'd ever eaten before. It was like… ambrosia. Wasn't that what they called the food of the gods?

He paused as a sound drew his attention… a whisper of noise that a normal human wouldn't have noticed. The sound of a bowstring being drawn taut.

Sayers was watching him, an arrow notched and ready. The sight of her shocked him back to himself and he dropped what he'd been gnawing on. He looked down at himself, at the blood on his hands and then back at her. Her expression was calm – empty. There was no disgust there, no fear. Just caution.

"You good?" she asked after a moment.

"I'm good," he said hoarsely. He wasn't sure whether he was glad she'd reacted the way she had or upset that she hadn't put him out of his misery.

"You sure?"

He wiped his bloody hands on his trousers and spat out the bits of Brady he hadn't swallowed yet. "I'm sure."

Sayers nodded and thrust her arrow back in its quiver. "Good. Because I found the others and I'm going to need some help."

CHAPTER TWENTY-SEVEN
Overboard

"Are you sure about this?" Imogene asked doubtfully, as she helped Kahwihta across the deck. "Your wound…"

Kahwihta winced, but kept walking. "Is going to hurt regardless of where I am." She took a deep breath and paused, one hand against her side. Hawser had stapled the wound shut and bandaged it, but the painkillers were starting to wear off. The truth was, she'd been getting bored just sitting in the infirmary, even with the visitors.

Rain fell, pattering against the tarpaulins and making puddles in the places where the deck had buckled slightly. It was getting on toward night, or maybe that was just the clouds. The wind was up, too, rustling the tarps and blowing wet leaves across the deck. The whole ship was singing ever so slightly. The wind sawing through the structural damage made for a mournful tune. The deck was trembling ever so slightly beneath her feet.

"Westlake and Sayers get away OK?" she asked, as Imogene helped her sit in a deck chair. Attila was right beside her, his square head on her lap and his eyes on her. A whimper escaped him, and she stroked his head.

"Grillo came back in one piece, so I expect so." Imogene frowned. "What's going on?" Kahwihta followed her gaze and saw Jessop and Grillo hurrying toward the prow, accompanied by several armed survivors. Calavera was with them. Imogene called out to him, and he stopped and turned.

"An airboat. It appears Ramirez is aboard," Calavera said as he joined them. He bent down and offered his hand. "Would you like to see?"

Kahwihta took him up on his offer despite the growing ache in her side. If Ramirez was here, what did that mean? Had her captors released her? If that was the case, what about the others? Imogene and Calavera helped her to the rail.

Spotlights shone down on the water, illuminating the walkers that floundered at the edges of the clearing and a single airboat idling a short distance from the ship. As Calavera had said, Ramirez was there, but she didn't look happy about it. Maybe it had something to do with the boat's pilot. He didn't look particularly friendly.

"Is that one of the guys who shot at us?" she asked Imogene.

The other woman nodded. "Looks like it to me. This should be good."

Jessop had a bullhorn out and was calling down to the new arrivals. Other survivors lined the rails, trying to get a look at what was happening. Kahwihta took in the scene; something about it seemed off to her.

She realized what it was a moment later – the zombies were acting odd. They weren't all converging on the airboat the way they should have been. Instead, some of them were retreating or milling about, as if confused. Or maybe they were hearing something the people on the ship couldn't. She watched them for a moment, then caught Imogene's attention. "We're in trouble," she said softly.

Imogene frowned. "What do you mean?"

"The zombies – the way they're acting... there's something else out there and we can't see it. Whatever is going on here, it's definitely not on the up and up." Kahwihta made her way to Jessop, but was stopped by Grillo. "I need to talk to him."

"Not right now," Grillo said, glancing toward the water.

Kahwihta tried to peer past her. "What's going on? What do they want?"

"A parley, according to your friend. Face to face. Or rather, boat to boat."

Kahwihta hesitated. "Are you going to?"

Grillo frowned. "She's your friend. Are you saying we shouldn't?"

"I'm saying something's up. The zombies aren't acting right."

Grillo's eyes narrowed. "So?" She sounded doubtful.

"So she's a damn zombologist," Imogene said. "She knows what she's talking about."

Grillo's frown deepened but before she could say anything, Jessop noticed them and waved them over. "She says the zombies–" Grillo began.

"I heard," Jessop said. "Calavera says that's your friend Ramirez down there. Is she actually an FBI agent?"

Kahwihta nodded. "She was, when there was an FBI." She paused. "I think they're forcing her to do this." She was also pretty sure it was a trap of some kind. Her grandmother had told her too many stories about cannibals – men and women haunted by the spirits of the lonely places – to believe they were anything but treacherous. Eating people was the ultimate betrayal; one who ate the flesh of their own people couldn't be trusted.

Jessop nodded slowly, a pensive look on his face. "Me too. Unfortunately, I think we need to hear them out. At the very least, we might be able to find out if the rest of your friends are still alive."

"So we're going to send the raft out?" Grillo asked.

"No. The lifeboat. We'll lower it halfway and stop out of reach of any walkers." Jessop looked at Kahwihta. "Would you come with me? A friendly face might do her some good." Kahwihta nodded and Jessop looked at Grillo. "Get a patrol going. I want eyes in motion up and down the deck, just in case they try some commando crap while we're distracted."

"I will help," Calavera said. He paused and looked down at Kahwihta. "Be careful. Ramirez would not want you to risk your life."

Kahwihta put on her best smile. "Wouldn't dream of it," she said. She joined Jessop at the edge of the rail where he'd pulled off a tarp to reveal an old-fashioned lifeboat hung from the side of the ship with chains. He caught her expression and smiled.

"We found a stash of them in a nautical museum in Palm Beach. They're basically seaworthy, but can't hold much. Meant for show not tell, as they say." He patted the chains. "Shamekia fixed this up for us. Simple pulley system. Pull the bottom chain, boat descends. Pull the top chain, she rises. Good for getting supplies on board, not for much else."

He climbed into the boat and offered her his hand. She took it, and Attila leapt after her. Jessop raised an eyebrow, but said nothing. One of the other ship survivors, a young man named James, joined them. He had a rifle, and settled into the prow of the boat where he'd have a clear shot.

Kahwihta peered over the side. There were walkers everywhere, most of them stuck in the mud or tangled up in tree roots. Floaters as well, pale faces peering up from beneath the scummy surface of the water. "Do you see many of the larger ones?" she asked.

Jessop shrugged. "A few. Less of late. We think the alligators have been feeding on them. Not many runners, either." He paused. "Never thought much about it honestly."

Kahwihta nodded and then jumped slightly, startled, as the boat began to descend unsteadily toward the water. The airboat was circling slowly below, Ramirez at the prow. She looked tired, unsteady. That was a bad sign. The guy driving the airboat looked nervous. That was a worse sign. Something was definitely up.

Attila growled softly and Kahwihta stroked him. His eyes were on the swamp, not the walkers below. Something else was out there. When she said as much to Jessop, he nodded. "Yeah. From what that Brady fellow said, these Watkins folks are bad news and sneaky to boot. I wouldn't be surprised if there's a few of them out there, watching us."

The boat juddered as it came to a halt about six feet above the water. Jessop waved the airboat forward and it puttered toward them. Ramirez caught sight of Kahwihta, and a look of relief came into her eyes. But it vanished quickly, and her poker face re-established itself. Jessop leaned over the edge of the boat and looked down. "Well?" he asked, without preamble.

Ramirez hesitated, and then said, "I'm honestly not sure what I'm supposed to say here." Her gaze flicked down to the tarp at her feet, and Kahwihta saw that there was something under it. Attila was growling steadily, his eyes on the tarp.

Jessop was taken aback by Ramirez's greeting. "Hello, for a start? Or you could cut the bull and tell me what your friends want."

"I didn't think this was the time for small talk." Ramirez looked around. "Can I – can *we* – come aboard?" she asked, glancing at the pilot. "We have a lot to discuss."

"Hey now," the pilot began. He was looking distinctly unhappy. Kahwihta had a feeling Ramirez had gone off script.

"Like how your friends have been killing my people?" Jessop asked, staring hard at the pilot. The man flinched and swallowed, clearly startled by this.

"Among other things," Ramirez said, with a tight smile. Again, she glanced down at the tarp. There was warning in her gaze. Kahwihta touched Jessop on the knee, and he cut his eyes toward her. The pilot must have noticed. He cursed and made to turn the airboat.

"They know!" he bawled. "Wilbur, they know!"

Several things happened all at once. James raised his rifle – then toppled over the side of the boat, an arrow in his throat. Another arrow struck the side of the boat a moment later, nearly pinning Kahwihta's hand in place. Rifle shots sounded from the tree line, and Kahwihta flinched as one of the spotlights above exploded. As the airboat veered away, Ramirez lunged toward the pilot, who was still yelling. The tarp was thrown back, and a woman rose, sighting Jessop through the scope of her rifle. Kahwihta tackled him to the bottom of the boat as the rifle boomed, and nearly screamed as the wound in her side twisted painfully. The shot struck the chain, causing it to rattle.

The rifle barked twice more, punching holes in the side of the boat. Jessop fumbled for his sidearm as Attila began to bark. Kahwihta could hear splashing below, as the floaters converged on James' body. Jessop rose, swinging his weapon up, but paused.

Kahwihta risked a look. Ramirez had managed to dump the pilot over the side, but not before getting hold of his weapon. Zombies converged on him, rotting hands rising from the water to yank him back and down as he tried to swim for the dubious safety of the trees. The woman with the rifle lay slumped against the front of the airboat, clearly dead. Ramirez was in the pilot's seat and as she skimmed close, she said, "They're in the trees! Tell your people to aim at the tree line!"

Even as she spoke, an arrow thudded into the headrest of the pilot's seat. Kahwihta spied a tall figure standing among the trees, taking a bead on the airboat. She shouted wordlessly and pointed. Ramirez followed her gesture and sent the airboat hurtling in the direction of the bowman.

Jessop was shouting up to his people, but there was no need. They'd already figured out what was going on and directed their fire at the trees. Kahwihta couldn't tell if they'd hit anyone, but the zombies were certainly getting excited. She looked down and saw what was left of James being pulled under. Jessop followed her gaze and cursed softly.

"I'm sorry," she said.

He shook his head. "Not your fault. Those bastards are really starting to annoy me. Hand me that rifle." He gestured to James' fallen rifle. "They must have hoped they'd draw us all out and pick us off. Luckily, we had some warning, thanks to you and your friends… otherwise we might just have fallen for it."

"Thank me after we get back up there safely," Kahwihta said. She touched her side and winced. The staples were still in place, but the painkillers had definitely worn off. She looked for Ramirez and saw that the other woman was having trouble controlling the airboat. It was skidding across the water, going too fast… and heading right for the archer.

Ramirez leapt over the side at the last moment as the airboat left the water and pinwheeled into the trees with a loud crunch. The fan burst loose from its cage and spun across the water like a farmer's scythe, chopping apart several walkers before it embedded itself in the mud. Ramirez started swimming toward Kahwihta and Jessop. Kahwihta looked around for something she could use to help and spotted a coil of nylon rope. She flung it over the side and shouted for Ramirez.

Jessop, seeing what she was up to, shot any walker that got in Ramirez's way. But there were still the ones right below them to worry about. Kahwihta snatched up Jessop's pistol and stretched herself over the side. The floaters hadn't noticed Ramirez yet. She took aim and squeezed off a few shots at the ones closest to the other woman, sinking several of them for good, opening up a path to the dangling rope.

"Hurry up," Kahwihta shouted. Ramirez caught the rope

and began to haul herself out of the water. Jessop dropped his rifle and grabbed the rope, holding tight. Kahwihta made to shout encouragement when she saw a floater, dressed in a bright red diver's costume, lunge upwards with sharklike ferocity. Kahwihta fired – and the floater fell back, skull burst open. A moment later, Kahwihta helped pull Ramirez over the side into the boat.

Ramirez looked at her, her expression one of relief. "I'm glad you're alive."

"Me too," Kahwihta said. "What say we keep it that way?"

CHAPTER TWENTY-EIGHT
Rescue

Music danced on the evening air, barely audible over the wind and rain. Westlake and Sayers were huddled in a knot of broken trees just past the outer boundary of the Watkins' place. There were a lot of broken trees; it looked as if something big had come this way, and more than once. Westlake thought about the thing Brady had called "King Crunch" and wondered if it were somewhere close by now, watching them.

He hadn't said anything to Sayers about it, but then she didn't seem interested in talking to him either. For good reason, obviously. He wondered if she would tell Ramirez. Part of him hoped so. Maybe it was time to retire from his second life.

He pushed the thought to the back of his mind as Sayers gestured to the set of concrete bulwarks that separated the Watkins' home from the swamp. "There's wire fencing stretched between them, just at the water level," Sayers said. "It's enough to keep out floaters and the odd walker, but not someone who knows what they're doing."

"Not very secure," Westlake said. He wiped ineffectually at his face. He could still smell – still *taste* – Brady's blood and it was driving him to distraction. Sayers' smile was cold in the dim light cast from the bulwarks.

"You'd think. But I got a look at what's waiting past them."

Westlake saw where she was going. "Walkers," he said.

She nodded. "It's like one of those ponds seeded with trout for fishermen. They probably dip in and pull one out every so often when they need protein." She drew her knife and handed it to him. "For the wire. Cut through it and slip in. They're not watching the pond. They're looking at the swamp."

Westlake took the knife. "They'll notice when I climb out of the water."

"No, they won't. They'll be too busy keeping their heads down." She patted her quiver of arrows. "Once you get clear of the water, find the others and make some noise. Blow up a generator or something. Keep them guessing."

"And while I'm doing that, you'll be playing Robin Hood?"

She gave a feral grin. "No, I'll be securing transportation. You just get everyone out the front. There's a jetty leading into the sawgrass. Get them on it and don't stop until you reach the end. I'll meet you there."

"If you don't, it'll be messy."

"I will. Trust me." She paused. "Watch out for Calvin for me." She hesitated. "If he's alive," she added reluctantly.

"And if not?"

"Eat a few of the bastards," she said harshly. Then she was pushing away from him, vanishing into the gloom. He gave her a few moments to get clear, and then made his way toward the bulwarks. There were spotlights rigged up on every other bulwark, and as he slid into the water, he took note of the power cables stretched across the top. They'd lead him to a generator, if he got the opportunity to look for one.

Westlake dropped low into the water, sinking until the top of his head was barely above the surface. There were floaters around him, broken things impaled on branches or chopped to pieces by something. They barely noticed him, their eyes fixed on the dim forms walking across the plywood planks stretched across the tops of the bulwarks.

He paused, waiting for a sentry to go past. He counted three. Not many. Then, what did they have to worry about besides floaters and alligators? He stayed low anyway, brushing aside floaters until he was right up against the fence. Then he went to work with Sayers' knife. It was easier than he'd expected. The metal was rusted, and he soon had a hole big enough to squeeze through. The rain hid the sound of him wedging the gap open.

The dead barely reacted as he joined them. Some moans, some swipes, but he kept things civil and ignored them. As always, they returned the favor. The sentries were obviously used to the noise, and they paid no attention to him as he shoved his way through the crowd. The walkways were easy to spot, lit by Christmas lights that twinkled in the gloom. He could hear music and laughter. They were having a grand old time somewhere in there. That was fine by him. Let them enjoy themselves.

There were ropes and chains dangling over the side of the walkway. He grabbed one, gave it an experimental tug, and began to climb. The nearest zombies groaned in puzzlement as he ascended, and he felt them fumbling at the rope in his wake. He wondered if they could learn to climb. Then he was up and crouched at the edge of the walkway. It was crowded with pallets and empty fuel drums. A forest of junk, left over from more prosperous days perhaps.

From the look of things, everyone was inside the house out of the rain. That was good. He turned, paused. One of the sentries on the bulwark was missing. As he watched, one of the remaining two pitched backward into the zombie pool, an arrow jutting from his throat. The remaining sentry noticed that he was alone and turned as if to shout. Westlake caught his eye and waved. The man opened his mouth – and the broad head of a hunting arrow emerged. His eyes fluttered and he spun away out of sight, clutching his head.

As he turned away from the bulwark, Westlake heard a door clatter, and the thump of someone striding across the walkway. He watched whoever it was go to the edge of the rail, unzip their pants and begin to urinate on the zombies below.

Westlake crept toward him, but paused just short of grabbing him, worried that it might alert the others inside. The man was big, bulky. A frayed baseball cap hid the top of his head, and his cheeks were rough with dead skin. He squinted toward the bulwarks. "What the good goddamn…?" he began. Westlake hit him on the back of the head with the pommel of the knife. The big man went down like a sack of potatoes.

He hesitated, wondering why he hadn't simply killed the other man. It was the smart thing, but he didn't feel like doing the smart thing. Not after Brady. He did, however, take the man's gun and stuffed it into the back of his jeans.

Moving as quickly as he could, he made his way toward the cages that hung over the water. It took him a moment to figure out the pulley system to bring them in, but once he did, he got it moving. The storm covered the sound. The first cage was empty. The second held Gable and Ptolemy. The third, Terry and a woman Westlake didn't recognize. Whoever she was, she looked in bad shape. The fourth and fifth cages were empty. As soon as the second cage thumped against the dock, he asked, "Where's Ramirez?"

"They have taken her to the ship," Ptolemy said. If he was startled by Westlake's sudden appearance, he gave no sign. Instead, he indicated the cage door. "The cages are locked. I do not suppose you have the key?"

Westlake paused. The simplest option would be to shoot the locks off. But that would attract too much attention. Plan B it was, then. He grabbed one of the bars, braced his foot against the frame of the cage and *pulled*. "Are you mental?" Gable hissed. "These things are designed to withstand shark attacks."

The bar popped loose from its upper housing. "Took her to the ship, huh? Let me guess, they intend to bushwhack them the way they did us?" Westlake felt a grim sort of admiration for such duplicity.

"I can only assume that's the idea." Ptolemy paused. "Elizabeth… did she…?"

"Out in the swamp, waiting for us." Westlake finished prying the bar loose and cast it into the water below. He started to work on the next bar. As he did so, he felt a looseness in his shoulder. A ligament had torn, or the muscle fibers were finally starting to fray. He ignored it and kept working on the bar. Shark cages were tough, but so was he. "And the people on the ship can handle themselves."

"We have to warn them," Ptolemy began. "These people—"

Whatever he'd been about to say was interrupted by the crack of a rifle. Westlake felt something tug at his back. He turned, drawing the pistol he'd taken from the unconscious man as he did so. He fired blind, hoping to make whoever it was think better of taking another potshot at him. Shouts and yells pierced the rain noise. But they weren't directed at him. He paused, startled by the sight of a walker hauling itself up onto the dock. It joined the others stumbling toward the house.

They'd copied him, he realized. They'd seen him climb the rope and figured out how to do it for themselves. Earlier he'd wondered if they could do something like that. Now he had his answer. More walkers shimmied up the ropes and chains, following the leader the same way they always did. The people in the house had realized something was amiss and were shooting at the dead.

He turned back to the cage and fired, busting the lock. "Guess we do it the quick way. Get out and find cover, I'll get the others." He hauled the next cage in and did the same. Down below, the dead were seething, agitated by the smell of blood and the sound of shots. The ones that weren't climbing were shoving against the support struts of the walkway and the wire fencing, trying to go somewhere, anywhere.

Westlake freed Terry and his cellmate a moment later. "You in one piece, kid?" he asked. Terry nodded, though he had a bruise covering half his face and looked as if he'd been dragged backward through a thorn bush. Westlake glanced at the woman. She shied away from him, eyes wide. She looked as if she were going to scream, but Terry caught her hand and murmured quietly to her.

Westlake gave Ptolemy a questioning glance. He and Gable were sheltering behind a stack of pallets. "She is from the ship," Ptolemy said. "There were three others with her."

"Where are they now?" Westlake asked. Ptolemy looked toward the house.

"Our... hosts are celebrating," he said. Recalling what Brady had told them, Westlake shook his head and gestured toward the far side of the house. There were at least twenty walkers scattered across the walkway and back porch of the house now, trying to get inside. A few were already down, and Westlake had no doubt the Watkins family would clear them all out in time. But for the moment, they were a good distraction.

"Let's leave them to their fun. It's time to go. There's a jetty on the far side of the house..." he began. Ptolemy nodded.

"It's where we were brought in."

"Sayers will be waiting there with transport. Let's go."

"You ain't going nowhere, mister," a woman's voice called out. "Except maybe into the paddling pool with the rest of the dead." A gunshot followed this assertion, and Westlake felt a punch in his stomach. He stumbled back against the cages and slid down. He saw a man resembling the one he'd knocked unconscious approaching, a rifle in his hands. Beside him were two others, similarly armed. They stepped over fallen walkers with the easy confidence of experienced killers as they approached Ptolemy and the others.

A young girl pushed an old woman in a wheelchair after

the trio. It was the latter who'd spoken, and her eyes gleamed with curiosity as she studied Westlake. "You look like something that's been marinating in a gator's belly, boy."

Westlake pushed himself to his feet. The big man shot him again, but he didn't fall this time. The other two joined in. Westlake looked down at the holes in his chest and stomach and then back up. "You must be Brady's kin. He says hi, by the way."

"Brady...?" the old woman said. "What you know about Brady?"

"He was delicious," Westlake said, and lunged forward.

CHAPTER TWENTY-NINE
Getaway

Terry saw Westlake lunge and did the only thing he could think of: he lunged, too. Not as big a one, obviously – Westlake had some reach on him – but toward the closest of the cannibals. And there was a word he never thought he'd use, even in the context of the apocalypse. His target was distracted by Westlake, thankfully, so it came as a surprise when Terry caught him in the jaw with an elbow.

While he'd never been a big football guy, Terry had watched enough professional wrestling to give him some idea of what to do in a fight. Knees and elbows were the key; at least, that was what Calavera claimed. The guy he hit staggered, but didn't go down. He did thrust out his rifle, trying to shove Terry away. Terry grabbed the rifle and belted the guy twice more in the brief tug of war that followed.

Terry was tired; everything hurt. But his adrenaline was going now, taking away the pain and replacing it with fury. Riggs was dead. He'd seen it happen, had watched it and been unable to do anything about it. It wasn't that they'd been friends, because they hadn't. It wasn't that he felt guilty; he didn't. It was that Riggs was a part of their group, and you tried to keep your group alive, whatever else. The way Terry saw it, everyone breathing was on the same side, or at least they ought to be.

But these guys hadn't gotten the memo. They were eating people for God's sake! The thought fired his desperation, and he threw a final punch, dropping his opponent to the planks. Panting, Terry wrestled the rifle free of the dazed man's grip and immediately turned it on a walker in an oil-stained jumpsuit that was reaching for Cheryl. The young woman flinched as the walker's head burst like an overripe melon, spattering her with oily blood. It slumped to the ground, fingers trailing down her leg.

Cheryl jerked away from the dead man, her eyes wide and her face drained of all color. She didn't scream, though, just made a low moaning sound. She gestured frantically to him, and he signed back without thinking, telling her to stick close. She nodded.

His Uncle Jack had been deaf, thanks to a youthful indiscretion with a firecracker. Terry and his cousins had learned ASL just so they could figure out what sort of obscenities Jack was flicking at them. He'd never imagined it would come in handy after the apocalypse.

Terry and Cheryl had spent their time in the cage getting acquainted. She'd been relieved to find someone who could understand her. There'd apparently only been one person on the ship who could do so, and they'd been first in the pot when the Watkins had gotten hungry, after he and Cheryl had been captured. She'd been in the cage for a week when Terry got tossed in with her. The others from the ship had been in for longer than that. Apparently, their captors had been picking people off since the *Dixie Jewel* had arrived.

And hadn't that been a kick in the head? An actual cruise ship sitting in the swamp. Terry had thought nothing could surprise him, but that came close.

He checked the rifle and looked for the others. Ptolemy and Gable had followed Terry's example and were wrestling with the third gunman. Westlake had the other down and was systematically bouncing his head off the planks. The old lady in the wheelchair was staring daggers at them as she reached around for a–

"Hold it," Terry shouted, pointing the rifle at her. "Don't even think about it, lady!"

She froze, her hand inches from the pistol hanging from the back of her wheelchair. The younger woman behind her stared at Terry in shock. Then she bolted rabbit-quick for the house, shouting for all she was worth. She dodged between two walkers and made it inside. Terry didn't know whether to be relieved or worried.

The old woman smiled, the rain plastering her white hair to her scalp. "The rest of them going to be out here in a minute, boy. Ain't got enough bullets for that."

"He's got enough for you," Westlake said, in a voice like a rusty can full of stones. He rose to his feet, leaving his opponent unconscious on the ground. A legless walker crawled toward the latter, and Westlake stepped over it without pause. Terry considered shooting it, but decided not to waste the bullet.

"What are you?" the old woman asked. She wasn't afraid, Terry thought, just curious.

"The guy who's going to take you for a little ride." Westlake caught the back of her wheelchair and spun it around. "You're coming with us." He looked at Terry. "Come on."

Terry looked around and saw Ptolemy and Gable waiting. "We should hurry. The dead are distracted right now, but that won't last," Ptolemy said. Terry figured he was right. The flow of dead climbing up out of the water had slowed to nothing, and the ones that had made it were clustered around the house. The music and the lights had drawn them, but eventually they'd realize there was easier prey to hand.

"Lead the way," Westlake said. "Grandma and I will make sure no one follows us." He leaned toward the old woman and exposed his teeth. "Won't we, Grandma?"

"My, what big teeth you have," she said, seemingly unafraid.

"All the better to eat you with," Westlake said. Terry flinched. Cheryl touched his arm and signed, asking what was wrong. Terry didn't know how to explain. Westlake glanced at him, and Terry saw what might have been regret on the dead man's face. But it was hard to tell with Westlake. His face was like a mask, hung over true features of bone.

Westlake had come close to killing him back in South Carolina. He knew that, whatever anyone else said. Westlake knew it, too. That he seemed unhappy about it didn't matter. Terry found himself pointing the rifle at Westlake without thinking.

Westlake met his gaze, but said nothing. Terry suddenly had the feeling that Westlake wouldn't resist. Maybe he wanted it to end. But, after long moments, Westlake said, "Come on, kid. Time to get out of here."

Ptolemy and Gable led the way. Terry and Cheryl followed,

with Westlake and his captive bringing up the rear. They made for the front, away from the walkers and the Watkins both. As far as Terry was concerned, they could have one another.

The porch was one of those big wraparound things. Terry couldn't recall the name. It encircled the house and branched off at points where the inhabitants had made jetty-like additions. He could see shed-like outbuildings and lean-tos crouched in the sawgrass that spread out around the front and sides of the house. There were airboats in various stages of disassembly and thickets of bones and alligator hide hung up on drying racks.

The rain was coming down hard now; it all but hid the walkers clustered around the house from sight. But he could hear gunshots and breaking glass. Cheryl caught his hand and squeezed it. "I think they're making a breakout," he called. He couldn't tell whether the others heard him over the rain or not. He glanced back and saw Westlake shoving the wheelchair along, occasionally darting a look toward the rear of the house.

Cheryl squeezed his hand again. Terry looked at her. Her eyes were on the sawgrass that rose wild around them. She'd seen something he hadn't, noticed something. Uncle Jack had said that being deaf meant you noticed things like strange vibrations or sudden movements more. He made to call out to the others, but the sound died on his lips as he felt the planks under his feet shift. Something big passed beneath them, nosing through the grass.

He was so preoccupied with that, he barely noticed the walker lurch out of the grass, its withered frame stewed and baked to a bundle of twitching sticks. It wore the tattered rags of a fast food server's uniform, and the leathery flesh was peeling from its extremities. It came out of the grass, jaws wide…

Then, it was gone. Snatched out of sight by an armored leviathan who bore it into the grass with a splash. The alligator was big, covered in unsightly barnacles of broken fiberglass and zombie meat. Eyes and mouths blinked and flapped in splatters of rotten meat that clung like algae to its hide. Terry stared at the monster as it chewed down on the walker, rolling over and over, instinctively trying to drown something that couldn't be drowned. Cheryl had to drag him away from the sight.

"You won't get away," the old woman said loudly. "My kin will find you wherever you go, whatever you try. That airplane ain't going to save you."

As if to prove the validity of those words, a rifle shot sounded. Terry and the others stopped, turned. The old woman laughed. "Glad to see you're good for something, Elmer."

"Love you too, momma," Elmer replied. He was a heavyset man dressed in camouflage, and he had a hunting crossbow in his hands. He looked like he knew how to use it as well. Three more of the Watkins clan stood behind him, their weapons aimed at Terry and the others. "You let her go, dead man, or we'll kill your friends," Elmer continued, blinking rain out of his eyes. "Hate to waste the meat, but needs must." He gestured. "You bring her back here real slow, and your friends can go on breathing – at least for a few more minutes."

"Elmer, don't you let them go," the old woman snarled.

"Momma, I'm handling it," Elmer said, almost plaintively.

Terry didn't go so far as to feel sorry for him, but he didn't figure the old woman had been a loving parental figure. Didn't explain the cannibalism, though.

"If Wilbur were here…" she continued, leaning forward in her chair.

"He ain't," Elmer barked. He kept his eyes on Westlake as he said it. "You do what I tell you, now. Bring her back."

For a moment, Terry thought Westlake might do it. Then, with a raspy sigh, he dumped the old woman out of her chair and into the water. As he did so, Terry fired and saw one of their captors yelp and stumble back. Ptolemy fired as well, but with more accuracy. Elmer staggered, clutching at his arm.

The alligator chose that moment to make its return. It plowed through the grass, only its eyes above water. The old woman squalled like an angry cat and her kin leapt to help her get out of the water. Elmer bellowed orders and those with guns turned them on the alligator. Westlake backed away toward the far end of the jetty, gesturing for Terry and the others to do the same.

The alligator bellowed and slammed itself onto the jetty, causing parts of it to buckle and splinter. Shouts of alarm mingled with gunshots. Then the rain hid everything. They reached the end of the jetty, where a number of airboats waited, floating in the water. The smell of fuel slithered through the rain, and Terry realized the jetty was soaked in it.

Sayers rose from the front of one of the airboats, bow in hand and arrow notched. The arrow was wrapped in cloth, and a flame sputtered on it, resisting the rain. "Down," she shouted. Terry caught Cheryl and flung them both to the planks. Westlake did the same.

Sayers' arrow hissed overhead and struck the man who'd been pursuing them without their knowing. The guy was big and ugly and he stumbled back, clawing at the arrow in his chest as flames spread across his body. He howled like a hit dog, but didn't go down. Instead, he lifted the machete he held and lurched toward Terry and Cheryl.

Westlake interposed himself at the last moment. The machete thudded into the meat of his forearm and snagged on something. Westlake tore it from the man's grasp and kicked him backward onto the jetty. Flames leapt from his thrashing body and spread across the fuel-doused wood. It spread fast, even with the rain.

"Up, up," Westlake said, as he ripped the machete free of his arm and sent it spinning into the sawgrass. Terry needed no further encouragement. He hustled Cheryl toward Sayers and the airboat. Ptolemy was already helping Gable aboard.

"Hurry up," Sayers said, as she lit another arrow with a Zippo. It took her several tries; long enough for Westlake to reach them. He hesitated at the edge of the jetty and Terry wondered whether he might stay. Part of him hoped so. Sayers looked at Westlake, arrow nocked. "You coming?" she snapped.

"Yeah," he said after a moment, and climbed into the boat as Sayers loosed her arrow and sent it thudding into the seat of one of the other airboats. Flames rose up, feeding on the spilled fuel. Terry saw the plan, then. Burn the jetty and the other boats, and maybe keep anyone from coming after them. Unless the rain put the fire out. But the fuel would help with that. He hated seeing machines burn, though. Not when they could still be put to use.

Sayers got into the pilot's seat and their craft pulled away from the jetty as it began to burn. Westlake looked at Terry.

"You OK, kid?"

Terry turned away. He squeezed Cheryl's hand. She smiled at him.

"Better once we're out of here," he said.

CHAPTER THIRTY
Discussions

Ramirez dried her hair with a threadbare first-class towel. She was still soaked through from her swim in the swamp, and the rain wasn't helping matters. "They'll be back," she said. "They want this ship, and they want it bad. But next time, they're not going to waste time on the subtle approach."

"That was the subtle approach?" Jessop asked. He and the others sat on chairs beneath a sun awning that was currently keeping the rain off. Ramirez had been introduced to Jessop and the other officers of the *Dixie Jewel*. They seemed like a good bunch; then, dangerous times made for sure bedfellows. She'd read that somewhere, and had found it to be largely true. Bad times made people more inclined to work together. It was one of the few things that gave her hope in these dark days.

"Compared to what they're probably going to do now, yeah," Ramirez said, hanging the towel over her shoulder. "I saw maybe thirty people at that house, counting kids, but I get the impression that there are more of them than that."

She paused. "Them and… the other thing." She suddenly saw Riggs flying through the air again, his body rupturing like a wet sack as the monstrosity battered him to pieces.

"King Crunch," Westlake said. "Sounds like a cartoon character." His voice sounded odd, and she wondered what was going on in his head. He'd come back with Ptolemy and the others, minus their prisoner, not long after Wilbur and his bunch had skedaddled.

Neither he nor Sayers had anything to say about the missing prisoner. She wasn't inclined to ask about it. She was just glad to see them alive, and Jessop had been similarly grateful to have Cheryl back.

"That thing is no joke," Ramirez said. "It's big and it's mean."

"I saw what it can do. I believe you," Westlake said.

Jessop nodded. "We've never seen it up close, but it sounds like the creature that's been sniffing around our hull the past few weeks." He flinched as the rising wind carried a loose branch across the deck. Ramirez peered out from under the awning. The wind was getting stronger, and the sky was a deep, unsettling gray.

"We'll need to start battening down the hatches tonight," Jessop said, following her gaze. "I doubt these… Watkins people will attack before tomorrow, and the hurricane will be here by then."

"I don't think a little thing like a hurricane is going to stop them," Ramirez said. "At least not Wilbur and his mother."

"Wilbur… the big one?" Jessop asked.

"That's the guy," Ramirez said. She'd hoped the airboat might have taken care of him, but no such luck. Maybe an alligator had gotten him, but somehow she doubted it. Wilbur wasn't the sort of guy to get eaten by anything as ordinary as an alligator. "He'll be back. He's not the type to give up easy."

"If they just wanted the boat, I think I'd give it to them at this point," Jessop said. He sat back. "Only that's not all they want, is it?"

"No," Ramirez said. She took her seat. "No, it isn't. These people – these kinds of people – see any resistance as an insult. You shot at them... killed a few... they'll want blood."

"She's right," Westlake said. "No way out of this now but to fight. Even if you left this boat behind–"

"Ship," Jessop corrected.

Westlake ignored him and continued, "Even if you left it, they'd hunt you down. And there's no way to get everyone out on our plane. Somebody would have to stay here, and whoever it was would be as good as dead."

"Even you?" Phipps asked hesitantly. Everyone fell silent. Westlake looked at him.

"Even me," he said, after a moment. Ramirez studied him as he spoke. There was a tremor in his face – nerve death, maybe. Or something else. His voice was rougher than normal, like the words were harder to come by. Sayers had told her a little bit about what had happened to him. Ramirez didn't like to think about Westlake alone. Something told her that he needed to be around people. That it was one of the only things keeping him... human.

She hadn't discussed it with Kahwihta yet. Part of her didn't want to. She didn't want to be right. Because if she was, that meant it was her responsibility to keep a watch on him until the inevitable. That wasn't how she wanted to spend her life. She was fairly certain Westlake wouldn't want that either.

"So, we fight," Jessop said. He looked around at his fellow officers. The woman, Grillo, nodded. Phipps looked a little green around the gills, but he nodded as well.

"Some of us will fight," Sayers said. "Some of us are going to go get those supplies out of the hold. Or at least as many as we can carry."

Ramirez looked at her. "Are you volunteering, then?"

"Already did." Sayers nodded to Calavera. "Him, too."

Ramirez looked at them both, then nodded. "Fine." She looked at Jessop. "You don't happen to have schematics for this ship, do you?"

Jessop nodded. "We do. Why?"

Ptolemy cleared his throat. "With the schematics, we can figure out the quickest route to the supply hold, as well as the best areas to cache supplies if necessary." He took off his glasses and cleaned them on his shirt. "It may well take several days to do it, if your description of the amount in the hold is accurate." He lifted his glasses and peered at them, checking for smudges. "Unfortunately, I do not think we have several days."

Jessop leaned forward. "In my experience, we've got maybe a few hours. By my estimates, the hurricane will make landfall tomorrow morning at latest." He shook his head. "I don't know what'll happen after that."

"What do you mean?" Ramirez asked.

"He means the ship might capsize... or just crack in half," Grillo said bluntly. "We took a lot of damage when we got blown inland by the last one. We haven't repaired any of it. That means a year of God knows how many problems just... getting worse."

"What kind of problems?" Ptolemy asked.

Jessop sighed. "A fuel leak, for one. The lower decks are probably full of fumes. Oil. Chemicals. The hull is definitely holed in places, which means structural damage. There's probably flooding as well. I have no idea what that'll look like after a year."

"Hazard a guess," Ramirez said.

"Bad," Jessop said bluntly.

Sayers grunted. "Wonderful."

"So we put a time limit on it," Ramirez said. "Get what you can get, if anything, and get out. Meanwhile, we'll get ready for... everything else." She looked toward the rail and the swamp. Wilbur was out there somewhere. She'd have bet money on it, if there was still such a thing as money. She looked back at the others. "What was the plan for when the hurricane hit?"

"Like I said, we batten the hatches. We've got everyone in the dining room currently. It's a big room, but the windows are reinforced. Unless something goes really wrong, I hoped we'd ride things out there. We're far enough above the water line that flooding shouldn't be a problem. I'm mostly worried about debris and..."

"Capsizing," Ramirez finished. He nodded.

"I don't think even one hundred and twenty mile per hour winds would shift us, but we're on unstable ground. We're basically stuck in a giant mud puddle. It'd be different if we were on the water, or in motion. But like this... there's nothing to hold us up if we start rocking but some broken trees. Not to mention the hull damage we've already sustained. If the winds get bad enough, there's a chance that part of the ship might just... collapse."

Ramirez ran her hand through her hair, trying not to imagine what that might look like. "OK, good to know. What do we have in the way of guns and ammunition?"

Jessop scratched his chin. "A few rifles, a couple of shotguns, some handguns. Ammunition is… scarce. Shamekia has that crossbow of hers, too."

"A crossbow would come in handy down in the hold," Sayers said speculatively. "Less chance of accidentally setting off a pocket of fumes. Or of attracting attention."

"We'll ask for volunteers," Jessop said firmly.

Ramirez nodded and sat up. "So, one team goes down while the rest of us stay up here and hope that no one comes calling." She looked at Westlake. "I want to talk to you."

"So talk."

"Privately."

Westlake grunted and turned away. Ramirez stood and they went toward the prow, away from the others. They stuck to the rain shelters that had been erected along the center of the deck, but it was still windy enough that she had to lean closer to him than she liked. "Sayers said you guys had a prisoner."

"We did," Westlake said, after a moment's hesitation.

"What happened to them?"

"They made a bad play."

Ramirez studied him. Even when he'd been alive, Westlake's poker face had been impressive. Dead, there was almost no way to tell what was going on in there. "What really happened?" she asked quietly. A normal person wouldn't have been able to hear her easily, not with the wind and the rising storm. But Westlake heard her just fine.

He was silent for several moments, and at first, she'd

thought his brain had sprung a gear again. Then, he said, "I was so hungry. You got no idea, Ramirez... no idea how hungry I am all the time. It's like a pit where my stomach ought to be, but there's no good way to fill it. Most days, I ignore it. I know it's not real. But it's getting harder." He looked at her. "He got loose. My fault. Inattentive. Tried to bash my skull in. So, I did the same to him."

"And then?"

Westlake looked away. It was all the answer she needed, though she wished it were otherwise. They stood in silence for a time, listening to the rain. After a moment, Westlake said, "You remember what we talked about, after I got bit at the Villa?"

"Yeah."

"You promised to put a bullet in me, if I ever turned into one of those things."

"Yeah," Ramirez said, her voice soft.

"After this is over, I'm not going back to the Villa."

"You're staying here?" she asked, even though she knew the answer.

He gave a short, raspy laugh. "God, no."

Ramirez's hands curled into fists. She knew what he wanted, even if he hadn't asked yet. "I won't do it," she said.

"You promised," he said, still not looking at her.

"You're still you, Westlake. Still the same asshole who dodged his protective detail and almost got buried in the Pine Barrens."

Westlake made a sound that might have been a chuckle. "Sometimes, I wonder. I think maybe I might actually be dead. This is all just... the last few neurons firing. Me trying to make sense of the bullet in my head." He tapped the side of his head for emphasis. "Wouldn't that be something?"

"That is possibly the most screwed up thing I've heard today, and that's saying something." Ramirez tried to laugh, but couldn't find the energy. She glanced at him. "Ptolemy told you about Riggs?"

"Yeah."

"Coop's dead too. They..." She trailed off, unable to complete the thought. She felt suddenly sick and put her hand to her mouth. She turned away, fighting for control. "They ate him," she said finally.

Westlake grunted. "I didn't like him, but he didn't deserve that." He hesitated. "He was right, though. You can't trust me anymore. Not really."

"The fact you said that means I can."

Westlake looked at her. "You know that doesn't make any sense, right?"

Ramirez took a deep breath and met his gaze squarely. "I'm not shooting you today. Maybe not tomorrow either. Because I still need you, Westlake. For one more job. Just one."

Westlake's eyes narrowed. "You want me to go into the hold, don't you?"

"I want you to go into the hold." She hesitated, and then touched his arm. It felt like touching a lump of something pulled out of a meat locker. "We need those supplies. We need to get everyone off this boat alive. We need to get everyone home. After that..." She trailed off, unwilling to finish the thought.

"After that," Westlake said simply.

CHAPTER THIRTY-ONE
Volunteers

"You sure about this?" Ramirez asked. Jessop nodded, though he wasn't. But the first rule of command was never let them see you sweat. Not easy to do in the Everglades.

He plucked at his shirt front. "I'm still wearing a uniform, but I'm not captain. This isn't a dictatorship, though lord knows there are times it would have been easier if it was. They need to have some say in things." He paused. "Are you absolutely certain your folks will welcome us?" There was a desperate edge to his voice that he wished wasn't there, but she took no notice.

"They will. That's part of why we've been flying up and down the east coast. We've been trying to find other survivors and get them to safety. If there is such a thing these days." She touched his arm. "We just have to get through this in one piece."

"Easier said than done," Grillo said. She stood a polite distance away, one hand resting on her sidearm. She hiked a thumb over her shoulder. "Everyone's here." Jessop followed her gaze and saw the crowd gathering under the main awning, talking amongst themselves.

Phipps, standing nearby, coughed into his fist. "We need to be quick. No one's watching the hatches at the minute."

Jessop nodded. He raised his hands for quiet. "We need volunteers," he said, when everyone had fallen silent. Fifteen sets of eyes fixed on him. The only two people missing from the ship's survivors were Ogilvy and Hawser. Hawser wasn't going; he was their only doctor. Currently, he was sitting with Ogilvy, trying to keep him calm. The storm was making the other man's issues worse. Or maybe it was just a coincidence. Either way, Ogilvy had slipped out of his cabin twice since the attack. Never for very long. But sooner or later, he'd do something stupid.

Jessop pushed the thought aside. He was going to have to handle it one way or another… but afterwards. Maybe if they got Ogilvy away from the ship, he might snap back to reality. At the very least, it'd keep him from accidentally feeding them all to the dead. "We need to go into the hold – to the galley – and get as many supplies as we can. A small group. Six or seven, no more than that."

"How many you got so far?" Shamekia asked. She was often the spokesperson for the group when it came to these matters. She'd been with them since before the ships had left dock. She'd even led teams to the other ships to check for survivors when things started going bad. Jessop glanced at Sayers and her people.

"Three," she said. "Me, Calavera… and Westlake." She indicated the dead man, and that caused some eyebrows to go up. Jessop had expected more curiosity about Westlake from the others, but people just seemed to accept the dead man at his word. Then, they'd seen every other kind of zombie... why not one that could talk?

"Why are we trying this now?" another person spoke up – a heavyset, former dockworker named Carballo. "What's going on? Who were those folks earlier?" Heads nodded at this. Jessop winced. He'd been trying to figure out how best to share the news that a clan of cannibals was intending to take the ship, but hadn't come up with a way of softening the news.

He took a deep breath. "Hostiles," he said. Maybe simplest was best. "They want to take the boat. I'm inclined to let them..." He paused and gestured for silence as everyone spoke at once. "I'm inclined to let them," he repeated. "The *Dixie Jewel* was never meant to be a permanent place for us. It was always temporary. And now we need to leave."

"Them bastards coming back, ain't they?" Willy asked. He spat tobacco into a cup. Jessop wasn't entirely certain where Willy was getting the chewing tobacco. They'd been on the boat for a year and he hadn't yet run out.

"Most likely. And in force."

"What does that mean?" Deborah asked. She was sitting by two children, both of them too young to really remember what the world had been like before the apocalypse. The sight of them, as always, put a knife in Jessop's heart. He'd been married, before the end. He and his husband had wanted to adopt. There'd been so many children in the world without parents. He tried not to think about them these days. He tried not to think about Joe either. They'd spoken once on the radio, after things had started to fall apart. But Joe, like so many others, hadn't made it out of Fort Lauderdale.

Ramirez spoke up. "It means they've got the numbers and the willingness to take this place. I've seen it myself."

Jessop nodded, and continued before anyone else could add their two cents. "But our new friends here have a solution for us. A place inland in the Adirondacks. They've even got a plane that can take us there." Voices rose with questions, but he gestured for them to wait. "Not all at once, and not right now. Not with the hurricane out there. So, here's the deal… we send a group down to acquire supplies. Then, when the hurricane is over, we leave before our unfriendly neighbors come knocking."

"We've only got the one decent raft and some patchy ones," someone said.

"There are a number of inflatable rafts in with the supplies. Get some rope, tie them to the motorized raft, and we convoy to the airstrip." Jessop gave his most confident smile. "It won't be easy, but it'll work."

"If they get the stuff out," Shamekia said. Jessop nodded.

"That's why I'm asking for volunteers. Many hands make for quick work."

After a moment, Willy stood. "Guess I'll go. I'm almost out of chaw, and the rest of my supply is down there." He spat in his cup for emphasis.

Shamekia nodded. "I'll go too." She looked around, as if waiting for someone to argue. No one did, though. Shamekia and Willy were their most competent scroungers and had been since the beginning. It only made sense that they'd both go.

Jessop took a deep breath. "Anyone else?"

Grillo put up her hand. "We should probably have an

officer riding herd on things. That's me." She smiled at the look on his face. "Besides, I've been bothering you to do this for months. Can't very well back out, can I?"

"You don't have to," Jessop began, but she cut him off with a shake of her head.

"Got to be me. Phipps wouldn't last two minutes – no offense, Phipps," she said, glancing at the man.

"None taken," Phipps said, and almost sounded like he meant it. "I'd prefer to oversee the evacuation preparations anyway. We'll need to gather what we need and get it ready to move as soon as possible."

Jessop sighed and nodded. He trusted Grillo; she'd been a good officer, if a bit aggravating. But she'd always had his back when it came down to it. There was no one else he'd trust more to see the job done. "We could use one more warm body," he said. He looked around. "Anyone?" They could do it with six. But seven was better. His mother had always maintained that seven was a lucky number. Then, she'd also regularly blown her paycheck at the craps table, so maybe she'd been mistaken.

For long moments, there was no reply. He looked at the small band of survivors and felt a flicker of guilt that he was even asking this of them. They'd been through so much, and there was still the worst to come if Ramirez was right – and there was no reason to think she wasn't. If they were lucky, the cannibals would wait until after the hurricane to mount an attack. By then, they might already be gone. But if they came with the storm, things would get very complicated, very quickly.

A dozen people weren't enough to cover the upper deck.

Even with the help of Ramirez and the others, they'd be at a disadvantage when it came to numbers. Especially since any gunshots would bring the dead out of the swamp. The waters below would become a seething cauldron of monsters, and there was no telling what would happen if a brute or a runner took it into its head to climb the hull. Or worse, something resulted in the hatches opening. He pushed the thought aside. They'd cross that bridge when they came to it.

Jessop was about to ask again when he heard Dr Hawser clear his throat. Surprised, Jessop turned to see Ogilvy and Hawser at the hatch that led to the cabins. "I'll go," Ogilvy said too loudly.

Jessop frowned. "What?"

"I'll go, I said," Ogilvy repeated. Hawser stood beside him, a resigned look on his face. "It's my responsibility. I'll go." He looked shaky, and sounded like he'd just woken up from a long sleep. "They want me down there. If you're going, I should go." He blinked, taking in the new faces in what might have been surprise, until he got to Calavera. The big man gave him what might have been an encouraging nod. Ogilvy swallowed and turned his attention to Jessop. "I have to go, Daniel. I have to."

Jessop stared at him, uncertain how to respond. He looked at Grillo, who shook her head. But Calavera stepped forward and said, "I will watch out for him." Jessop looked at the big man and came to a decision.

"Fine," he said. He looked at Ogilvy. "Glad to have you along, captain."

Ogilvy nodded jerkily and then turned away to mutter something to Hawser. Probably in need of a drink, Jessop thought, somewhat uncharitably. He sighed. "All right. I guess that's it. I need everyone else on hurricane duty... we need to strap down anything that can be strapped and move anything that can be moved inside. I want the gardens harvested of anything still left, and then covered. I want water jugs set out and zip tied to the rails."

He paused and pointed at Carballo and two others – a lean, spare man named Oscar, who dressed all in black, with rhinestones on his button up shirt, wore a set of snakeskin cowboy boots and had a gold-plated pistol he was inordinately fond of; the second was a short woman named Patricia who wore military fatigues and had a battered prosthetic hand in place of her own flesh and blood one, which she'd lost to a shark. "You three are on patrol. I want you to keep an eye on the swamp and an ear on the internal hatches. You hear or see anything untoward, you come and get me."

"And untoward means...?" Oscar drawled.

"Bad," Patricia supplied. She detached the white plastic hand from her forearm and replaced it with something that resembled a cross between a bayonet and a zip gun. Shamekia had designed the strange weapon for her, and Jessop had seen the short woman put it to good use more than once.

"Got it," Oscar said. He drew his pistol and gave it a theatrical twirl. Jessop recalled he'd been a singer or something before the apocalypse. It explained his outfit, if nothing else.

"Remember, save your ammo for when you really need it," Jessop said. He left them to it and turned to find Ramirez watching him.

"Ogilvy... he was the captain, wasn't he?" she asked.

"Is," he corrected. "He is the captain."

"But he's not in charge, is he? Doesn't that make you captain?"

"Not until he's formally removed from command," Jessop said. He'd given the answer so many times it came instinctively. Ramirez nodded.

"And you haven't done that… why?"

Jessop paused. "He saved us. All of us. Ogilvy figured out that the ships were the safest place for us and got everyone together and got us all out to sea in one piece. We had to fight like hell, but we managed it. We were safe…" He took a deep breath. "Then we weren't. People died. A lot of people. He blames himself. It wasn't his fault, but I think… it broke him. He wanted to die, but couldn't. Not as long as he's captain. He's got his duty, his responsibility."

"And if you took that away…" Ramirez said, nodding.

Jessop smiled sourly. "Then he'd have thrown himself over the side months ago. As it is, we can barely keep him from going down and apologizing in person to the dead. But if your big friend Calavera thinks he can keep an eye on him, it might just help snap him out of it." He hesitated. "Why did he offer to do that, by the way?"

Ramirez shrugged. "Who knows? Calavera is… weird."

"Weirder than the talking zombie?"

Ramirez laughed. "A bit, yes. Westlake's fairly normal other than being dead. But Calavera is Calavera, and always has been as far as I know." She touched his arm. "But there's no one I'd trust more to watch out for your captain. If Calavera says he'll keep him safe, he will. No ifs, ands or buts."

"I hope you're right," Jessop said. He looked out over the rail. The sky had gone black, and the rain punched against the deck with enough force to make him wince. The wind was picking up as well. Another hour or two, maybe less. He looked back at Ramirez.

"I hope you're right about all of it."

CHAPTER THIRTY-TWO
Blasphemy

Wilbur sat slumped in the airboat, anger simmering on a low heat. They'd made it out with almost everyone, save Roy and Sandy. Roy was no big loss, but Sandy'd had some grit. There were a few flesh wounds to go around, and Dale had been bit by a walker, but otherwise he'd managed to get everyone out. He counted that as a win.

He'd figured Ramirez for a tough nut on first sight, but she'd caught him by surprise nonetheless. He grunted and lifted his shirt, studying the puckered bullet wound. It was more of a crease really, and the bleeding had largely stopped. That didn't mean it didn't hurt. He wasn't sure who'd shot him; hadn't even noticed the injury until he'd joined up with the others.

"Bad?" Ava asked. She leaned toward him. She was a pretty woman, all lean firmness. But her eyes were gleaming like those of a cat and she licked her lips as she studied the bloodstain on his shirt. Wilbur dropped his shirt and fixed his cousin with a warning look.

"I've had worse."

Ava sat back and raised her hands in a gesture of surrender. Wilbur glared at her for a moment longer, just to emphasize his annoyance. He didn't care for the look in her eyes, or the tone of her voice. Like they were equals, rather than him being in charge. Once, his place in the familial pecking order would have been unquestioned but of late some of the others were starting to think they could do a better job seeing to the family's affairs. Ava was one. Her brother Elmer another.

When he'd been young, he'd thought it a great pleasure to have so many cousins around. Kinsfolk were a blessing, as his momma said. Only of late, he'd started to see it as a curse. Too many mouths to feed, too many idiots to ride herd on. Oh, they'd made a strong start when the world had gone topsy-turvy; having a veritable army in place had helped thin the numbers of the dead before they got too large. But then food had gotten scarce, and momma had decreed that no one was to eat the dead if they could help it, on account of the changes some of the family had undergone.

Wilbur had dealt with most of the changed himself. Uncle Gideon, all swollen up with mutant muscle and leaking pus, his mind lost to pain; Aunt Jessie, whose body had dried up like a prune, and who had taken a bite out of her own brother before they'd brought her down; Abe, Beaumont, and Sarah... all convulsing and moaning like animals as the tainted meat made them something worse than dead.

But the truth was, they were all changed to one degree or another. The eyes were the least of it. Most of the younger cousins had near-constant rashes and digestive issues; the older ones went vague in the head and complained about being hungry, even with full bellies.

The kids were the worst; they weren't quite human anymore. Dickie and her peers were basically feral, willing to strip meat from bone without much regard for where it came from. When they finally took over, there wouldn't be a family anymore – a pack maybe. But not a family. Wilbur wasn't sure how he felt about that. Maybe it was time.

Maybe…

"Smoke," Ava said, sitting up.

Wilbur blinked and straightened. "Oh, goddammit. What now?"

"Something's on fire," Ava said helpfully.

Wilbur ignored her. It wouldn't have been the first time Elmer or one of the other idiots had spilled some propane in the wrong place and flicked a cigarette butt into it. If it weren't for Keziah and Wilbur himself, he was fairly certain the others would have burnt themselves out of house and home long ago.

"The dock," Ava said, as the jetty came into sight. The length of wooden planks that ran through the sawgrass was on fire, as were most of the other airboats. Wilbur lurched to his feet, cursing. There was nothing to be done that the rain wasn't already doing. It was more that it had happened in the first place. It wasn't just carelessness. This was something else.

"Keep going," Wilbur said. "Take us around back."

They nosed through the grass and saw that the house was lit up like Christmas. Not that they celebrated Christmas anymore. Momma didn't approve of pagan holidays, or so she claimed. Everyone was out in the rain, and there was a pile of dead walkers near the back of the house. Elmer and the others were standing around near a dead gator that had been strung up by its tail and back legs from a skinning frame. They were talking and laughing like they'd done something to be proud of.

Ava whistled. "That's a big one. Think he's the cause of all this?"

"In my experience, gators are not known to set fire to things," Wilbur said. As soon as they reached the edge of the back dock he climbed out. Elmer greeted him loudly.

"Conquering hero returns," he called out. "You missed some fun, cousin!"

"So I see," Wilbur said. He glanced down at Ava. "Go take the boat around, check the perimeter," he said. "Make sure whoever hit us ain't still out there."

"It was them from the plane," Elmer said. "They came to get their people back."

"Wonderful," Wilbur grunted. "I knew we should have killed them when we had the chance. How'd they get away?"

"Momma..." Elmer began. Wilbur looked at him.

"She ain't your momma, boy. You her nephew. Don't put on airs."

Elmer grimaced. "They took her. Hostage, I mean. Dragged her halfway down the damn jetty before we caught up to them..."

"Took her?" Wilbur growled. "What do you mean 'took her'?"

"He means they used me to get away," Keziah said, as she wheeled herself toward them. "They tossed me in the swamp when Elmer showed up. That gator would have had me, if he hadn't killed it." She indicated the alligator with a flick of her fingers. Elmer swelled, looking pleased with himself.

"And how did they get hold of you in the first place, momma?" Wilbur asked softly. Keziah glanced at Elmer, who wasn't looking so pleased now.

"Your cousin convinced me we were in sore need of some recreation."

Elmer hesitated. "We were celebrating you taking that ship." He peered at Wilbur. "You did take it, didn't you?" There was an insinuation in his words that Wilbur didn't like. A veiled challenge. The eyes of his cousins glinted. Watching. Taking stock. Momma was wrong. They weren't a family anymore.

"You had a party and… what? They snuck up on you?" Wilbur shook his head. "You had a damn party while we was out getting shot to bits." He looked at his hands – then lashed out, catching Elmer by the throat. He hefted Elmer by his thick neck.

Elmer pawed at his wrist, trying to break his cousin's grip. Elmer was almost as big as Wilbur, but it was mostly fat. He was lazy; preferred taking his kills from a distance. "I ought to squeeze your fat head until your eyeballs pop, boy," Wilbur said.

"*Wilbur!*" Keziah snapped. "You put him down right now, you hear me? We start turning on each other, it's over and we might as well feed ourselves to God."

Wilbur let Elmer fall to the ground with a heavy thump. "Ain't no god, momma. Just a damn big turtle and you know it." Kezia glared up at him, and if looks could kill Wilbur knew he'd have been stiff and cold on the floor.

"Blasphemy," she said softly.

Wilbur didn't bother to reply. He looked down at Elmer. "They all gone then? Every goddamn one of 'em?"

Elmer nodded, rubbing his throat. "Never seen nothing like it," he wheezed. "That fella must have had six bullets in him, and some arrows. He didn't even twitch. Like he didn't feel a damn thing we was throwing at him." He gave Wilbur a sidelong glance. "Only person I ever seen do that is you."

Wilbur grunted and ran his hands through his hair. Some of it came away in his hands, a common occurrence these days. He didn't mind. He knew he was changing the way Gideon and the others had, slowly but surely. But he was sure he wasn't turning into some groaning hulk. Not that he knew what he was becoming, only it wasn't like anything they'd seen.

He could feel whatever it was inside him churning around, like a gator rooting in the mud at the water's bottom. Sometimes, when he looked at himself in the mirror, he fancied he saw something like scales growing beneath his peeling skin. His mother saw it as well, he knew, though he'd never asked her what she thought about it. Whatever he was turning into, it'd be an improvement over his current circumstances. At the very least, he might not itch so bad anymore. He looked at Elmer. "How'd they find us?"

Elmer frowned. "Someone must have showed them."

Wilbur frowned. An unpleasant thought occurred to him. "Have we heard from Cole and them others yet?" he asked. Elmer shook his head.

"Nope."

Wilbur was about to ask whether they'd bothered to send anyone to check on Cole when he heard Ava call out from the direction of the bulwark. He waved her over, tossing a final glare at Elmer as he did so.

"We found something," Ava said, as she reached the walkway. "Looks like Brady. He was out there just past the bulwarks. Looked like something got at him."

"Gators?" Wilbur asked. Brady wouldn't have been the first to be caught out past the perimeter by one of the big reptiles. The family had learned the hard way that they needed to keep the creatures out early on. That had been part of the reason they'd set up the bulwarks.

Ava shook her head and grimaced. "Not unless they're getting awful picky about which bits they chew on. A walker, maybe. There were a few of them around."

Keziah hunched forward in her chair. "No walker would ever have got the best of Brady. Nor them others. You taught them too well for that. It was that Federal and her friends; bank on it." She knotted her fingers together and stared toward the tree line.

Wilbur waved the others away. He waited for them to absent themselves before he said, "You should have let me kill her."

Keziah looked up at him, her expression unreadable. Then, "You're right, son. I should have. But I did not. Oh, I had my reasons. I wanted to do this clean. Without risk to us." She paused and looked back up at the house. "This house has been in our family for damn near a century, you know that?"

"You might have mentioned it a time or two."

She swatted him lightly on the arm. "Don't sass me. A century is a drop in a bucket. We only been around a minute, as the swamp judges things." She frowned. "Y'all are going to tear yourselves apart when I'm gone. I know that. All we're doing is buying time." She looked up at him. "We need that ship. We need them supplies. We need that good meat. You understand, boy? Not just because we need to eat, but because they need to see you win."

"What do you mean?"

She laughed softly. "You going to be in charge when I'm gone. Elmer and all the others, they're going to look to you – or try to kill you. But most of them, they'll be in need of a strong leader. Someone who can keep them safe and well fed."

Wilbur ran his hand through his wet hair once more. His mother tilted her head up, letting it wash over her. The rain had never bothered them much. It was part of life in the swamp. "That's why you came up with this dumb idea, ain't it?" he asked, after a moment. "You made a big deal out of it for my benefit? That what you're telling me?"

Keziah clutched his hand. "It was a gift from God."

"God should have thought to give us a way to get on that damn boat," Wilbur said, pulling his hand free of her grip. He went to the edge of the walkway and looked down at the remaining walkers fumbling in the water. Then he looked up, at the place where they hung the sacrifices. A thought occurred to him. "Huh."

"What are you thinking, boy?"

"That maybe you're right," he said. He turned back to his mother and smiled, showing his teeth. "Maybe God can help us after all."

CHAPTER THIRTY-THREE
Lower Decks

The first hatch was clear when they started the descent. There were scorch marks and signs of gunfire on the internal bulkheads, and bodies lying in contorted heaps where they'd fallen. Some looked as if scavenging animals had been at them; either walkers or rats, Westlake couldn't say which. He kept his hand on the pistol he'd brought back from the Watkins' place. The thought of being eaten alive – undead – by rats wasn't a pleasant one.

He led the way down the corridor, Grillo just behind him. "I haven't been much past this point in over a year," she said softly, as the beam of her flashlight skittered across the walls and floor. "For the first few weeks we tried to keep these passages clear. Jessop thought we might be able to take the ship back deck by deck."

"Guess that didn't work out," Westlake said, not looking at her.

She gave a terse chuckle. "Not so as you'd notice. Too

many of them, not enough ammunition. After a while, no one wanted to chance it anymore. We just sort of gave up on the idea." She looked around, eyes narrowed. "Then they went quiet, and we started pretending they weren't there at all."

Westlake grunted and glanced at the others. Ogilvy was quiet. He'd said little since they'd begun the descent. Westlake had him pegged as an alcoholic, probably in the early stages of liver failure, given the pasty hue of his skin. He started and flinched at every faint clink or rustle, but said nothing. He carried nothing other than a flashlight and a collection of flares taken from the survivors' dwindling stash.

The other survivors were made of sterner stuff. Shamekia and Willy were tough in the way of a lot of survivors; hardened by a hard life, even before the apocalypse. Grillo was harder to read, but he had her pegged as a by-the-book type.

He stopped. The corridor bifurcated ahead. One way led around the curve of the hull, the other took an internal route. He glanced at Grillo. "Which way?" Grillo indicated the internal route.

"That's the quickest way."

"And the other one?" Sayers asked from behind them.

"The safest, depending."

"On what?" Calavera asked.

Shamekia answered for Grillo. "If they managed to break through into the access passages. Me, I'd rather not chance it. It's a tight space to be dealing with a horde of walkers – or worse." She paused. "Every other time, they were all over us by now. I wonder where they are."

Westlake had no answer for her. He was wondering the same thing. "Speaking of which, how did you... you know, wind up like this?" Shamekia asked in a low voice. Westlake looked at her.

"Like what?"

"You know what she means," Sayers said in an annoyed tone. Calavera chuckled.

"I'd like to know that myself," Willy asked.

Westlake didn't reply. He could hear something shuffling up ahead. The sound was too arhythmic for a walker. It was... jittery. Erratic. He waved the others to silence and advanced alone to peer around the corner. A single zombie stood shivering in the center of the corridor. It had been a woman once. Its clothing was stiff with filth and its body was shriveled, shrunken. Dried out like leather.

It was looking at nothing in particular. It simply stood there, twitching. Then, without warning, its head snapped around, empty gaze fixed on him. Its jaw sagged, and a thin whistle of warning escaped it.

Westlake shot it. It collapsed in a quivering heap. He paused, listening. No groans. No cries. No pounding feet. Nothing. Just... silence. He glanced back at the others. "Something isn't right. We should hear something."

"They've been quiet a long time," Grillo said. "Maybe they ate each other."

"Maybe," Westlake said, but something told him it wasn't that simple. He looked down at the body, noting the odd injuries that marked its limbs. Bite marks, he thought. From other zombies, or something else. He felt a faint flicker of worry, but swiftly pushed it aside.

"Sally Heffer," Ogilvy said suddenly.

Westlake and the others looked at him. "Her name was Sally

Heffer. She was a– a CPA, I think. From Miami. Two kids, both grown. At college. Her husband turned in the first few days. She was forced to kill him with a meat tenderizer. She'd been preparing steaks for their anniversary dinner." Ogilvy knelt beside the dead woman. "She was a good person."

"Do you know all their names, then?" Sayers asked.

Ogilvy nodded without looking at her. "I know the names of everyone on my ship. Living and dead alike." He stood. "Last time I saw her, she was down in the hold. She's traveled far since then."

"They walk until they can't anymore, or something stops them," Westlake said.

"So what stopped her?" Willy asked. He looked around. "Something must have."

"Doesn't matter," Grillo said. "Let's go." They kept moving, along narrow passages and then down internal stairways that expanded into wide landings, until they reached the central part of the ship. The interior of the vessel was dark and stank of rotting meat and gasoline. The light from their torches danced across shuttered shopfronts and restaurants. It reminded Westlake of the inside of a mall.

There were bodies everywhere, ruined and crushed and rotting. A carpet of filth covered the deck; rotten meat, congealed blood and ash mingling in a glutinous shroud. Every step they took crunched or crackled unpleasantly. But no zombies.

"How many people were on this ship, before... all of this?" Calavera murmured, as he stared at the pitiful remains of a gnawed body hanging from a web of electrical cables and snapped wires. It had been stripped to the bone in places.

"Two hundred, or near abouts," Willy muttered. "Maybe a hundred after we broke away from the other boats. Got less real quick after that."

"What happened?" Calavera asked.

Sayers snorted. "You know what happened. It's what always happens. Someone turns, they turn somebody else, until pretty soon there's zombies everywhere and you're out of bullets. It's the new way of the world." Bone crunched under her boot, but she didn't pause. "How far to the galley?"

"We need to keep going down." Grillo paused, and played her light over the far wall, illuminating a bank of elevators. "There's our ticket."

"No power in the ship," Westlake said. He could hear something now, a faint skittering sort of sound. Rats, he thought. Rats and ships often went together. Something about the thought bothered him.

"We thought of that, before it all went wrong," Shamekia said. "Took out the car on one of them and put in ladders. Took us forever, but it means we can get below fairly quickly without drawing too much attention."

Westlake turned, trying to follow the sound. It raced about the edges of his hearing, refusing to resolve itself into one thing or another. "And how about coming up?"

"We'll have to take the stairs," Grillo said. She looked around. "Let's hurry. I don't like being out in the open like this." She took a step and something shrieked and scurried away from her.

Grillo played her light across the floor and Westlake heard her sudden intake of breath. Something was moving across the floor. Something hairy. The skittering sound was suddenly loud now. "Oh Jesus…" Grillo began softly.

It leapt. Then another and another. They sprang from all sides and hit Grillo like hairy bullets. Ogilvy cried out and tried to go to her aid, but Calavera held him back. Her light fell to the ground and spun wildly, illuminating her final moments in strobing flashes. She was dragged to the ground by the horde of furry bodies, her final cry strangled in its inception.

Westlake shoved Shamekia toward the elevators. "Go! Now!" The others needed no further encouragement. Rats poured across the deck in their hundreds, most of them converging on the writhing mass that had been Grillo. They were foul things; bloated on dead flesh, rotting on the bone, and driven mad by a hunger that could never be sated. Westlake paused only to snatch up the dead woman's light and then joined the others.

Shamekia and Willy were trying to lever the elevator doors open with a pair of pry bars, but it was resisting. A year of neglect had obviously rendered the mechanisms faulty. Calavera shoved them aside none too gently and wrenched the doors partially open in a show of strength. Unseen gears squealed, matching the chittering hordes of rats for volume. Calavera grunted and braced himself, giving it another go. "Help me," he growled. Willy thrust his pry bar into the gap.

In the meantime, the rats were advancing. Grillo had ceased moving, and while some of the creatures were preoccupied feasting on her, the rest had turned their attentions to Westlake and the others. They came in a wave. Westlake fired, plucking off a handful. The ones he shot were swiftly devoured by their kin, but it did little to stem the tide. Shamekia and Sayers joined him. Sayers shish-kebabbed two of the rats with an arrow, and Shamekia killed another with a crossbow bolt. But the rats swirled around them, cutting them off from the elevators.

A sudden flare of light lit up the area. Westlake turned and saw Ogilvy holding a sputtering flare aloft. He sidled away from the elevator, and the rats retreated before him. They shied back from the flare's radiance as if it stung their eyes. Ogilvy flung the flare toward the largest concentration of vermin, scattering them, if only momentarily. The flare sputtered and flames snarled up as the sparks caught a puddle of something moderately flammable. He waved Westlake and the others back as he lit another flare. The first had begun to spread, creeping across sodden wreckage and crawling up the walls.

Ogilvy sent his second one spinning toward where the rats were gathering, sending them scuttling back into the dark. "Get those doors open," Ogilvy shouted. "The light will keep them back."

He was right. The rats had gotten used to the dark, and they found the light blinding. But they were too hungry to flee far. As soon as the flares died, they massed and attacked again. Ogilvy sent another flare pinwheeling through the air, and rats scattered, chittering in frustration and anger.

Westlake joined Willy and Calavera in getting the doors open. It took several moments, during which Ogilvy was forced to toss several more flares. And the rats crept ever closer as they grew used to the glare. Or maybe they were simply trying to escape the fire. It was consuming the tattered bodies, slowly but surely. Everything was wet, making its progress slow, but it wasn't going out.

Then, finally, the elevator doors shrieked open, and stayed that way, thanks to Calavera planting himself between them so that everyone could squeeze through. There was a platform beyond, made from rebar and plywood.

Westlake was the last through, save for Ogilvy and Calavera. The captain hesitated, a lit flare in one hand, and the rats closed in. Westlake saw what he intended. Calavera did as well. They both reacted at the same time, reaching out to grab the man by his arms and drag him back through the aperture. Westlake wrestled the lit flare from Ogilvy's hand and chucked it at the pursuing rats, even as Calavera allowed the elevator doors to slam shut.

"Uh, Westlake?" Shamekia said hesitantly. She pointed at his leg, and he looked down. A rat clung to his calf, gnawing away enthusiastically. Westlake tore it loose and studied it. It looked diseased. Something oily wept from its pores, matting its fur. Its eyes were like balls of yellow fungus flowering from its eye sockets. It squirmed in his grip and snapped at him until he broke its neck and dropped the body to the platform.

"Guess that explains where the zombies went," Sayers said, nudging the rat with her foot. "Rats will eat damn near anything, even walking corpses." She looked at Westlake. "No offense."

"None taken," Westlake said. He tried to imagine it, the horde prowling about in the dark, being consumed one by one. Had they understood what was happening? Had they realized that they'd become the prey? Probably not. At least he hoped not.

He looked around. As Shamekia had said, the elevator car

had been removed entirely, leaving the cramped shaft empty save for the platform they were on, and a set of steel industrial ladders that had been spot-welded to the shaft frame. "Clever," he murmured.

"We thought so," Willy said. He touched the side of the shaft and sniffed his fingers. "Fuel. Not from a leak, though."

"Seepage," Shamekia said. "Fumes from below mixing with damp and condensation." She shook her head. "This whole ship is a fire waiting to happen."

"She's dead," Ogilvy said, staring at the doors. He sounded confused. The others fell silent and looked at him.

"Bad way to go," Willy said, breaking the silence. "Can't say we got along, her and me, but I never wished that sort of end on her." He glanced at Shamekia, but she said nothing. Westlake recognized the look on her face. The thousand-yard stare of the determined survivor, focused on the job at hand, rather than what had just happened.

"The galley is about twenty minutes down from here, depending on how fast we climb and whether there's anything waiting for us," she said, after a moment.

Before anyone could reply, the elevator doors creaked; buckled. As if a great weight were pressing against them. Westlake frowned. How many rats were out there? Hundreds from the sound of it.

He thumped his fist against the metal of the doors. Once, twice. A third time. The sound echoed through the shaft. Boom. Boom. Boom. And the rats responded. A light went on in his head. Maybe his brain wasn't quite kaput yet.

"What are you doing?" Calavera asked, as Westlake continued to knock on the elevator doors as he shuffled toward the far edge of the platform. The fumbling on the other side grew more agitated.

"They follow noise, just like the dead," Westlake said. "We make enough noise, we can draw them away from where we need to be." He looked back at the doors, and then up. Another set of ladders led up toward the top of the shaft. "You get to the supplies. I'll keep the rats busy."

"I'll go with you," Ogilvy began, but Calavera caught him by the arm.

"No. You will go with us and leave him to it."

Ogilvy frowned, but didn't argue. Westlake started up the ladder. The metal trembled in his grip and he wondered if it was the hurricane causing it. "And if they catch up to you?" Shamekia asked, causing him to pause. He looked down.

"Well then, you should hope I give them indigestion."

CHAPTER THIRTY-FOUR
Attack

Imogene stood beneath a lean-to and watched the hurricane approach. She'd always thought of hurricanes as rain and wind, but it was so much more than that. A black wall of water, falling down and rising up simultaneously as it advanced across the horizon. Beautiful, in an awful sort of way.

She scraped one of her knives across a whetstone as she watched the storm. During her time as a chef, she'd bought her own knives and the whetstone, preferring the latter to an industrial sharpener. The knives had saved her life more than once since it had all gone sour. Zombies were no different to any other slab of meat, or so she told herself.

She thought about Atlantic City. About the sewers and the underground parking lots that had been her home for months. This was better. At least there was fresh air out here. Another thing she told herself. She glanced back at Kahwihta. The other woman sat with her back against the wall, Attila sleeping beside her despite the storm.

Imogene hadn't been seeing anyone when the world ended.

She hadn't had the time, or the interest. Work occupied most of her hours, and when she wasn't working, she was out with coworkers, drinking and making a nuisance of herself, just like a professional chef. The world had spun from day to night to day with no real distinction, save the severity of her hangover. She paused. She hadn't had a hangover in over a year. She almost missed them.

She studied Kahwihta's face, the way she sat, and felt that familiar flutter in her belly. She hadn't even given thought to liking someone – caring about them – until she'd spent time with Kahwihta in the aftermath of events in Atlantic City. She still wasn't sure what she was feeling, but she desperately wanted time to find out.

Kahwihta, noticing her attention, looked at her and Imogene hastily looked away. She tried to distract herself by thinking of other things, like the group that had gone below. It had been almost an hour since the others had made their descent. They'd heard no gunfire, no screams. Maybe that meant everything was fine. Maybe they were all dead.

There was no way to tell which it was without someone else going down after them, and Jessop had nixed that idea right off the bat. Imogene didn't think they were dead, however. They'd all survived worse, except Westlake, and even he was still kicking.

She flinched as a broken branch thudded against the rail and fell away. The wind was picking up, and there was a lot of debris in the air. Some of it was even still moving. A legless zombie had been flung onto the deck, where it had been swiftly dispatched. But there was a chance it wouldn't be the only one.

She peered toward the bow of the ship, where Jessop and Ramirez were huddled in conversation, likely going over plans for the evacuation. She wondered if they'd factored flying zombies into their strategies. Knowing Ramirez, probably. There was a woman with a plan for everything, at least as far as Imogene could tell.

The wind rose, and a faint tremor ran through the hull of the ship. They'd fastened down everything that could be fastened, but they'd already lost a lean-to. The way the rest twitched in the wind hinted that they might not last either. Soon, they'd have to seek shelter inside. Most of the ship survivors were already in the dining hall. Only a few were braving the weather on guard duty.

"Do you think they'll really try something now?" she asked, glancing back at Kahwihta. "They'd have to be crazy, right?"

"They eat people," Kahwihta said. She looked better than she had earlier. The painkillers had clearly taken some of the edge off.

"Point taken," Imogene said, as she turned back to the storm. She tried not to think about Riggs or Coop. Both dead, and not in pleasant ways. She hadn't liked either man much – Coop had been an asshole and Riggs was just… weird – but that didn't mean she'd wanted them dead. And frankly, someone like Coop would come in handy right about now.

Her attention was caught by movement below. Walkers, wading unsteadily through the shallows. Floaters bobbing in tangled reefs of flesh. And the alligators prowling through it all, occasionally dragging down one of the walkers. What would happen when the humans were gone? Would the walkers leave as well? What would the alligators eat then?

Even as the thought occurred to her, the alligators suddenly thrashed about and vanished beneath the surface of the water as one. Nor were they the only ones making a precipitous departure. The walkers at the edges of the trees were stumbling away from the ship. But why? The only reason she could think of was that they'd detected easier prey.

She frowned and turned to ask Kahwihta about it, but paused as she spotted Ptolemy and Gable approaching, both of them wrapped up in hooded raincoats and carrying rifles. "Hey Gable," she called out. "Think the plane will be OK?"

Gable made an obscene gesture in reply. Imogene laughed. The truth was she wasn't much worried about it either way. One place was as bad as any other, or so it seemed to her. Maybe the apocalypse was making her philosophical. She put away her whetstone and joined them. "So, what are our chances, really?"

Gable grunted and leaned against the rail. "If the plane's in one piece when we get there. If the hurricane don't chuck her into the swamp like it did this ship." She looked at Imogene. "Lots of ifs. Not a lot of answers."

"Answers are rarely as satisfactory as we hope for them to be," Ptolemy said, as he looked down toward the trees, as if trying to detect a sign of movement through the sheeting rain. "Worrying about things one has no control over is a waste of mental energy."

Imogene laughed. "Aren't you the one who believes in aliens?" She hesitated as she caught a snatch of sound beneath the rising wind. Not the moaning of the dead, or the bellow of an alligator. Something else. But before she could focus on it, the wind snatched it away. It had almost sounded like… music?

Ptolemy glanced at her. "I believe that the idea of intelligent life being confined to this world is a flawed one."

"So, yes, then," Imogene said, grinning. As she spoke, she spied something, out in the rain. On instinct, she grabbed Gable and dragged her down as an arrow cut through the curtain of rain and thunked into the wooden paneling of the walls behind them. More arrows followed the first, and more than arrows. Gunfire licked from the trees, forcing them to keep their heads down. It seemed inconceivable – impossible – that anyone with any smarts would be out in this sort of weather, but maybe cannibals thought the weather didn't apply to them.

"Incoming," Ptolemy shouted. "Find cover!" He ducked below the rail. Gable shoved Imogene aside and scrambled up, raising her rifle. Imogene crawled back toward Kahwihta. She could hear shots coming from other parts of the ship, and Jessop and the others shouting. The wind whipped across the deck, tearing loose another lean-to and sending it sailing out over the swamp.

Imogene risked a glance through the railing. She spotted several airboats zipping through the trees. Music rose from one of them, as if someone had strapped a boombox to the front. Incongruous gospel hymns blared out, accompanied by gunfire. She jerked back as an arrow clattered against the railing.

"Are they playing music?" Kahwihta asked. She was flat on the deck, covering Attila's body with her own. The dog was barking, nails scrabbling against the deck as he tried to free himself from her grip. Kahwihta calmed him with a hand on his neck.

Imogene heard a shout and saw Terry running toward them from the bow. He still had the handgun he'd scavenged from his captors, and his eyes were wide. "Are you OK?" he shouted, ducking low as another arrow bounced off the rail and was carried away by the wind. "Ramirez sent me to check on you."

"We're fine," Kahwihta said. "Are Cheryl and the others OK?"

Terry nodded. "They're all hunkered down in the dining room, packed and ready to dip. If it comes to it, we can get everyone out through the emergency exit. But Jessop swears it won't be necessary." He flinched as a tree branch whirled past them and shattered a porthole. "I hope he's right."

Imogene brushed wet leaves from her arm. "I'm guessing these guys are everywhere, huh?" Down below, the wind was ripping across the top of the swamp and the rain was pounding down, obfuscating the horizon in a shroud of gray.

Terry nodded. "They're all around us. Ramirez figures they'll have to pull back when the hurricane hits. We just need to sit tight."

Rifles cracked and Imogene flinched. "Easier said than done. They're trying to pick us off." She sought out Gable and Ptolemy, and saw that they were moving back toward the prow, pausing only to take the occasional shot at their attackers.

"It doesn't make any sense, though," Terry said. "It's not like they can board us. So what's the point?" He paused. "Are they playing... music?"

"Yeah. Maybe they need a soundtrack." There didn't seem to be much sense to it. Then, as Kahwihta had pointed out, they were crazy. But something about it didn't seem right. She'd dealt with more than her fair share of raiders in Atlantic City, and even the most desperate among them would think twice about using a hurricane as cover. It was almost as if they were simply trying to keep the survivors on the ship pinned down. But why?

"They played music back at that house of horror of theirs, too… when they wanted to call that big ass turtle in for supper." He braced himself as the ship swayed slightly. Or at least it felt that way to Imogene. Jessop had insisted that the ship could ride out the hurricane, but she was beginning to doubt that. From down below came a burst of music. The volume was cranked, and the airboat was just… circling the ship.

Imogene looked at Kahwihta. "You don't think…?"

"I think it's time we got you inside," Terry said, making to help Kahwihta stand. Kahwihta shook her head as Attila began to bark loudly.

"Somehow I don't think that's going to be any safer – look!"

Imogene turned and saw the trees closest to the ship bend and snap. Suddenly, she realized why the alligators had vanished, and why the walkers had been moving away from the ship. A massive form burst through the tree line with a thunderous bellow. "Oh Jesus," Terry said in a hushed voice. "I knew it! It's the thing that killed Riggs."

"I think we've figured out what they were waiting on," Imogene said in a hollow voice. She had never seen a snapping turtle up close, but she'd seen them on television. This thing looked like nothing so much as an outsize turtle, swollen to a monstrous size. It was nearly as tall as the ship and as it shoved aside the broken trees, the entire vessel shuddered as if caught in an earthquake. When it saw the ship it paused, as if startled.

Then, with another roar, King Crunch lumbered toward its prey.

CHAPTER THIRTY-FIVE
King Crunch

Wilbur watched King Crunch lurch out of the swamp and barrel toward the ship with a sense of satisfaction. He slapped his knee and glanced back at his mother, sitting just below the pilot's seat of the airboat. "I told you this would work. Didn't I say it?"

"I don't recall saying it wouldn't," Keziah said loudly, fighting to be heard over the storm. "What I said was that you shouldn't!" She pointed at King Crunch. "This is blasphemy, Wilbur – plain and simple."

"You didn't have to come, momma," Wilbur said pointedly.

"You watch your damn mouth," Elmer growled from the pilot's chair. Wilbur fixed him with a yellow-eyed glare, but didn't reply to the provocation. Elmer hadn't learned anything from their last go-round. He was still bucking to be Keziah's favorite, though there wasn't a hope in hell of that. He looked at Keziah.

"Why did you come anyway, momma?"

"To make sure this works," she said flatly. Her wheelchair

was strapped to the sides of the boat, anchoring her in place. Ava crouched beside her with a rifle, making sure Elmer's erratic piloting didn't throw Keziah out of her seat. "It didn't go so well last time. I'm here to make sure you don't screw it up again."

Elmer and Ava snickered at her words, and for a moment, Wilbur considered shooting them both. He was just going to have to do it later, after all. But then where would that leave Keziah, since she'd insisted on coming – despite his objections. Instead, he turned away and tried not to think about how much his teeth had started to hurt. It was like new growth was trying to push out the old, and it ached something fierce.

It had taken him longer than he'd liked to convince Keziah of his plan. He'd known she wouldn't approve, but once she'd reluctantly agreed she'd insisted on overseeing its implementation herself. She kept telling him it was all for him, but he could sense her frustration. He wasn't acting grateful enough for her liking.

The other airboats had stopped at the edge of the tree line, and the others had scattered themselves out in a loose circle around the ship. They'd left barely anyone behind; just the kids, mostly. One or two of the young folks to watch them. Wilbur had wanted as many guns as possible to throw at the ship, and thankfully, Keziah had agreed. They needed to keep the folks there on board, keep them from making a break for it somehow. He didn't want any of them sneaking away to cause trouble later. Besides, King Crunch needed to eat.

The monstrous turtle hit the side of the ship like a falling tree. It wasn't quite tall enough to reach the upper deck, but that didn't bother Wilbur. All he wanted was for King Crunch to tear the guts out of the ship, to humble it and crush it.

He felt no awe at the sight. No religious fervor, no transcendence. He never had. Not really. Only the children really felt it. They were the ones most susceptible to Keziah's dogma. He guessed they were too young to know any better. Wilbur could remember better days, when God had been notional and abstract. Before Keziah had gone away for a stretch and gotten religion. That was when she'd started seeing something holy in the swamp. As if the Everglades was Eden, rather than a suburb of Hell.

She'd chosen to call everyone together then. To bring all the disparate Watkins families in from whatever redneck hollers they'd been lurking in, in South Carolina, Georgia, and Kentucky. To bring together all those petty criminals, meth-dealers, and poachers under one roof, and teach them about Jesus.

Only it hadn't quite worked out that way. Keziah was still too much of a criminal herself. She'd quickly set them up as private security for a bunch of big-time drug dealers from south of the border. And hadn't that been a fine old time?

The people on the ship were panicking now, he figured. Shooting at Crunch or looking for escape. He could hear their cries over the storm and the music. He felt something like pleasure at the sound. Not because he was a sadist, but because they had something he wanted and now they were going to give it up to him. He watched the giant turtle tear into the hull and wanted to laugh. Keziah looked at him. "What's so funny?" she asked.

"Us," he said, picking at his neck. More dead skin came

away beneath his persistent fingers, and he felt hard, scaly flesh beneath. "We trained that damn ugly brute that music – church music – means food. Hear the music, come get the food." He looked down at her. "All this time, that damn thing would have killed whatever we aimed it at, so long as we played the right tune."

Keziah glared at him. "It ain't a thing, it's a god. It's what kept us safe out here. Kept the dead from taking us all."

Wilbur crouched before her. "Not out of the kindness of its heart, momma. It's an animal. It eats the dead same way it eats the living. It's big because it's a mutant. We've all seen them big zombies, the ones all swollen up with muscle; the fast ones, that move like greased lightning... freaks. Just like this thing is a freak." He smiled and pulled a strip of dead skin off his neck and held it up in front of her eyes. "Just like us."

Keziah looked away and Wilbur snorted and turned back to the ship. It had been right in front of them the whole damn time and they'd never noticed. Too busy surviving, perhaps. Or maybe Keziah's willful blindness had affected them all. She thought of it as a god, but it wasn't. It was just another dead thing. Bigger than most, maybe, but no smarter.

"You're saying we could have done this any damn time?" Ava asked after a moment.

"No," Keziah snapped.

"Yep," Wilbur said, glancing at his cousin. "Don't that beat all?" He signaled to Elmer. "Take us around again, but watch out for the big boy. Don't want to accidentally get stepped on, now, do we?"

"So what happens after, cousin? I don't think that thing is

gonna wander off just because we ask it nice," Ava asked. "You got a plan for that?"

Wilbur smiled. "Don't need a plan, do we? Once he's wrecked things and eaten his fill, we'll turn off the music and he'll wander off like always."

"What if he decides to stay, huh?" Elmer asked, angling the airboat around a congealed mass of thrashing zombie bodies. Wilbur ignored him and studied the dead. The things had rotted to such an extent that they were stuck together like a reef of twitching carrion. He'd heard tell from a few of their prisoners that such things were common in the ocean – enormous conglomerations of bodies swept out to sea or tossed overboard, all smashed together but still hungry… still hunting, wherever the tide took them.

They turned the corner and King Crunch rose up before them, tearing at the ship with bestial fury. The turtle bellowed, and the sound reminded him of thunder. Elmer cursed as pieces of the hull rained down around them. They swept past and Wilbur saw bodies clinging to the edges of Crunch's shell, stuck there by tracks of moss and dried effluvia. The zombies twitched and clawed at the monstrosity's shell, trying in vain to free themselves.

"I bet he's eaten a damn city's worth of walkers," Ava said admiringly.

"He was eating men before the dead rose, I'd reckon," Wilbur said. He scratched his arm, drawing a bit of blood. He felt something in him shift and move, and he wondered what would be left of him once he'd scratched all his skin off.

Maybe something like King Crunch. Just an appetite that could never be sated. Maybe that wouldn't be so bad. The swamp could be peaceful, once you knew your place in it. No more Elmers or Avas to test his patience. Suddenly reminded of her existence, he glanced at his cousin. "They say snapping turtles can live a century, easy. There was one somewhere that was around during the War Between the States. Lived under a restaurant or some such."

"He's older than that. Older than the world," Keziah said, like a preacher beginning a sermon. "For he is nothing less than God's wrath, wrought in the shape of a mountain. Feared by everything that walks or crawls, and stronger than any gun."

Wilbur nodded absently. He had a few theories in that regard himself. Guns might not do the trick, but he was pretty sure a rocket launcher might crack King Crunch's shell good and proper. He looked forward to trying it out at the first opportunity, but until then, the beast could prove valuable. Especially if they could get it going out of the Glades and into one of the nearby towns. It'd clear out the dead in a few days, and any living folks holed up there as well. So long as they had batteries for the boombox and a CD of church music, they had themselves a one-turtle army.

"For he is our intercessor in this fallen world; God and messenger in one," Keziah went on, her eyes shining now. She grabbed Wilbur's forearm. "Do you remember when we first saw him?" she asked, so softly that he almost didn't catch it. Her grip on his arm tightened, and her nails drew blood. "When he rose up under your Uncle Cecil's airboat and snapped him and Willy-Jack up, like they was crackers on a cheese plate." Her smile was ugly. "I wasn't too broken up about it, I admit. Cecil was a pain in my ass and Willy-Jack...

well, he had that trouble back east. I'd have had you take him for a walk out in the swamp sooner or later."

Wilbur grunted. He remembered Willy-Jack and agreed with his mother's assessment. Wilbur was many things; murderer, cannibal, grave-robber, horse thief, encyclopedia salesman and gunrunner, but there were lines even he wouldn't cross for love nor money. Bad as things were, they were better off without Willy-Jack's sort.

He shook the memory off. "Right. Get me over near the trees, then get moving again. Time for me to make sure this goes right." He checked his revolver and holstered it. Excitement rose in him, prompting what might have been a pulse of hunger. Not for food; not exactly. Something else.

Keziah touched his arm. "You don't need to do this, boy. You wanted God to do the work, let him do it."

"I got a few scores to settle, momma. And it's like you said… I need to prove myself. So this is how I'm going to do it. I'm going to make sure that we're fed for the next goddamn year. How's that for leadership?" He glanced at Elmer as he said it. "You keep momma safe, Elmer – or I'll feed you to that giant asshole piece by piece, you hear me?"

Elmer blanched. "I– I hear you, Wilbur."

"Good." He glanced at Ava, but she refused to meet his gaze. Satisfied that they were both safely intimidated, he hefted the coil of rope he'd brought and dropped it over the side as the airboat passed beneath the bow of the ship.

He'd thought long and hard about how to board the ship, pondering the matter in his idle moments, though Keziah had forbidden them from even attempting it. It wouldn't be easy, but he was strong. He'd made himself a grappling hook out of a boat anchor and knew he could throw it a fair distance, for he'd practiced with it when no one was paying attention.

There were plenty of gaps in the hull. Places where the steel frame was exposed, where the hull plates had shifted and fallen away into the water. More now that King Crunch was at work. If he could get to one, he could get to the top, he was sure of it. If not, he'd just work his way inside and get up on the deck that way, zombies or no zombies.

Wilbur started toward a stable patch of hummock, only his eyes and ears above the water. He could almost taste the feast that awaited him and couldn't help but grin.

CHAPTER THIRTY-SIX
Shaft

Calavera was descending the ladder when Santa Muerte began to sing somewhere above him in the elevator shaft. Her voice echoed eerily, freezing him to his core. Sayers and the others hadn't noticed, of course. They continued their descent, staying as quiet as possible. Calavera paused where he was, listening.

It wasn't a pleasant moment. The shaft stank of fuel and rot. Shamekia was right; the ship was a leaky drum of gasoline, waiting for the ignition of an errant match. He felt the hull flex around them, pummeled by the rising winds.

Far above, he could hear Westlake hammering on the walls of the shaft, trying to draw the rats upwards and away from them. But there was something else as well. Something he only noticed because Santa Muerte had drawn his attention to it. A rumbling, coming from outside the ship. It was getting more noticeable by the moment. He made to alert the others when he heard the sudden rip of metal and felt the ladder shake beneath him.

Out of the corner of his eye, he saw an old power conduit tear loose of the shaft wall and there was a sound like the scratch of a striker on a flint. No power in the cable, but metal on metal could make its own fire. Santa Muerte enfolded him in her dark shroud as the fume-laced air caught and flames roared upwards, following the shaft. Instinctively, Calavera loosened his grip on the ladder and slid down, trying to outrace the flames that were now spilling toward him. "Look out below," he roared. He hoped they heard him.

It was like sliding into Hell. The metal tore his palms, even through the athletic tape wrapped around them. But pain was better than death. He hit the bottom with a clang, muscles bunching automatically to absorb the impact the way he might've done in the ring. The others were already down, trying to get the doors open and having no luck. Flames boiled above them, crawling down the shaft.

"It ain't budging," Willy shouted, pushing vainly against his pry bar. Sayers was trying to help, but the doors were even more stubborn than the ones above. As before, Calavera shoved past them and gripped the doors. He took a deep breath and felt Santa Muerte's hands on his shoulders.

"When I get it open," he said, "Don't hesitate. Just go."

Then he pulled. The doors resisted but the metal was old and warped and rusted. They began to move with a shriek. Fire dripped from the shaft above, and out of the corner of his eye, he saw Ogilvy looking upwards and Santa Muerte stood beside him.

The doors parted and Calavera braced himself in the gap, holding them open. "Go, go," he barked. They went. Sayers first, then Willy. The gap shrank despite his best efforts. He could feel it straining against him. He knew then that he wouldn't have time to extricate himself from the doors before the fire hit. Not as heroic an end as he'd imagined, but good enough. He looked at Shamekia and Ogilvy. "There is no time – come on!"

Ogilvy hesitated, and Shamekia caught his hand. Calavera saw death in his eyes and over the captain's shoulder, Santa Muerte shook her head. "Captain, come on," Shamekia urged. Ogilvy resisted her pull.

"I cannot hold it much longer," Calavera said. Ogilvy stepped back and took off his satchel full of flares. He extended it to her.

"Go," he said. Shamekia took the satchel but hesitated, clearly wanting to argue. But fire was falling on them from above, a rain of heat and cinders. Calavera decided. He reached out with one hand and caught the back of her jacket, pulling her close. Ogilvy leapt forward and caught the doors, holding them in place just long enough for Calavera to haul Shamekia out into the open space beyond.

His last glimpse of Ogilvy was of the captain smiling beatifically as the doors closed and the flames reached down to envelop him. Smoke speared from the thin gap between the doors as Calavera and the others were forced to back away by the sudden wash of heat.

Shamekia hit him. "You left him," she shouted. "You said you'd watch out for him and you left him!" She made to hit him again and he caught her fist.

"He saved us," Calavera said simply. His body ached where the fire had kissed him, but he had become good at ignoring pain. "Do not cheapen that sacrifice." He took the bag of flares from her and slugged it across his shoulder and chest.

"Where to now?" The corridor was tight; undecorated. Two directions, one toward the front of the ship, one toward the rear. In the glow of the flashlights, he could see old blood on the walls and gnawed bones on the floor. But no zombies.

Shamekia gestured toward the bow of the ship. "That way. Should be right along this corridor." The ship shuddered again, nearly knocking them all from their feet. Something told Calavera it wasn't because of the storm.

Willy looked around nervously. "What the hell is going on out there? They using mortars or something?"

A strange, shrill sound echoed through the ship, muffled by the hull but not completely blocked. The cry of something alive, something hungry. Santa Muerte pointed down a dark corridor, away from the galley. Calavera nodded and realized Sayers was snapping her fingers in his direction. "Hey, you with us?"

"No. My fate lies elsewhere." He looked at them. "Santa Muerte is with us. She will see you safely to the galley, but it is up to me to buy you the time you need to collect the supplies." He patted the bag of flares. "So I will do so."

"What are you talking about?" Sayers asked.

"It's the dinosaur, ain't it?" Willy asked. Calavera nodded. He looked at Sayers.

"Can't you feel it? The ship is under attack – one it may not survive. Unless someone intervenes. I will do so, as is my right and duty." He started down the corridor that Santa Muerte had indicated, ignoring Sayers' calls. She would know what to do. Like the others, she was a born survivor. This new world held no terror for them – save the one he now rushed headlong to confront.

He moved lightly, resisting the ship's efforts to toss him from his feet. Santa Muerte raced alongside him, as eager as he to meet the monster that called out to them. King Crunch, that was its name, and he was thankful he knew it. A warrior needed to know the name of his enemy. Was it a devil from Xibalba, or simply another mutant? It did not matter. Whatever it was, he would meet it in battle and destroy it – or die in the attempt.

Since the world's end, he had wondered why Santa Muerte had chosen to guide him. He knew that there was something he was meant to do. Some task which only he could accomplish. Perhaps this was it. A monster worthy of the attention of a hero.

The ship convulsed and he felt the deck plates begin to rip free of their housings. The darkness ahead was split by streaks of gray light, and wind howled through the corridor, nearly buffeting him from his feet. It was as if something had torn a gaping wound in the side of the ship. He could hear the faintest blare of music rising from somewhere beyond.

Then, an avalanche of dark flesh punched into the ship ahead of him and ripped away more of the hull. The impact threw him against the wall, and that was the only thing that saved his life as a talon as large as a car entered the ship and tore at the corridor. It narrowly missed him, and he marveled at its sheer mass as it was retracted.

This was no brute; it wasn't even like the monster he'd fought in the Adirondacks. This was something else again. A massive head pressed itself against the hole, and a yellow eye as large as a hubcap peered inside, searching for prey. Calavera stepped forward and spread his arms. *"¡Hola!"*

As he'd hoped, its eye fixed on him. And as he matched its gaze, he saw himself reflected. But not as he was – as he would be. A skeleton stripped of meat. Forgotten. For a moment, he hesitated. Then he felt the cool hands of Santa Muerte on his shoulders and heard her voice in his ear. Urging him on, reminding him that he had survived this long not for himself, but so that he might be her hand on Earth. He bared his teeth.

"Hello, monster. Wait there, I will be with you shortly."

CHAPTER THIRTY-SEVEN
Inferno

Westlake was on fire and climbing. It didn't hurt, though part of him was screaming inside his mind. Part of him wanted to just… let go. To let the fire do its work. But the rest of him was too stubborn to quit. So he just kept climbing, ignoring the pieces of himself he left behind, stuck to the ladder.

Hungry.

Hungry.

Hungry.

The need echoed through him, making his limbs shake like he was in withdrawal. The hunger was driving him on as much as his own stubbornness. He was starting to understand how walkers could endure the punishment they did before going down. The hunger was riding him like a jockey, urging him on, digging its heels into his ribs. Making him climb until the ladder ended and there was a hatch above him.

No way to tell where it went. He didn't much care. He figured he only had a few more minutes before his eyeballs cooked in their sockets. He hit the hatch with his elbow and shoulder, ignoring the way his bones cracked. Hit it again, and again. Again, again, again, *again*. His skin split and curled away from bone, his head was a torch, but he didn't cease until the hatch gave way with a cry of abused metal.

Westlake hauled himself out through the hatch in a plume of smoke. He collapsed onto the deck, and for a moment, his body resisted his best efforts to get it moving. He felt like a rubber band that had been stretched to breaking point. He felt the rain, but only as a spattering of pressure points on his battered carcass. His clothes had been burnt into his skin, and the scorched cloth crackled as he dragged himself away from the hatch.

Hungry.

Where were the others? The last he'd seen of them, they'd been climbing down. He'd lost sight of them after a while. Maybe that was a good thing. Maybe they'd gotten away from the flames. But they might well have nowhere to run to.

The ship was quaking like it was gripped with convulsions. He could hear a familiar roar rising from the swamp. He thought of alligators being torn apart, but the image only increased his hunger. He heard gunfire. Shouts and screams. More roaring. The boat was being torn apart. People were running around in a panic. Some of them were trying to get others inside, but not having much luck. He couldn't motivate himself to care.

Instead, he concentrated on crawling across the deck. The sharp, iron tang of blood drew him on. Someone lay near the rail, moaning in pain as someone else tried to pull an arrow out of them without causing more damage. He focused on them, using his elbows to push himself in their direction, their pulses thundering in his ears. They couldn't see him because of the rain and the debris. Wouldn't see him, until it was too late. He wanted to warn them, but couldn't.

Hungry.

"...how the hell did they get that thing to come after us?" Ramirez's voice. Sharp. Piercing the rain like a knife. It was familiar enough that he paused and sought her out. She was striding across the deck like a hurricane was no more bother than a spring rain. Jessop was with her. Westlake wanted to call out to them, but his vocal cords still weren't responding.

Instead, he pushed himself to his feet. Ramirez and Jessop whirled. "Jesus," Ramirez said, startled. She raised her weapon, and he tried to focus on her. To tell her that he was still him. But all that came out was a gurgle. And as he looked at her, he felt himself rise. Not because he wanted to, but because he had to.

Because he was hungry.

Hungry.

His jaws fell open, and he hissed. Body burnt black where it wasn't blistered red, he took an unsteady step toward her. His arms rose, hands grasping.

Hungry. HUNGRY.

He wanted to tell her to shoot. To beg her. But all he could manage was a dull growl as he lunged for her. Ramirez stepped back and clocked him with her pistol. The blow rattled him, knocked him to one knee. He felt like a good breeze might blow him away. Something struck the ship, knocking everyone sprawling for a moment.

Westlake went for Ramirez. She rolled aside, calling for help. Jessop came at him, swinging a pry bar. Westlake avoided the blow and sent Jessop staggering back with a wild flail of his arm. The effort overbalanced him, and he fell to his knees.

Others on this part of the deck were realizing what was going on, despite the rain and the wind and the monster beating on the side of the ship. He saw a man in black turn toward him, and nearby, Terry, Imogene and Kahwihta. The latter made him pause. Attila began to bark. "It's a damn walker," the man in black said. He brandished a golden pistol and made as if to shoot. Westlake wanted him to, but Kahwihta stopped him.

"It's Westlake," she said, staring down at him. Attila crouched beside her, growling. There was no recognition in the dog's eyes, no sense that the animal saw Westlake as anything more than another walker.

Hungry.

Westlake tried to get to his feet, but failed. Instead, he rested on his knees. Ramirez looked down at him. "Westlake," she said. "Are you in there?"

He rolled his eyes toward her. His voice thrashed in his throat like an animal with its foot in a trap. Finally, he said, "It's me."

"You tried to take a bite out of me," she said.

Westlake bowed his head. "Shoot me."

"No."

"What do you mean, no? Shoot him," the man in black said.

"Quiet, Oscar," Jessop said. Westlake ignored him. Ignored all of them except Ramirez. She was the one who'd made the promise, after all. The one he could count on to do the smart thing. He could feel the ship quivering, hear the roaring, but all he could concentrate on was Ramirez.

"I'm... hungry," he said.

Ramirez shook her head. "We're a little busy right now, Westlake. You might have noticed that there's a giant turtle trying to eat us." She was trying to make a joke, but it wasn't working. He shook his head.

"I'm done. Shoot me."

Ramirez stared at Westlake for a moment, then looked at the others. "Oscar, you and Patricia get Kahwihta inside with the others. Terry, go grab Gable and Ptolemy, and let's make sure those access stairs are still clear. I think it's time we started the evacuation." She glanced at Jessop, and he nodded.

"Long past time," he said. He looked down at Westlake. "What about Grillo and the others? Are they still down there?"

Westlake shook his head. "Don't know. We got separated." He hoped the rats hadn't got them. Or the flames.

Jessop looked suspicious, but Ramirez simply shook her head. "If they're still alive, they can find their own way out. We need to get the noncombatants somewhere safe." The ship shook again, and Jessop caught Ramirez as she fell against him. "Preferably before that damn monster tears the ship out from under us!"

The others were already moving, heading back along the ship toward the bow. Kahwihta paused once to look back at him. Westlake couldn't bring himself to meet her gaze. Couldn't bear to see what she might be thinking. He wondered if he could make it to the rail. A fall might not stop him, but it would smash him up good enough that he might as well be dead. As if reading his mind, Ramirez stepped between him and the rail.

"No," she said.

"Get out of my way," he croaked, as he pushed himself to his feet.

"Ramirez," Jessop began, looking back and forth between them.

Ramirez didn't take her eyes off Westlake. "Jessop, go take charge of the evacuation. I'll handle this."

Westlake stared at her as Jessop left, albeit reluctantly. The world was soft at the edges, and black. The fire had damaged his eyes after all. He blinked and shook his head. "Please…"

"No. I still need you. The job isn't over yet."

Hungry.

"Ramirez…" he pleaded. He didn't understand. She had to see he had nothing left.

She held out her hand. "Come with me."

Westlake looked at the hand and then at her. He took her hand.

Hungry. Hungry. HUNGRY.

"OK," he said.

CHAPTER THIRTY-EIGHT
Boarding Action

Wilbur made it to the top after what felt like hours, out of breath and his muscles burning with fatigue. But he forced himself over the rail and checked his gear. His daddy's hunting knife was on his belt, where it always was, and the pistol sat opposite it. That was all he needed. That and his own two hands. He scraped rain and sweat out of his face and braced himself against the side of a cabin as the ship lurched slightly with a groan of abused metal.

He heard King Crunch roar, though whether in pain or hunger he couldn't say. The ship shuddered again, and there was a sound like sheet metal tearing. The giant turtle was working hard, ripping the ship open. Sooner or later, the whole thing was likely to collapse. That was fine by him. Let it. They'd skim the water and take whatever survived. But first, he had some business to take care of.

He wanted a piece of Ramirez's hide for how she'd suckered him. He wanted to prove he was in charge, and that meant showing Elmer and Ava and all the rest that he was stronger than them and meaner. Mean enough to snatch food out of King Crunch's mouth if need be. The ship trembled, and for a moment, he wondered if he was doing something monumentally stupid. Or maybe crazy. Then the world had gone crazy, hadn't it? And in a mad world, only the mad prospered.

He staggered, suddenly gripped by a pain inside him. A twisting, coiling sensation that wasn't quite hunger. He closed his eyes, trying to push it down and away. For a moment, it resisted him. He felt something in his throat, as if it were trying to escape. Then, it faded. But not completely. His hand came away from his neck covered in shreds of dead flesh. So much of it… like he was rotting on the bone. Whatever was in him, whatever he was becoming, the time was near. Not yet, but soon.

He pushed himself forward, finding his balance now. He could hear shouting and gunfire beneath the thud of the rain and the bellowing of the turtle. Someone burst through the rain, running toward him: a man in black. He looked like a country singer, complete with fancy snakeskin boots. Gold flashed in his hand as he skidded to a stop – a gold-plated pistol, of all things. He started to speak, weapon trained on Wilbur, but Wilbur was too quick. He snatched his own pistol from its holster even as he flung himself against the rail.

Despite his speed, he still felt the whistle of the bullet as it creased his sleeve. His own shot plucked at the deck, making the other man dance back with a curse. He swung his golden gun up, but never got off a second shot. Wilbur pounced, bearing him flat, and proceeded to pistol-whip him until his boot heels ceased drumming against the deck.

Still on his knees, Wilbur reared up and looked down at the bloody mess he'd made of the other man's face. It made his stomach growl, and for a moment he hesitated – distracted by the thought of all that meat, his for the having.

"Oscar? What is it?"

Wilbur looked up. More shapes in the rain. A whole gaggle. Three and something else. A dog? Where were they going to? The first in sight was a short woman in military fatigues. She skidded to a stop as she saw him and what was left of the man he'd killed. "Oscar…" she said, even as she raised a bladed prosthetic. Wilbur took a moment to admire it before he shot her. She pitched backward with a yelp, startling the other two. Still alive, but he'd correct that in a moment.

"Attila – sic 'em!"

Wilbur was on his feet an instant later, and then back down just as quick when the dog hit him. It wasn't a big animal, but it was sturdy, and its teeth hurt as they sank into his flesh. He roared in pain and swung the dog around, trying to dislodge it.

The pain ran up and down his spine, dancing along his nerve endings. He drew strength from it, the way he always had. But there was something different about it now. Something was in him and clawing at the walls of him, trying to get out. He wanted to let it out but didn't know how. Instead, he focused on the dog. He finally managed it by slamming the animal into the rail. The dog fell from him with a whimper and he kicked it aside, sending it tumbling across the deck.

"Now that that bit of nastiness is done, y'all will tell me where Ramirez is," Wilbur said, looking at his bloody arm. It ran black in the rain. He stepped over the dog. It was still alive, and he felt something that might have been relief. He didn't like hurting animals unless he had to, and he took no pleasure in it. Not like with people.

The two young women facing him looked frightened. Good. They were smart to be frightened of him. Maybe that meant they were smart enough to give him what he wanted. He studied them. One looked like a girl he'd taken up with in Miami. The other was covered in knives. "Y'all look like you might know a Federal named Ramirez. I'd be grateful if you could tell me where I might find her."

"Go to hell," one of them said. She glanced at the dog, and he saw the concern in her eyes. He smiled and aimed his weapon at the animal. She flinched and he chuckled.

"I don't like hurting animals, but I will do it if that is what is necessary to loosen your tongue. Where's Ramirez?"

"Back there," she said reluctantly. "At the prow."

"Yeah? Organizing a defense or some-such, I bet." Wilbur licked his teeth. "Not going to be no defense. Not no more." He looked around. "Y'all were planning to evacuate, I expect. Got some rafts somewhere? Yeah. You do." He pointed his weapon at them. "Tell you what – you take me to them, and I'll let you live."

A vague plan was coming together in his blood-addled mind. He'd find the evacuation point and wait. Ramirez would turn up sure as hell, and he'd pop her then. But he'd get the others that way, too. Get them all off the boat before King Crunch tore it apart and save them for the family. Just like momma wanted.

The thought pleased him so much that his attention wandered, just for a moment. The woman with the knives came at him then, quicker than a flash. He snapped to attention just as she got a knife out and swung it toward his head.

The knife in her hand cut through the rain and then his wrist. He cursed and dropped his weapon, staggering back. She hesitated, and he smiled. He ducked toward his pistol and got to it before she did. Her friend tackled her out of the way as he fired, but in doing so put herself too close to him. His hand snapped out and he caught her by the hair, yanking her back into his embrace, even as he booted the one with the knives in the stomach, flattening her. Hand around his captive's neck, he looked down at her friend.

"You take me where I want to go, or I'll kill her."

"No need for that," Ramirez called from behind him. He spun, dragging his prisoner with him. Ramirez stood behind him, her weapon out and aimed at him. He hadn't even heard her sneak up on him. He smiled at her.

"I been hoping to see you again," he said. There was another shape behind her, something broken and stinking of burnt meat even with the rain. A walker? He pushed the thought aside. Ramirez was the danger.

She glared at him over the barrel of her weapon. "I'm right here, Wilbur. Now let her go!"

CHAPTER THIRTY-NINE
Main Event

Calavera raced down the contorting length of the corridor, lightly springing from wall to floor as the underlying structure buckled from the monster's continued assault. There was no pain now. No ache in his joints. Santa Muerte saw to that. He laughed as he ran, adrenaline singing through him.

This – THIS – was his reason for being. Not simply to fight the dead, but to fight the monsters that came after. Rain and wind pelted him as he continued his headlong charge toward the opening ripped in the side of the hull. Ramirez and the others were afterthoughts. That they would capitalize on his action was an assumption. They all had their struggles, their own battles to fight and this was his.

Somewhere, a bell rang. Calavera reached the gap and sprang through as gracefully as he had ever leapt into a ring. The monstrous turtle barely noticed him as he slammed into its shell and swung himself up. It was bigger than he'd imagined, taller than a house and wide. It stank of deep, dark places and stagnant water. A part of him shied away fearfully from the sensation, but it was swiftly overridden by the desire to fight.

The zombies encrusting the hardened carapace clawed weakly at his arms and legs as he fought to get his balance. He ignored them, focused on his opponent. He needed to catch the monster's attention, to draw it away from the ship somehow. It was too big for his usual tricks. If he could get to its face, maybe. He swung from one encrustation to the next, but as the turtle moved, he lost his grip and almost fell from his perch.

Panting, he wedged his fingers in a crack and let his shoulders and thighs carry his weight. He shouted, trying to catch its attention, but it couldn't hear him. Rainwater cascaded down the contours of its shell, threatening to wash him down into the swamp.

Calavera reached into the satchel Ogilvy had given him and pulled out a flare. He popped the flare, hoping the sudden blaze of light would catch King Crunch's eye. He was rewarded by a quaking grumble from the beast as it turned awkwardly, trying to catch a glimpse of the light. It turned with all the ponderousness of an avalanche, and Calavera caught hold of a chunk of metal embedded in its shell to keep himself from being flung off. He hurled the flare out and away from the ship, toward the swamp.

King Crunch gave a shriek of frustration and took a booming step in pursuit. Then, from below, came a blare of music, barely audible through the cacophony of the hurricane. It caught King Crunch's attention and it swung back around toward the ship. Calavera reached for another flare but something grabbed his arm. He heard a sickly, ripping sound and looked down.

A walker – several walkers, all hideously conjoined into a singular hulking morass of twitching limbs and gaping maws – wrenched itself free of the turtle's shell and rose to grapple with him. He cried out in disgust as a half dozen flailing limbs pawed at him. He kicked out, and the whole disgusting mass tumbled away, falling like dandruff from the monster's back. But it wasn't alone. More zombies were pulling themselves free and scaling the shell like insects. He needed a new plan, and fast.

Calavera risked a look down, and spotted the airboat where the music was coming from. The monster seemed to be following it. Ramirez had said something about music when she'd described the beast – they'd trained it somehow. There were three passengers, one in a wheelchair. The oddity of it struck him, and he gave a sharp bark of laughter.

Santa Muerte met his gaze from the boat. She stood beside the pilot, her hand on his shoulder. She pointed and Calavera knew what she wanted of him. Instinct took over. He waited for the boat to begin its approach again and popped another flare. Then... jumped. It was a leap of faith in many ways. There was no guarantee he'd make it and no second chances if he missed. But he did it regardless.

And as Santa Muerte had promised, he landed where he'd aimed. He felt the impact in his knees and hips, and a jolt of pain ran up his spine, but he ignored it, concentrating instead on the boat's passengers – especially the young woman swinging the rifle in his direction. The barrel slapped into the palm of his hand, and he wrenched it out of her grip before she could fire. She went for a knife, and he slammed the stock of her rifle into her face. She went over the side without a sound.

"Ava!" the pilot roared and unlimbered a pistol. Calavera sent the rifle hurtling toward the big man. It caught him in the chest and knocked him out of his seat. The airboat began to slew sideways, as the pilot fought to climb back into the craft. The old woman in the wheelchair let out a wild cat shriek and went for her own weapon. Calavera lunged and seized her hand, twisting the weapon out of her grip.

Stuffing the weapon into his waistband, he leapt to the front of the boat, caught up the boombox and tore it free of its bindings. Then, with a thankful wave to the old woman, he leapt into the water, still holding the boombox. The airboat continued its wild trajectory as Calavera surfaced. He paid it no mind. The boombox was still blaring, despite the water. He hefted it onto his shoulder and struck out for the edge of the swamp.

The rain made it hard to see, but any direction was fine as long as it was away from the boat. He still had the flares. He could draw the beast away, into the swamp. Give the others time to evacuate. Ahead of him, Santa Muerte stood among the trees, beckoning him on. Gunshots plucked at the water; the rest of the Watkins family. Zombies clawed at him.

He ignored them all and plunged on until he reached something solid. He wedged the boombox into a nest of roots just above the water. Shapes moved toward him, and he heard voices crying out – in panic, rather than anger. The reason for that was obvious. King Crunch was coming, following the song.

The turtle lumbered through the water, on two legs and four. It was an awkward thing, made invincible by its size and fury. A monster out of a film. He felt a flicker of pity for it. In the end, it was just an animal. Like the alligators. Like the birds, the rats, the bear. An animal twisted into something awful by the folly of mankind.

Calavera hauled himself up above the boombox and checked the satchel. The flares were mostly dry. Good enough. He let it hang from his hand. The Watkins were no longer shooting. He could hear airboats revving. They were retreating. He heard a grunt from close by and saw the eyes of an alligator peering at him from just above the water line. As if it was waiting for something – but what?

A shadow fell over the trees. King Crunch. Broken pieces of the ship hung from its claws. The king of the Everglades. But every king's reign ended. The turtle stared down at him and Calavera met its gaze. There was no intelligence there, no malign wisdom. Just empty hunger. He felt almost disappointed... here was no great battle, no furious foe. Only another victim of the world's ending.

Calavera drew the pistol from his waistband and began to whirl the satchel of flares over his head. King Crunch eyed him curiously for a moment – then it lunged, beak wide. Calavera slung the satchel straight into its gullet and fired a shot from the pistol after it. There was an eruption of light, so bright as to be painful. Calavera flung himself backwards into the trees, away from those awful jaws.

King Crunch reared back, its mouth full of molten magnesium. The turtle screamed and the swamp seemed to scream with it. Calavera watched as the beast turned away, clawing at its head, body shuddering. Its throat bulged white-hot and its scaly hide split, venting noxious smoke. And, as one, the alligators that had been lurking at the edges of the clearing swam toward it. Zombies as well, drawn by the noise and the smell of blood.

They ignored Calavera, lurching toward the towering monster, now screeching in agony. First a few, then a dozen, then more… so many more. Calavera watched them converge on the behemoth with sickened fascination as the hurricane at last vented its full fury on the Everglades. Calavera looked away, to Santa Muerte, who held out her hands to him. He took them, and she led him away from the storm and into the trees.

He was tired, and pain from his exertions crept through him. He wanted to rest, but knew he could not. Not just yet. "Where are we going?" he murmured.

But as ever, she did not answer.

CHAPTER FORTY
Last Stand

"Wilbur Watkins," Ramirez shouted, taking a shooter's grip on her sidearm. "Throw down your weapon and let her go!" She'd been coming to help with the evacuation when she'd spotted Wilbur. Westlake hovered behind her, but he wasn't in any position to be helpful. He could barely walk, barely hold himself together. She tried not to think about it.

She wasn't surprised Wilbur was here. She'd known he'd come back. Known as soon as she'd seen King Crunch and the airboat with the music. He was the sort who'd keep coming until he was dead. She'd almost shot him in the back, but the last vestiges of Quantico had compelled her to draw his attention, to pull him around for one last face to face. It was stupid, but she'd gotten by on it so far.

Wilbur's yellow eyes burned with feral malice as he stared at her. "Federal," he croaked. "Not dead yet? Guess we'll have to fix that, won't we?" He pressed the barrel of his pistol to Kahwihta's head. "You throw down your weapon or I'll put one in her."

"You do that, I put you down," Ramirez said. She could see Imogene on the deck just beyond Wilbur. The young woman was reaching for her knife, but slowly. Patricia was there as well, injured and trying to pull herself to her feet.

Wilbur's smile was ghastly. "I think you'll try. But I don't think you'll manage it." His smile widened and the flesh at the corners of his mouth frayed and tore like paper. "I think I am beyond you, now. Beyond momma and all of this world. I am becoming something blessed and holy in this hell and you cannot stand against me." A flicker of what might have been pain passed across his face. "I feel it in me, waiting to be born…"

"It'll have to wait a minute," Ramirez said. She caught Kahwihta's eye, and the younger woman glanced down at her hand. Ramirez saw something in her sleeve – the ice pick. "Let her go," she said again. "It doesn't have to end this way."

Wilbur laughed harshly. "Maybe I want it to," he growled. His finger tapped the trigger teasingly and Kahwihta flinched. Ramirez cursed under her breath.

"Let her go. Take me instead. One hostage is as good as another, right?"

Wilbur appeared to think this over. "I'm not altogether sure about that, Federal… but I will consider it if you like." There was something like black tar running from the corners of his mouth as his smile turned into something like an animal's snarl. "You know what? I think I'm going to shoot her and take my chances." His arm tensed, and Ramirez fired.

The shot took him high in the shoulder and he roared in pain. His grip on Kahwihta loosened, and the ice pick slid into her palm. She twisted in his grip and drove it into his side. At the same moment, Imogene leapt up and thrust a knife into his back.

He bellowed again, grabbed Kahwihta by the hair, and flung her toward the rail. She hit it – and went over. On instinct, Ramirez dove for her. Out of the corner of her eye, she saw Wilbur slug Imogene and knock her flat again. How was he still standing?

She caught Kahwihta's arm and found herself nearly dragged over the rail. "Hold on," she cried, bracing herself. Kahwihta cried out as she slammed against the hull of the ship. Ramirez tried to haul the younger woman up, but it felt as if her shoulder were about to pop out of its socket. She glanced around, looking for help, but saw only Wilbur, leaning against the wall of the cabin. "Westlake," she called out. "Westlake!"

Wilbur reached down and plucked the ice pick from his side and let it fall to the deck. Panting, he raised his weapon – fired. Ramirez jolted as the slug tore through her. A second joined the first, and she nearly let Kahwihta go. There was no pain, not at first. Just the impact and the sensation of something going wrong inside her. But then it started to hurt and she almost blacked out.

When her vision cleared, Wilbur was still there, still aiming his weapon at her. He made to fire again, but it clicked dry. He tossed it aside and reached for his knife.

Ramirez brought her own weapon up and tried to aim, but her world went topsy-turvy for a moment. The weapon slipped from her hand. Wilbur approached in slow motion, his grin threatening to unzip his face. She could see it now, inside him. Like a snake in a bag, twisting and writhing as it looked for an escape.

The edges of her vision turned a crackling red. The sound of the storm beat against her senses, drowning out everything but the raw tingle of pain spreading out through her midsection. She turned away from Wilbur and reached out with her free hand to Kahwihta. If she could just get her up and over – that was all she needed to do – just that one thing.

She stared down into Kahwihta's face, saw her mouth move, shouting a warning that she couldn't hear. Saw the young woman try to climb, feet slipping against the wet hull. Saw the dead far below – a lake of corpses, slashed through by monstrous reptiles. Saw the hideous form of King Crunch, head burning like a torch, swiping at those same reptiles as they swarmed about its bulk. Saw fires dancing on the water as spilled fuel burned in defiance of the storm. Felt something sharp bite into her back, and heard a grave-deep voice say, "You one tough Federal, I'll give you that... but not tough enough."

Cold steel pierced her back, twisted inside her... a lightning strike of cold fire, filling her up. The bullets had been bad, the blade was worse. The world was shards, tumbling all around her, but she couldn't let go of Kahwihta. *Wouldn't.*

Instead, she flung her head back, heard it – felt it – strike something with a crunch, and felt the knife leave her back. She drew together what was left of her strength and heaved, dragging Kahwihta up close enough to the rail that she could grab it. Her limbs felt like water as she stumbled and fell. She saw Wilbur, one hand pressed to his face. He'd be on them again in a moment, and there was nothing she could do about it.

Then Westlake was there... body burnt, skin in tatters, not much of him left at all, but what was there was intent on

Wilbur. Where had he been? Hands like claws seized the big man by the front of his shirt and bent him back over the rail. Wilbur was raving, howling, but Ramirez could hear nothing but the sound of her own heartbeat. It had been so fast a moment ago, but now it was so... slow. So slow.

A moment later, they were gone. It happened so fast she didn't even notice. Had they gone over the rail? She wanted to get up, to see, but nothing was working. The rhythm of her heart was barely there at all. Westlake was gone. She knew it. Felt it. Gone for good.

Relief mingled with regret. He'd deserved better, but then they all had. None of them had deserved this. Not even the Watkins family. But like the song said, deserving had nothing to do with it. It was what it was, and now it was done.

Kahwihta was on her knees beside her, hair plastered to her face and neck by rain, tears running down her cheeks. She clutched at Ramirez, and Ramirez wanted to tell her that it was OK, but she couldn't find her voice, couldn't make her mouth work.

She hoped she wouldn't come back.

Her heartbeat slowed

Slower.

Done.

CHAPTER FORTY-ONE
Do or Die

When Westlake hit the water, he was chewing on Wilbur's throat. Wilbur was returning the favor with gusto. He twisted and thrashed in Westlake's grip like an animal, making a low grunting sound as they plummeted down.

Hitting the water from that height was like hitting concrete. He made sure Wilbur hit it first and was rewarded by a sudden limpness in the giant's body. He wasn't sure whether Wilbur was dead or just... broken, but didn't much care. He was smashed up himself. Everything felt loose and deflated. For a moment, just a moment, he thought he'd let the swamp take him.

Hungry.

He surfaced. Wilbur didn't. The big man vanished beneath the water and didn't come back up. But his eyes were open and wide and luminous as he sank down into the mud. There was awareness there, and a dreadful hunger. Then it was gone. The moment brought no satisfaction. It had taken him too long to pull himself together, to will his body into motion, and Ramirez had paid the price.

Westlake heard an airboat's engine cutting the water and managed to push himself aside before it struck him. He saw the old woman, Keziah, looking disheveled. She was shouting something to the boat's pilot, but he couldn't make it out due to the storm. Maybe she was looking for her boy. He decided to help her out.

His hand, burnt clean to the bone, snagged the side of the airboat as it passed and he hauled himself up onto the side of the craft, much to the passengers' surprise. "Wilbur...?" Keziah began, as the pilot passed her his sidearm.

"No," Westlake wheezed. His throat felt like a torn open balloon, bleeding air and sound. Keziah shot him, point blank. The bullet caught him in the jugular and tore away what was left of his throat, but he didn't fall. Instead, he finished pushing himself up and over the side, into the bottom of the boat. He felt his spine click in a disturbing fashion as he tried to stand. Keziah shot him again and again. She was shrieking curses – or maybe prayers – as she did so. The pilot was shouting.

Westlake grabbed Keziah's weapon and twisted it out of her grip. Then he shot the pilot. The airboat dipped and spun out of control. He fell back against the side as it whirled itself into a hummock and got hung up. The fan shrieked and stuttered to a halt, its cage busted open by the crash. Keziah hung from her chair, hair plastered to her scalp by rain, her eyes blazing through it. She looked like a trapped animal as she spat curses at him.

Hungry.

The compulsion to eat was stronger than ever. It had gone

from a whisper to a shout to an all-pervasive roar thundering in his ears. He pushed himself erect, his eyes fastened on her. She laughed. "You look like shit, boy. You think you're going to eat me?" She drew a knife from somewhere on her person and made a come-hither gesture.

Hungry.

His jaw sagged. He wondered what she'd taste like. Then, a sudden shifting of the boat caught his attention. The prow was still in the water, and something had hold of it. A hand – or something like a hand. A head broke the surface a moment later, with two yellow eyes like balls of sickly fire.

Wilbur. Or what was left of him. He came out of the water with a bestial roar and landed on the prow of the stalled boat. His body was… changing. Twisting and swelling. Excretions of bone pushed through his flesh as he eyed Westlake with mad hunger. Keziah laughed. "My boy, my beautiful boy – take him! Kill him and then you'll feast on his–"

She didn't get a chance to finish. Wilbur lunged, shoving Westlake out of the way as he did so. His new jaws, long and reptilian, snapped shut over his mother's head. He reared back, stub-tail twitching as he swallowed her head whole and left her decapitated body twitching in its chair. Only when he'd finished did he turn to Westlake. His yellow eyes were empty of anything human. There was only hunger there.

Westlake fell back, resigned to the mauling to come. Wilbur took an awkward step toward him, his body still changing. Death had been the catalyst, apparently. Whatever he was turning into, he hadn't quite finished yet. Westlake heard a shout, and suddenly a tall form crashed into Wilbur, knocking him back against the busted cage of the airboat fan.

Calavera.

The luchador struck Wilbur again and again, but the giant refused to fall. Wilbur shoved Calavera back, slicing his chest open with newly sprouted talons. Calavera staggered, clutching at his wound. Westlake flung himself into Wilbur before the creature could renew its attack. Using the dead weight of his own body, he muscled Wilbur back against the fan cage again. Unable to speak, he kicked out at the controls, hoping Calavera would get the hint. Thankfully, he did.

Calavera activated the fan. It sputtered, coughed, and began to spin. Wilbur's struggles became more frenzied. He tore chunks out of Westlake's midsection and torso, exposing bone. Westlake braced himself against the cage and, with his free hand, forced Wilbur's head back – directly into the spinning fan blade.

Wilbur's head – and Westlake's hand – exploded into a morass of chopped meat. Wilbur's body jerked and spasmed, but finally fell limp. Westlake stumbled back, and only Calavera prevented him from falling into the water.

"Do you live?" the big man asked, panting.

Westlake gave him a look and Calavera laughed. Westlake looked up. The rain all but hid the ship from view, but the wind was dying down. He straightened and climbed out of the boat. Calavera followed him. Westlake stopped him and gestured for him to back away.

It was time to go.

He'd seen Wilbur stab Ramirez. There was no walking that sort of thing off, not unless she came back the way he had. He doubted she was that unlucky, however. There was no Ramirez to watch out for him. And not much left of him to watch. He could feel his insides pulling apart. Every movement made him lose a little more of himself. He didn't want Kahwihta or the others to see that.

Calavera looked at him for long moments, and then nodded. "You will not say goodbye, at least?"

Westlake shook his head. He wanted to speak, but his voice box was mangled. Calavera nodded in apparent understanding. "I will tell them that you are gone. That you perished in the fall." He hesitated and then held out his hands. "Do you wish me to…?"

Again, Westlake shook his head. He pushed himself away from the tree and started away into the swamp. He didn't know where he was going, or what he would do when he got there. Maybe, if he was lucky, he'd simply collapse into pieces before he got close.

Calavera called out to him. He paused and turned. Calavera held out a pistol. "Just in case," the luchador said. Westlake paused, and then went back and took the weapon. Automatically, he attempted to check the magazine. Something he'd done a hundred thousand times in his old life, and in his new. Only now, he lacked the dexterity – not to mention the additional hand – to do it without concentrating. He doubted he could even pull a trigger now, but it was the thought that counted. He met Calavera's gaze and tried to muster words. He failed, but Calavera nodded regardless.

"I will," he said. "I will tell them."

Westlake turned away and made his departure. There was a path of broken trees marking where King Crunch had fled its dying. There was a smell of big death on the hurricane wind, and every zombie in the area was following the trail.

Whatever was left of the giant turtle would be stripped to the bone by the end of the week, he figured. One less monster in the world. Two less, counting whatever Wilbur Watkins had been.

Hungry.

Rain hammered down, pulling pieces of his cooked flesh off. He kept walking. At some point, the pistol fell from his grip. He didn't see where it went, didn't much care. He thought about Ramirez, about Kahwihta.

Then, oddly, about Tommy Waingro, who'd taken him out to the Barrens to kill him as the apocalypse began. The last he'd seen of Tommy, the thick-necked little asshole had been stumbling along with most of his throat missing.

Westlake wanted to laugh, but couldn't muster the air. Poor Tommy. Poor him. The old world was slowly rotting away. There was no telling what would be left. Maybe that was a good thing. Maybe that was what it would take to give people like Kahwihta and Calavera and all the rest a clean start. He hoped that whatever judgement was waiting for him on the other side would take good behavior into account.

Hungry.

He stopped. Trees rose around him like the pillars of some ancient temple. He looked up and saw a spiral of empty sky above him. The eye of the hurricane. The moment of calm before the storm finished its job. The swamp was quiet, save for the groaning of the dead. It sounded almost like a benediction. Or maybe a funeral hymn.

It was as good a place as any.

It was as good a time as any.

Past time, really.

Hungry. Hungry. Hungry.

He tilted his face upwards as the rain began again and closed his eyes.

Then Westlake waited for it to wash him away with the last of the old world.

CHAPTER FORTY-TWO
Tomorrow

Kahwihta sat on the stack of pallets, watching as the plane was refueled. It had come through the storm mostly intact, save for a few dents and dings. It was airworthy, or so Gable insisted. It was still raining, but only lightly. The Everglades were quiet, for the moment.

The airstrip was bustling with activity. Jessop and Sayers were overseeing the erection of defenses around the safehouse – rolls of wire and cinder blocks, fences made from pallets and fuel drums. It wasn't ideal, but it would serve in a temporary capacity. Between them, Terry and Shamekia had repaired the generators and gotten them running. The safehouse had some power, enough to run an electric current through the wires strung up at the edges of the cleared space. That would serve to hold the dead back when they inevitably came calling.

She looked down at her notebook and finished her sketch of King Crunch. They'd found the creature, or what was left of it, a good distance from the ship. Every zombie in the Glades was feasting on it. And the alligators were eating them. The new cycle of life – or undeath, if you preferred. Attila whined and she reached down and scratched his head.

With their monster dead, the Watkins had melted back into the Glades. Maybe they'd gone home, or maybe the hurricane had taken them. Maybe they just didn't have the stomach to press the issue. No one felt like checking. So long as the clan stayed clear of the survivors, they'd leave them to it. Kahwihta still wasn't sure how she felt about that. What she did know was that she was ready to get back to the mountains.

Everyone else felt the same, the survivors of the *Dixie Jewel* especially. Her eyes strayed to the front of the safehouse where Ptolemy was speaking with Jessop and Sayers. All three of them intended to stay behind and wait for the second flight. Ptolemy and Sayers were in their element, building defenses and making supply logs. She spotted Patricia nursing her injured side. She'd come through her encounter with Wilbur mostly intact, but for some blood loss and a few cracked ribs. Small mercies.

Calavera sat nearby, talking animatedly to several of the younger survivors from the ship. He leapt up, and they cheered and clapped excitedly. For a giant in a mask, he was good with kids. For a moment, their gazes met, and he nodded to her. She nodded back.

Imogene joined her. She had a vivid bruise on her face, but no other signs of injury. "Ptolemy says we've got a few more boxes of supplies to load up, and then we can make the first trip back to New York," she said. Sayers and the others had found the supplies in the galley mostly intact. The discovery had been anticlimactic, compared to everything else.

They'd taken what they could. It wasn't much, but it was something. Enough to keep the safehouse fed until a plane could get back to pick up whoever drew the short straw. Even if they returned straightaway, there was no guarantee how long it would take. Flight duration in the apocalypse was an iffy thing.

"Still planning to wait for the second trip?" Kahwihta asked. Imogene shrugged.

"I've waited this long to see the Villa, I can wait a few more days. What about you?"

Kahwihta hesitated. Her eyes strayed to the swamp. Westlake was somewhere out there, she was certain of it. Calavera claimed otherwise, but she knew – *she knew* – that Westlake wasn't dead. He'd survived too much just to fall off a boat and die. Or die again. But even so, she wondered if maybe, wherever he was, it was better that he stayed there. It was sad, but not. Maybe it was for the best.

Imogene nudged her. "Thinking about him?"

Kahwihta sighed. "Yeah. Him and Ramirez." Her eyes strayed to a flat place near the safehouse, where a number of newly dug graves clustered. On one of them hung Ramirez's leather jacket. She rubbed her eyes. "A part of me... I– I hoped... I wanted her to come back, you know? Just like Westlake." But she hadn't. Ramirez was dead, just like Hutch and Labrand and Coop and Riggs and a dozen others she'd known since the world had ended and she'd begun her new life.

People died every day, even before the apocalypse. But now it seemed that when they went, a piece of the world went with them. Ramirez had been a constant in her life since she'd come down out of the mountains that day and found things irrevocably changed. And now she was gone, too.

Maybe there was a lesson there, but if so, she wasn't seeing it at the moment. Maybe it would come later, when the hurt wasn't so raw. Or maybe never. All you could do was keep moving forward. Ramirez had taught her that.

She looked at Imogene. "Feel like some company? I wouldn't mind getting another look at one of those alligators before we go back. Calavera said he'd help me."

Imogene laughed. "I bet he did." She hesitated and then took Kahwihta's hand. "And... I'd like that." She smiled nervously. "If– if you're willing, I mean."

Kahwihta covered Imogene's hand with her own. The dead would keep. Maybe it was time to live for a little bit. "Yeah. I think so."

Attila lifted his head, his eyes fixed on the sawgrass beyond the airstrip. Kahwihta followed his gaze and saw a fire-blackened figure standing in the grass. Her eyes narrowed. "Westlake...?" she murmured. A moment later, it was gone, if it had ever really been there at all. Imogene gave her a curious look.

"Did you see something?"

Kahwihta smiled sadly. "No, nothing." She rose to her feet and pulled Imogene with her. "Let's go see if anyone needs some help."

ABOUT THE AUTHOR

JOSH REYNOLDS is the author of over thirty novels and numerous short stories, including the wildly popular *Warhammer: Age of Sigmar*, *Warhammer 40,000*, *Arkham Horror* and *Legend of the Five Rings*. He grew up in South Carolina and now lives in Sheffield, UK.

joshuamreynolds.co.uk
twitter.com/jmreynolds

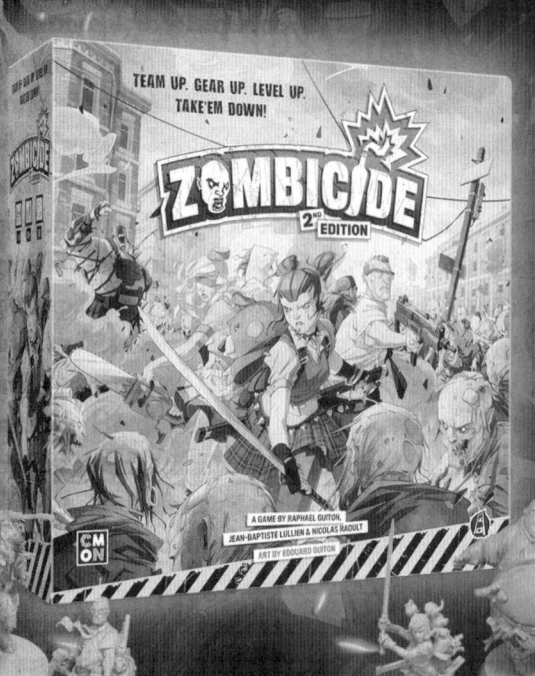

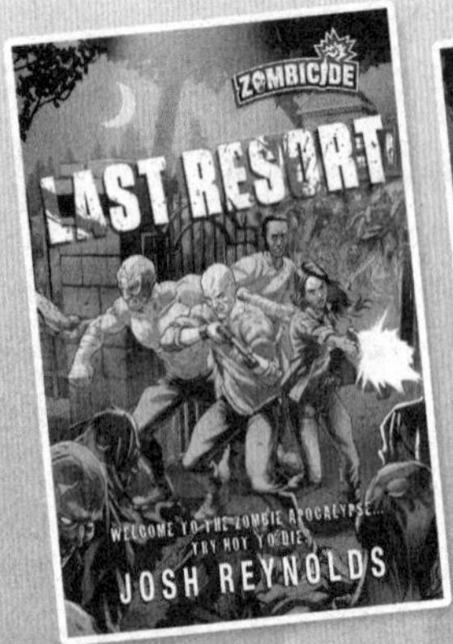

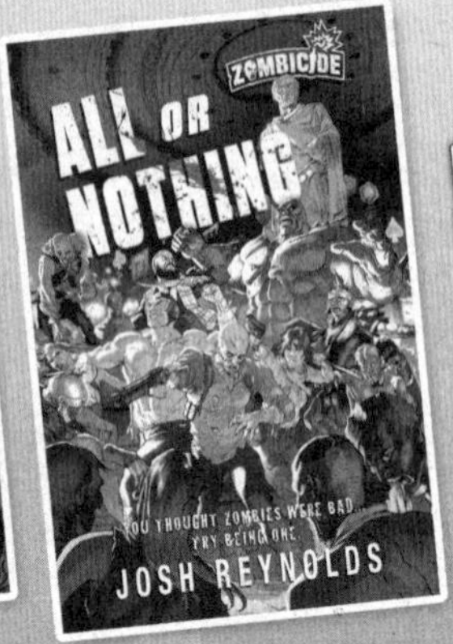

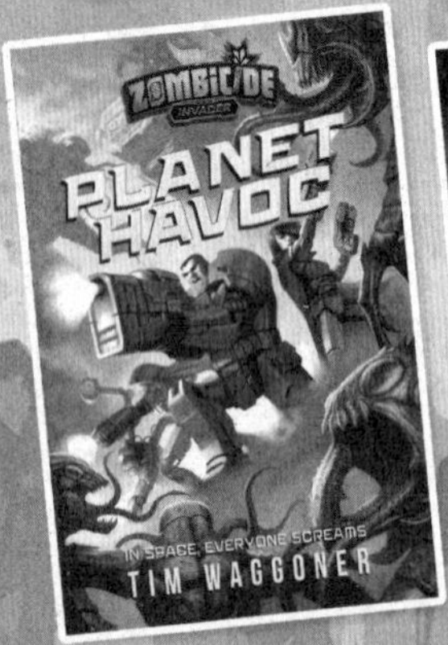

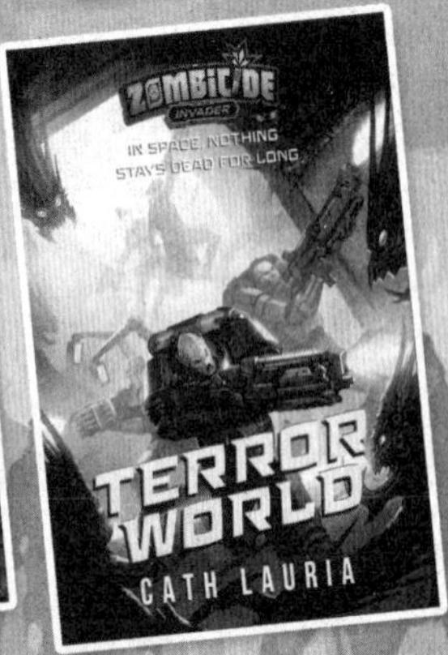

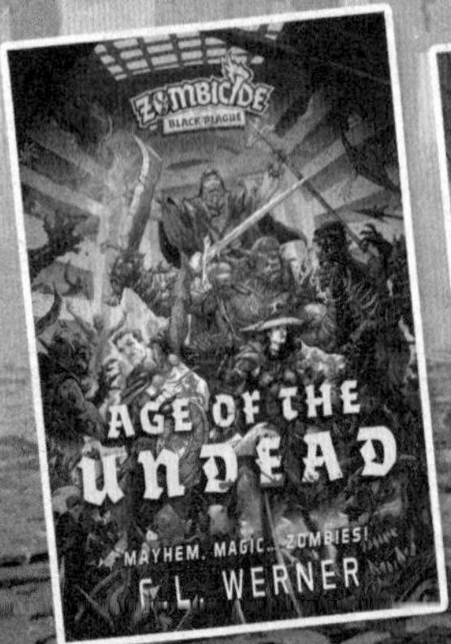

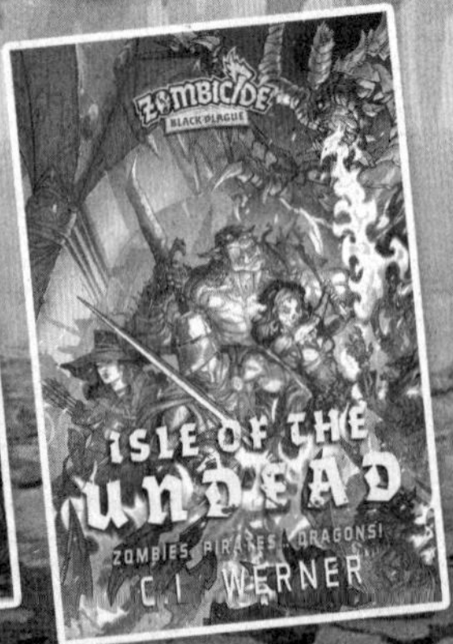